THE TEXAN'S MISSION

USA TODAY BESTSELLING AUTHOR

Delores Fossen

NEW YORK TIMES BESTSELLING AUTHOR

Elle James

Previously published as *Lucas* and *Triggered*

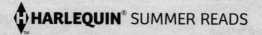

HARLEQUIN® SUMMER READS

ISBN-13: 978-1-335-00524-3

The Texan's Mission

Copyright © 2018 by Harlequin Books S.A.

First published as Lucas by Harlequin Books in 2017 and Triggered by Harlequin Books in 2013.

Recycling programs for this product may not exist in your area.

The publisher acknowledges the copyright holders of the individual works as follows:

Lucas
Copyright © 2017 by Delores Fossen

Triggered
Copyright © 2013 by Mary Jernigan

Printed in U.S.A.

HARLEQUIN®
™ www.Harlequin.com

CONTENTS

Delores Fossen, a *USA TODAY* bestselling author, has sold over fifty novels, with millions of copies of her books in print worldwide. She's received a Booksellers' Best Award and an RT Reviewers' Choice Best Book Award. She was also a finalist for a prestigious RITA® Award. You can contact the author through her website at deloresfossen.com.

Books by Delores Fossen

Harlequin Intrigue

The Lawmen of McCall Canyon

Cowboy Above the Law

Blue River Ranch

Always a Lawman
Gunfire on the Ranch
Lawman from Her Past
Roughshod Justice

The Lawmen of Silver Creek Ranch

Grayson
Dade
Nate
Kade
Gage

HQN Books

A Wrangler's Creek Novel

Those Texas Nights
No Getting Over a Cowboy
Branded as Trouble
Texas-Sized Trouble
Lone Star Blues
The Last Rodeo

Visit the Author Profile page at Harlequin.com for more titles.

LUCAS

Delores Fossen

CHAPTER ONE

TEXAS RANGER LUCAS RYLAND stared at the bed in the room at the Silver Creek Hospital.

It was empty.

He touched his fingers to the sterile white covers, already knowing they wouldn't be warm. According to the doctor, no one had been in that bed for at least the last fifteen minutes.

Maybe longer.

Mumbling something that Lucas didn't catch, Dr. Alfred Parton paced across the room. The doctor had already told Lucas that he wasn't sure how long the *patient* had been missing. That was one of the first things he had told Lucas when he called him. Of course, first Dr. Parton had dropped the bombshell.

Hailey Darrow is gone.

Lucas had rushed to the hospital to see for himself. And now that he had seen the empty bed with his own eyes, it didn't help with the jolt of adrenaline he'd gotten.

"How the hell did this happen?" Lucas demanded.

"No idea." Dr. Alfred Parton scrubbed his hand over his balding head, something he'd been doing a lot since Lucas had arrived. "I've asked everyone on the staff, and no one knows. But Hailey must have had some help. She wouldn't have been able to get up and just walk out of here."

No. Not after being in a coma for three months. She wouldn't have been able to stand on her own, much less get out of the bed and leave the building.

Of course, that only brought on a boatload of questions for Lucas—had she awakened and managed to talk someone into helping her leave? It was a valid concern, because the last time Lucas had seen Hailey conscious, she'd been nine months pregnant with their child and running. Not just from some guy who'd been chasing her.

But also running from him.

He'd found her, finally, unconscious from a car accident. She'd plowed into a tree, and a limb that'd come through the windshield had given her a nasty head injury. She'd also had a fake ID and enough cash for Lucas to know that she had planned on disappearing.

Even now, three months later, that felt like a punch to the gut, but a "punched gut" feeling pretty much described his entire relationship with Hailey for the year he'd known her.

"We have some security cameras," the doctor explained, "but none back here in this part of the hospital. They're at the front entrance, the ER and the pharmacy. We're still looking, but she's not on any of that footage."

Which meant she might still be inside the place. It wasn't a huge hospital, but there were clinics, storage closets and probably some unoccupied rooms.

"You think she'll try to go to the Silver Creek Ranch?" the doc asked.

Lucas cursed and yanked out his phone. He'd been so shocked by the news that Hailey was missing that he hadn't even considered the next step of how this might play out.

But, yeah, if she was capable of moving, she would almost certainly try to get to his cousins' ranch, where Lucas now lived. Hailey would try to get to the baby.

Camden.

His three-month-old son.

But he was Hailey's child, too.

And Hailey would go after him. Or rather, she would try. As far as Lucas was concerned, Hailey had given up her rights to their precious little boy when she'd gone on the run before Camden was born. Hailey had endangered herself and the baby in that car wreck.

"Search every inch of the hospital," Lucas ordered the doctor, though that was just the frustration talking because the staff was already looking for Hailey. "And let me know the second you find her."

Lucas headed out the door, hurrying, but he didn't call Camden's nanny because he didn't want to alarm her, yet. Instead, he called his cousin, Mason Ryland. Mason was a part-time deputy in Silver Creek, but since it was nearly 8:00 p.m., he'd already be home, and his house was just up the road from Lucas's new place.

"I'm not coming into the office," Mason said instead of a greeting. His cousin wasn't the friendliest of the Ryland clan, but he would protect Camden with his life.

Lucas prayed it didn't come down to that, though.

"Hailey's missing from the hospital," Lucas tossed out there. "I'm on my way home now, but make sure she doesn't get anywhere near Camden."

Mason cursed, too, and it was ripe enough that Lucas heard Mason's wife, Abbie, give him a scolding about saying such things in front of their two young sons.

"You can explain when you get here," Mason said. "I'll head over to your place now."

Lucas thanked him and hoped he did indeed have something to explain—like Hailey's whereabouts and how she'd managed to escape. Right now, he didn't know nearly enough.

He ran out of the building and across the parking lot to his SUV. The November wind swiped at him, but he didn't duck his head against it. Lucas kept watch around him. A habit that had saved him a time or two while he'd been a Texas Ranger. But nothing seemed out of the ordinary.

The moment he was behind the wheel, Lucas started the engine. However, before he could throw the SUV into gear, he caught the movement from the backseat. Lucas whirled around, already reaching for his gun.

But it was too late.

Hailey was there.

She was sitting right next to the baby's empty car seat, and thanks to the security lights, he could see that she had a gun pointed right at him. *His* gun. The one he kept as a backup in the glove compartment. Since he hadn't seen her when he first approached the vehicle, it likely meant she'd ducked down out of sight. Hiding from him so she could—well—do whatever the heck she was doing.

"Leave your weapon in your holster," she ordered, and it was indeed an order.

That was a hard look Hailey gave him. But the hardness didn't mesh well with the beads of sweat on her forehead. It was chilly, definitely not warm enough weather for sweating, so this must have been from exertion. There was no color in her cheeks. She looked weak, and no doubt was, but she didn't need much strength considering the gun she had in his face.

Lucas had no idea if she'd actually shoot him, because she clearly wasn't thinking straight. Couldn't be. Or else she wouldn't have him at gunpoint. Then again, she had run from him three months ago, so it was obvious she hadn't trusted him.

Still didn't, apparently.

The head injury that had put her in the coma had healed with the exception of a thin scar near her scalp. Her blond hair was pushed back from her face now so the scar was easier to see, but in another month or two, it'd be practically gone. No signs of the trauma that had nearly killed her and the baby.

No visible signs, anyway.

Lucas would always remember. *Always.*

"Start driving," Hailey insisted. "We can't stay here."

Because the hospital staff would look in the parking lot. But that didn't explain why she was hiding and clearly trying to escape.

Hell, it didn't explain a lot of things.

Lucas did drive. Not far, though, and only after he hit the child safety button to lock all the doors so that Hailey wouldn't be able to get out. He drove out of the parking lot and went two blocks up before pulling over.

He purposely didn't choose a spot in front of any businesses in case something went wrong when he wrestled that gun away from her. Instead, he stopped in front of the town park. Since it was already dark, the park was empty.

"All right. Now talk." Lucas had a string of questions but went with the easiest one first. "How'd you get from your room to my SUV?"

"I walked."

"Impossible," Lucas fired back. He glanced around

to make sure someone wasn't out there ready to help her with more than just getting out of that hospital bed. "People who've been in a coma for three months just don't get up and walk."

She nodded. Dragged in a thin breath. That's when he noticed she was shaking. "I've been out of the coma for nearly a week now, and I've been exercising my legs when no one was watching."

Nearly a week.

Damn.

"And none of the medical staff noticed?" he snapped.

"I was never in a vegetative state, just a deep coma, so the monitor already showed plenty of brain activity for me. The activity increased when I woke up, but I tampered with the machine so that it looked as if it malfunctioned. I kept doing that, and the staff thought they had faulty readings."

A nurse had indeed told him about the readings, and the hospital had called in someone to repair the machine. The Silver Creek Hospital wasn't big or modern by anyone's standards so they hadn't had another monitor to use on Hailey. That's why the nurses had been keeping a closer watch on her. Obviously, they hadn't watched nearly close enough.

"How'd you know how to tamper with the monitor?" he pressed.

She glanced away. "I'm good with computers and such."

This was the first Lucas was hearing about that, but it didn't matter. Not when there were so many other things they needed to talk about.

"When I was trying to regain my strength, I made sure no one else saw me," she added.

Obviously. Just as she'd made sure he hadn't noticed her before he'd gotten in his vehicle.

Her gaze dropped to her stomach for just a second. "I listened to try to find out if I'd had a boy or a girl, but no one mentioned it. Not even you when you visited me on Monday."

Clearly she'd known he was there. Lucas had indeed visited her, something he did a couple of times a week. Why, he didn't know, because he couldn't get answers from a woman in a coma. It riled him to the core, though, that she'd been awake during that visit and hadn't said anything.

But what had he said?

Lucas wasn't even sure—maybe nothing—but he'd almost certainly glared at her. He still was glaring now.

"So, you faked being in a coma for the last week, built up your strength, and just walked out of the hospital?" he asked, going through the probability of that as he said it.

He was skeptical.

Hailey nodded. "I ducked into a supply room, and when I heard the doctor call you, I knew you'd be arriving soon. I made my way to the parking lot and hid behind some shrubs."

"And then you broke into my SUV," Lucas snarled.

"The back door was unlocked," she answered as if that was something she did all the time. To the best of his knowledge, she didn't, but then, he really didn't know much about this woman.

The mother of his child.

"Why didn't you let me know you'd come out of the coma?" Lucas demanded.

Hailey stared at him a long time. "I'll tell you that if you'll tell me what I had—a boy or a girl?"

He debated bargaining with her. Even with that gun aimed at him. But it was probably best to give her the information so they could move on to something else. Something that involved his ripping that gun out of her hand.

"You had a boy," he finally said. "He was born three months ago."

"Three months?" she repeated. It sounded as if she had to choke back a sob. "That long."

Yeah, that long. "The doctors had to deliver him by C-section because you weren't conscious when you went into labor."

She shook her head, her breath shuddering. "I don't remember."

"Comas are like that," he said, and he didn't bother to sound even marginally sympathetic. "I named him Camden David. But I have sole custody of him," Lucas added.

Not a lie, exactly. He did have custody of him and had tried to make it permanent, but the judge had refused on the grounds that Hailey might come out of the coma and her parental rights could be reinstated.

Could be.

Lucas would make sure that didn't happen.

Something went through her pale green eyes, and Hailey made a sound, part groan, part gasp. At first he thought maybe the reaction was due to his custody comment, but the tears proved otherwise. It was the reaction of a woman who'd just learned she had a son.

But she was a mother in name only.

"And he…Camden's all right?" Hailey asked, still blinking back those tears. "There were no problems with the delivery?"

"Yeah. No thanks to you."

"Is he safe?" she asked before Lucas could finish what he was about to say.

"Of course he is." Lucas couldn't stop himself from cursing. "What the hell were you thinking when you went on the run like that? And what happened to you? Were you driving too fast? Is that what caused the accident—and that?"

He pointed to her scar, but Lucas didn't pull back his hand. He knocked the gun away from her, and it fell on the front passenger's seat. Hailey immediately scrambled to retrieve it, but Lucas was a whole lot faster. He dropped it on the floor, well out of her reach.

"Don't make me draw my gun," he warned her and took hold of her wrist in case she was about to try to get out the door.

But she didn't try to escape.

A hoarse sob tore from her mouth, and Hailey eased away from him. Just in case she had another weapon back there, Lucas leaned over the seat and did a quick check around her. He frisked her, too. Since she was wearing a pair of loose green scrubs, a thin sweater and flip-flops, there weren't many places she could conceal a weapon.

Still, after what'd happened three months ago, Lucas looked.

His hand brushed against the side of her breast, and she made a soft sound. Not the groan she'd made earlier. This one caused him to feel that tug deep within his body. But Lucas told that tug to take a hike.

Their gazes connected. Not for long. Lucas finished the search and found nothing.

"Now, keep talking," he insisted. "Tell me what happened to you. Why did you go on the run, and why didn't you tell anyone before now that you were out of the coma?"

She opened her mouth and got that deer-in-the-headlights look. What she didn't do was answer him.

"Enough of this," he mumbled.

He took out his phone to call Mason and then the sheriff, but as he'd done with her earlier, Hailey took hold of his hand. "Please don't tell your cousins. Not yet."

Since most of his Ryland cousins were cops, that wasn't what he wanted to hear. "Did you break the law? Is that why you were on the run?"

"No." She closed her eyes and shook her head. Her head wasn't the only thing shaking, though. She started to shiver, the cold and maybe the fear finally getting to her. "But I'm in trouble. God, Lucas, I'm in so much trouble."

He was about to curse at her for stating the obvious, but something else went through her eyes.

Fear.

"It won't take long for word to get out that I'm awake," Hailey said, speaking barely louder than a whisper. "And he'll find out."

"He?" Lucas snapped.

Hailey's voice cracked. "There's a killer after me."

CHAPTER TWO

HAILEY CLOSED HER eyes a moment, hoping it would help with the dizziness.

It didn't.

It was hard to think with her head spinning, the bone-deep exhaustion and the muscle spasms that kept rippling through her body.

Hard to think, too, with Lucas glaring at her as if she were the enemy. Of course, in his eyes, that's exactly what she was.

He obviously didn't believe her. Didn't trust her, either, but somehow Hailey had to make him understand. First, though, he had to take care of what was most important—the baby.

"Are you sure Camden is safe?" she asked.

That caused a new slash of anger to go through his eyes. Probably because he believed she was dodging the news she'd just dropped on him.

There's a killer after me.

"He's safe," Lucas finally said, but he spoke through clenched teeth. "Now, tell me why you need to make sure of that. Does it have something to do with the so-called killer?" He didn't give her a chance to say a word, though. "Or are you trying to lie your way out of why you ran from me three months ago?"

"It's not a lie." She wished it was. "But I didn't tell the truth about some other things."

That tightened the muscles in his jaw even more. "Start from the beginning, and so help me, there'd better not be any lies this time."

Hailey nodded but glanced around them. Since it was Tuesday and a school night, Silver Creek wasn't exactly teeming with activity, but she did spot someone jogging in the park. She kept her attention on him until he disappeared around the curve of the tree-lined trail. Maybe it was nothing. Maybe the guy was just that—a jogger— but he could have been someone after her.

"We need to find a better place to talk," Hailey told him.

Lucas gave her a flat look. Cursed. "I'm not taking you to the Silver Creek Ranch."

That was no doubt where the baby was.

Camden.

Hailey mentally repeated that, something she'd been doing since Lucas had first mentioned her precious son's name. Learning something—anything—about her baby caused her heart to ache. It felt as if someone was squeezing it hard.

Mercy, she'd lost so much already. Three months. And there was a lot more she could lose. Thank God the baby was okay, but it was up to her to make sure he stayed that way.

"I can't see Camden," Hailey answered. Saying it aloud added an even deeper pain. "Not until I'm sure it's safe."

"You won't see him at all," Lucas snapped. He spewed out more of that profanity. "You don't have a right to see him."

No, in his eyes, she didn't. But if and when this was over, she would see her son. Even if she had to push her way through an army of Ryland lawmen. No one would keep him from her.

Since it was obvious Lucas wasn't going to budge, Hailey tried to figure out the fastest way to convince him that it wasn't safe for her to be out in the open like this.

That meant starting from the beginning.

"I'm not who you think I am," she said.

A burst of air left his mouth, but it wasn't a laugh. "Obviously. You slept with me and then sneaked out, leaving me a note saying you couldn't see me again."

Hailey didn't need a reminder of that. She could have recited the note word for word.

Lucas, I'm sorry, but this was a mistake. I can't get involved with you.

"That was the truth," she continued. "I shouldn't have let things get so...intimate between us."

"But you did, and you got pregnant."

Yes, she had. Since they'd used a condom, the pregnancy definitely hadn't been something Hailey had been expecting. But that hadn't stopped her from wanting the child right from the start.

"Mistakes aside," Lucas continued, "you had no right to run away from me while you were carrying my baby." He cursed again. "If you hadn't had that car accident, I might have never found you. Of course, that was probably the plan, wasn't it? To run away so that I'd never be able to see my child?"

Hailey didn't even have to think about that answer. "No. That wasn't the plan."

He didn't believe her, but it was the truth.

"I was trying to stay alive, trying to keep the baby from being hurt," Hailey explained.

He tapped his badge. "I'm a Texas Ranger." That was probably his way of saying that if something was wrong, she should have gone straight to him.

But Lucas had been in danger, too.

Something he didn't know.

Yet.

Figuring she would need it, Hailey took another deep breath. "Two years ago, I was employed as a computer systems analyst in Phoenix for a man named Preston De-Salvo. I found out he was working with someone in the FBI. A dirty agent. And they were selling confiscated weapons. I went to the cops, DeSalvo was eventually arrested, and after I testified against him, I was placed in witness protection and given a new identity. The marshals relocated me here to Silver Creek."

She paused, giving him a few moments to let all of that sink in, but Lucas didn't take the time. He whipped out his phone again, and before she could stop him, she saw him press the contact for one of his cousins.

Sheriff Grayson Ryland.

"Don't tell him I'm with you," Hailey insisted. "The sheriff's office could be bugged."

She saw the debate Lucas was having with himself, but he didn't stop the call. He did put it on speaker, though, and it didn't take long before Grayson answered.

"I heard about Hailey," Grayson said right off the bat. "I've sent two of the deputies to the hospital to help look for her."

"Thanks," Lucas said. And he paused. A long time.

"Can you look up info on a guy named Preston De-Salvo?"

Grayson paused, too. Hailey knew the sheriff well because she'd worked for him as an emergency dispatcher shortly after her arrival in Silver Creek. Grayson had a lot of experience as a lawman and was probably suspicious.

"Is DeSalvo connected to Hailey?" Grayson asked, though she could hear the clicks of his computer keys.

"Maybe."

More keyboard clicking sounds. "Well, Preston De-Salvo was sent to prison about eighteen months ago. He's dead. Killed in a fight at a maximum security prison in Arizona a little over three months ago."

"Why was he in prison?" Lucas pressed.

"A laundry list of charges, including murder, extortion and gun running. An employee, Laura Arnett, testified against him, and she's in WITSEC." He huffed. "Now, what does this have to do with Hailey?"

"Maybe everything. I'll call you back when I know more. In the meantime, can you make sure the ranch is on lockdown?"

"Already have. Mason called and said you'd asked him to go to your house. You think Hailey could be headed there?"

"I'll call you back," Lucas repeated, probably so that he wouldn't have to lie to his cousin.

But the stalling wouldn't last long. Soon, very soon, his cousins would be demanding answers. Especially Grayson, since he wasn't just the sheriff but also the head of the Ryland clan. However, Lucas would be demanding them first.

"Laura Arnett?" Lucas repeated. "That's your real name?"

She nodded. "I haven't thought of myself as that since all of this happened. I'm Hailey Darrow. For now, anyway. But I'll have to come up with another identity. De-Salvo's dead, but no one knows who his partner was," she added.

"The dirty FBI agent," he spat out like the profanity he tacked onto that. "And you believe he's after you?"

"I know he is. Well, one of his henchmen, anyway."

She glanced around again, praying that one of those thugs wasn't nearby, looking for her.

"I don't know how he found me," Hailey continued. "Maybe he hacked into the WITSEC files, or he could have bribed someone to give him the info. But three months ago, I found an eavesdropping device in my house here in Silver Creek, and I knew my identity had been blown."

"You should have come to me." His jaw muscles were at war with each other again. "Or since you were in WITSEC, you could have called your handler."

"I didn't get a chance. Before I could do anything, a hired gun showed up at my house. I hid, but he yelled out that if I didn't give myself up, he'd go after you and use you to get me to cooperate."

The skepticism was still written all over his face. "Cooperate with what?"

Oh, he was not going to like this. "I have some computer files that I didn't turn over to the cops. Files that incriminate Preston's son, Eric. Nothing as serious as murder, but it would have put him away for a few years."

"I'll want to see those files." And it wasn't a suggestion.

She nodded. "It'll take a while to access them. I put them in online storage with some security measures. I set it up so the files won't open until twelve hours after I put in the password."

"Clever," he mumbled, but Hailey didn't think that was a compliment. No. Lucas was silently cursing her for not bringing this to him sooner.

"I let Preston know I'd leak the files if anything happened to me," Hailey explained, "and that his son would head to prison right along with him. It was my insurance, a way of making sure he didn't send his hired thugs after me."

Lucas lifted his shoulder. "But he sent them anyway?"

"No. Preston was dead by then. I think the person who sent the thugs is the dirty agent. First, though, he wants those files."

"Or it could be his son who's after you," Lucas quickly pointed out.

"Maybe. But I didn't personally mention anything to Eric about having incriminating info on him."

Of course, that didn't mean Eric hadn't found out. Eric hadn't visited his father in prison. Not once. But Preston could have said something to one of his lackeys, who in turn passed the info on to Eric. Which wouldn't have necessarily been a bad thing. Because it could have kept Eric off her back, too, had he ever decided to come after her.

"How did you get away from that hired gun?" Lucas asked a moment later.

"I sneaked out the back of the house. I had a car, some cash and new identity papers in a storage unit." Hailey huffed. "I'll answer all your questions. I promise. But we can't stay here. In fact, you can't be with me."

He looked at her as if she'd just sprouted wings. "You think I'm going to dump you out here on the street?"

"No, but I was hoping you'd arrange to get me a car. Or let me use this SUV for a couple of hours."

"That's not going to happen. But I am taking you somewhere—to the sheriff's office."

"No." She couldn't say it fast enough, and Hailey went to the edge of her seat so she could take hold of his arm again. "Didn't you hear me? The office could be bugged. My hospital room was. That's why I didn't say anything to any of the medical staff. I wasn't sure who'd put it there or if I could trust any of them."

Lucas had already put the SUV in gear to drive away, no doubt to head toward the sheriff's office, but that piece of information stopped him. He turned, studying her, probably to decide how much of this was the truth.

Before he could make up his mind, his phone rang, and again she saw Grayson's name on the screen. She doubted Lucas would keep her secret much longer. He would spill everything to the sheriff.

And that meant she had to get out of there—fast.

But how? Lucas had all the doors locked, and she wasn't nearly strong enough to break the windows.

"We might have a problem," Grayson said when Lucas answered, and he put the call on speaker. "Dr. Parton called, and he said right after you left, a man showed up looking for Hailey. He claimed he was her brother."

Oh, God. "I don't have a brother," she mouthed.

"Doc Parton got suspicious," Grayson went on. "And he just sent me the surveillance footage of the guy coming in through the ER entrance. I put his photo into the facial recognition program and got an immediate hit."

Lucas groaned, no doubt because he knew what that

meant. If the guy was in the system, he had a record. "Who is he?" he asked the sheriff.

"Darrin Sandmire. A low-life thug." He paused. "Sandmire often works as a hit man."

Her heart slammed against her chest. It was happening. Her worst fears. The killer wasn't just after her. He was here in Silver Creek.

"Sandmire left the hospital before the security guard could stop him, so he could be anywhere in town. Now, you want to tell me what this is all about?" Grayson demanded.

"Yeah. I'll be at the sheriff's office in a few minutes." Lucas paused. "Hailey's with me."

The panic shot through her, and she tried the door handle even though Hailey knew she was trapped. If Lucas took her to the sheriff's office, she might be putting not only herself in danger but also all of them. Lucas put the SUV in gear again, but something must have caught his eye, because his attention zoomed to the driver's side window.

To the park.

Hailey saw it then, as well. The jogger she'd spotted earlier. But this time, he wasn't on the trail. He was coming straight toward the SUV.

And he had a gun in his hand.

CHAPTER THREE

"GET DOWN!" LUCAS shouted to Hailey.

His first instinct was to draw his gun and take aim at the man running toward them. But Lucas didn't want to get into a gunfight on Main Street where innocent bystanders—or Hailey—could be hurt.

Lucas wasn't sure he believed everything she'd just told him, but it was obvious she had someone after her. Later he'd find out who that was, but for now he wanted to put some distance between this armed man and them. He hit the accelerator.

Just as the guy took aim.

And fired.

The bullet slammed into the side of the SUV, missing the window and Lucas by only a couple of inches.

"I need a gun," Hailey said, climbing over the seat to get to the passenger side. She started to fumble around for the weapon that he'd knocked away from her.

"Stay down," Lucas warned her, but her search took care of that. Hailey crawled onto the floor.

At least, it took care of it for a couple of seconds. Once she had the gun, she got back in the seat and took aim out the back side window.

She fired.

The sound blasted through the SUV, causing Lucas to curse. He hadn't actually expected her to shoot. Too bad she missed, because the gunman sent another bullet their way.

Lucas sped off. The thug got off one more shot before Lucas took the first turn he reached. He wasn't driving in the direction of the sheriff's office, but he could double back.

Lucas tossed Hailey his phone. "Call Grayson and tell him there's an armed man near the park at the intersection of Main and Everett Road."

Hailey made the call, but she kept watch behind them, making sure that goon wasn't in pursuit. The moment Grayson answered, she rattled off the information. Then she hit the end call button. No doubt because she didn't want to answer Grayson's questions. That was okay. For now.

But as soon as they reached the sheriff's office, Hailey had better come clean about everything.

Lucas took another turn. Then another, meandering his way back to Main Street. That particular part of the park was only about seven blocks away from the sheriff's office, so it wouldn't take Grayson long to get a pair of deputies there to catch the guy.

"Do you know if that was Darrin Sandmire?" Lucas asked her.

"I have no idea. But I'm pretty sure that was the same man who came after me three months ago."

Hell.

Lucas had to rein in the anger that sliced through him. That was the SOB who'd put Hailey—and therefore, Camden—in danger. Too bad Lucas hadn't managed to shoot him. But then he rethought that. He didn't want the guy dead, not until he had answers from him.

Like who hired him.

Thugs like Darrin Sandmire always worked for bigger thugs. Maybe DeSalvo's son, Eric. Maybe that unidentified rogue agent. Soon, Lucas intended to find out who'd paid this killer to come after Hailey.

Lucas took another turn, the tires squealing against the asphalt. The moment he was on the side street, he saw something he didn't like.

A truck.

It wasn't right in the middle of the road, but the front end was jutting out from the parking space in front of a motorcycle repair shop.

Lucas hit his brakes.

"You think someone's inside the truck?" Hailey asked. Her voice was shaking like the rest of her.

Lucas didn't know, and it was next to impossible to see inside the truck's cab. There was a streetlight and a lit sign for the motorcycle shop, but the tint was so dark on the windshield that he couldn't tell. He pulled up a little farther though so he could get a better look at the front license plates.

"Out-of-state plates," he mumbled under his breath.

Maybe that in itself meant nothing, but Lucas got that feeling in his gut. The feeling that told him to get the heck out of there.

He threw the SUV into Reverse.

But the second he did that, the truck door opened, and a man bolted out.

The guy had a rifle.

"Get down," Lucas repeated to Hailey. "And this time, stay there."

Whether she would or not was anyone's guess, but he didn't want to have to worry about her being shot. He hit the gas, the SUV speeding backward. But he didn't get out of the path of that rifleman fast enough.

The bullet slammed into the windshield.

Since this wasn't the vehicle he used for work, the glass wasn't reinforced. The shot tore through the safety glass, the bullet exiting out the back.

Great. Just great.

Now he had two thugs after them, and Lucas had no choice but to go back in the direction he'd seen that other shooter in the park. Maybe the guy was long gone by now. Or better yet, maybe one of the deputies had managed to capture him.

When Lucas reached the side street, he spun the SUV around so he could drive forward. He definitely didn't want to head right into the middle of an ambush, so he headed for a better lit area.

"The truck's coming after us," Hailey said.

And that's when he realized she'd lifted her head and was looking out the side window.

Lucas pushed her right back down. "Don't make it easier for them to kill you," he snapped. Yeah, it was harsh, but Hailey was clearly the target of some very determined attackers.

Whoever was in the truck fired another shot at them, this one slamming into the rear end of the SUV. A second shot quickly followed.

Then a third.

"There must be two of them," Hailey muttered. She hadn't figured that out by looking at them, though. She was still on the floor.

But Lucas knew there had to be two, as well. Those shots were too well aimed for someone who was trying to negotiate the turns and dodging the cars parked along the street.

"Hang on," Lucas told her a split second before he turned onto another side street. He was thankful he'd grown up here and knew these streets like the back of his hand.

His phone buzzed, and since Hailey still had hold of it, she answered it and put it on speaker.

"Where are you?" he heard Grayson immediately ask. "Someone just called about shots being fired near Henderson's Motorcycle Shop."

"Someone in a blue pickup is shooting at us. We're on Bluebonnet Street, coming up near the Corral Bar." It was a risk since there'd be customers still inside, but Lucas didn't plan on stopping or even slowing down. "I'll turn back on Main Street and head in your direction. Please tell me you found the first shooter."

"Not yet. But I'll send Dade and Josh your way to help," Grayson said, and he ended the call.

Good. Dade and Josh were both cousins, both deputy sheriffs, and maybe having backup would cause these thugs to quit firing.

The parking lot of the Corral Bar was lit up better than the rest of the street, and Lucas glanced in his side mirror at the truck. Definitely two men. And the one on the passenger side was doing the shooting.

"I can return fire," Hailey insisted, already climbing into the seat and lowering the window. "Please don't stop me. This is all my fault, and I have to do something to stop them."

"No way." And he meant it. It might indeed be partially her fault for not coming to him sooner, but she wasn't sticking her neck out to fire any shots.

Hailey didn't get a chance to argue with him. That's because the sound of sirens stopped anything she was about to say. In the distance, behind the truck, Lucas saw the flashing blue lights of a police cruiser.

Dade and Josh, no doubt.

The driver stopped following Lucas and took a very quick turn off a side street. A street that would lead them straight to the highway.

No, hell, no.

Lucas didn't want these clowns getting away, but it wasn't smart to go in pursuit with Hailey in the vehicle. Besides, Dade and Josh went after them, and Lucas could only hope they'd catch them.

"Keep watch for the other shooter," Lucas told Hailey.

He hated to rely on her for help, but with the glass in the front, back and side windows cracked and webbed, they had reduced visibility. That would make it hard for them to see the guy hiding between one of the buildings where he could shoot at them as they drove by.

Lucas held his breath, going as fast as he could, and he didn't release that breath until he made it back onto Main Street. Definitely no sign of the shooter, so he headed for the sheriff's office.

"Can you run?" he asked her.

"I'll try," she assured him. Which meant she couldn't. "I had to use a cane to walk to your SUV."

Definitely couldn't.

The SUV squealed to a stop directly in front of the door to the sheriff's office, but he didn't get out. Lucas waited until Grayson hurried to the door and threw it open.

"I'm carrying you in," Lucas insisted, and he didn't leave any room for argument.

He scooped her up in his arms and rushed her inside the building, with Grayson locking the door behind them. But Lucas didn't stop there. He hurried her past the squad room to the hall that led to Grayson's office and the break room. That way, if someone did come in with guns blazing, she'd have some protection.

"Dade and Josh are in pursuit," Lucas told Grayson. "Arizona plates, but there was something covering the numbers. Mud, I think." Probably not an accident.

"Arizona?" Hailey repeated.

Lucas knew the reason for her concern. DeSalvo had been from Arizona, which meant his son, Eric, likely was, too. So, had Eric sent those goons after Hailey?

Now that they weren't in the SUV, Lucas got a better look at her. Especially a better look at the fear in her eyes. And the fact that she was having to grip the door to steady herself.

"As soon as it's safe, I'll have the doctor come over to see you," Lucas told her.

But she was shaking her head before he even finished. "I can't trust Dr. Parton. Or anyone in the hospital. Someone planted that bug on the table next to my bed."

Lucas certainly hadn't forgotten about that. The device needed to be checked, but that would have to wait, because Grayson no doubt had every available deputy on this manhunt for the shooters.

"When there's time, Hailey will need to give you a statement," Lucas told Grayson.

Grayson nodded. He still had his gun drawn, was still keeping watch on the area just outside the building. "Is she in WITSEC?"

"Yes," Hailey answered. "But I don't want the marshals to know I'm here."

Grayson mumbled something Lucas didn't catch, but he didn't need to hear the words to know that Grayson wasn't pleased about all this going on right under his nose.

"Hell, you worked for me," Grayson added.

She nodded. "I figured it was a way to keep an eye on what was happening in town, just in case something went wrong." Hailey paused. "And something did go wrong."

Yeah. And Lucas wondered if sleeping with him was in that something-gone-wrong category.

"I'll call Mason and give him an update," Grayson said after he shot Hailey a glare.

Hailey dropped back a step, holding onto Grayson's desk. Lucas was volleying his attention between her and the outside. However, she got his complete attention when she made a soft gasp.

Lucas hurried to her, following her gaze to the computer on the desk. It was obviously the security feed that the doctor had sent Grayson. In the shot, the tall, lanky man was coming through the glass doors of the ER. Grayson had paused it and zoomed in on the man's face.

Darrin Sandmire, no doubt.

Lucas had no trouble seeing the renewed fear in Hailey's eyes. "That's definitely the man who came to my house three months ago. And the man who ran me off the road that night."

Lucas hadn't needed to hear anything else about the guy to know that he wanted him caught, questioned and punished.

Hailey touched the screen to get the security feed moving again. Darrin disappeared from view when he walked past the camera and to the hall. Since it would

have taken him several minutes to get to her room, Lucas
sped up the footage, watching for Darrin to reemerge.

He did.

But the man wasn't alone.

There was a woman with him, walking right by his
side, and it was obvious they were talking. The woman
was a blonde, and she kept her head down. Right until
she was close to the camera.

Now Hailey's gasp wasn't so soft.

"I know her. That's Colleen Jeffrey."

The name meant nothing to Lucas, and he didn't recognize her, either. "Who is she?"

There were tears shimmering in Hailey's eyes when
she looked up at him. "My half sister."

Damn.

Lucas was about to assure her that maybe this was
a coincidence. But it didn't look like that to him. He
needed to get this woman in for questioning right away.

He heard the footsteps. Hurried ones, and they put
Lucas right back on alert again. Though he hadn't exactly been relaxing.

"We've got a problem," Grayson said, stepping into
the doorway. "Someone tripped the security sensor near
the back fence at the ranch. One of the ranch hands spotted a gunman."

CHAPTER FOUR

HAILEY'S BREATH FROZE. She wanted to scream, to shout out for Lucas to hurry to the ranch so they could protect their son, but the words and sounds were wedged there in her throat.

No. This couldn't be happening. This monster couldn't get to her baby.

Even without her warning, Lucas thankfully understood just how dangerous a situation this could be, because he took off running toward the front of the building. Hailey followed him. Or rather, she tried.

Lucas must have remembered she was still hobbling, because he spun around, scooped her up in his arms and hurried toward his shot-up SUV still parked just outside the door.

"We need to use a cruiser," Grayson called out to them. "Because this could be a trap to lure you into the open."

Lucas stopped, and while everything inside Hailey wanted to move, to hurry to the ranch, she knew Grayson was right.

"Wait right here for me," Grayson insisted. "I'll bring the cruiser around to the front."

Hailey didn't want to waste precious minutes while he did that, but they didn't have many options here. Lucas and she waited, the time crawling by slower than a snail's pace, and it seemed to take an eternity for Grayson to drive up. Even before the cruiser came to a stop, Lucas and she jumped into the backseat, and Grayson took off again.

"I'll call the ranch and get an update," Lucas said.

As much as she wanted to know what was going on, Hailey didn't want anyone there distracted right now. She wanted all the focus on protecting the baby.

Camden.

The name seemed foreign to her. Probably because she'd yet to see her son, but maybe that would change soon. Maybe they'd get to the ranch and put an end to the danger.

"Tillie," Lucas said to whoever answered his call.

"One of the nannies," Grayson provided to Hailey, but he didn't even glance back at her when he spoke. He looked all around, no doubt in case someone was trying to follow them.

Or attack them again.

Hailey couldn't hear what the nanny was saying, but since Lucas's arm was pressed against her, she felt his muscles relax just a little. "We'll be there as fast as we can." He paused. "Hailey's with me."

The nanny perhaps hadn't even heard she was out of the coma, so this could be a real shock. An unwanted one. Hailey didn't know Tillie, but she doubted she was going to get a warm reception from anyone at the Silver Creek Ranch. It wouldn't matter that she thought she'd done the right thing.

Still did think that.

But a family of lawmen wouldn't see it that way. They would believe she should have trusted them. However, maybe they could see now that all the trust in the world wouldn't have put an end to the danger.

Oh, mercy.

That reminder came at her hard, like a heavyweight's fist. The reason she'd tried to escape was to avoid this. To keep her child safe. And now he wasn't safe because of her.

"Whoever's behind the attacks will use Camden to get to me," Hailey said under her breath.

She hadn't intended to say that aloud, and it stung even more when Lucas made a sound of agreement. He'd finished his call with the nanny and now was keeping watch. Along with glancing at her.

"That doesn't mean you're going to try to take him and disappear," Lucas snapped. There wasn't a shred of gentleness in his tone. In fact, it was the same tone he likely used with criminal suspects.

"It's too late to take him and hide," Hailey agreed. "Too late for me to disappear, as well. Because now that they know I'm awake, they won't stop, and they'll try to use the baby to come after me."

That meant she needed to find out who *they* were. And fast. For that to happen, she needed to rely on Lucas.

Something that wouldn't please him.

It didn't please her, either, but no one would work harder than Lucas to keep Camden safe. Of course, once that happened, and this snake was captured and behind bars, Lucas and she would have another battle to fight.

For custody.

But that was a fight that would have to wait for another day. Right now, Hailey had enough to deal with.

"The fences are all rigged with security alarms?" she asked.

"Yeah," Grayson and Lucas answered at the same time. It was Lucas who continued. "There are also sensors on the grounds. Cameras, too. Since this clown tripped a sensor, the ranch hands and my cousins will be able to pinpoint his exact location before he can get near one of the houses."

Good. But pinpointing him wasn't the same as stopping the threat.

"Hurry," Hailey said to Grayson. She was speaking purely out of frustration, because he was going as fast as he safely could.

The rural roads that led to the ranch weren't exactly straight. Plenty of sharp curves and turns, and it certainly wouldn't help them if Grayson wrecked.

Something she knew all too well.

Hailey couldn't quite choke back a gasp when the cruiser tires squealed around one of those turns and it felt as if Grayson was losing control of the vehicle. All the memories of that other night came flooding back.

The frantic rush to get away from the person trying to kill her. The adrenaline and the fear. Even the feeling of the impact.

The pain.

But more intense than the pain and the fear had been the sickening dread that she'd failed.

"Flashbacks?" Lucas asked.

She nodded. "I remember that you're the one who found me that night. If it hadn't been you…"

Hailey didn't finish that thought. No need. Lucas had found her, and while it hadn't made things perfect, it had allowed her to deliver the baby safely.

Grayson took the final turn, and Hailey saw the ranch come into view. To say it was sprawling was an understatement. It'd been huge, but now that the Ryland cousins were buying up the adjacent land and building their own homes, the place stretched out for miles and miles.

They'd also added more security since the last time she'd visited. There was now a large security gate, and she saw several men near it. Ranch hands, probably, since she didn't recognize any of them.

"Get down," Lucas told her as they approached the gate. He lowered the window. "Anything?" he asked the men.

"Yep. Just a few seconds ago Sawyer called to say he shot at a guy who'd crossed over the fence. He and two of the other hands are chasing him."

Hailey sucked in her breath. Sawyer was his cousin as well as an FBI agent. "Did Sawyer have to fire shots anywhere near the houses?"

The guy volleyed glances among Lucas, Grayson and her. Maybe he was trying to figure out if it was okay if he answered since he probably didn't even know who she was.

"No, the shooting happened in the back pasture," the guy said after Lucas gave him a go-ahead nod. "Mason said, though, that y'all should wait down here until they've made sure there's only one."

Oh, mercy.

As hard as that was to hear—and it was even harder for her to stay put—Hailey knew he was right. The attacker might not be alone. Heck, he could have brought an entire army with him, and it was best to aim that army at her rather than launch an attack near the houses.

Still, waiting was hard.

Even if she lifted her head, something Lucas wouldn't like her to do, Hailey couldn't see Lucas's house from this part of the road, but she knew it was less than a half mile away. She knew because he'd taken her there for the one night they'd been together. The night she'd had a serious lapse in judgment and gotten way too personal with a man she should have avoided. Or so it'd seemed at the time. But without that night, she wouldn't have her son, and despite everything that'd gone on, the one thing she was certain of was that she loved her baby.

Lucas didn't seem to be having an easier time waiting than she was. He put the window back up, mumbled some profanity and took out his phone. This time she saw that he was calling the nanny again.

"Just checking to make sure everything is okay," Lucas said when Tillie answered.

Hailey automatically scooted closer so she could hear what the nanny had to say, but that only earned her a scowl from Lucas. He put the call on speaker, her cue to inch away from him. She did.

"The baby's fine," Tillie assured Lucas. "He went straight to sleep after his bottle. And Mason's still here just in case."

Just in case everything went from bad to worse. Hailey hated that it was a possibility, but Mason was another lawman, so it was good to have him there. She prayed, though, that he wouldn't be needed and that the danger would end soon. With this idiot intruder not just in custody but also willing to tell them the name of the person who'd hired him.

"You said earlier that Hailey was with you," Tillie went on. She paused. "Is, uh, everything okay? Did that man try to get onto the ranch because of her?"

"Yeah," Lucas admitted. Now he was the one who

paused. "I'll need to take the baby someplace safe. Will you be able to come with us?"

"Of course," Tillie quickly agreed.

Hailey was shaking her head before the nanny even answered.

The head shaking caused Lucas to scowl again. "I'm going to protect my son," he snarled as if she didn't want the same thing.

She did. More than anything, she wanted him safe. Lucas and his family, too. "But I want to see him."

That got Lucas's muscles tightening again. "And then what?"

It was a good question. Hailey didn't have anything resembling a good answer. "I don't know," she admitted. "I need some answers, and I think the place to start is with my sister."

"I agree," Lucas said without hesitation. "I'll want her contact info and anything recent you have on her. I'll especially want to know why she could want you dead."

"I don't know any of those things," Hailey had to admit. "I haven't seen or heard from Colleen since I've been in WITSEC."

Lucas huffed, clearly not pleased that she hadn't given him something to go on. "You two were close?"

"Once." But that was another round of bad memories. "We were both working as computer systems analysts for Preston DeSalvo's company. I testified against him, but Colleen didn't. She claimed she didn't see the incriminating evidence that I found."

Lucas jumped right on that. "She lied?"

"Maybe. But I can't believe she'd be the one behind this. I'm still her sister."

He gave her a flat look. "Cain and Abel were brothers, and you know how that ended."

Yes, with one murdering the other, but Hailey had to hang on to something, and that something was that her only sister hadn't betrayed her like this. Still, she wanted to talk to Colleen and get this all sorted out.

She nearly reached for his phone to make a call, but there was no one who came to mind that she could trust. Well, no one other than Lucas.

"I'll bring Colleen in for questioning," Lucas said as if reading her mind. He didn't get a chance to add anything else because the sound got their attention.

A shot.

Even though it was in the distance, it still caused Hailey's heart to slam against her chest. She held her breath, waiting, and even though she tried to steel herself for whatever would happen next, she still gasped when Lucas's phone buzzed.

"Mason," he said looking at the screen before he answered it and put the call on speaker.

She hadn't thought her heart could beat any faster, but she'd obviously been wrong. Mason was with the baby, and if he was calling then maybe that meant the shot had been fired close to the house.

Or in it.

Hailey pressed her fingers to her mouth and listened, praying.

"Sawyer fired the shot," Mason said. "The guy's alive for now."

"Is he talking?" Lucas asked.

"No, but I just called an ambulance, so maybe he'll say something on the way to the hospital. Sawyer has a way of getting dirt to talk."

Good. But that didn't mean this was over. "Are there any other attackers out there?" Hailey pressed.

Just as the ranch hand had done, Mason hesitated. "No. Nothing else is showing up on any of the security feeds, either. It looks as if this clown came alone. And I don't think he came here to kill anybody. He had surveillance equipment on him."

So there could be others on the way. It was too much to hope that this guy's injury and arrest would get the person behind this to back off.

"It's safe for you to come to the house," Mason continued. "If you want to come, that is."

She knew what he meant by that. Mason was giving his cousin an out in case Lucas didn't want her to see the baby. Hailey was about to insist that happen when Lucas gave Grayson the go-ahead to get moving.

Toward the house.

Hailey sat back up, keeping watch around them, but she was also looking for the house. It finally came into view since it was the first building on the ranch road. All of the interior lights were off, probably as a safety precaution, but there were security lights on all four corners of the property. Enough for her to see the barn and corral that hadn't been there a year ago.

Lucas was making this place a home.

Part of her was thankful for that. Their son deserved it. But she was betting there was no place in this home for her.

Grayson pulled to a stop directly in front of the porch, and the door opened. Mason. Yet another unfriendly face, but then, Mason usually looked unfriendly. As he'd done at the sheriff's office, Lucas got her in—fast. This time, though, he didn't carry her. He looped his arm around her waist to steady her, and the moment they were inside, he moved away from her.

Hailey immediately looked around for the baby. But there was no sign of him or the nanny. She was about to demand to see him, but Mason stepped in front of her.

"Just got a text from Sawyer," Mason said, his voice low and dangerous. "The guy he shot is drifting in and out of consciousness, but this is what the guy said."

He held his phone screen up for her to see, and the words there caused her to drop back a step.

Hailey Darrow paid me to take the kid.

CHAPTER FIVE

LUCAS DIDN'T KNOW who looked more shocked by the accusation that the wounded gunman had just made. He or Hailey.

"I didn't," she said, her gaze firing between Mason and him. "I only left the hospital a couple of hours ago."

Mason didn't seem convinced. "You were conscious for a week. You could have called someone and set this whole thing up."

The anger flared through Hailey's eyes, and she opened her mouth as if ready to return verbal fire, but she was obviously spent. Heck, so was Lucas, and while part of him hated to defend the woman who'd tried to run from him, he couldn't see how this would have played out.

"There was no phone in her hospital room," Lucas explained. "And yes, she could have borrowed one from someone on the staff, but that kind of thing doesn't stay a secret very long."

Lucas could have gone on and mentioned the part about Hailey not having touched her bank accounts since she'd been in the coma, and it wasn't as if she'd had wads of cash lying around the hospital to pay someone to carry through on something like this.

Even Lucas's own explanation didn't seem to convince Mason. "You trust her, then?" Mason asked.

"No," Lucas readily admitted. "But if Hailey intended to take the baby, she wouldn't have done it this way."

At least, he hoped like the devil that she wouldn't. The baby and other members of his family could have been hurt by the thug who'd trespassed onto the ranch.

"Thank you," Hailey said to him.

For some reason, that riled Lucas. Maybe because he didn't want to do anything for her that would cause her to say something like that.

"So, who did hire the *lying* sack of dirt?" Mason asked.

Hailey shook her head, but it was clear from the way she was looking around that her attention was elsewhere. She obviously wanted to see the baby, and Lucas tried to remind himself that if their positions were reversed, he would have wanted the same thing.

Of course, their positions would never be reversed because he would have never gone on the run from the law.

"I'll question Hailey's sister, Colleen, and Eric De-Salvo in the morning." Lucas tipped his head to the hall that led to the bedrooms. "Is Tillie in the nursery?"

Mason lowered his phone and nodded. Even though he didn't voice his disapproval as to what was about to happen, it was on his face. "I'll wait here until I get the all-clear from Sawyer."

Lucas thanked him and made a mental note to thank all the others who'd pulled together to keep Camden safe. For now, though, he had to focus on getting through this. And *this* was having Hailey see the baby.

From the moment Camden had been born, Lucas had known it might come down to this. But as every day had passed with Hailey in a coma, he'd also considered that she might never wake up. That she might never have a claim on their child. Now, here she was, and Lucas was having to face one of his worst fears.

That he might lose his son.

Not to a kidnapper, either. But to Hailey. She wouldn't be able to get full custody of Camden. No way would Lucas allow that, but she would be entitled to visitation rights. Considering she was in WITSEC, that was going to be tricky. And not very safe for any of them.

Moving ahead of her, Lucas led her down the hall. She caught onto the side of the wall to steady herself, and she was probably moving as fast as she could go.

When they reached the nursery, Lucas stepped in, his gaze immediately connecting with the nanny's. There was just as much concern in Tillie's expression as there had been in Mason's. But she stepped aside so that Lucas—and Hailey—had the crib in their direct line of sight.

Where Camden was sleeping.

"I'll be in the living room if you need me," Tillie said, but her offer seemed to be a question, as if maybe he wanted her to stay.

Lucas nodded, giving her the go-ahead to leave, but Hailey didn't wait for Tillie to be out the door before she hobbled her way to the crib. The sound that left her mouth crushed at his heart. Part moan, part sigh.

All love.

It was a sound and a look that Lucas felt all too well because he got that same punch of emotion every time he was near his son. And even when he wasn't.

"He's so beautiful," Hailey whispered, touching her fingers to the wispy strands of dark brown hair.

Lucas had to agree with her, but he was certain that was the reaction of most parents. Certain, too, that Hailey would want to do more than just touch his hair. She looked back at him, as if waiting for permission. She didn't wait long, though, before she scooped Camden up in her arms.

She made that sound again and kissed his cheek. Even though Camden stirred a little, he went right back to sleep. Good. Even though his son was too young to know what was going on, Lucas didn't want to risk Camden being upset by having his sleep interrupted. He also didn't want to risk Hailey falling with the child, and since her legs were obviously still wobbly, he helped her to the nearby chair.

"Is he healthy?" she asked.

"Yeah." It was hard for him to talk about something so—well—normal. "He's right on target for his height, weight and milestones."

She nodded and looked up at him, and that's when he saw the tears in her eyes. "I was so scared that he'd been hurt in the accident."

"He could have been," Lucas quickly pointed out, but then instantly regretted the jab. It was the truth, but stating the obvious didn't make him feel any better.

"I know. I'm so sorry. When I ran, my only thought was to keep him safe."

Lucas nearly went for another jab by reminding her that the safe thing to do would have been to come to him, but that ship had already sailed. They were here now and had to deal with this. Not just the danger, either. But all those old feelings.

He'd been attracted to her once and vice versa. That's what had landed them in bed in the first place. And while there were still some lingering traces of the attraction, it wouldn't play into this. He hoped the bitterness he felt over what'd happened wouldn't, either. Right now, bitterness wouldn't help.

He was about to question her more about the night of the accident, to see if she remembered any details that would help them find out who was responsible for the attacks, but Hailey spoke before he did.

"Tell me about the delivery," she said.

Lucas paused, not because he intended to hold anything back, but because remembering that night still felt like a punch to the gut.

"I was scared," he admitted. "We didn't know if there'd been trauma to the baby, and since you were so close to your due date, the docs did a C-section on you. But everything turned out okay. Everything except that you were in a coma," Lucas added.

She, too, paused. Then nodded. "I've heard that some people remember and hear things while they're in comas. I didn't." She brushed another kiss on Camden's cheek. "I wish I could remember seeing him as a newborn. He's already so big."

Camden was, but while Hailey had indeed missed a lot, the baby wasn't old enough to have noticed that his mom hadn't been around.

Hailey looked up at Lucas again, those tears still shimmering in her eyes. "I know this is hard for you. You haven't had to share him with anyone for the past three months."

Lucas wasn't sure how to respond to that and didn't get a chance to say anything anyway, because Mason appeared in the doorway. One look at his cousin's face and Lucas knew something else had gone wrong. Apparently so did Hailey, because she slowly got to her feet, her attention nailed to Mason.

"The gunman died on the way to the hospital," Mason said.

Hell. Lucas had wanted him alive so they could get answers. But maybe they could still do that. "Did he have a phone on him? Maybe his boss's number is in his contacts?"

Mason nodded. "Grayson will check for that, but there's more." He paused. "The ranch hands did a thorough search of the fence line in that back part of the ranch, and it appears the dead thug didn't come alone. There were enough tracks back there for three people."

Lucas bit back the profanity that he nearly blurted out, something he'd been training himself to do now that he was a father. Still, it was hard not to curse about that. "Any other signs of the men?"

"No. They're apparently gone. For now, anyway."

That didn't mean they wouldn't be back. Maybe even tonight, since the darkness would give them an advantage for an attack.

"I've got men patrolling the entire ranch," Mason went on. "I also called everyone and told them to lock down and stay inside."

By "everyone" he meant his brothers and their cousins. No one would be leaving and coming onto the ranch unless Mason gave the okay. Which he wouldn't do until he was certain it was safe. And Lucas knew what that meant.

This time he wasn't able to stop himself from cursing.

Because it meant Hailey would have to stay there.

Of course, he probably wouldn't have been able to talk her into budging since she'd want to be near the baby, but Lucas had planned on having her sleep far away from the Silver Creek Ranch. Far away from Camden, too.

"I'm so sorry," Hailey whispered. Maybe she was apologizing again for the danger. But one look in her eyes and Lucas knew the reason for this "I'm sorry." She had also figured out what the sleeping arrangements would be.

"You can stay in the guest room," Lucas growled. It was at the end of the hall, as far away as he could get her while still having her under the same roof.

Hailey mumbled a thanks, and while Lucas thought part of her looked relieved, that was still fear he saw in her eyes. Worry, too. Especially worry when she looked at Mason again. His cousin wasn't budging. Mason continued to stand there, his hands bracketed on the doorjamb.

"What else happened?" Hailey asked Mason. Her voice was shaky again, probably because she knew they were about to get another dose of bad news.

"Grayson tried to get in touch with Colleen, so he could bring her in for questioning." Mason paused again. "But there's a problem. Colleen is missing."

HAILEY HOPED THIS medical exam wasn't a mistake.

She wasn't certain about the ER physician, Dr. Parton, but Lucas had assured her that Parton wasn't the one who'd planted that bug in her hospital room, that the doctor was trustworthy. So, that's what Hailey was going to do—trust him. Besides, she needed to make sure she was okay. Not just for her sake but to soothe some of the concern on Lucas's face.

Of course, she had plenty of her own concerns, too. There were so many things for her to worry about, and that's what she'd done through the night and now the morning. The constant threat of an attack. Her missing sister. The obvious tension between Lucas and her. Between her and his family, too.

But it was hard for Hailey to focus solely on all of that when she was looking at her son's face while Lucas was holding him.

For the entire time she'd carried him, she had considered how he might look. Considered as well the love she would feel for him, but she'd way underestimated that love. She couldn't believe how deep it was for this child, and even though it crushed her heart, she knew that same feeling of love was the very reason that Lucas would do everything to hang on to his child.

Everything, including attempts to exclude her.

Those attempts wouldn't work, of course. Or maybe they wouldn't. If they couldn't stop the threat of another attack, then she might have no choice but to disappear. She'd do that if it meant keeping Camden safe.

She'd started that process by using Lucas's laptop and putting in her password for the storage cloud for the files she'd gathered on Eric DeSalvo. It'd be a few more hours before she could open them, but once Lucas had a chance to go over them, maybe he could find something he could use to arrest Eric. It might not put an end to the attacks, but at least it would get him off the streets for a while.

"Follow the light with your eyes," Dr. Parton instructed her.

Hailey did, though it meant taking her attention off her son. And Lucas. Lucas was feeding the baby his bottle while he had his phone sandwiched between his shoulder and his ear. She wasn't sure who was on the other end of the phone line this time, but Lucas had obviously adapted to juggling his work with fatherhood.

"From what I can tell, you're fine," the doctor said, stepping back from her. "You'll need a thorough exam, though, and some tests that I can do only at the hospital. Any idea when it'll be okay for that?"

It was the million-dollar question, and Hailey didn't have a clue what the answer was. She shook her head. "We're waiting on some information." Information that would ideally lead to an arrest.

The doctor didn't seem especially pleased with an indefinite delay to those tests, and Hailey knew why. There could be brain damage. And damage to her legs. The muscles felt a little stronger, but she was nowhere near a hundred percent and might need physical therapy to regain all her strength. No way could she risk going to PT or taking those tests now, though, and she didn't want to speculate how long it would be before that happened.

The doctor gathered his things and headed to the door, where Mason was waiting to escort him back to town. They left, leaving Hailey to sit there and watch as Camden finished his bottle. As if it were the most natural thing in the world, Lucas put the bottle aside and moved the baby to his shoulder to burp him.

A year ago, if someone had told her that the tough cowboy cop would be the doting father, she wouldn't have believed it. Lucas likely wouldn't have, either.

Tillie came out of the kitchen and made eye contact with Lucas. "You want me to take him?" Tillie mouthed.

"No, thanks. I'm finished with my call." He put away his phone and looked at Hailey. "That was Grayson. Still no word on your sister, but Eric DeSalvo should be arriving at the sheriff's office any minute now."

Good. Hailey figured the best place to start with getting those answers would be with Eric. And Colleen. It sickened her to think that her sister might be involved in this.

"What about the other gunmen who were around the ranch last night?" she asked. "Any signs of them?"

"No. And the dead guy, Darrin, was using a burner cell phone and didn't have any contacts stored there. In fact, the phone hadn't been used, so there's nothing to trace."

Another dead end. Literally. Since Darrin had lived only long enough to accuse her of hiring him.

"Grayson had the medics take Darrin's picture," Lucas went on. When he reached to take his phone from his jeans pocket, it caused the baby to move, and Camden stirred, lifting his head just a little.

Hailey figured Camden was too young to see her from across the room, so she went closer. Lucas didn't scowl, exactly, but it was close. He took out his phone and handed it to her.

"Take a look at the picture Grayson sent, and see if you recognize Darrin. Is he the same man who went after you the night you were trying to get away?"

She took the phone, her fingers brushing against his. Lucas noticed. Noticed, too, that she was volleying glances between the baby and him. He pulled in a long, weary breath.

"Sit down," he growled. "You can hold Camden while you tell me about the picture."

Hailey moved as fast as she could, making her way back to the chair. Lucas went to her, easing the baby into her arms.

There it was again. That punch of emotion.

Though it was hard to focus with Camden staring up at her, Hailey studied the photo. It wasn't the best shot since the man's face was twisted with pain, but Hailey picked through the features.

And remembered.

She sucked in her breath so fast that she nearly got choked. "He definitely looks like the man who ran me off the road."

Other memories came flooding back. The car following her. Her frantic attempt to get away. Then the crash.

"He rammed into the back of my car, forcing me into a ditch," she explained. "That's when I hit my head."

Thank goodness she'd been wearing a seat belt. That had prevented her from being thrown from the car, but it hadn't stopped the tree limb from coming through the windshield and hitting her.

Lucas stared at her, clearly waiting for more details. Hailey had more, but she had to fight the panicky feeling rising in her again. It wasn't that night, but it suddenly felt as if it was.

"After I crashed, Darrin came to the side of the car," Hailey continued. "He looked at me." But then she stopped, her attention going back to Lucas. "Why didn't he just kill me then? I was helpless, barely conscious."

"Maybe he didn't want you dead," Lucas said. "He probably wanted those computer files and would have been willing to torture you to get them."

Yes. That had to be it. "But he didn't get a chance to kidnap me, because that's about the time you drove up. Did you see Darrin leave?"

"I saw his SUV speeding away. I couldn't go in pursuit."

That's because she had needed medical attention

ASAP. Lucas had saved her life. Camden's, too, by staying with them. Lucas didn't seem any more comfortable
thinking about that night than she did, and he looked
relieved when Tillie came back into the living room.

"Is Camden ready for his bath?" the nanny asked, her
voice tentative, probably because she knew that Hailey
wanted to continue holding him.

Lucas nodded. "Best if he sticks to his routine," he
told Hailey. "Plus, we need to do reports for the attack."

Yes, paperwork. Necessary, but she still hated having to hand her son over to the nanny. She'd gotten so
few minutes holding him. Of course, a lifetime would
be too few.

"You can watch," Tillie added, glancing at Hailey.
"That way, you'll know how to do it." She also glanced
at Lucas, and Tillie seemed to ignore the slight scowl
that was on his face.

Maybe a scowl because it would mean a delay in
doing those reports, but also because Tillie was including her.

Hailey didn't give Lucas a chance to veto Tillie's
offer. She stood, following the woman as best she could
to the bathroom just across the hall from the nursery.
Lucas followed, too. Good thing, because just before
Hailey reached the door, she stumbled and would have
fallen flat on her face if Lucas hadn't caught her.

And just like that, she was in his arms.

The memories came. No way to stop them. Not with
Lucas and her being body to body. Hailey got some
flashes of even more body contact. Of when they were
naked in bed.

Mercy, that caused the heat to flood through her
again. Worse, Lucas noticed, and he looked as if he

wanted to curse again. He didn't. He moved her away from him. Well, he moved so that her breasts were no longer pressed against his chest, but he looped his arm around her waist to steady her.

"You should be resting," he grumbled.

"Would you rest if you were in my shoes?" she countered.

That only deepened his scowl. Both knew the answer to that—no, he wouldn't.

Lucas kept his arm around her when they went to the doorway, but it was obvious that he was trying to touch as little of her as possible. Hailey soon didn't notice it because her attention was on the baby. Or at least, it was until Lucas's phone buzzed. She was close enough to see Grayson's name on the screen.

She felt the muscles in Lucas's arm tense. Probably because this could be bad news. He stepped back into the hall, answered the call and put it on speaker.

"Is Hailey there?" Grayson said without even issuing a greeting. Yes, this was bad news. Hailey could tell from his tone.

"I'm here," she answered.

"San Antonio PD found your sister," Grayson continued.

"Where is she?" Hailey immediately asked.

"The hospital. She's hurt, and she's asking to see you. Colleen says she knows who's trying to kill you."

CHAPTER SIX

A CAR ACCIDENT.

That's what had put Colleen in the hospital. And not just any ordinary accident, but one that'd happened on the same stretch of road where Hailey had nearly been killed. Lucas figured that was either an eerie coincidence or someone was trying to send them a message.

If it was a message, Lucas hadn't needed it. He knew just how much danger they were in. That's why it was almost certainly a mistake to take Hailey off the ranch and to the hospital, with the threat of an attack still hanging over their heads. But he also knew this meeting with Colleen could give them critical information to put an end to the danger.

Maybe an immediate end.

If Colleen confessed to helping Darrin when he tried to run Hailey off the road.

Lucas doubted that would actually happen, but he wouldn't rule it out. Heck, he wasn't ruling out anything right now. After all, he'd sworn that Hailey would never be under his roof again, and she'd not only spent the night there but also was back in his arms. Sort of. As he'd done earlier, he had to help her out of the cruiser, and that involved touching her.

He didn't have to remind her to hurry, and she did. As much as a hobbling woman could hurry. Lucas only hoped all this moving around wasn't doing anything to harm her leg muscles. The sooner he put some physical distance between them, the better, and that started with her getting back to a hundred percent.

Lucas believed her story about someone trying to kill her. And he felt a little sorry for her. But he wasn't ready to welcome her back into his and Camden's lives.

There was a deputy at the door to the hospital. Another inside. Since his cousins Dade and Gage had escorted Lucas and Hailey to the hospital, that meant Grayson had three other lawmen plus himself tied up with this.

"Thank you for not saying it was a stupid idea for me to come here," Hailey whispered as they made their way down the hall.

Lucas glanced at her from the corner of his eye. "Just because I didn't say it doesn't mean I agree with this. You could have demanded that Colleen tell you everything over the phone."

She glanced at him, too. "I did demand," she reminded him.

Yeah, but Hailey hadn't stood her ground when Colleen had insisted that she speak to her sister in person. This felt like a trap, and while the baby wasn't in danger at the moment, Hailey clearly was.

When they reached the patient ward of the hospital, Lucas spotted yet another lawman cousin. Josh. But he wasn't alone. There was a lanky, dark-haired guy in a black suit standing next to him. Judging from their scowls, neither Josh nor the suit were happy.

Hailey had an equally unhappy reaction to the man. She sucked in her breath. "That's Brian Minton. He was one of the FBI agents who worked on the DeSalvo investigation."

Even though they were only a few yards from Minton, Lucas stopped. "You don't trust him?"

The question was valid, considering Lucas could feel Hailey's suddenly tight muscles. She hadn't exactly been relaxed on the trip over, but the tension was even worse now.

"I don't trust anyone involved in that," Hailey answered without taking her attention off Minton. "Remember, Preston DeSalvo had a dirty agent on his payroll. I'm positive of that."

No way could Lucas forget it, especially now that he'd read the file about it. The problem was, there'd been at least a dozen agents involved in that case and countless others who might have distanced themselves from it just so there'd be no obvious connection to the DeSalvo family.

"Any proof that Minton's dirty?" Lucas pressed.

"No," Hailey readily admitted, and she got moving again. "What are you doing here?" she asked the agent.

"I've asked him the same thing," Josh provided. "I've also told him he's not getting into Colleen's room until I get the okay from the sheriff. I haven't gotten that okay," he added, directing his glare at Minton.

Minton tapped his badge. "I'm here to interview two witnesses—Colleen and Laura—or, rather, Hailey, as she's going by these days. This investigation belongs to the FBI."

"How do you figure that?" Lucas said, but he didn't wait for an explanation. "Hailey is in WITSEC, and the marshals are in charge of that. As for Colleen, she was in a car accident in the jurisdiction of the Silver Creek Sheriff's Office."

Minton gave him a blank stare and huffed. "You and I both know this is connected to the DeSalvo family."

Lucas almost hoped this guy was dirty just so he could arrest him. "I know no such thing. I'm just bringing Hailey here to visit her sister."

"A sister who could have information I need," Minton countered.

Welcome to the club, but Lucas was first in line to question Colleen.

"Who ran Colleen off the road?" Minton asked, volleying his gaze between Hailey and Lucas.

Lucas shrugged. "Don't have a clue. Yet. How about you? Do you know who did this?"

"Probably the same thug who caused Hailey's accident."

"That thug is dead," Lucas said. "He died last night. From what I understand, Colleen's accident happened hours later."

Judging from the startled look in Minton's eyes, he hadn't known that. Or else he was pretending not to have known. "Eric could be behind this," Minton added after a long pause.

Yes, he could be. Or Colleen. Or even Minton himself. Lucas kept his speculations to himself to see if Minton would continue. He did.

"Whoever did this had a chance to kill you that night," Minton reminded Hailey. "He might have had the same chance to kill Colleen. But he didn't take it." He paused. "Why?"

Hailey shook her head. "I don't know."

No more startled look in Minton's eyes, but the comment seemed to rile him. "There are rumors that you have some files. Files that could incriminate Eric. If you have something like that, it's illegal to withhold them."

Hailey didn't back down from the agent's suddenly lethal stare. "It's illegal only if I know about the files. I don't. Truth is, I have huge gaps in my memory."

Normally, Lucas hated lying and liars, but in this case, the lie was warranted. His gut told him to hold off on giving Minton anything until they'd sorted all of this out. The *sorting* began with Colleen.

"Once you get approval from the sheriff, I'll let you in to see her," Lucas said to Minton.

Minton protested, of course, but Josh blocked his way while Lucas ushered Hailey inside. Josh wouldn't let the agent in without a fight, but just in case that happened, Lucas stayed near the door. That meant letting go of Hailey while she stepped around him and turned toward her sister.

"Thank God you came," Colleen said.

Lucas had never met the woman, but he recognized her from the hospital surveillance tapes. Colleen was a blonde, and despite the fact that there were cuts and bruises on her face, she looked as if she'd recently combed her hair and put on some lipstick. That sent an uneasy feeling up his spine. People who'd just had a brush with death didn't usually think about their appearance.

Of course, maybe Colleen had faked the accident to make herself appear innocent.

"Laura, it's been so long," Colleen added.

"Hailey," she automatically corrected her. "I don't use Laura anymore." Hailey limped closer until she was finally able to catch onto the end of the bed for support.

"Has anyone been in here who could have planted a bug in the room?"

Colleen's eyes widened, and then she shook her head. "Only the doctor and some nurses have come in to check on me. I would have noticed if they'd planted something."

Maybe, but just in case, Lucas took a look around. When he didn't find anything, he went back to his guarding duties.

"Did Minton leave?" Colleen asked, and it took Lucas a moment to realize she was talking to him. Since she hadn't asked for introductions, she likely knew who he was.

"He's still in the hall. The sheriff will stall him, but eventually he'll get in here to see you. Is that a problem?"

"Of course." Colleen didn't hesitate, either. "I don't trust any of the agents who helped put Preston behind bars."

Preston.

Interesting. Colleen certainly didn't say the man's name with the venom that Hailey did.

"Preston's dead," Colleen went on. "And Minton is one of the people responsible for that."

"Preston was killed in a prison fight," Lucas pointed out. "Are you saying that Minton arranged to have him killed?"

Colleen opened her mouth but then closed it just as quickly. "I don't know. But there was a lawman involved in the dirty stuff Preston was doing, and if I trust the wrong person, I could end up like Preston."

Yes, she could. So could Hailey, and it might happen even if she withheld that trust.

Hailey went a few more steps toward the bed and

looked surprisingly steady. Maybe because she was trying to look strong for what was no doubt about to be a confrontation with her sister.

"Aren't you even going to ask me if I'm all right?" Colleen asked before Hailey could speak.

Hailey paused a long time. "Are you okay?"

"No," her sister snapped. "Someone tried to kill me." And she stared at Hailey as if she were somehow responsible for that.

"Are you going to ask me if I'm all right?" Hailey fired right back. Heck, she sounded stronger, too. "After all, I was in a coma, and not long after coming out of it, someone tried to kill me, too."

And she waited for Colleen to respond to that.

Lucas watched Colleen's expression and her body language, but the woman seemed clueless as to what was going on. Again though, she could have been playing dumb like the agent outside the door.

"The hospital surveillance footage," Lucas finally prompted her. "We saw you on it with the man who tried to kill Hailey."

Colleen gasped and pressed her fingers to her lips. "That man tried to kill my sister?"

"Not once but twice," Hailey confirmed.

Colleen gasped again and frantically shook her head. "He said he was a marshal, and he showed me a badge. It looked real."

"It was fake," Lucas told her. "And he was a hired gun. Any idea who he was working for?"

More head shaking from Colleen. "I honestly thought he was a marshal and that he was here to protect Hailey."

Hailey drew in a long, weary breath and sank down onto the foot of the bed. "Start from the beginning. We need to know everything about him, everything that he said to you."

There were tears shimmering in Colleen's eyes now, and while Lucas wasn't immune to those tears, he wasn't fully buying them just yet. The woman could be crying because she'd just gotten caught and could be arrested.

"The marshal called me yesterday," Colleen started. "He said his name was Donald Silverman."

"It was Darrin Sandmire," Lucas corrected her.

"Was?" Colleen questioned.

"He's dead. Killed in a shoot-out with one of my cousins while he was attempting to get to Hailey."

Colleen pressed her fingertips to her mouth for a moment. "I didn't know. I swear I didn't," she added, her attention shifting to Hailey.

Like Lucas, Hailey still didn't look convinced. "This man asked you to meet him at the hospital?"

She nodded. "He said you were in danger, and that he needed my permission to access your personal things, like your computer."

So that he could get those files that Hailey had hidden. Files that Lucas needed to know more about as soon as they were finished here with Colleen.

"I told him that I didn't know where the rest of your personal things were," Colleen went on. "That the only things I had were what was collected from the car the night of your accident."

"It wasn't an accident," Hailey said. "That man ran me off the road and put both my baby and me in grave danger."

Colleen blinked back the tears, and her expression changed a little. Not so much alarm on her face but concern. "You're not suggesting that I was working with this snake?"

Hailey stayed quiet a moment. "I only need to find out the truth. So we can keep Camden safe."

"Camden?" Colleen asked.

"My son. That's what Lucas named him, and I will make sure no one, including you, does anything to harm him."

That didn't do much to ease Colleen's alarm. "You think I was together with him on this," she concluded. "I'm your sister."

"Yes, but we haven't always seen eye to eye in the past. You refused to testify against Preston."

Colleen's alarm turned to something else, and Lucas was pretty sure that something else was anger. It flashed through her eyes. "Because as you well know, I didn't witness the crimes you said he did."

There it was. Not just her words but Colleen's tone. Yeah, there was bitterness. Maybe because Colleen had been personally involved with the man? Or maybe she'd been doing more than only IT work for him.

"Why would Darrin want you dead?" Colleen came out and asked Hailey.

Lucas hoped she wouldn't mention those files, and she didn't. Hailey only shook her head. "Is it possible he was working for Preston and that Preston left orders to have me killed?"

"No," Colleen answered. Way too fast. She was definitely in the defensive mode when it came to her former boss. "Preston wouldn't have done that."

"How do you know that?" Lucas snapped.

Colleen volleyed some annoyed glances between Hailey and him. "Because I visited Preston in jail a few times."

Lucas rolled his eyes, took out his phone. "If I call the prison, I can find out exactly how many visits you made."

Her mouth tightened. "I saw him every week. And I'm not going to apologize for that."

"You should," Lucas argued. "Because even from behind bars, Preston could have arranged for the attacks against Hailey."

"He didn't," Colleen practically yelled. It took her a moment to regain her composure, and then she shifted her gaze back to Hailey. "You always believed the worst about Preston, but I believe it was the dirty agent who set him up. The same agent who's been trying to get into this room. Probably to kill me. Maybe he's the one who wants to kill Camden and you."

That was entirely possible. "You have any proof that Agent Minton is dirty?" Lucas asked her.

"No, but since you're a lawman, you should be the one getting that proof. Because someone put me in this hospital bed, and the next time, he might succeed in putting me in the grave."

Because that was possible, too, Lucas decided it was time to have a more thorough chat with Minton. Of course, that meant Hailey spending a little more time in the room with her sister, but Lucas could chat with Minton in the doorway. That way, he could keep an eye on Hailey.

Lucas opened the door, expecting to come face-to-face with the riled agent, but Minton wasn't there. However, Josh wasn't alone. There was another man standing in front of him. A man that Lucas recognized from the research he'd done the night before.

Eric DeSalvo.

Like Minton, Eric was wearing a suit. But he sure wasn't scowling. The man was smiling. A slick kind of smile that reminded Lucas of a snake oil salesman.

"You're supposed to be at the sheriff's office for an interview," Lucas immediately reminded Eric.

"I'm on my way there, but I decided to make a detour." His smile widened. "Lucas Ryland, Texas Ranger," Eric greeted him. Obviously the man had done his research as well. "I understand you think I'm guilty of all sorts of assorted felonies."

"Are you?" Lucas growled.

"No, but I think I can help you solve this." He tipped his head to the end of the hall, where Lucas saw Minton walking away. "Arrange a plea deal for me, and I'll give you what you need to put Agent Minton behind bars."

CHAPTER SEVEN

HAILEY HADN'T WANTED to make this trip to the Silver Creek Sheriff's Office. She'd wanted to be back at the ranch with her son. But these interviews could be critical to helping Lucas and her make sure that Camden stayed safe.

Well, there was one official interview anyway—with Eric.

But since Agent Minton had shown up, Grayson would be questioning him, as well. Of course, that didn't mean Minton would answer anything. Especially anything that could incriminate him, but maybe he would spill something that would be helpful. For that matter, maybe Eric would do the same, and this nightmare would stop right here, right now.

"They're about ready to start," Lucas said, joining her by the observation window of the interview room. He handed her a cup of much-needed coffee.

Eric was already seated at the gray metal table, an attorney on each side of him, and even though he couldn't see Hailey through the one-way glass, he occasionally looked in her direction. And he smiled again.

No doubt to unnerve her.

There was certainly no love lost between them, and after his father had been convicted, Eric had issued plenty of veiled threats to get to her. Not because he'd wanted to defend Preston. He hadn't.

Eric hadn't had much love for his father, either, but he hadn't wanted Hailey to do anything that would include him in the charges against Preston. Father and son still had plenty of business ties. Ties that Preston would have gladly continued because from all accounts, he'd wanted to protect his son.

Hailey now understood the lengths a parent would go to to protect a child. Even when that child—Eric— had done everything to distance himself from his father.

"Where's Minton?" she asked.

Lucas hitched his thumb to the hall. "In the other interview room, where Dade will question him. Let's just say he's not happy about being questioned by a *local yokel* deputy sheriff, and he's on his phone to his boss to find out if he can get out of it."

Maybe his boss would side with Grayson. And even if he didn't, perhaps they could get the information some other way.

She glanced back at Eric when he smiled at her again. "Any idea what kind of plea deal he wants?"

Lucas shook his head. "After dropping the bombshell at the hospital, he clammed up, claimed he didn't want to say anything else without his attorneys present."

That didn't surprise her. "Eric always hides behind his attorneys. So did his father. Not the same attorneys, of course. Preston would have shared, but Eric never trusted his father enough to mix his personal stuff with the family business."

Lucas stared at her. "After this, you should be able to access those files. Too bad you can't do that before Grayson talks to Eric, because there might be something he could use for leverage. Just how much jail time would Eric get with what you have?"

"Not nearly enough. It's an illegal sale of some land. He paid off some officials one county over and got the land rezoned so he could in turn sell it to one of his puppet companies. There's also a sale of confiscated weapons."

That got his attention. He moved even closer. So close that his arm brushed against hers. It was just a slight touch, but she felt it head to toe.

"How many weapons?" he asked.

"Not nearly enough," she repeated after she gathered the breath to speak. Mercy, she had to figure out how to stop these flutters when she was around Lucas. She also had to focus since this was an important conversation. "It's a felony, but since he's got a spotless record, he might not get more than a year."

Lucas's forehead bunched up. "Yet it was enough to keep his father from coming after you."

"Preston loved him. Despite everything."

"Exactly what is *everything*?" he asked.

Because he was looking her straight in the eyes and because he was so close to her, it took Hailey a moment to realize they were still talking about Eric. And not this attraction between them.

"I don't know all the details," Hailey explained, "but Preston was a widower since Eric was a little boy, and Eric always blamed his father for his mother's death."

"Was Preston to blame?"

"I don't know, but she did die in a car accident. The cops did investigate it. Nothing concrete turned up, though."

Lucas made a sound, one of skepticism. A sound

that Hailey totally understood. "Three car wrecks, and I know mine wasn't an accident," she said. "Perhaps the others weren't, either."

"You think Colleen's telling the truth about that? About any of this?" he asked.

Hailey drew in a long breath. "I want to believe her. But things have sometimes been—well—tense between us. She was three when her father married my mother, and I think once I was born a couple of years later, she thought our parents doted on me more than her. And maybe they did when I was little. Then our mother died of breast cancer, and my father ended up abandoning us. Colleen blamed me for that, too."

She stopped and realized she'd never told anyone that. "Sorry," Hailey said. "Didn't mean to dump all of that on you."

"No. I wanted to hear it because it's motive. People have certainly killed for a lot less, and coupled with her disapproval over you testifying against Preston, maybe Colleen decided she'd had enough."

That turned Hailey's stomach. Because *enough* nearly cost her Camden.

"What happened to Colleen and you after your father left?" Lucas continued.

"Foster care. That's when we got closer. I think because we only had each other."

And now Colleen might be trying to kill her. Of course, her sister wasn't their main suspect. That person was sitting on the other side of the observation mirror, and Eric smiled again when Grayson finally came into the room.

Lucas reached over to turn on the audio so they could hear the interview, and again his arm brushed against hers. The other time he hadn't noticed. Or at least, he'd pretended not to notice. But this time their gazes met.

And held.

He mumbled some profanity and looked away. "This isn't going to happen," he said, but she wasn't sure if he was trying to convince her or himself.

No way did he want to get involved with her. She totally understood that, but the attraction was undeniable. The heat was still just as strong as it had been the night she'd gone to his bed. Thankfully she didn't have to keep remembering it, because Grayson got her attention when he spoke.

"Tell me about this plea deal you want," Grayson demanded.

Eric looked directly into the mirror. "I've heard that Hailey might have something she believes could be incriminating about me. It'll be all fake, of course, but I need the chance to clear my name."

"You said you thought that Eric didn't know about those computer files," Lucas reminded her.

"I didn't think he did. The only one I personally told was Preston."

Lucas stayed quiet a couple of seconds. "Is it possible Preston told Colleen?"

Hailey sighed. Nodded. Yes, it was possible. "But why would Colleen have told Eric?"

Lucas didn't get a chance to answer because Grayson continued. "What kind of incriminating info?" Grayson pressed. He knew all about the computer files they'd soon be able to access, but he no doubt wanted to hear Eric's take on this.

"I'm not positive, but I think it's supposed to be about illegal arms. It could be anything since it's fake."

Grayson just stared at him. "And you think Hailey manufactured this?"

Eric shrugged. "Probably not her, but my father could have."

"From everything I've heard, your father cared about you. In fact, I heard he'd do pretty much anything to prevent you from going to jail."

"That's what he wanted everyone to believe, but as a lawman, you certainly know what he was capable of. It's not much of a stretch to think he'd come up with something to keep me in line."

Oh, mercy. Was it false evidence? "It looked real," she said to Lucas. "And besides, if it were fake, why wouldn't Preston have sent someone after me? He hated me for testifying against him."

"Maybe even Preston didn't have the stomach for murdering a woman in a coma. Still…the latest attacks didn't happen until after he was dead."

True. And that led them right back to Eric.

"All right," Grayson continued. "You want a look at these so-called files. What are you offering in exchange?"

"Some files of my own," Eric said without hesitation. "They won't be admissible in court, but they're recordings that my father made when people visited his office."

Judging from Eric's smug look, there was something critical on the recordings. Judging from Grayson's scowl, he wasn't pleased about it.

"Any reason you didn't turn these recordings over to the authorities when the investigation was going on?" Grayson snapped.

Eric's smug look went up a notch. "Because I only recently found them. Yesterday, in fact."

Hailey groaned. He was lying. He'd probably had them all along. But why had he held on to them?

"Eric's up to something," Hailey mumbled.

Lucas made a sound of agreement, but before he could say anything, the door to the observation room opened, and she saw Dade and Minton standing there.

"I've played along with this fiasco long enough," Minton snarled. "I'm an FBI agent and won't be treated like this."

"Let me guess," Lucas said to his cousin. "The interview went well." His voice dripped with sarcasm.

"No, it didn't." Minton's tone was full of sarcasm, too. "I don't know anything that can help you end whatever the hell's happening to Hailey. And I won't know until you tell me everything that's going on." He glanced at the mirror. "Including what's going on with that piece of slime."

Hailey wanted to tune Minton out and focus on Eric's conversation, but Grayson, the lawyers and the DA had moved on to the details of the plea deal, and from what Hailey could tell, Eric was asking for immunity from prosecution.

Which meant there was likely something incriminating him on those recordings or in the files Hailey had.

Hailey hadn't intended to bring up anything to Minton about what Eric had just said, but Lucas obviously had something different in mind.

"Eric claims he has recordings that he got from his father's office," Lucas tossed out there. "He's working out a plea deal now."

And Hailey soon knew why Lucas had done that. He pinned his attention to Minton, clearly looking for a reaction.

He got one.

Minton charged toward the window to have a closer look. "Any recordings come under the jurisdiction of the FBI."

Lucas huffed. "You seem to keep forgetting that this isn't an FBI matter. The recordings could be evidence in the recent attacks against Hailey. Attacks that happened right here in Silver Creek." He glanced at Dade. "Did anyone here in the sheriff's office request FBI assistance? Because that's the only way Minton could be involved in this."

Dade pretended to think about that. "Nope. No one here made a request like that. Grayson said if we needed help, we'd call in the Rangers. Of course, we won't have to call very loud since a Texas Ranger is standing right here in this room."

Minton's mouth tightened, but instead of verbal fire at any of the men, he turned toward Hailey. "I'm trying to keep you and your son alive." He nodded toward Eric. "You'll need all the help you can get with that piece of slime. He's dangerous. That's why you should give me copies of anything you have on him."

Lucas's huff was even louder this time. "This conversation is over." And he took Hailey by the arm and maneuvered her around Minton and Dade.

"It's not over," Minton insisted. "One way or another, I will get the evidence you have."

It sounded like a threat. Worse, it felt like one.

Hailey reminded herself that Minton could just be focused on the job, but if he was the dirty agent Preston had on his payroll, then she had two snakes to watch out for—Eric and Minton.

"I'll take you back to the ranch," Lucas said once they

were out of earshot of Minton. "We'll wait there until you can get into the files. Maybe by then Grayson will have worked out something with Eric."

They went to the front where Lucas had left the cruiser, but before they reached the door, his phone buzzed. Hailey saw Josh's name on the screen. Since he was at the hospital, she instantly got a bad feeling.

Lucas obviously did, too, because he belted out some profanity under his breath. "A problem?" Lucas greeted his cousin.

"Yeah. Please tell me we have something to hold Colleen. Because if not, she's about to leave the hospital."

Hailey released the breath she'd been holding. She'd braced herself for something worse, like an attack. "Did the doctor say it was okay for her to go?"

"No. But she's leaving anyway unless we've got grounds to hold her."

"She was on the surveillance tape with a hit man," Hailey reminded Lucas.

But Lucas shook his head. "Not enough since she had an explanation for that, and there's no proof that she knew who he was. Can Colleen hear me talking right now?" he asked Josh.

"No," Josh repeated. "She's in her room getting dressed, and I'm in the hall."

"Good. Then let her leave, but I want a tail on her. Tell me where she goes and who she sees. Because if she's behind this, she might try to meet with her hired thugs."

True. Hailey hated to think Colleen would do that, but this might be a way to be sure.

"Will do," Josh said. "Hold on while I send a text to the reserve deputy who's in the parking lot. He's dressed in plain clothes."

Maybe Colleen wouldn't notice the man and would do whatever it was she was setting out to do. Part of Hailey wished, though, that her sister had had no part in any of this.

"Colleen's coming out of her room now," Josh added a moment later.

Josh said something else, something that Hailey didn't catch. Ditto for whatever her sister said to the deputy.

"Colleen just handed me a note that I'm supposed to give to Hailey," Josh finally explained.

"A note?" Hailey asked. "Why didn't she just talk to me?"

"Don't know. You want me to unfold it and read it to you?"

"Yes," she answered as fast as she could.

Hailey heard the rustling around on Josh's end, and a moment later he mumbled some of the same profanity that Lucas had just used. "It says, 'I'm sorry, Hailey. I know you'll never understand, but I did what I had to do.'"

CHAPTER EIGHT

"I DID WHAT I had to do."

Lucas hoped Colleen was referring to checking herself out of the hospital, but he had a bad feeling in the pit of his stomach.

It certainly hadn't helped when Colleen had managed to ditch the tail they had on her. Now she was in the wind. Could have been anywhere. Heck, she could have been out there planning another attack. Colleen had a lot of questions to answer, but first they had to find her and somehow force her to tell them the truth.

Of course, in addition to Colleen, Lucas had plenty of other things adding to that bad feeling. Minton, Eric.

And Hailey.

Hailey, though, was a bad feeling of a different kind.

Once again, he had no choice but to take her to his house at the ranch. It was either that or spend more time at the sheriff's office, and neither of them wanted that. In fact, Hailey had jumped to say yes when he suggested they go.

Hailey had *jumped* yet again when they'd arrived home and Tillie had offered to show her how to give Camden his bottle. Now Lucas was supervising that while he waited for updates on both the plea deal and Colleen.

"He really is a little miracle," Hailey said, smiling at Camden while she burped him.

Of course, Hailey was in heaven over doing something as simple as feeding and burping their son. "You might not call him a miracle when he wakes up every three hours," Lucas joked, because he thought they could use some levity.

At least, he could use it, anyway. His muscles were knotted so tight that his back and shoulders were hurting.

Hailey smiled, and he got a knot of a different kind. This one in his stomach. He remembered that smile. It was one of the first things that had attracted him to her, and even now it stalled his breath in his chest. Then she chuckled when Camden let out a burp that sounded as if it'd come from a grown man drinking beer. Lucas didn't join her on the chuckling, but he'd had the same reaction the first couple of times it had happened.

His phone dinged with a text from Josh.

Lucas glanced at his watch. "You should be able to get into the storage cloud to retrieve those files." That would get his mind off her smile and back to what he should have been focusing on.

She nodded, her forehead bunching up. Obviously she didn't want to let go of the baby just yet, but Lucas needed to see exactly what Hailey had against Eric.

Hailey kissed Camden, and she waited for Tillie to come and take the baby before she got up from the chair. She made her way to Lucas's office just up the hall. It seemed as if each hour she was walking a little better, but she still caught onto the wall to steady herself.

And she also caught onto him when she eased into the chair.

"Sorry," she said. No doubt because she felt his muscles tense. "I know it bothers you for me to touch you."

Yeah, it did. But not in the way she was thinking. It bothered him because it reminded him of things he shouldn't have been remembering. Instead of mentioning that, though, Lucas just motioned for her to get busy on the laptop.

She nodded, looked disappointed that he hadn't addressed the elephant in the room—the attraction. Something he had no plans to address.

"It'll take a couple of minutes for me to get through the passwords and security questions," she said just as his phone rang.

Since it was Grayson's name on the screen and no doubt a call about the investigation, Lucas answered it on speaker. That way Hailey wouldn't have to lean too close to him to hear.

"We worked out a plea deal with Eric," Grayson said. "A limited one for both of us. He'll get immunity only if there's something of evidentiary value on the recordings. The second condition is that the immunity will cover only one criminal count. A count that doesn't include murder or accessory to murder."

Lucas looked at Hailey. "Any chance of Eric having murdered someone?"

"Not that I know of," she answered. "From what I learned, the DeSalvo family crimes seemed to be limited to money laundering and the sale of illegal arms. Of course, it's possible someone was killed during those deals, but the deals I had knowledge of were mainly Preston's, not Eric's."

That didn't mean Eric didn't have any side deals of his own. But then, if he had, there was no way the man would give Grayson evidence to incriminate himself for murder.

"What did you mean about the deal being limited for both Eric and you?" Hailey wanted to know.

"The recordings are on old compact disks, and Preston set it up so they can't be copied. Eric wants the disks to stay here in the sheriff's office, and that means I'll have to tie up some manpower to listen to them."

Eric had probably added that into the deal to make sure Minton and the FBI didn't get their hands on them. Or maybe Eric had another reason for doing that.

"Did Eric give you any idea what was on the recordings?" Lucas asked Grayson.

"He says he hasn't listened to them all. Which I find hard to believe."

So did Lucas. Eric didn't seem like the sort to shoot himself in the foot by handing over anything that could be connected to him beyond the limits of the plea deal. Still, there might be something that Eric had missed.

"But what Eric did say," Grayson went on, "was that there are dozens of recorded conversations with his father and his business associates. Of course, he didn't get permission from any of these people. But there are names, he claims, that we can use to make some arrests if we can link those names to the crimes."

Yeah, because the recordings themselves probably wouldn't be admissible in court since Preston didn't get prior consent from at least one of the people he was recording. Then there was the problem of the tapes being in the hands of one of their suspects, one who could have doctored the conversations.

"I'll call you as soon as we have the recordings. Let

me know what you find out from Hailey's files," Grayson added before he ended the call.

Lucas put away his phone and watched as Hailey accessed the site. Thankfully her fingers were working better than her legs. She had no trouble typing.

No trouble cursing, either.

That bad feeling in his stomach went up a couple of notches.

"The files are gone?" Lucas concluded, but he hoped he was wrong.

Hailey didn't answer him. She kept mumbling profanity. Kept searching through the storage cloud. Even though Lucas was far from a computer expert, he could see that all the files were empty.

Except one.

Hailey clicked on it, and when Lucas saw what was there, he was the one cursing. Not files to incriminate Eric. There was just a single document with one sentence written on it.

I did what I had to do.

It was the exact wording of the note Colleen had left with Josh, but in this case it didn't make sense.

"Why would Colleen want these files deleted?" Lucas asked. "From what I can tell, Colleen despises Eric."

Hailey groaned, obviously still dealing with the bombshell of what her sister had done. Or else what someone wanted them to believe Colleen had done.

"She does," Hailey confirmed. But then she shook her head. "Or maybe that was all a pretense. I just don't know anymore."

Another groan, and she buried her face in her hands

for a couple of seconds. When she lowered them, Lucas spotted the tears in her eyes.

Oh, man. Not tears. Not now. He was already feeling raw and exhausted, and he was a sucker for a woman's tears. Especially this woman. Because this was quickly turning into a very bad day for Hailey and this investigation.

She stood and looked around as if trying to decide what to do, but Lucas could see that there wasn't much fight left in her. "Colleen must hate me to side with a snake like Eric."

"Maybe she didn't have a choice. Maybe Eric has some dirt on her. Something that would send her to jail."

The tears continued. "Yes, but she knows those files are meant to protect Camden and me from Eric. Or from any of Preston's thugs who might be out there ready to carry out their late boss's dying wish to see me dead."

She was right. And Lucas had had enough of the tears. Before he could talk himself out of it, he reached out and pulled her into his arms. Of course, Hailey had been in his arms since she'd come out of the coma. It'd been necessary to keep her from falling.

This was different.

Lucas could feel it. And Hailey could feel it, too. She didn't go stiff as she had the other times they'd touched in the past twenty-four hours. She sort of melted against him.

"I'm just so scared," she admitted. "Not for me but for Camden and you. For your family."

"No one is going to hurt Camden or my family," he assured her. Not that he was in a position to give that kind of assurance. Not with hired guns after them. Still, those hired guns would have to get past him, and since he was protecting his son, Lucas had no intention of making that easy for them.

Hailey looked up at him at the exact moment he looked down at her. Lucas silently said more of that profanity. He was so not ready for this. Well, his mind and heart weren't, anyway, but the rest of him seemed to think it was a good idea to kiss her or something.

Especially *something*.

The heat came. Memories, too. Vivid memories of Hailey naked and beneath him in his bed. The very bed that was just up the hall.

She didn't look away from him, and hell, he didn't look away, either. They just stood there with all those bad thoughts running through his head. Lucas was within a fraction of a second of acting on those bad thoughts by kissing her, but Hailey cleared her throat and stepped back.

"I'm sorry," Hailey said, rubbing her forehead and dodging his gaze. "I know that makes things worse."

It did, and Lucas didn't want her to clarify that. Or talk about it. Hell, he just wanted to concentrate on anything but this ache that was begging him to have sex with her right here, right now.

"You should try to call Colleen and ask her about this," he managed to say, and he handed her his phone.

Focus. He needed to deal with the problems of the investigation and not create new problems by having his body go rock hard with thoughts of Hailey.

She nodded. "I'm not sure if Colleen still has the same number. Until I came out of the coma, I hadn't been in touch with her since Preston's trial, and that was over eighteen months ago."

It was a long shot, but it was one that paid off. In a

way. Colleen didn't answer, but when her voice mail greeting kicked in, Hailey and he got verification that her sister had kept the old number.

"Call me ASAP," Hailey said when she left the message, and there was a definite urgency in her tone.

But whether Colleen would phone her back was a different matter. After all, even though she'd been injured in that car accident, Colleen had still managed to elude the reserve deputy. Something Lucas wished he'd handled differently. He should have requested one of the regular deputies to follow her.

Hailey sank back down onto the chair and gave a heavy sigh. At least she wasn't crying, but this was obviously getting to her. Or rather, it was, until she looked up at him again, and there was something in her eyes. Not attraction this time.

"What if Colleen and Eric believe I have hard copies of everything that was in the online storage?" she asked.

It didn't take long, only a few seconds, for Lucas to figure out where this was going. And he shook his head. "You're talking about setting a trap. Definitely not a good idea, because it could send those hired killers after you again."

"The hired killers will come no matter what. I'm not sure why, but obviously the person behind this sees me as a threat. Or maybe the things that I know are what he or she considers the threat."

That was true, and it didn't rule out any of their suspects. Minton could want anything destroyed that could link him to being a dirty agent. Eric could be trying to save his butt from going to jail. And Colleen? Well, Lucas still didn't know why she was seemingly playing on Eric's side in this, but it was obvious she didn't want her sister to have any incriminating evidence about the man.

Or maybe the information in the file incriminated someone else? Like Colleen herself?

Too bad they didn't have the real files to examine.

"Just think this through," Hailey pressed. "We could leak that the computer files have been erased and that I'm getting the hard copies to give to Grayson. We could say that I'm getting them from a safe deposit box or something."

Lucas huffed. It would still put Hailey in immediate danger. Unless...

"Maybe we could get a cop to go in posing as you," Lucas said. "There's a reserve deputy, Kara Duggan, who has a similar height and build. We could arrange for there to be eyes on her and give her plenty of backup." But then he paused. "Of course, the gunmen might be expecting a trap and come here after you."

She pressed her lips together a moment. Clearly this thought had already occurred to her, but then Hailey's gaze drifted in the direction of the nursery. If the gunmen came here, Camden would be in danger.

"How about you and I go to the sheriff's office and then leak the info?" she suggested. "That way, if they do smell a trap, they'll go after me there and not come to the ranch."

Lucas went through all the things that could go wrong. And with hired killers, there was plenty that could go wrong.

"You know that none of our suspects will go after the decoy, right?" he reminded her. "He or she will send a lackey."

Hailey nodded. "But if we have a lackey—alive—we might be able to find out who hired him."

True. Once they had the hired thug's name, then they could search for a paper trail or maybe work out a plea deal. Still, it wasn't without huge risks.

"You're sure you want to do this?" Lucas asked.

"I'm sure," Hailey said without hesitation.

Lucas hesitated, but he knew this was the only straw they had a chance to grab right now. He took out his phone, but it rang before he could call Grayson to set all of this up.

Dade's name popped up on the screen. "We got the recordings from Eric," Dade told Lucas. "They're actual disks. Dozens of them. He flagged one that we should listen to first. It's a conversation between Preston and Colleen." He paused. "I really think Hailey should hear what her sister had to say. Then we can figure out what we need to do."

CHAPTER NINE

HAILEY DIDN'T KNOW what she was dreading more—this return trip to the sheriff's office to hear the recorded conversation that Dade had said she'd definitely want to hear, or leaving Camden.

Still, it was necessary. Not just for the recordings but also because they needed to work out the final details for the trap to lure out whoever was behind this. She hated that the reserve deputy would be in possible danger, but Hailey was hoping that Lucas would be able to set it all up so they could minimize the risks.

"Maybe this won't take long," Lucas said as they got into the cruiser.

They weren't alone. Josh and one of the armed ranch hands, Avery Joyner, were with them. Josh was behind the wheel with Avery riding shotgun. Lucas and she took the backseat.

"And I'm still not sure this is a good idea," Lucas added.

She'd lost count how many times he'd said a variation of that, and Hailey agreed with him. She wasn't sure it was a good idea, either, but at the moment they didn't have a lot of options as to how to put an end to the danger. Plus, she really did want to listen to those recordings. Of course, she could have had Dade play the conversations for her over the phone, but from the sound of it, there'd need to be some follow-up action when it came to her sister.

"Colleen or Preston must have said something bad for Dade to have called," Hailey remarked.

Lucas made a sound of agreement, but what he didn't do was take his attention off their surroundings. Like Avery and Josh, his gaze was firing all around them, watching for anyone who might attack them. "Not a surprise, though. After all, she's the one who likely deleted those computer files."

True. But there was something about it that didn't feel right. People with solid computer skills could have hacked their way in and then set up her sister to take the blame.

"What the hell?" Josh mumbled, and he slowed the cruiser.

Hailey followed his gaze to the end of the road, where someone had parked a black car. The road was barely a few yards off Ryland land, which was probably why the security system hadn't detected it, but there were also two ranch hands armed with rifles. They weren't pointing the rifles at their visitor, but Hailey figured they would if he tried to get on the ranch road.

"You know that man?" Avery asked Lucas.

And that's when Hailey spotted Minton stepping from the car.

"Yeah," Lucas answered. "That's FBI Agent Brian Minton."

Both Lucas and she groaned. She definitely didn't want to deal with the agent today. Especially since he was one of their suspects. But from the way Minton had parked, they wouldn't be able to get around him without speaking to the man. Judging from the way Lucas was cursing, the *speaking* wouldn't be friendly.

"Wait here, and I'll see what he wants," Lucas said to Hailey. He drew his gun, reached for the door but then glanced back at her. "And I mean it about waiting inside the cruiser. If Minton's behind the attacks, he could have snipers in the area."

That caused her heart to jump to her throat, and Hailey caught onto his arm. "If there are possible snipers, it's too risky for you to go out there."

"I won't be long," Lucas insisted, as if that made everything okay. Hailey wanted to remind him that it took only a split second for someone to gun him down, but he was out of the cruiser before she could even gather her breath.

Josh opened his door, as well. So did Avery. And they drew their guns while continuing to watch around them. Hailey tried to do the same, but it was hard not to focus on Minton and Lucas. Thankfully, with the front doors open, she could hear Minton when he *greeted* Lucas.

"These men wouldn't let me onto the ranch," Minton complained.

"Because they're smart and following orders. *My* orders. No one's getting onto the ranch unless you live or work here. Neither applies to you."

In addition to hearing them well enough, Hailey had no trouble seeing Minton's steely expression. "We're fellow peace officers. You'd think we could cooperate long enough to bring someone to justice. Especially since that someone is obviously after Hailey and now you since you're trying to protect her. They'll kill you to get to her."

"Cooperate? Right. You and I have a different notion

about what that means. You want me to give this investigation to the FBI, and it's not mine to give. Sheriff Grayson Ryland is in charge."

"Well, he shouldn't be," Minton snapped. Every muscle in his face was tight, but he said something under his breath. Something she didn't catch. And then it appeared he was trying to rein in his temper. "I just need the information, that's all. I need to know what Hailey has. Eric, too. Especially Eric, because he could have altered those recordings." Minton paused. "I think Eric's trying to set me up."

"And how and why would he do that?" Lucas asked.

"I'm investigating him, and I think I'm close to giving him a dose of the justice he deserves. He'd obviously do anything to stop me, and that includes doctoring the tapes that he claims he just found. Eric's got the money and resources to do something like that."

Interesting. Maybe Minton was trying to do some damage control beforehand just in case there was anything in those conversations about him.

"Did you and Preston have conversations in his office?" Lucas pressed. He was still keeping watch around them, and while Hailey knew this chat could be important, she didn't want Lucas out there any longer.

Minton nodded. "A couple of them, in fact. Remember, I was investigating both Eric and him, and I interviewed Preston. Anything I said could be altered or taken out of context, and I just don't want my name sullied because of a snake like Eric."

"I get that, but it still doesn't mean you can listen to the recordings. Eric worked out a plea deal, and we have to abide by that." Lucas glanced around again. "If you want to keep up this little chat, then call the sheriff's office and make an appointment." With that, he headed back to the cruiser.

Obviously Minton didn't like being dismissed that way, because the flash of anger returned on his face. "Not cooperating with me is a huge mistake," the agent snarled, and he, too, turned back toward his car.

He didn't get far.

Because a shot slammed through the air and smashed right into the front end of Minton's car.

HELL.

Lucas had known right from the start that something like this could happen, but he'd hoped he would get lucky. Apparently not, though.

He was still a few yards from the cruiser and started to run so he could dive in, but the next shot stopped him. It didn't go toward Minton's car but right at Lucas. He had to drop to the ground, and it wasn't a second too soon.

Because if Lucas hadn't, the next shot would have hit him.

"Get in!" Hailey yelled.

He had no trouble hearing her and the fear in her voice, but Lucas hoped like the devil that she was staying down. The windows in the cruiser were bullet-resistant. That didn't mean, though, that these shots wouldn't eventually tear their way through the glass and reach her.

Another shot came.

This one landed near Minton again, and like Lucas, the agent had no choice but to go to the ground and use his car as cover. The ranch hands outside took cover, as well. They scrambled into the ditch.

Good.

Lucas didn't want them in the line of fire, but he also needed the attack to stop. Because they weren't the only ones in danger. Anyone else on the ranch could be hit if this idiot trying to kill them had a long enough range.

Judging from the sound of the shots, they were coming from a heavily treed area across the road. The oaks were huge there and would make the perfect catbird seat for a sniper. But that wasn't all that Lucas realized. There was more than one gunman.

"Can you see who's shooting?" Minton called out to him.

"No. But I think they're at your eleven and one o'clock."

Lucas only hoped there weren't more, but considering the other attacks, there was no telling how many the sick person behind this had sent after them.

The two gunmen were clearly working together to keep all five of them pinned down while also keeping watch on the cruiser. When Josh tried to open the door, no doubt to return fire, one of the gunmen sent a bullet his way. Definitely not good because it didn't stop with just one shot. A barrage of bullets went into the cruiser, each of them with the possibility of being deadly.

Lucas had to do something *now*.

"Minton, somehow you need to get in your car and move it," Lucas ordered.

Because until he did that, they wouldn't be able to move the cruiser forward and get the heck out of there. There was no way Lucas wanted to go in reverse and have these hired guns just follow them onto the ranch.

Minton did try to move. He made it a few inches before the shots turned in his direction, and he had to scramble to the ground again.

By now, someone had called for backup, and even though there were several of his lawmen cousins on the grounds, they wouldn't be able to get to them right now without putting themselves in grave danger.

The shots shifted again. Some went in the direction of the ditch. No doubt because Avery had tried to fire. Since the hands were armed with rifles, they would stand a better chance of putting an end to this than Lucas would with his handgun. It was obvious, though, that the thugs weren't going to give the men a chance to shoot.

Lucas glanced over at the cruiser to make sure Hailey was staying put. She wasn't. She was by the door nearest him, and she was opening it as wide as it would go. Of course, that caused the gunmen to fire at her.

"Get down!" Lucas told her.

He didn't want her risking her life, but he was thankful about the door maneuver. It would make it easier for him to get back into the cruiser if he could just get a break from the gunmen. Even then, though, he'd still need Minton to get the devil out of the way.

"I'll create a diversion," Lucas said to Minton. He didn't shout and hoped his voice didn't carry so the gunmen would hear him. "When they start shooting at me, get to your car."

Minton nodded. Lucas had to admit that the man looked just as concerned about this as Lucas was. Maybe that meant Minton wasn't a dirty agent after all. But then, this could all be a ruse to make him look innocent, especially since no one had actually been shot. The gunmen would have had ample opportunity to do that when Minton and he had been talking out in the open.

Anything that Lucas did at this point was a risk, but doing nothing was even riskier, so he got into position the way a sprinter would at the start line, and after saying a quick prayer, he bolted toward the cruiser.

"No!" Hailey shouted when Lucas started moving.

But he was already doing that diversion that he hoped would work. It did. The shots started coming right at him, each of them smacking into the ground and kicking up bits of asphalt right at him. Still, Lucas didn't stop. He barreled to the cruiser and jumped inside.

"You shouldn't have done that," Hailey cried out. She grabbed him and pulled him into her arms.

Lucas could feel her shaking. Could feel the relief, too. Relief he understood because he was feeling it as well. But he couldn't think about that right now. Instead, using the cruiser door for cover, he took aim and started shooting in the direction of those gunmen. They were perhaps out of range, but it might distract them enough to buy Minton a little time.

Avery joined Lucas, and both of them fired. For the first time since this attack had begun, the gunmen stopped shooting. It was just enough time for Minton to dart around to the side of his car and get in.

"Put on your seat belt," Lucas told Hailey.

He didn't have to tell Josh to get ready to move because his cousin had already put the cruiser in gear. Thankfully it didn't take long for Minton to start his car engine, and as soon as he'd done that, he hit the accelerator.

Josh did the same.

Minton sped out onto the main road, turning toward town. The majority of the bullets followed him, slamming into the back of his car. But some of the shots came at the cruiser, too.

"Don't go the same direction as Minton," Lucas instructed Josh.

His cousin didn't question that, probably because he already knew that Lucas considered Minton a suspect. Josh went in the opposite direction. That would also get them to town. Eventually. But it was a longer route. Still, as long as it got them out of the path of those shots, Lucas didn't mind the extra miles.

Well, provided he could keep Hailey safe by going that extra distance. Lucas didn't want to be near Minton, but he also hoped they weren't heading straight for another attack.

"I've already called Mason," Josh explained. "He heard the shots and was already putting the ranch on lockdown. Grayson's sending someone to find those snipers."

Lucas figured they wouldn't be easy to find. They'd probably had a darn good escape route mapped out before either of them ever pulled their triggers. Still, that didn't mean they wouldn't leave some kind of evidence behind.

"Is anyone following us?" Avery asked, looking around.

Lucas was looking, as well, but he didn't see anyone. Not at first, anyway. And then, just ahead, he spotted the black SUV that had pulled into an old ranch trail. Josh no doubt saw it, as well, because he muttered some profanity under his breath.

No way could it be the shooters because they wouldn't have had time to leave those trees and make it to this point. But Lucas doubted that it was a coincidence that someone happened to be on this rural stretch of the road at the same time someone had been trying to kill them.

"Turn around," Lucas said to Josh. He kept his attention pinned to the vehicle while he pushed Hailey down onto the seat. "Go back in the other direction."

It was dangerous, but he didn't want to risk driving past that SUV in case someone started shooting at them again. Best to get Hailey to safety, and then he could have the deputies go on the search for the SUV.

"Don't stop by the ranch," Lucas added. "Just keep driving to the sheriff's office."

Josh hit the brakes, and even though the road was barely wide enough to do a U-turn, his cousin managed it by using the gravel shoulder of the road. He got the cruiser headed in the other direction. But not before Lucas caught a glimpse of the people inside the SUV.

"No," Hailey said under her breath. And Lucas knew from her tone and her gasp that she'd seen them, too.

There was a man behind the wheel. Someone that Lucas didn't recognize, but he sure as heck knew the person in the front passenger seat.

Colleen.

CHAPTER TEN

ONE MINUTE HAILEY felt numb from the spent adrenaline, but the next minute she wanted to scream. Yet another attack could have killed them.

Attacks perhaps orchestrated by her own sister.

It turned her stomach to relive the image of Colleen in that SUV. Less than a half mile from those snipers at the ranch. Had she been sitting there, staying close to her hired thugs? Because she certainly didn't look like a hostage.

From the glimpse that Hailey had gotten of her, she'd seen no restraints on Colleen, but her sister had looked surprised to see her. Maybe because Colleen had figured they'd be heading toward town and not her direction.

The one good thing in all of this was that Camden and the rest of the people at the ranch were safe. Their attackers hadn't tried to get onto the grounds to continue their rampage there. Even more, Mason had sent additional armed ranch hands to guard Lucas's house. Of course, they wouldn't be able to go outside, but that was better than putting themselves in harm's way.

"Are you okay?" Lucas asked her.

Hailey didn't even try to pretend she was. She just shook her head and hoped the truth didn't worry him too much. There was already enough worry on his face without her adding more.

Josh pulled to a stop directly in front of the sheriff's office, and Lucas quickly ushered her in. She'd already prepared herself that Minton would be there, and he was. He was also glaring at them.

"I blame you two for this," Minton snapped. "I could have been killed because of you."

Lucas returned the glare. "How do you figure that?"

"You should have already called in the FBI on this. Obviously this is too big an investigation for the locals to handle."

Now that got Grayson glaring, but it was Lucas who took up the argument with Minton.

"And by calling in the FBI, you mean *you*?" Lucas challenged the man. He huffed. "I didn't have a lot of reasons to trust you before this latest fiasco, and this didn't improve things."

"You think I had something to do with this?" Minton howled. He didn't wait for Lucas to answer. "I didn't, and because you're so stubborn about handling this yourself, you put Hailey right back in danger. Is that what you want, huh?"

"I've had enough of him," Hailey managed to whisper. She was barely hanging on by a thread, and she needed a moment to compose herself. Maybe during those moments she'd figure out how to put an end to all of this.

That's all she had to say to Lucas to get him moving. He still had his arm around her waist from when he'd ushered her in from the cruiser, and now he got her moving toward the hall, heading to the break room.

"I'm sorry," she added. "I should have just stood up to him—"

"No, and we shouldn't have stayed in the squad room

for as long as we did. It could have been a ploy to keep us near the windows so that the snipers can finish us off."

Mercy. She hadn't even considered that, but she should have. She needed to be thinking clearer because the stakes were sky-high.

"I need to call Colleen again," she said, figuring that Lucas would hand her his phone to do that.

He didn't. He took her into the break room, had her sit on the sofa. "Grayson can talk to Colleen. In fact, he'll bring her in for questioning."

Yes, because her sister was more than just a person of interest. She'd been in the vicinity of a crime scene and had likely deleted those storage files. Grayson no doubt had lots of questions for her. Anything Colleen said at this point should be part of the official investigation. Still, Hailey needed to hear what her sister had to say, and if Grayson couldn't get her in soon, then she'd try again to call her.

Lucas handed her a bottle of water that he took from the fridge. "This will have to do for now, but you probably could use something stronger."

She could indeed use it. And she got it when Lucas dropped down next to her and pulled her into his arms. It was such an unexpected gesture that Hailey went stiff for a moment. Lucas noticed, too.

He eased back a little, glanced down at her. "I know. This isn't a smart thing for me to be doing, but you look ready to drop."

"I am," she admitted. "And you're right about it not being a smart thing."

It brought back the memories of when they'd been lovers, and Hailey didn't have the energy to fend off those old images. Or the heat, which wasn't old at all.

Anytime she was around Lucas, that heat flared up with a vengeance. Now was no different.

"I'm also scared," she admitted. "For Camden. For you. For all of us."

He didn't try to dismiss those fears. He couldn't. Because they were real. The danger just kept coming at them.

Lucas made a sound of agreement and eased his hold on her a little. Hailey was certain he would just pull away. But he didn't. He stayed there right next to her, and he slowly turned his head to look at her again. Since she was already looking at him, their gazes met. Held.

The air was suddenly so still it felt as if everything was holding its breath, waiting. Hailey certainly was. She had no idea where Lucas was going to take this, but she knew what she wanted.

She wanted him.

Hailey saw that want in Lucas's eyes. Saw the storm that was brewing there, too. He hadn't forgiven her for what she'd done. Probably didn't completely trust her, either, but that didn't stop this attraction.

He cursed. His voice hardly had any sound. And she saw the storm get much stronger as he lowered his head and touched his mouth to hers. It was barely a kiss, but it caused that fire inside her to blaze out of control. A simple kiss from Lucas could do that.

And then he did more. Much, much more. His mouth came to hers again, and this time it was for more than just a touch. He kissed her. Really kissed her.

His taste was a reminder of all those memories and images she'd been battling since she'd come out of the coma. A battle she was losing because the memories came flooding back and mixed with this new firestorm that the kiss was creating.

A sound rumbled in his chest. Definitely not one of agreement this time. It was one of protest and a reminder of a different sort. He didn't want to be doing this, but like her, he seemed helpless to stop it.

The kiss lingered on a moment. Then two. And just when Hailey was ready to pull him even closer Lucas stopped.

"I think I've complicated things enough for one day," he grumbled.

That made her smile even though there wasn't anything to smile about. What he'd said was the truth. The kiss had complicated things. Heck, being together upped the complications, as well, but until they found a way to put an end to the danger, they were joined at the hip.

And afterward…well, Hailey wasn't ready to go there just yet, though she knew a future without danger also meant a future in which Lucas and she had to work out a custody arrangement for Camden.

There was a knock at the door, and a moment later Grayson opened it. He stared at them, and even though he didn't say anything about how close they were sitting, he probably noticed that they looked as if they'd just been doing something they shouldn't have been doing.

"Everything okay?" Grayson asked.

"I was about to ask you the same thing." Lucas got to his feet. "Bad news?"

Grayson lifted his shoulder. "Josh filled me in on the details of the attack. Two of the deputies just arrived in the area where those snipers were. They're not there, of course, but there are tire tracks. It's a long shot, but CSI might be able to get a match from them if they were driving a custom vehicle. The gunmen might have left prints or trace evidence behind as well."

That seemed like such a long shot, but everything was at this point. "What about the black SUV?" Hailey asked.

Grayson shook his head. "No sign of it, either. I don't guess either of you got the license plate numbers?"

"No," Lucas and she said in unison.

Hailey added a sigh. Again, she wasn't thinking straight. The shock of seeing her sister had prevented her from looking at the plates. Plus, Josh had been so fast at turning the cruiser around that she'd barely managed a glimpse of Colleen, much less any specifics about the SUV.

"Any luck getting in touch with my sister?" Hailey wanted to know.

"No. I've left her a message, and San Antonio PD will go out to her place and see if she's there."

She wouldn't be. In fact, Colleen was likely on the run right now, and there was no telling when she'd surface.

"Minton finally left," Grayson went on. "But we haven't seen the last of him."

"No, we haven't," Lucas agreed. "Either he's the most persistent FBI agent in the state or else he's dirty."

Yes, too bad they didn't know which. Because if Minton was clean, then he might truly be able to help them with this investigation.

"I know you wanted to lure out the person who's doing all of this, but we'll have to put the trap on hold for a little while," Grayson added. "I need all the reserve deputies out looking for that SUV and dealing with the snipers."

Understandable. He had a new crime scene to process.

"Is Eric still here?" Lucas asked.

"No. He's at the DA's office getting a copy of the plea deal." Grayson paused, looked at Hailey. "If you're feeling up to it, you need to come to my office. We have Preston's recordings set up in there, and we listened to something else that you should hear."

Lucas CERTAINLY HADN'T forgotten about the recordings that Eric had given Grayson. After all, that was one of the reasons Hailey and he had been on their way to the sheriff's office.

The other reason they had come was to set that trap that was now on hold. No way did Grayson have enough manpower to cover protecting the reserve deputy, and there'd been enough people put at risk today without adding that.

"You're sure you're steady enough to do this now?" Lucas asked her as they made their way to Grayson's office.

She nodded, didn't stop walking. He suspected Hailey was nowhere near *steady*. Not so soon after nearly being killed. But it was clear she was going to steel herself up and listen to what he hoped would give them information they could actually use. As opposed to information that would just make Hailey feel worse than she already did.

Grayson had two laptops in his office, and Josh was listening to one with headphones. Since there were hours of recordings, there was no telling how long it would take to go through them all.

"I've loaded the recordings into audio files that we can access from several computers," Grayson explained, and he hit the play button, motioning for Hailey and Lucas to sit. "This is the first conversation that's connected to you," he added, looking at Hailey. "It was re-corded about two weeks before the start of Preston's trial."

It didn't take long before Lucas heard a man's voice. Preston, no doubt. "We need to do something about your sister," he said.

"I could talk to Laura." It was Colleen who responded. Lucas recognized her voice from the phone conversation she'd had with Hailey.

"Talking won't help," Preston snapped. "She could send me away for life. Is that what you want?"

"No. Of course not." Colleen paused for several seconds. "What do you want me to do?"

Preston, however, didn't hesitate. "Find something I can use against her, something to neutralize her."

"There wasn't anything to find," Colleen insisted. "Nothing illegal, anyway."

"Then make Laura believe that I'll hurt you if she doesn't back off. She loves you. She'll protect you. If that doesn't work, plant something that'll get her to stop."

"Plant what?" Colleen asked.

"Anything illegal. I don't care what, just something to make the cops think she's trying to cover up her own crimes by pinning them on me. You're a whiz with the computer, so hack into hers and see what you can do."

Grayson hit the pause button and turned to Hailey. "I'm guessing this is the first you're hearing of any of this?"

Hailey nodded. "I knew Colleen didn't want me to testify against Preston, but she never said anything about this false threat of making me think he would hurt her."

"Maybe because Colleen thought something like that wouldn't work with you?" Grayson pressed.

"No. It might have worked." Then Hailey groaned softly. "But I wouldn't have just stopped pursuing Preston. I would have just figured out a way to keep Colleen safe."

Lucas hoped Hailey would have done that by going to the cops. She didn't know him then. They hadn't met until after Preston's trial and after she'd entered WITSEC, but she'd obviously been working with some cops that she'd trusted.

"As far as I know," Hailey continued, "Colleen didn't plant anything illegal on my computer." She took a deep breath as if to steady her nerves. This was no doubt only adding salt to the wounds, but Lucas knew this wasn't the last of the things she probably wouldn't want to hear.

"Preston and Colleen sound *friendly*," Lucas commented. "Just how friendly were they?"

"I don't know for sure, but since Colleen didn't do what Preston wanted her to do—I mean, by planting something to frame me—then maybe they weren't as friendly as Preston seems to think they were."

Lucas latched right onto that. "You think Colleen was afraid of him?"

Another headshake from Hailey. Then a shrug. "Maybe, but Colleen never gave any indication of that."

"Of course, we haven't had a chance to listen to all the recordings," Grayson said. "But so far there's nothing about Colleen being afraid. Nothing about the specific nature of Colleen and Preston's relationship, either." He paused. "In fact, I'm betting that the recordings have been edited with parts cut out."

"You think Eric did that?" Lucas asked.

"Maybe. But it could have just as well been Colleen or Preston. The CSI lab is analyzing the originals to see if there have been any alterations. If not, it makes the second recording—well—all the more interesting. It's the last one, made the final day of Preston's trial. He was out on bond, but since he was convicted just a few hours later and put in jail, he didn't have a chance to go home again."

Grayson pressed the play button again, and like on the other recording, Lucas immediately heard Colleen's voice. "It's true. Hailey does have something incriminating on Eric. I'm not sure exactly what, but she won't use it against him. She wants to hold it over your head to make sure you don't go after her."

Preston cursed, "If I end up behind bars, you need to fix that for me. Swear that you will."

"I will," Colleen answered without hesitation.

"You'll also need to pay your sister back for what she's doing to me," Preston continued. "Understand?"

Again, Colleen didn't hesitate. "I understand."

Even though Hailey didn't make a sound, Lucas could see her body tense, and he put his hand over hers. It must have felt like a punch to the gut to hear her sister basically say that she would get revenge for Preston. Was that what the attacks were all about? Payback?

Colleen didn't say anything else because Preston's phone rang. "I need you to step out while I take this call," he told her. He didn't continue for several seconds, probably until Colleen had left. "How's my favorite FBI agent?" Preston said to the caller. There was plenty of sarcasm in his voice. "Have you tied up the loose ends for me?"

Lucas moved closer to the computer so that he wouldn't miss a word. This had to be the dirty agent.

"Please tell me that Preston gives us a name during this conversation," Lucas said to Grayson.

"Sorry, there's no mention of a name, but there's other info that might be able to help us ID him."

Good. Lucas kept listening.

"If the worst happens and I'm convicted," Preston continued, "go to my bank in San Antonio and destroy everything in the safe deposit box."

Too bad they couldn't hear how the agent responded to that, but Lucas knew what Grayson meant about that *other info.* "You're getting surveillance footage from Preston's bank?"

Grayson nodded. "It'll take a while, though, because I need a court order." Which he would get for something like this. Eric might have been telling the truth when he said the recordings could help them arrest Minton.

"One final thing," Preston said to the caller. "If Colleen doesn't take care of the situation, I want you to kill Laura."

Lucas didn't think it was his imagination that Hailey became even paler than she already was, and he did more than hold her hand this time. He slipped his arm around her. Yes, she already knew someone was trying to kill her, but it was hard to hear it spelled out like that. But Hailey eased out of his grip and reached for the phone.

"I'm calling my sister," she insisted, snatching up Grayson's desk phone and putting it on speaker.

No one stopped her, mainly because Lucas didn't expect Colleen to answer. But she did. She answered on the first ring.

"I just heard proof that Preston asked you to kill me," Hailey said without issuing a greeting. "Don't bother to deny it. What I want to know is if you're carrying through on his wishes."

"No." Colleen's voice was shaky, and she didn't jump right into an explanation. She took several moments. "I couldn't go through with it."

"You're sure about that?" Lucas snapped. "You were near the ranch today when there was another attack."

"I was lured there." Colleen paused again. A long time. "I thought I was meeting someone who could give me information. But it turned out to be a hoax."

"What kind of information?" Hailey demanded.

More hesitation. "About this nightmare that's happening. Hailey, I'm so sorry, but I'm not behind the attacks. Things haven't always been good between you and me, but I'm not a killer."

"Then who is?" Hailey pressed. "Who's the dirty agent who was working for Preston? Is it Minton?"

"Maybe." Colleen gave a heavy sigh. "I wish I could say it's him, but I'm not sure there is an agent. Not a real one, anyway. I think it could have been one of Eric's henchmen posing as an agent."

Interesting. This was the first Lucas was hearing of this possibility. "Why would you say that?"

"Some things just aren't adding up, and I think Eric duped Preston into believing he had an agent on the take. I also believe Eric might have used that fake agent to spy on his father. I'm so sorry," Colleen repeated. Lucas heard something in her voice. Guilt maybe. Maybe fear.

It wasn't fear, though, that he saw on Hailey's face. It was pure frustration. Something he felt as well. Because Colleen was stalling, and he wanted to know why.

"Why did you erase the files that Hailey had on Eric?" Lucas demanded.

"I swear, I didn't have a choice."

Lucas huffed. "That's not an answer. Why did you do it?"

Colleen hesitated again before a hoarse sob tore from her mouth. "Because it was part of the ransom demand."

Lucas looked at Hailey to see if she knew what the heck Colleen was talking about. Clearly she didn't.

"A ransom?" Hailey questioned.

Colleen sobbed again. "For my baby with Preston."

And with that, Colleen ended the call.

CHAPTER ELEVEN

A BABY.

Hailey sat there for a moment, stunned with the news her sister had just dropped on them, and then she pressed Redial. Colleen didn't answer. The call went straight to voice mail.

"Colleen could be lying," Lucas pointed out.

Yes. This could all be some kind of ploy to make them believe that her sister was being manipulated into doing these things. But it was also possible.

"Preston and she could have had an affair." Hailey was talking more to herself than anyone specific, but it prompted Grayson to take out his phone.

"I'll have someone run a search of birth certificates," Grayson explained. "Any idea how old a baby would be if it exists?"

Even though the thoughts were racing in Hailey's head, she forced herself to think. "Preston went to prison eighteen months ago, so unless he had conjugal visits, the baby would have to be at least nine months old. But possibly older. Colleen never said anything about being pregnant, though."

Not exactly surprising, because Colleen and she hadn't been on the best terms when Hailey had entered WITSEC.

"If there really is a baby, then Eric could have kidnapped it to get Colleen to cooperate," Lucas suggested. "*If*," he emphasized.

Yes, that was a big if. But even if Colleen did have a child, that didn't mean it was Preston's. She could have gotten pregnant by someone else after he went to prison.

Grayson was still on the phone, but Hailey heard a familiar voice coming from the squad room. And she groaned. It was Minton, and she didn't want to go another round with him today. Obviously, though, that's what was going to happen, because he was demanding to see Lucas and her.

"I'll handle this," Lucas said, getting to his feet.

It was tempting to let him do just that, but Hailey got up as well so she could see what had prompted this latest visit from one of their suspects. Of course, he was no longer at the top of her list because Colleen was now in that particular spot.

"I'm getting a court order for those recordings," Minton informed them the moment he caught sight of them. "My boss will be here any minute with it. You need to turn over copies of those recordings Eric gave you along with the files you have on Eric. And I want them now."

"We'll just wait for that court order if you don't mind," Lucas answered. "Even if you do mind, we'll wait."

Hailey had no idea if there really was a court order or if this was a bluff on Minton's part. But she could clear up one thing for him now. "My sister hacked into my online storage and erased the info I had on Eric."

Minton's eyes were already narrowed, and they stayed that way. "You expect me to believe that?"

She lifted her shoulder. "I don't care what you believe, but it's the truth."

Now Minton cursed. "No way would Colleen help Eric."

Not voluntarily. But Hailey had to rethink that, too. With all the possible lies being bantered about, Hailey had no idea if Colleen even despised Eric.

"Why would Colleen have done something like that?" Minton pressed.

Hailey looked at Lucas to see if he had an opinion on how much or how little she should say, and he took the lead from there.

"Colleen perhaps had a child who's been kidnapped. You know anything about that?" Lucas asked.

Hailey carefully watched Minton's reaction, and now his eyes widened in disbelief. Or perhaps he was faking that response. Because if someone had indeed taken Colleen's child, it could have been Minton. Yes, Eric had a stronger motive, but Minton could have done it to force Colleen to do whatever was necessary to make sure his crimes weren't revealed.

Anything, including those attacks to murder Hailey.

"This is the first I'm hearing of a child," Minton answered. "It's true?"

"We're trying to confirm it now," Lucas assured him.

Minton took out his phone. "I want to talk to Colleen. Where is she?"

Hailey shook her head. "Your guess is as good as mine."

It didn't surprise her that Minton had Colleen's number in his phone. After all, her sister was part of the investigation into Preston. And now Eric. It also didn't surprise her when Colleen didn't answer.

"I'll have someone from the bureau look for her," Minton said, and he fired off a text.

Finding Colleen still wasn't within the FBI's jurisdiction, but at this point Hailey just wanted her sister found so she could be brought in for questioning. She only hoped that whoever Minton had contacted wasn't as dirty as he possibly could be.

"What do you know about this so-called kidnapping?" Minton continued when he'd finished the text.

"Not much." Lucas took out his own phone. "But let me talk to someone who might know."

Hailey wasn't sure who he was going to call. When Lucas put the phone on speaker, though, the DA's office answered, and he asked to speak to Eric.

"Tell me about Colleen's baby," Lucas said the moment Eric came on the line.

"What baby?" Eric snapped.

He seemed as surprised as Minton had been. Of course, it was possible neither man had had much personal contact with her sister, so their reactions might have been genuine.

"Colleen claims someone kidnapped her baby with Preston," Lucas explained. "Was it you?"

Eric's profanity was even worse than Minton's had been earlier. "She's lying. She's doing this to get money from Preston's estate. Well, it won't work. He left everything to me in his will."

Hailey figured that was true, and maybe that was her sister's motive for this. Of course, if Colleen truly had been having an affair with Preston, then he'd probably arranged to have her receive some money before he was killed in prison. At least Hailey hoped that was the case. No way, though, would Eric want Colleen or anyone else, for that matter, to have a dime of his father's money. Eric hated Preston, but he loved the big bucks and trust fund that came with the family name.

"I want to talk to Colleen," Eric practically shouted.

"Welcome to the club," Lucas grumbled, and without even saying goodbye, he ended the call.

Minton jabbed his finger toward Lucas's phone. "That doesn't prove Eric's innocent. No way would he admit to kidnapping his half sibling. If a baby really exists, that is."

"A baby does exist," Grayson said as he came out of his office. For four little words, he got everyone's attention. He came into the squad room before he continued. "According to Texas Vital Statistics, Colleen gave birth to a daughter eleven months ago. Her name is Isabel."

The emotions flooded through Hailey. She had a niece. Colleen had been telling the truth. About that, anyway.

"And the father?" Hailey asked.

Grayson shook his head. "No name's on the birth certificate. In Texas, Colleen would have needed written consent to include the father's name."

Maybe because it would have been too much trouble to get the consent with Preston in jail. Or perhaps Preston wasn't the father after all.

"So, where's the baby?" Minton asked, his attention volleying among Grayson, Lucas and Hailey.

None of them had an answer. Only Colleen could give them that information, and they had to find her first. But if her niece had indeed been kidnapped, Hailey wanted to help. Especially now that she was a mother herself, she couldn't stomach the thought of a baby being taken.

"I'm sorry," Lucas said to her, his voice a soothing whisper. So was the slight touch on her arm.

She looked up at him, their gazes connecting, and the look he gave her was comforting, as well. For a second or two. Then he must have remembered that it wouldn't take much for the comforting to turn to something more.

The fire.

No, it wouldn't take much at all, and now wasn't the time for that. Maybe there'd never be time. Because, like now, Lucas would continue to fight this attraction. No way did he want to go another emotional round with her, especially since she wasn't in any position to renew a relationship.

Hailey cleared her throat, hoping that would clear her head, as well. "I'll try to call Colleen again. If she doesn't answer, I can leave a voice mail so she'll know I found out I have a niece."

She turned to go back into Grayson's office to do that, but the sound of the door opening stopped her. Hailey braced herself for another visit from Eric, but it was a bulky, dark-haired man she didn't recognize. Apparently neither did Lucas, because he instantly stepped in front of her and drew his gun.

But their visitor had a gun, too. And a badge.

"You can put your weapon away," Minton insisted. "This is FBI Agent Derrick Wendell."

Judging from the now smug look on Minton's face, this was someone he wanted to see, and it didn't take Hailey long to figure out why.

"Sheriff Ryland?" Agent Wendell asked, looking at Grayson. When Grayson nodded, Wendell took a paper from his pocket. "This is a court order. You're to turn over the recordings and all evidence that's connected to Eric DeSalvo."

Grayson mumbled some profanity under his breath and took the court order to read through it. However, Hailey figured it was legit.

"The FBI has been conducting a long-time investigation into Eric and his business operations," Wendell continued. "We have reason to believe some of these operations have crossed into other states, making it a federal case."

Lucas looked at her, and even though he didn't say anything, Hailey knew what he wanted to ask her. Did she know about any of Eric's illegal interstate deals? She didn't.

But that didn't mean there weren't any.

She shook her head and was about to tell Minton and Wendell that, but Wendell's attention went to her next. "Hailey Darrow." He didn't wait for her to confirm that. "I'm here to take you into custody."

"WHAT THE HELL do you mean by that?" Lucas growled.

Even though Lucas glared at the agent, Wendell only shrugged as if the answer were obvious. It wasn't. Not to Lucas, anyway.

"Miss Darrow is a material witness in this federal investigation. Plus, someone's trying to kill her. One of Eric's henchmen, no doubt. The FBI intends to put her in custody and keep her safe so she can testify against him."

"She's already in protective custody—mine," Lucas argued. No way was he letting Hailey go with this clown. "There's proof on the recordings that Preston was dealing with a dirty agent. How do I know that agent isn't you? Or him?" he added, tipping his head to Minton.

Judging from the way Minton's face went red, he didn't appreciate that. Apparently neither did Wendell, because he scowled. But it was going to take a lot more than riled FBI agents to get Lucas to hand her over.

"I'm not dirty," Wendell insisted. "And you haven't done a good job of protecting Hailey so far."

"I'm alive." She stepped out from behind Lucas. "I'd say that's a good job, considering that someone's been trying to kill me from practically the moment I came out of a coma."

No, he hadn't done a good job. Because if he had, Lucas would have already found the person responsible for the attacks. Though he did appreciate Hailey standing up for him. But part of him didn't like it, either.

Hell. They were on the same side of this argument, and that was tearing down more barriers between them. Barriers that Lucas wanted in place until he'd worked out a whole lot of things with Hailey. Including her intentions for custody of Camden.

"Hailey can't go with you," Grayson told the agents. "I haven't even interviewed her about the attacks."

"Again, our jurisdiction," Minton argued right back.

"Possibly," Grayson said. "But the attacks might not even be related to Eric. Or the dirty agent. This could be connected to some other things that went on in Silver Creek prior to Hailey's coma."

"What things?" Wendell challenged.

"I'm not at liberty to discuss that with you right now. But it's not federal."

Grayson was sticking up for them. Sticking his neck out, too, since he could be hit with obstruction of justice if the agents could prove he was stonewalling them. Which Grayson was. But he was also buying Hailey some time. She'd already been through hell and back and definitely didn't need to be around someone who might be trying to kill her.

Minton huffed, put his hands on his hips. "Then go

ahead. Interview her. Do what you need to do, but she'll
be coming with us when you're done."

Grayson shook his head. "Not anytime soon." He
glanced at the court order. "This applies only to the recordings, which you can have. But there's no mention
of Hailey being forced to be in your *safekeeping*." There
was plenty of sarcasm on that last word.

The muscles in Minton's jaw stirred, and he turned
toward his fellow agent. "Get the paperwork for Hailey.
I'll get the recordings."

Wendell didn't jump to leave. He glanced at all of
them as if trying to figure out how to resolve this without attempting to convince a judge that it was a necessity for him to take Hailey into forced custody. But he
must have realized this wasn't an argument he could win
with the Ryland lawmen, because he issued a terse "I'll
be back" and headed out.

"Give me the recordings now," Minton said the moment Wendell was gone. "But Hailey doesn't leave the
building until Wendell gets back."

Grayson nodded, headed to his office to get them.
Giving up the recordings was no big deal since Grayson had made copies of them, but Lucas needed to make
sure that Wendell didn't find a judge to do Minton and
Wendell's bidding. He took Hailey by the arm and led
her to the break room.

Lucas called one of his fellow Rangers and asked
him to keep an eye on Wendell for him, and once he'd
done that, he saw to Hailey. Who was obviously even
more shaken up.

"Please don't let him take me," she said, her voice
with hardly any sound.

"I won't." But Lucas only hoped it didn't come to a legal showdown between them and the FBI.

He sat on the sofa next to her, and because he thought they could both use it, he made a FaceTime call to the nanny. It was something he did often while away on business so he'd be able to see his son—if not in person, then at least on the screen.

"Is everything okay?" Tillie asked the moment she answered.

"Fine," Lucas lied. Of course, Tillie must have known it was a lie, but she managed a smile.

"Camden's sleeping," she said, whispering, "but I'll carry the phone to the nursery so you can get a peek."

Hailey moved closer to him, her attention glued to the screen, and she was holding her breath. A breath she released when Camden came into view.

The baby was sleeping, all right. He was on his side, a blue blanket draped over him. Tillie moved the phone closer to his face so they could have a better look.

Hailey touched her fingers to her lips for a moment. "I wish I were there to hold him."

Yeah. So did Lucas. Being away from his son created a horrible ache in his chest. "Maybe soon," Lucas told Hailey, and he hoped that was true. He didn't want this mess with the FBI to drag on so they'd be stuck here in the sheriff's office.

Even though Camden wasn't moving and certainly nowhere near being awake, Hailey and he continued to watch him for several minutes.

Lucas thanked Tillie before he ended the call. "We'll check in again with her in a couple of hours, when Camden will be awake," he added to Hailey.

She nodded, and he figured she was trying to look

a lot braver than she felt. "You're being nice to me," she said.

He wasn't sure how to respond to that, so Lucas didn't say anything. Big mistake. Because his silence caused Hailey to look up at him. Normally her looking at him wouldn't be a big deal, but they were close. Side by side. Arms touching. With their emotions running sky-high, something as simple as a look could become a trigger for this attraction.

And it was.

Lucas felt the slam of heat go through him, and before he could remind himself that kissing Hailey would be a dumber-than-dirt sort of thing to do, he lowered his head and put his mouth to hers.

He'd thought that the attraction between them couldn't get any hotter, but he had been wrong. It did, and along with the fire came the need. A need that his body remembered only a couple of seconds into the kiss. That fire and need were what had started this whole ordeal with Hailey. Apparently the ordeal was going to continue, too. Because he certainly didn't stop kissing her.

Hailey didn't stop, either. In fact, a soft sound rumbled in her throat. A sound filled with the same need and heat that Lucas was feeling. She slipped her hand around the back of his neck, pulled him closer. Not that he needed much encouragement for that, because Lucas was already moving in on her.

He deepened the kiss, took hold of her shoulder and dragged her against him. Great. Now they were body to body with the kiss raging on and on until finally he had to stop just so they could catch their breaths.

She looked at him again, silently questioning whether this was a good idea. It wasn't. But that didn't stop Lucas from going back for a second kiss. It didn't help, of course. But this time he stopped not because of air. If he didn't stop, he was going to drag her upstairs. There was an apartment up there. With a bed.

Definitely not good.

Kissing had already added too many complications to this mix, and sex would spin those complications out of control.

He was about to apologize to her, but Grayson opened the door to the break room. Hell. One look at his face and Lucas knew something was wrong.

"The FBI isn't taking Hailey," Lucas jumped to say.

Grayson shook his head. "Not yet, anyway. No, this is about Colleen."

Hailey slowly got to her feet. "What happened?"

"There's something you need to see." Grayson motioned for them to follow him, and he led them to his office.

Thankfully, Minton wasn't there. He was still across the hall in the squad room, pacing, and judging from his expression, he was riled about something other than not getting his way about taking Hailey.

"If that's something that pertains to the FBI's investigation," Minton called out, "then I want to see it."

"It's not about the investigation," Grayson assured him. "This is a family matter." Once Hailey, Lucas and he were inside the office, Grayson locked the door, no doubt to stop the agent from barging in.

Josh was no longer in the room listening to those recordings. Or rather, the copies of the recordings. Grayson had no doubt put him in one of the interview rooms.

"What's going on?" Lucas asked, but he was almost afraid to hear the answer.

Grayson tipped his head to his desk. There was a padded envelope, opened, along with several papers. "This just arrived by courier," he explained. "There's no name on it, but I've already called the courier's office and asked them to tell me who sent it."

Lucas went closer, Hailey following right behind him, and he saw the first piece of paper. It appeared to be test results.

"DNA," Grayson supplied. "According to the person who sent it, this proves that Isabel is Colleen's baby."

"Does the test really prove it?" Hailey immediately asked.

Grayson lifted his shoulder. "This sort of thing can be faked, but it looks real. It has both the baby's DNA and a sample apparently retrieved from Colleen. Josh is calling the lab to verify." He wore a plastic glove when he moved aside the test results to show them what was beneath.

A photo.

Of a baby girl.

Hailey leaned in even closer, her gaze combing over the picture. She nodded. "The baby definitely resembles Colleen."

Of course, they'd known Colleen had a child, but Lucas figured all of this was leading to something bad.

It was.

"This was the final thing in the envelope," Grayson said, showing them another piece of paper. "It's a ransom demand—for a quarter of a million. But there's another demand. The kidnappers say if Hailey doesn't personally turn over everything she has on the DeSalvo investigation, then Colleen will never see the child again."

CHAPTER TWELVE

HAILEY HEARD EVERY word of what Grayson said. Saw it, too, written in the ransom demand. But it still took a moment to sink in.

Mercy.

If this was real, then her niece could be in grave danger. It didn't matter that she'd never seen the child. Hailey still loved her and wanted to protect her.

"No," Lucas said before Hailey could speak. "You're not going to do this."

Since she was about to tell him that she would indeed do it, he'd obviously known what she was thinking. "I have the money in savings. It's from my father's life insurance. I've never spent any of it, and it's in a bank in San Antonio."

"The money's not the problem," Lucas argued.

Yes, she knew what he meant. It was the *personally* part of the demand. Someone wanted her dead, and this could be a trap to lure her out into the open.

"But we can't just let them disappear with the baby," she snapped. What she felt was pure frustration because Lucas and she were both right. She couldn't go out to deliver anything, but she also couldn't just give up on getting back the baby.

"Just sit," Grayson suggested to her. "We'll work this out somehow."

His phone buzzed, and he lifted his finger in a wait-a-second gesture. Since the caller had gotten Grayson's full attention, Hailey figured it had to be about the kidnapping.

"Eric or Minton could have taken the baby," Hailey tossed out there.

Lucas nodded. "Or this could be something Colleen concocted. We don't know what her real motives are."

True, but it sickened her to think that her sister might be using her own child to do whatever it was she was trying to do. Plain and simple, maybe this was about the money.

"Even though my mother adopted Colleen, she didn't leave Colleen any money from her life insurance," Hailey told Lucas. "She and my mother were on the outs at the time of her death, and she left it solely to me. I offered to share it with Colleen, but she was so angry at being cut out of the will that she refused."

"Was Colleen angry enough to do something like pretending to kidnap her own daughter?"

Hailey had to shrug. "Colleen was always angry about a lot of things. Still…this doesn't feel like something she'd do."

Of course, she'd been wrong about Colleen before. She hadn't thought her sister would delete those files she'd stashed away about Eric. Which was a reminder that she didn't have a key part of what the kidnappers were demanding.

"If we can work out a deal with the kidnappers so I don't personally have to deliver their demands, I'll need to put together some fake files to give them."

Lucas didn't give her his opinion on that because Grayson finished his call and turned to them. "That was the agency for the courier who delivered the package. The person paid in cash, and according to his driver's license, his name is Eldon Silverton. It's fake," Grayson quickly added.

Hailey didn't even bother to groan because it had been such a long shot, anyway. She seriously doubted that the kidnappers would have used someone who could be identified and therefore linked back to them. Or rather, linked back to the person who'd orchestrated all of this.

"What about security cameras?" Lucas asked. "Does the courier agency have them?"

Grayson shook his head. "I think we've struck out with the courier. With the lab, too, because it was Darrin Sandmire who ordered the lab results."

Darrin was the man who'd tried to kill her the night she'd been put in a coma. According to Colleen, he'd been behind the attack shortly after Hailey left the hospital.

Darrin was also dead.

So, yes, that meant they had indeed struck out since they couldn't question Darrin about it. But something about that didn't make sense.

"Why would the person behind the kidnapping use Darrin for this?" she asked. "Why not just use someone with a fake ID?"

"It was to convince us that this is real," Lucas answered, and it prompted Grayson to nod. Thankfully, Lucas continued with his explanation, because Hailey wasn't following this. "We know Darrin's a thug. *Was* a thug. The kidnappers wanted us to understand that a thug like this was involved. That way, we could be sure the baby was truly in danger."

All of that made sense, but it also tightened the knot

in her stomach. Because if a snake like Darrin had been involved, there was no telling who had the baby now.

"Let me take care of Minton," Grayson said. "And then we'll try to contact Colleen again. From now on, any conversation with her needs to be recorded."

And Hailey knew why. Her sister might be involved in this crime in some way, and anything Colleen said might lead them to the truth.

When Grayson unlocked the door and threw it open, Minton was standing right there. It was possible he'd heard some or even all of what they'd said, and he clearly wasn't happy about being excluded.

"You need to leave," Grayson ordered him before Minton could get out a word. Lucas went to his cousin's side. "Until you have papers putting Hailey in FBI custody, you have no right to be here," Grayson added.

Minton had never been a happy-looking person, and Grayson's words only made it worse. "I'm an FBI agent."

"Which gives you no right to be here. This is the sheriff's office, and last I checked, I'm the sheriff. You're leaving, and that's not a request. You can come back when and only when you have something to convince me to turn over Hailey to you."

Minton still didn't budge. He threw glances at all of them, his glare lingering on Hailey for a few long moments.

"You'll regret this," Minton said, and it sounded like a threat. He turned and stormed out.

Grayson and Lucas stood in the doorway and watched the man leave, and they didn't move until Hailey heard the front door slam.

"Make sure he doesn't come back," Grayson told one of the deputies.

He returned to his desk, handed Hailey the phone and put the recorder right next to it. Hailey pressed in the number, and it rang. And rang.

Her heart dropped when it went to voice mail.

"Colleen, I need to talk to you right away," Hailey said once she was able to leave a message. "We got a ransom demand from the kidnappers of your baby. Please call me back ASAP."

She was about to put the phone away, but it rang before she could do it. Hailey answered it as soon as Grayson hit the record button again, and she immediately heard her sister's voice.

"The kidnappers got in touch with you?" Colleen asked. "How? When?" She certainly sounded like a mother who'd had her child taken.

"A package was delivered to the Silver Creek Sheriff's Office," Lucas answered. "There's a demand for a quarter of a million and any info Hailey has on the DeSalvo family. They want her to deliver everything to them herself. Now, who's behind the kidnapping?"

"I don't know. I swear, I don't. But I'll pay them whatever it takes to get back my baby. Where and when do they want Hailey to make the drop?"

Colleen made this sound as if it were a done deal, that Hailey would indeed be involved in the exchange, but Hailey figured no way would Lucas let that happen.

"We'll go over all the details with you," Lucas said. "But only if you come here to the sheriff's office. I have some questions for you."

Hailey guessed that Colleen would come up with an excuse as to why that couldn't happen. After all, she'd stonewalled them practically from the start of this nightmare. And her sister did hesitate for a couple of seconds.

"All right," Colleen answered. "I'm just up the street and can be there in a few minutes. But please come out and watch for me. Draw your gun, too. Because when I come out in the open, they'll try to kill me."

"WHO'S TRYING TO kill you and why?" Lucas snapped. But he was talking to himself, because Colleen had already hung up.

Hell. It didn't make sense that someone was trying to kill Colleen. Especially not the kidnappers. They'd probably want her alive so she would push Hailey to pay the ransom.

Maybe.

And maybe the idea was to kill Hailey when she delivered the money and files. Then, also murder Colleen so that anything the sisters had learned about the De-Salvo family would die with them. Of course, that theory worked only if Colleen was innocent. The jury was out on that. Still, Lucas couldn't risk her being gunned down if she was truly out to rescue her child.

"Wait here," Lucas warned Hailey.

She took hold of his arm. "It's too risky for you to go out there." The very thing she'd said to him when he was meeting Minton at the ranch.

That hadn't turned out so well, but Hailey must have realized they didn't have much of a choice about this, because her grip melted off him. "Just be careful," she added.

There was plenty of emotion in her voice, and Lucas didn't think all that emotion was related only to what was about to happen. No. That kiss was playing into this. It had deepened things between them. Had upped the stakes. And that wasn't good, because they were both already distracted enough without adding higher stakes.

"I mean it," Lucas warned her. "Stay put."

He headed toward the front door with Grayson following right behind him. Both drew their weapons. However, they didn't actually go outside. They stayed in the doorway, Lucas looking up one side of the street and Grayson the other. One of the deputies hurried to the window. All of them preparing for what might be another attack right on Main Street.

But there was no sound of shots. No sign of Colleen, either. Not at first, anyway, but then Lucas spotted someone on the sidewalk just two buildings up from the sheriff's office. Not Colleen, though.

Eric.

Lucas didn't like the timing of the man's arrival, and apparently Eric didn't like it much, either, when he spotted Grayson's and Lucas's weapons. He cursed as he got closer.

"Are the guns really necessary?" Eric asked.

"They're not for you," Lucas assured him. "There might be gunmen in the area."

That put plenty of alarm on Eric's face. Alarm that he could have been faking, but it still got him running toward them. Lucas considered not letting him in, but if Colleen was innocent and she saw Eric out front, that might send her back into hiding.

"Frisk him," Lucas told the deputy when Eric went into the reception area.

Lucas barely spared Eric a glance. Instead he kept his attention on Main Street, and he finally saw more movement. It was in the same area where Eric had just been. But the person wasn't on the sidewalk but rather peering around the corner of a shop.

Definitely Colleen.

Lucas motioned for her to come to them. She didn't. Not right away. She kept looking around. Not just up and down the streets but also on the rooftops. Colleen definitely seemed concerned about being gunned down. Lucas was concerned about that, as well, but if she was in danger, then that alley wasn't a safe place. Heck, nowhere out in the open was safe.

Colleen finally came out and raced toward them. She was limping, maybe an injury from her car accident, and judging from her expression, she wasn't just afraid but also in pain. The moment she reached the door, Grayson pulled her inside.

"What's he doing here?" she snarled, looking at Eric.

"I could ask you the same thing," Eric countered.

"Take Eric to an interview room," Grayson told the deputy who was still in the process of frisking the man.

"I don't want to be put away in an interview room," Eric protested. "I need to talk to Colleen."

Lucas was about to tell him, "Tough." But Colleen spoke first. "Did you kidnap my baby?"

Her voice was shaking. So was she. And that was no doubt what prompted Hailey to come out of Grayson's office and go to her sister. Something Lucas definitely didn't want her to do. Especially when Eric stepped in front of her. Eric wasn't facing Hailey, though, but rather Colleen.

"You really had a baby?" he demanded.

"Yes," Colleen snapped, "and someone took her. Was it you?"

Eric stared at her as if trying to sort all of this out. Of

course, maybe he already had it sorted out if he'd been the one to kidnap the child.

"No. I didn't. Is there DNA proof?" Eric pressed. "Real DNA proof that hasn't been faked by you?"

"There is proof," Grayson verified. "Now, let's all move away from the windows." He pointed to Eric. "You either leave or go in the interview room."

Eric's chin came up. "I'm not leaving until I see solid evidence that I have a half sibling."

"Arrest him," Grayson told the deputy without hesitation. "He's obstructing justice."

Eric howled out a protest, moved out of the deputy's grip. He glared at all of them before he stormed out of the sheriff's office. Good. One less pain to deal with.

"What did the kidnappers send you?" Colleen asked the moment Eric was gone.

But Lucas didn't get a chance to show her. That's because his phone rang, and he saw Unknown Caller on the screen.

Usually not a good sign.

"Record it," Grayson said, and Josh hurried to get a recorder from his desk so that Lucas could do that.

Grayson's phone rang, too, and he stepped into the hall to take it. He motioned for Lucas to go ahead and answer his call. Lucas did, and he put it on speaker.

"Are you ready to talk?" the caller immediately said.

It was a man, but Lucas didn't recognize the voice. "About what?"

"The kids, of course. You want to get them back, right?"

Every muscle in Lucas's body tightened. "Kids?"

"Yeah. Colleen's girl and your boy. We have them both."

CHAPTER THIRTEEN

THE PANIC SLAMMED through Hailey so fast that she couldn't speak, couldn't breathe. But she could feel, and what she was feeling was the sheer terror after learning that someone had taken her son.

Lucas didn't respond to the caller. He looked at Grayson, and Hailey could tell from his expression that something had gone wrong.

Oh, God.

"The ranch is under attack," Grayson said, confirming her fears.

"Do they really have Camden?" Lucas asked.

Grayson shook his head, then cursed. "They're sorting that out now. An SUV armed with gunmen broke through the gate. Mason and the others responded, but it's chaos there."

"Told you," the caller taunted.

"They might not have him," Lucas tried to assure her. But he didn't look convinced of that any more than she was.

Hailey wanted to know how in the world this had happened. She wanted to scream, run outside, find the nearest vehicle and hurry to the ranch. Lucas must have known what was going through her mind, because he took hold of her arm and had her sit at the desk next to

Josh. No way could she stay put, though. She got up and started pacing.

"Let's just wait for a report from Mason," Lucas told her. He motioned to Josh who was at his desk, and Lucas mouthed, "Try to trace the call."

"Yeah, and Mason will soon tell you that we have the boy," the caller added. "And now it's time to talk about how you get both kids back."

"Prove to me that you've got him first," Lucas insisted. "You sent a picture of the girl, but I don't have anything to convince me that you truly have my son."

"Soon. I'll give you proof before our little exchange happens, and if you do what you're told, I'll give you the kids."

"I swear we'll do whatever you ask," Colleen blurted out. "Just please don't hurt them."

"Nobody will get hurt if you follow my instructions to a T."

Hailey didn't put much trust in a snake who would kidnap babies, but she moved closer to the phone so that she wouldn't miss a word of those instructions. It was so hard to focus, though, with the tornado of bad thoughts going on in her head.

"The price is now a half million," the man said. "All because there are two of them now. Go ahead and start gathering the money. I'll give you an hour—"

"That's not enough time," Lucas interrupted. He was almost certainly stalling the kidnapper to give Josh more time to trace the call. "The money has to come from a bank in San Antonio. It'll take a while for them to pull together that kind of cash."

"All right, you have until morning. And no, don't ask for more time than that, because it's all you're going to get. Along with the money, Hailey's got to give us the files she has on the DeSalvos."

Files that she didn't have. Because Colleen had deleted them. Colleen opened her mouth, maybe to tell the kidnapper just that, but Hailey shook her head, stopping her. If this man learned that the files were gone, it might compromise the ransom and rescue. Hailey would just come up with some fake files to give them.

But there was something about this particular kidnapper's request that didn't make sense.

Hailey had assumed that Colleen had deleted the files to appease the person who'd kidnapped her baby. If she'd done that, though, then this man wouldn't be demanding them now, because he would know the files no longer existed.

"Hailey won't be delivering anything to you," Lucas argued. "You'll get the money and the files, but someone else will be doing the drop."

The kidnapper paused for several heart-stopping moments. If this man insisted she deliver the goods, she'd have to do it, of course. But it would be a suicide mission. Still, she'd go through with it if it meant Camden and her niece were safe.

"All right," the kidnapper finally said. "Not Hailey."

Hailey's breath swooshed out, but she certainly didn't feel any relief. She waited for the other shoe to drop, and it didn't take long.

"You and Eric DeSalvo will bring the money and the files." The kidnapper's words hung in the air.

Grayson and Lucas exchanged a glance, but she could see Lucas's answer in his eyes before he even spoke. "Why Eric?" he asked.

"Let's just say Eric will be bringing some cash of his own. For those files."

So Eric was being blackmailed. Or at least, according to this man he was.

Lucas huffed. "I'll have to work it out with Eric—"

"Just do it," the kidnapper snapped. "I'll call you back with the drop-off point. Have everything ready to go."

"I got the kidnapper's location from the cell tower," Josh said the moment the man ended the call. "It's coming from Sweetwater Springs. I'll get the sheriff to send someone out there."

Hailey latched onto that like a lifeline. Maybe the sheriff could find them and put an end to this.

While Josh contacted the Sweetwater Springs sheriff, Hailey went to Grayson to see if he'd heard anything about what was happening at the ranch. He had the phone pressed to his ear, and while she could hear someone talking on the other end of the line, she couldn't make out what the person was saying.

Lucas came closer to her, and he slipped his arm around her waist. Waiting. And no doubt praying, as Hailey was doing.

"I'll wait to talk to Eric," Lucas explained.

Yes, but it would have to be done. Well, it would unless they managed to end this kidnapping. But Eric would still have to be brought in to answer questions about whether or not he was being blackmailed about those blasted files.

"I didn't know you two were back together," Colleen said.

Hailey glanced at her sister, ready to explain that it wasn't like that between Lucas and her, but she didn't want to waste the energy. Besides, it seemed a strange observation to make when their children could be in grave danger.

Grayson pressed the end call button, his attention going straight to Lucas and Hailey. "Mason and the ranch hands are closing in on the trespassers. There are three of them. And we still don't know if they took Camden. It shouldn't be long, though, before Mason calls back."

A second was too long, and Hailey's legs suddenly felt ready to give way.

Josh finished his call and joined them just outside Grayson's office. "I know the timing for this is bad, but I found out something about that surveillance footage from the bank."

Hailey certainly hadn't forgotten about that. It was the security feed that was supposed to show the dirty agent Preston had sent to destroy whatever was in his safe deposit box.

"It was Eric," Josh said.

It took Hailey a moment to get what he was saying. "Eric?" she asked. "Why would he be on that footage?"

Josh shrugged. "He'll have to answer that. Have to answer, too, what was in the box, since there's no security footage for that."

Hailey tuned out the rest of what Josh was saying when Grayson's phone rang. The sound shot through the room, shot through her, too, and Grayson answered it as fast as he could. What he didn't do was put the call on speaker. Probably because he wanted to buffer any bad news that he got. But that wasn't a bad news kind of look on his face. He blew out a quick breath.

"Camden's safe," Grayson relayed.

Suddenly she was in Lucas's arms. This time, though,

not because of a kiss but because they were both over-
come with relief. Relief that Colleen wasn't sharing. She
went back into the squad room and sank down into one
of the chairs. Hailey hoped she was having that reaction
simply because she was still terrified for her daughter
and not because her sister had planned this failed kidnapping.

"Is everyone okay?" Lucas asked Grayson.

"Yes. The attackers didn't get into your house. Tillie's shaken up, of course, but she said Camden's too
little to know what was going on. She hid with him in
the bathroom."

Good. That was probably the safest place for her to
have been, but it ripped at Hailey's heart to know that
her precious son, the nanny and everyone at the ranch
had been put in that kind of danger.

"One of the attackers is dead," Grayson went on. "The
other two escaped, but Mason called in help to look for
them."

She figured the men were long gone by now, but if
they could get an ID on the dead one, it might lead them
back to who'd hired him.

"I need to see Camden," Hailey insisted.

Lucas didn't even argue with that. He looked at Grayson. "Can you spare a deputy to go with us?"

"Josh can do it." Grayson didn't get to add more because Lucas's phone rang.

Unknown Caller was on the screen again. Lucas
waited until Grayson turned on the recorder before he
answered it.

"So, we didn't get your boy," the kidnapper said. It
was the same man who'd called earlier. "Not this time,
anyway. But there's always tomorrow."

The muscles tightened in Lucas's jaw, and Hailey could tell he wanted to go through the phone lines and rip this guy to pieces. Hailey did, too. But more than anything, she just wanted to hold her baby and make sure he truly was safe.

"You'll still pay the ransom if you want your sister's kid back," the kidnapper insisted. "Get that money together. Those files, too, and I'll be in touch." And he ended the call.

"I'll have the call analyzed," Grayson volunteered. "To see if he's still in Sweetwater Springs. The three of you go ahead and leave."

"But what about my daughter?" Colleen asked, getting to her feet. "You can't just leave while that monster has her."

"Staying here won't help her," Lucas answered. He hooked his arm around Hailey, and along with Josh, they started toward the door. "When the kidnapper calls with drop-off instructions, I'll come back."

Hailey hoped not. Maybe they could work out a different deal. One that didn't include Lucas, her or anyone in his family. Perhaps Eric could do this solo.

There was a cruiser parked out front, and the three of them hurried to get in it. Josh took the wheel. She thought Lucas would ride in the front, but he got in the backseat with her. He brushed a quick kiss on her forehead. A kiss no doubt of relief, and he kept watch around them. So did Josh.

There was a storm moving in, and the sky was already getting dark, but Hailey hoped the rain would hold off until they made it to the ranch. She didn't want anything to slow them down.

Josh certainly wasn't moving slowly. He was speeding through town, and like Lucas, he was also keeping watch.

"You think Colleen could have been the one to arrange this attack?" Lucas asked. It was a question that hadn't been far from her mind.

"It's possible. But even if she wasn't the mastermind, she could have known about it. Getting Camden could have been part of the kidnappers' demands to her."

Of course, Colleen hadn't said a thing about a demand like that, but it still could have happened. If Colleen was truly desperate to get her daughter back, then she might be willing to do anything. That could include having Camden taken.

Because if the kidnappers had him, they had the ultimate bargaining tool to get Lucas and her to cooperate.

Josh had just made it out of town when Lucas's phone rang again. Hailey hoped it wasn't the kidnapper calling to give them an immediate drop for the ransom. But it was Grayson. Hailey felt a new slam of fear and prayed that nothing else had gone wrong at the ranch.

"Pull over and check the cruiser," Grayson said the moment Lucas answered the call.

"What's wrong?" Josh and Lucas asked in unison.

"It might be nothing, but a waitress from the diner across the street said about thirty minutes ago she saw somebody walking by the cruiser. A man she didn't recognize. She said at one point the guy appeared to drop something, and he stooped down out of sight for a couple of seconds."

"Hell." Lucas added some more profanity as Josh pulled to the shoulder of the road. "Why didn't she tell you this sooner?"

"She got busy with some customers and just now got

a break. Like I said, it might be nothing. I just want to be sure."

Judging from Lucas's and Josh's reactions, though, it could be some kind of tracking device. Or worse.

"I didn't see anyone around the cruiser," Hailey said.

But then, they'd had plenty of distractions with Minton, Eric and Colleen all there. Plus there'd been the calls from the ranch about the attack and those from the kidnapper.

"Stay inside the cruiser until I check it out," Lucas told Josh and her.

She hated that he was going out there again, but Grayson was right. They had to be certain no one had tampered with the vehicle.

Lucas already had his gun drawn, and he stepped out. Josh opened his door, too, no doubt in case this became an ambush. But there really was no place for attackers to hide on this particular stretch of the road. There were no trees, just flat pasture, and the ditches weren't particularly deep. She also couldn't see any vehicles either ahead of or behind them.

Hailey held her breath, waiting as Lucas went around the cruiser. He was moving quickly. Until he got to the rear of the vehicle. Because she was watching him so closely, she saw the instant alarm on his face.

"Get out now!" Lucas shouted. "There's a bomb."

LUCAS FELT HIS heart slam against his chest.

He didn't take the time to kick himself for not checking out the cruiser before hurrying Hailey into it. He should have gone over every inch of it before they left the sheriff's office. But they'd been so eager to get to the ranch and check on Camden, so he hadn't done it.

Now it might cost them their lives.

Josh was out of the vehicle within seconds, mainly because his door was already open, but Hailey was struggling with hers. Lucas threw it open for her, dragging her out, and he started running with her in tow. But they weren't moving nearly fast enough. They had to put some distance between them and the car, so he scooped her into his arms and raced toward the pasture.

They made it only a few yards past the ditch, though.

The blast ripped through the air, throwing them forward and onto the ground. Lucas scrambled to cover Hailey's body with his and hoped that the flying debris didn't kill them.

Chunks of the cruiser came crashing down. Most of the pieces were in flames, and the other jagged shards fell into the pasture all around them.

"Josh?" she said, no doubt checking to make sure he'd gotten out.

He had. Lucas's cousin was on the ground only about two yards away, and from what he could see of him, he didn't have any injuries. In fact, he was already calling for backup.

"Josh is okay," Lucas assured her.

But Hailey was a different matter. When she looked up at him, he saw the two small cuts on her forehead. Probably from the fall. Maybe she hadn't broken any bones or suffered any internal injuries.

He glanced back at the cruiser. What was left of it, anyway. It was now a fireball, and if they'd been inside when that bomb had gone off, they'd all be dead.

"We need to get into the ditch," Lucas told them.

The sound of the blast was still causing his ears to ring, and it was hard to think. However, he didn't need to think hard to know they shouldn't stay out in the open like this. Someone could be coming to finish them off.

He helped Hailey to her feet, and despite the ringing noise, he still heard the grunt of pain she made. She'd need to be checked out by a doctor. First, though, they needed to get out of here.

"Grayson's on the way," Josh relayed.

Good. They were so close to town that it wouldn't take him long to get there, but trouble could arrive ahead of him. Lucas figured whoever had planted that bomb was probably nearby so they could finish them off.

And he was right.

Within seconds after having that thought, he saw the SUV coming up the road from the direction of the town, and Lucas knew they didn't have much time. They had to take cover now. He ran toward the ditch, dropping down into it. It was shallow, too shallow, but it was the only thing they had right now.

"Stay down as far as you can get," he warned Hailey, and both Josh and he got into crouching positions so they could return fire if necessary.

The SUV screeched to a stop just about twenty feet from them. It was hard to see just how many were inside, though, because of the black smoke coming from the cruiser. The gas tank was already gone, so there probably wouldn't be a secondary explosion, but Lucas wanted Hailey to stay down just in case. That's why he cursed when he felt her put her hand in the waist of his jeans and take his backup weapon from his slide holster.

"You might need an extra hand," she insisted.

He didn't have time to argue with her. Didn't want to turn his attention from that SUV for even a second, but he hoped like the devil that she didn't do anything to get herself hurt worse than she already was.

"Can you see how many of them there are?" Lucas asked Josh.

His cousin shook his head and then scurried down the ditch, no doubt to get a better angle. While Josh was still in motion, though, the front passenger door of the SUV flew open. The barrel of a gun appeared.

And the shot came.

Like the explosion, it ripped through the air, and the bullet slammed into the asphalt just a few inches from Lucas and Hailey. He shoved Hailey back down, took aim and returned fire. His shot smacked against the door and sent the gunman ducking back inside the SUV.

But not for long.

The driver lowered his window and started shooting. Not just one shot, either. These came at them. A barrage of bullets that tore right through the mud and dirt in the ditch. Soon it would tear into them, too, if Lucas didn't do something.

He couldn't lift his head for long. Too risky. And if these thugs managed to kill him, then Hailey would be left as easy prey. So Lucas glanced up just long enough to get his aim. Then he lowered his head.

And he fired.

Lucas could tell from the pinging sound of the shots that he was hitting the SUV. Ideally he was hitting the gunmen, as well, but if so, that didn't stop them from continuing to fire.

"Grayson," Hailey said.

It took Lucas a moment to pick through all the noise from the gunshots to hear a welcome sound. A siren. Grayson certainly wasn't making a quiet approach, and

Lucas was thankful for it. Thankful because the gunmen stopped firing.

But that wasn't the only thing they did.

Almost immediately, the driver threw the SUV into Reverse and hit the accelerator hard. He sped backward until he reached the dirt path at the edge of the pasture and then spun the SUV around so that it was heading in the opposite direction.

Lucas came out of the ditch and started firing, hoping to shoot out the tires. Just up from him, Josh did the same. But they were too late.

The gunmen were getting away.

CHAPTER FOURTEEN

HAILEY HELD CAMDEN close while he slept in her arms. She wasn't sure she would ever want to let go of him again. Lucas and she had come so close to losing him.

So close to making him an orphan, too.

But Hailey didn't want to think about that. She only wanted this time with her son. Of course, Lucas wanted time with him, as well, but he was on the phone, pacing and trying to get more information from Grayson about the attack. Especially more information about who'd been in that SUV.

Since they'd gotten back to his place, Lucas had learned that the camera at the bank on Main Street had captured some footage of the SUV used in the attack. The footage wasn't clear, but the CSI lab might be able to enhance it enough so they could see the license plate number or even their attackers' faces.

Outside, the storm was finally moving in, and the rain was starting to spatter against the windows. The air felt heavy and thick, almost as if it were bearing down on them. It didn't help that the house was nearly dark, too. Lucas had turned off all the lights when they'd gotten in. Probably so anyone watching them wouldn't be able to see their shadows and know where to aim.

Lucas finished his latest call and went to her, sinking down on the sofa next to her. He didn't say anything. He just looked at her. Or rather, he looked at the cuts on her face. Tillie had tended them after Hailey had showered and changed her clothes, but they were no doubt a clear reminder of what'd happened to them.

"I'm sorry this happened," Lucas finally said.

Hailey shook her head. "It's not your fault. Remember, we're in danger because of me."

Admitting it put a lump in her throat. Brought tears to her eyes, too. She blinked them back because it wouldn't do either of them any good for her to break down and cry. Still, she lost the battle fighting it, and tears spilled down her cheeks.

Lucas cursed under his breath, pulled her to him and kissed her forehead. She was almost positive he didn't want her in his arms. Or so she thought. Until their gazes connected again. Yes, he did want it. Even though he knew it was only breaking down more of those barriers between them.

"What about Colleen's baby?" she asked. "Have the kidnappers called back yet with the drop-off point?"

"No, but I suspect we won't hear from them until morning. I hope it's not sooner, because Grayson still hasn't convinced Eric to do the drop with me."

Hailey hoped the kidnappers changed their minds about that. She didn't want Lucas out there where he could be gunned down, and she especially didn't want him out there with Eric. If Eric was the person behind everything, then he could lead Lucas right into a trap and then use Lucas to draw her out.

And it would work.

No way would Hailey hide herself away and let Lucas be hurt or killed just to protect her.

"Grayson said there's no sign of the gunmen," Lucas

continued after he looked away from her and stared at Camden. He touched his fingers to the baby's toes peeking out from the blanket.

She hadn't expected there would be, and Hailey already knew it would take the crime lab a while to get to the camera footage from the cruiser, especially since they had so many other things to process from this investigation. Which was a reminder about Eric showing up on the security footage from the bank.

"Has Grayson had a chance to talk to Eric yet?" she asked. It'd been a couple of hours since the attack. Maybe more than a couple since she hadn't been keeping up with the time. But she figured Grayson would make that a priority.

Lucas nodded. "Eric claims the only reason he went to the bank was that he listened to the recordings and wanted to get to the safe deposit box before one of his father's lackeys did."

It could be true. Could. But this was Eric, so there was no telling. "What was in the box?"

"According to Eric, nothing much. Just some records of illegal land deals and such that Preston had done over the years. He says he destroyed them since those were his father's last wishes."

Since Eric hated his father, she seriously doubted he would care a flying fig about carrying out Preston's wishes. "There must have been something in the box to incriminate Eric."

Lucas made a sound of agreement. There was no way to prove that, though. Maybe Grayson could go after Eric for destroying possible evidence, but with everything else he and his deputies had on their plates, that probably wouldn't happen soon, either.

"Minton came by the sheriff's office again," Lucas continued. "Of course, he says this latest attack is yet another reason for you to be in his protective custody." He paused. "If that's what you want—"

"No." And Hailey didn't even have to think about it. "I want to be here with Camden and you."

Lucas stayed quiet a moment, just long enough for her to know something was wrong. It was also plenty long enough for the feeling of panic to start spreading through her.

"Please tell me I don't have to go with Minton," she said.

"No. Well, not unless he manages to get a court order, which hasn't happened. Even then, I think we could fight it."

Good. But something else was obviously wrong, because his forehead bunched up. "Grayson and I talked about Camden, and we don't think it's a good idea for him to be here. Those attackers could try to come after him again. The ranch is secure, but he'd be better off at the main house."

The place where Mason and his family now lived. It was in the center of the ranch, which would make it harder for kidnappers to get to Camden. Still, there was a problem.

"If the kidnappers have us under surveillance, they might see that we're taking him there," Hailey pointed out.

Lucas nodded. Hesitated again. "The kidnappers want Camden only to use him to get to you."

Because Hailey was fighting the spent adrenaline and the new wave of panic, it took her a moment to figure out what he was saying. "You don't want me to be with Camden."

Another nod.

Oh, mercy. That felt like a punch to the stomach, and it caused a fresh round of tears to fill her eyes. It broke her heart to think of not having Camden close to her.

But Lucas was right.

Her baby was much safer without her around. Plus, Lucas's house was close to the main road. Too close. It would be the first place that gunmen reached if they stormed the ranch.

"How soon would Camden have to leave?" she asked.

"Soon," Lucas said. "Now would be better. I already talked to Tillie about it when you were in the shower, so she's ready. Sawyer and two ranch hands are outside patrolling, but they'll drive Tillie and Camden to the house."

That punch felt even harder, and she saw Tillie peer out from the kitchen, where she was almost certainly waiting for Lucas to break the news. The nanny gave her a sympathetic look, but Tillie was probably ready to put some distance between her and Hailey. After all, Tillie was in danger, too, simply by being around her.

"I'll take good care of him," Tillie assured her.

Hailey knew she would, but it was still hard to let go of the baby. She gave him a kiss on the cheek. Added several more. And she handed him to Lucas so he could take him to Tillie. Once he'd done that, he sent a text. No doubt to Sawyer or one of the hands, because it wasn't long before Hailey heard the sound of a vehicle pulling directly in front of the house.

"We'll come up in the morning to see him," Lucas told the nanny.

When visibility would be better, and it would be easier to spot any attackers who were trying to get close to the ranch. Of course, the visibility wasn't that good right now, which only made her fears skyrocket.

"What if they start shooting when Tillie and Camden go outside?" Hailey asked.

"There's nothing to be gained from them hurting Camden," Lucas assured her. "They want to take him, but they can't do that if he's at the main house."

It felt like a horrible loss to have these next hours taken away. But maybe Lucas and she could use that time to figure out a way to put an end to the danger. They could still set the trap using the reserve deputy to try to lure out the culprit with the promise of getting those files that Colleen had deleted.

"Stand back," Lucas told her. "I don't want you by the door when it's opened."

Yes, because it might prompt the gunmen to fire shots at her. That would put everyone, including the baby, in harm's way.

Hailey tried to hold it together but failed miserably when Lucas disarmed the security system so he could get Tillie and Camden out of the house. They didn't spend but just a couple of seconds out in the open before Sawyer got them in a cruiser. He took off with them as soon as they were inside.

Two other ranch hands stayed behind, no doubt to keep guard. Lucas did his part in keeping them safe, as well. He locked the door and reset the security system.

As fast as she could, Hailey went to the windows on the same side of the house as the road and opened the curtains. She watched as Sawyer sped out of sight.

"That's not a safe place to stand," Lucas said. He not

only moved her back but also closed the curtains again. Shut off the lights, too. "You should try to get some rest," he added. "I'll call Grayson and see if there are any updates."

Hailey had every intention of moving toward the guest room where she'd been staying, but her feet suddenly seemed anchored to the floor. Her eyes seemed out of her control, too, because she started to cry again. She hated the tears. They wouldn't help anything, and in fact, they clearly made Lucas uncomfortable, because his forehead bunched up.

Lucas gave a heavy sigh and went to her. He pulled her into his arms. "It's just temporary," he reminded her.

She got the feeling he was talking about more than just Camden. He probably meant her being here in his house.

In his arms.

They stood there in the darkness with only the sound of the rain and their breaths. She could feel his heartbeat since his chest was against hers. At the moment Hailey could feel everything about him. Feel everything about herself, too.

Especially the heat.

It came, of course. It always came when she was anywhere near Lucas. It was especially there now because they were coming down from the nightmare of the attack and having to be separated from Camden.

"I'm okay," she told him, giving him an out so he could back away.

But Lucas didn't budge. "I always swore that I'd never go another round with you."

That stung, but it was exactly what she expected him to say. "Understandable. I made mistakes with you. Not the sex," Hailey quickly added. "That wasn't a mistake because we got Camden. But I messed up pretty much everything else."

A sound that could have meant anything rumbled in his chest. "I still don't think it's a good idea for us to get involved. Not like this." He glanced at the close contact between them.

Because she thought they could use some levity, she smiled. "Are you trying to convince yourself?"

"Yeah," he admitted.

The levity vanished. So did what was left of her smile. Now, that was not what she'd expected him to say. Lucas was the sort of man who kept his feelings, and his pain, close to the vest. She'd hurt him by not trusting him, and it would take him a long time to get over that.

Or maybe not.

"I'm not doing a good job of convincing myself," he added. "In fact, I'm sinking fast here. I'm trying to come up with a damn good reason why I shouldn't just strip you naked and take you to my bed."

That robbed her of what little breath she had. And it fired up every inch of her.

"I hope you can't think of a reason," she whispered.

There. She'd given him the green light that he probably didn't want. Probably wouldn't take, either.

But she was wrong.

He lowered his head, kissed her. Not a gentle I'm-still-thinking-about-this kind of kiss. It was the real deal. Long and deep. It didn't do anything to cool down her body. Just the opposite.

The kiss went on for so long that Hailey staggered a little because she couldn't breathe. Lucas caught her, tightening his grip around her, and he pulled back so they could take in some air.

He also cursed himself. And he looked down at her. Despite the darkness, she could still see a storm of a different kind brewing in his eyes. Fire mixed with the bitterness of the past.

The fire won out.

Because Lucas scooped her up in his arms, kissed her again and headed in the direction of his bedroom. He stopped along the way to kiss her again. Maybe to make one last-ditch effort at rethinking this, but they were obviously past the point of no return.

Later there'd be consequences.

But Hailey didn't want to think about those now.

She wanted only to feel, wanted to let Lucas take her to the only place she wanted to go. A place with no tears, no gunmen. It was just the two of them, giving in to the heat that had been blazing since they'd first met.

He carried her to the bed, eased her onto the mattress. He was being too gentle with her. Probably because she didn't have her full strength, but she didn't want gentle. Not with this ache starting to throb inside her.

Hailey caught onto him, dragging him closer, and ideally letting him know that she wasn't fragile. Also letting him know that there was already a need to finish what they'd started. In case he didn't get the message, she put her hand over the front of his jeans.

Yes, he got the message, all right.

He lowered the kisses to her neck. Foreplay. Definitely not overrated when it came to Lucas, though there really was no need to fan these flames any higher.

She was wearing a loaner dress that had been in a stash that some of the Ryland wives had sent over. It was loose, so Lucas had no trouble pushing it up, and she felt his hand on her bare skin. His mouth, too, when he took those kisses to her breasts. Then her stomach. He lingered there a moment before he stripped off her bra and panties.

And he kept kissing her.

Hailey didn't want to be the only one naked, though, so she went after his shirt. Not an easy task, though, since Lucas was still wearing a holster. He had to put the kisses on hold to help her with that, and the battle started up again. Hailey wanted his clothes off *now*, but Lucas was back to the kisses.

Which kept going lower.

If they continued in that direction, he was going to make her climax. Something she desperately wanted. But not like this. She wanted him inside her.

Hailey caught onto him, pulling him back up. The movement created an incredible sensation with his body sliding over hers. That made her reach for his zipper. She fumbled around and cursed, causing Lucas to smile. As he'd done with the shirt, he helped her get off the rest of his clothes.

But then he stopped. And moved away from her.

She could have sworn her heart stopped, too, but then she realized he was only getting a condom from the nightstand drawer. It brought back the memories of the other time they'd been together.

The memories got a whole lot better, though.

Lucas came back to her, and once he had on the condom, he gathered her into his arms again. Kissed her. And entered her slowly, easing into the heat of her body. Hailey hadn't thought she'd wanted gentle and easy, but this was working just fine for her. He took his time, building the fire even hotter.

It didn't last.

Couldn't.

The need soon took over, and slow and easy was done. Now it was all about finishing this. And he did. Lucas moved in her, the pace as frantic and deep as the need. Until both of them went flying right over the edge.

CHAPTER FIFTEEN

LUCAS TRIED TO get some sleep. Hard to do, though, with a naked Hailey right next to him. Especially hard to do with the thoughts racing through his head. Thoughts of tomorrow's ransom drop and of the danger to his son.

Thoughts, too, of what'd happened between Hailey and him.

He figured he should regret the sex. And in some ways he did. It was a distraction that he didn't need at a time when he should have been focused on the investigation. Still, it was hard to regret something that'd been damn good.

At least she was sleeping now. That was good. But he figured her body hadn't given her much of a choice about that. Hailey had been running on adrenaline since coming out of the coma, and she needed to rest. Because tomorrow would be a hellish day for her, as well.

Lucas only hoped he could get back Colleen's baby without anyone getting hurt or killed. While he was hoping, he added that Eric would cooperate and do the drop with him. So far, he hadn't agreed, which meant Lucas would have to convince him or else renegotiate with the kidnappers.

Maybe Colleen wouldn't do something stupid before then.

Shortly after Hailey had fallen asleep, Lucas had gotten a text from Grayson telling him that Colleen had refused to stay at the sheriff's office any longer. Grayson hadn't had any grounds to hold her, and even though he'd reminded her that the kidnappers could be watching the place, Colleen had left anyway. At best, she was just going somewhere else to wait for the ransom drop. At worst, she was in grave danger. And Grayson didn't have the manpower to send someone out to make sure she didn't get herself into trouble.

Right now, the Rylands had enough trouble on their hands.

Lucas glanced at the laptop that he'd brought into the bedroom after Hailey had fallen asleep. It was on the nightstand next to him, and it showed the feed from the security cameras positioned all around the ranch. No doubt several of his cousins were watching the cameras, too, as was the head ranch hand. All of them looking to make sure someone didn't try to sneak onto the grounds.

So far, so good.

It was a bad night, though, for any kind of sneaking around outside. The rain was steady and heavy, and there was the occasional jag of lightning in the sky. Maybe the storm would be enough to keep the thugs from another attempt to take Camden or Hailey.

With a few strokes on the laptop keyboard, Lucas pulled up the feed from another camera. This one was in the nursery at the main house. Tillie had set up the camera so that they could see Camden. And there he was, sleeping in a crib. He was sharing the room with Mason's son, Max. Tillie was in the guest room just up the hall and would no doubt have a baby monitor next to her bed so she'd be able to hear the babies if they woke up.

As if she'd sensed what Lucas was doing, Hailey

stirred, her eyes opening and her attention going straight to the screen. She smiled. Sat up.

"It's not the same as having him here with us, but it's still nice to see him," she said.

Yeah. It was. But the *us* gave Lucas some hesitation. She'd said it so easily, as if it were normal. It wasn't. And Hailey must have realized her slip, because she muttered an apology under her breath.

Lucas hated that she felt the need to apologize. Hated even more that he felt as if he should have one. Because despite the fact that she was in his bed, they were a long way from getting to the *us* stage.

Once he'd taken care of the danger, they could start working on that. And Lucas refused to believe he couldn't put an end to the attacks, because if he couldn't, it would mean Hailey and Camden going to a safe house. Or her even returning to WITSEC, but this time she would have to take Camden with her since as long as he was out there, the snake behind this could use the baby to get to Hailey.

"Colleen left the sheriff's office," Lucas told her. "Grayson couldn't talk her out of it."

Hailey gave a heavy sigh. "No, he wouldn't have been able to do that. Did Colleen say where she was going?"

Lucas shook his head. "But unless she manages to get her hands on the money, she can't do the ransom exchange." And he hoped she didn't even attempt it.

She looked at Camden again. Then Lucas. "You're no doubt thinking we messed things up big-time," she said. "And yes, I'm talking about the sex."

He let that hang in the air for a couple of seconds. Then lifted his shoulder. "Well, yeah, when I mess up, I aim for big."

She laughed, but it wasn't exactly from humor. More nerves. Something he understood. Reality was quickly settling in, and there was no way they could go back to where they'd been just hours earlier. There was no such thing as casual sex when it came to Hailey.

The silence settled between them. And it wasn't exactly comfortable. Hailey fixed her attention to the laptop and on Camden. As much as he wanted to continue looking at their son, though, he had to switch the camera back so he could help watch the security feed. That didn't do much to ease the discomfort between them.

"Just how bad do you think it'll get tomorrow?" she asked.

He considered lying and saying "not bad at all," but he couldn't make that kind of guarantee. He looked at her, though. Saw the worry on her face again, so Lucas decided to go with a half guarantee.

"I'll make it work," he assured her and brushed a kiss on her cheek.

Of course, that sparked the attraction again, along with sparking another kiss. This time not on the cheek but her mouth. Hailey moved right into the kiss, too, sliding closer and touching him.

Not good since they were naked.

That didn't stop him, though, from deepening the kiss and hauling her right against him. However, then something stopped Lucas.

It was just a soft beep, barely audible because he had the sound turned down on the laptop, but it was a sound that went through him like the lightning bolt that slashed outside.

Because it meant something or someone had triggered one of the dozens of sensors positioned all around the ranch.

The laptop was showing six different cameras, the ones positioned on the most vulnerable points of the ranch. The fence lines and the road. He looked at each of them but didn't see anything.

"Does that sound mean what I think it means?" Hailey asked. She moved away from him, her attention back on the screen.

"It could be nothing," Lucas tried to assure her. "Sometimes animals trigger the sensors. The storm could, too, if the wind knocked down a tree branch or something."

Lucas held on to that hope, but it was hard not to think the worst. Hard to stave off the knot that was already tightening in his gut. A knot that got even tighter when his phone buzzed, and he saw Mason's name on the screen.

"Any idea why the alarm went off?" Lucas immediately asked him.

"No. I'm looking through the camera feeds now, all of them, and I don't see anything. You?"

"Nothing." Lucas put the phone on speaker so he could get dressed, but he also tapped the keyboard to scroll through some of the other security feeds. "But I'll keep watching."

"Yeah, be ready just in case," Mason said, ending the call.

That sent Hailey scrambling from the bed. There were no signs of the heat and attraction on her face now. Just the fear as she grabbed her clothes and started putting them on. Fear that Lucas needed to rein in right now, because this could be a long wait to find out if anything was truly wrong.

"No one can get near the main house," he reminded her. "Not without going through a dozen ranch hands and plenty of other houses."

Since those places all had lawmen inside them, Lucas was pretty sure Camden was safe. But "pretty sure" didn't ease the knot in his stomach. He wanted a hundred percent guarantee when it came to his son, and it didn't matter where Camden was. He wouldn't have that guarantee until the person responsible for the attacks was dead or behind bars.

Hailey finished dressing—obviously she was preparing herself in case they had to go outside, but Lucas was hoping that didn't happen.

Lucas put back on both his weapons, and even though it was hard to force himself to sit down, he did for Hailey's sake. So that she'd sit, too. She did, right beside him, and they both watched the screen as he scrolled through all the feeds.

She shook her head. "I still don't see anything."

Neither did he, but it was dark, and even with the security lights, there were still plenty of shadows. Plenty of places for someone to hide, too, what with all the fences, trees and outbuildings. But if someone was out there and that person moved, then the sensors would pick him up, and the alarm would ding again.

The seconds crawled by, turning into minutes, and just when Lucas was ready to try to level his breathing, he saw something. Movement not near the fence line but near the road. It was just a blur of motion, barely in camera range and not actually on ranch land.

"What?" Hailey asked. She'd obviously noticed that he'd tensed.

"Maybe nothing," he repeated.

Lucas clicked on that specific screen, enlarged it and zoomed in on the area where he'd seen the motion. He was hoping it was a deer or an illusion caused by the rain.

But it wasn't.

It was a man dressed all in black. And he had a rifle aimed right at Lucas's house.

HAILEY COULDN'T STOP herself from gasping when she saw the man. He was lurking behind one of the trees directly across the road from the ranch.

"Oh, God," she said, and she scrambled to get the gun from Lucas's nightstand.

He took hold of her hand and had her sit next to him again. He also adjusted the view of the camera so that she could see the truck that was parked at the end of the road. Unlike the man with the rifle, the truck was actually on the ranch.

"Two of the hands are in the truck," Lucas explained, and he took out his phone and fired off a text. No doubt to warn them that there was definitely a problem.

Lucas went back to the camera angle so they could see the man, and Hailey realized he wasn't alone. There was another armed guy directly behind him.

The skin crawled on the back of her neck. Because she knew what those men wanted.

They wanted her.

And they'd try to use Camden to get her.

"Get down on the floor," Lucas instructed.

She did as he said, and he grabbed the laptop to bring

it to the floor with him. The difference was he had her lie all the way down while he stayed in a sitting position. Probably so he'd be better able to respond if things turned bad in a hurry.

Hailey tried not to panic. Hard to do, though, when all she could feel was the panic and fear. Both went up a significant notch when she saw the headlights of an approaching car on the screen. The vehicle no doubt carried more thugs arriving to launch a full-scale attack.

Both the hands in the truck opened their doors, and they put out their rifles. Ready to return fire.

She gasped again when the dinging sound shot through the room. But it wasn't a security alarm. It was Lucas's phone to let him know he had a text. She saw Mason's name on the screen.

"Mason's on the line with the hands at the road," Lucas said when he read the text. "He's sending them backup right away." He cursed. "But I need to stay here."

She knew the profanity wasn't for her but the situation. He wanted to be down there helping the hands, but all of this could be designed to have him do just that. So that she'd be alone and an easy prey.

The car came to a stop directly in front of where the hands were parked. Hailey saw another vehicle, too. A cruiser barreling down the ranch road toward the hands, the two armed men and the newly arrived vehicle. A moment later, another cruiser followed the first. So there were plenty of lawmen responding to what was no doubt about to become the scene of another attack.

"What the hell?" Lucas said, moving closer to the laptop screen.

Hailey watched as the driver of the car got out. Colleen. And her sister lifted her hands into the air as if surrendering. Colleen said something to the ranch hands, but since there was no audio, Hailey had no idea what.

But this couldn't be good.

Either her sister was part of the oncoming attack, or else she was going to be right in the middle of it.

Even though it was pouring rain, Colleen stayed outside the car, and after a very short conversation with the hands, she took out her phone. A moment later, Lucas's own phone rang. He answered it and put it on speaker.

"Hailey?" Colleen asked. Her voice was frantic. As was her expression. "You have to tell these men to let me onto the ranch."

Hailey debated how to answer that. But Lucas had no such debate with himself. "Did you bring those gunmen with you?" he asked.

"What gunmen?" Colleen's gaze began to slash all around her.

"The ones across the road."

A sob tore from Colleen's mouth, and she ducked back into the car. "No, I didn't bring them, but I think they want me dead."

"If they wanted that, you already would be," Lucas pointed out. "They had a clean shot and didn't take it."

And it wasn't as if the men had left. Hailey could still see them on the corner of the screen. Could see the approaching cruisers, too. They pulled to a stop behind the ranch hands' truck. The doors opened, and four of Lucas's cousins—Dade, Sawyer, Josh and Gage—all took aim at the gunmen while they used the doors of the cruisers for cover.

"You're just going to let me stay out here?" Colleen protested.

Hailey was torn about what to do. Her instincts were

screaming for her to protect her sister, but her instincts were even stronger to keep Camden safe.

"Answer me!" Colleen practically shouted.

"I can't let you near my son," Hailey said. "Leave and go to the sheriff's office. You'll be safe there."

That brought out some vicious profanity from Colleen. "I stopped Preston from having you killed. You owe me!"

That chilled her to the bone, but then Hailey reminded herself that it might not even be true. It could be Colleen who wanted her dead. Or even Colleen just carrying through on Preston's old wishes.

Colleen added some more profanity, but Hailey shut her out when Lucas's phone dinged, indicating he had an incoming call.

Unknown Caller popped up on the screen.

"I have to put you on hold," Lucas said to her sister, and he answered the other call.

"I know I said I'd be in touch in the morning," the man said by way of greeting, "but I just couldn't wait." It was the kidnapper, the same one who'd been communicating with them.

"Where are you?" Lucas asked.

"Nearby but out of range of all those pesky cameras you got all around the ranch. You might be able to see a couple of the fellas I brought with me, though."

"I do, and you probably see that there are six men with guns aimed right back at them."

"Yeah, they know. None of us want a gunfight. Especially not Hailey and you. Not with your boy and all those Ryland kids and babies so close. Somebody might get hurt."

Instead of ice in Hailey's blood, that sent some hot

rage through her body. How dare this snake threaten not only her son but also everyone else on the ranch? She nearly yelled at him and wanted to use some of those same curse words that her sister just had, but Lucas spoke before she could say anything.

"If you don't want a gunfight, what do you want?" Lucas asked the man.

"I thought you'd like to see who's with me," he said, obviously not answering Lucas's question. "I'm sending you a pretty picture now."

Almost immediately, Lucas's phone dinged with a text. Again from Unknown Caller, and it did indeed have a picture attached. It took a moment to load.

Hailey's heart went to her knees.

Because it was a picture of Colleen's baby. Not alone. Minton was holding her in the crook of his arm.

And there was what appeared to be a bomb strapped to Minton's chest.

CHAPTER SIXTEEN

HAILEY SNAPPED TO a sitting position, and she practically snatched the phone from his hand so she could get a closer look of the photo that the kidnapper had just sent them.

But Lucas didn't need a closer look. He'd already seen more than enough.

"It could be fake," Lucas reminded Hailey. "Minton could be their boss, and he could have set all of this up."

She gave a shaky nod, repeated that last part. But he wasn't sure she was buying it. Her breathing was already way too fast, and she was no doubt having to battle the panic that had to be crawling through her. Lucas felt some of that same panic, too, but he had to rein it in so he could focus on what exactly he was seeing.

And how to fix it.

"Let me speak to Minton," Lucas told the kidnapper.

"Thought you'd want to do that. I'll put him on the line, but for just a few seconds. After that, you and I will have a little chat about what you need to do for this to turn out good for all of us."

Lucas didn't have to wait long before he heard Minton's voice. "They hit me with a stun gun when I was going into my office," Minton said, his voice a snarl. His expression in the photo matched the snarl, as well. Either he was one unhappy camper or he was pretending to be one. "Now I have a bomb on me, right next to the baby."

"Yes, I saw the photo. Is it real?" Lucas came out and asked.

"Hell, yes, it's real!" Minton's shout must have startled the baby, because she began to cry.

Not good. Hailey's nerves were clearly already frayed enough, and the baby's cries only added to the urgency of this situation.

"How do you know the bomb is real?" Lucas pressed. "Do you have personal knowledge of explosive devices?"

"Yes, I do, but not in the way you're insinuating. I didn't put this bomb on myself. These idiots did after they kidnapped me. And I don't know who they're working for, but if you don't do as they say, they're going to start the timer. After that, I'd have only two minutes before this kid and I get blown to bits."

Lucas glanced at the photo again, at the placement of Minton's hands, and he saw that they were literally tied around the baby. Two minutes probably wouldn't be enough time to get out of those ropes and remove the bomb. Especially since it was possible the kidnappers were also holding Minton at gunpoint and wouldn't give him a chance to escape.

"Well?" the kidnapper said, coming back on the line. Lucas could still hear the baby crying, so obviously the little girl and Minton weren't too far away. "Convinced that we mean business?"

"I was convinced of that before you put an innocent baby in danger. Get the baby away from that bomb and then we'll talk."

"We'll talk now," the man snapped.

"All right," Lucas snapped right back. "You want the baby alive to collect the ransom. Well, you're risking a half million dollars by keeping her that close to the explosive."

"There's no real threat to her," the kidnapper said. "Not at this moment, anyhow. You gotta do something, though, to keep it that way. You can have the baby in exchange for Hailey. And before you go all cowboy cop on me, this isn't your decision. It's Hailey's. I'll give her five minutes to decide."

Lucas was about to tell him that he didn't need a second of that five minutes, that the answer was no. But the kidnapper hung up.

"You're not going out there," Lucas insisted.

She moved as if ready to get up, but he caught her arm to force her to sit back down. He needed to convince her to stay put, but he also had to keep watch on the security screens in case those gunmen started firing.

"These men want you dead," Lucas reminded her. "And along with two of our suspects, Colleen and Minton, there are gunmen. Going to meet them won't get the baby rescued. It will only get you killed."

She stopped struggling to get away from him, and even in the darkness, Lucas saw the tears shimmer in her eyes. "I have to do something to help that baby. She's my niece."

Lucas got that. Hell, he had a niece, and he would have done anything to keep her safe. But a suicide mission wasn't the way to go, especially since it was possible the child wasn't even in any real danger.

"So, what do we do?" Hailey asked.

He looked at the screen again. Still no movement from the gunmen. Lucas panned around, trying to get a glimpse of the vehicle holding Minton and the baby, but he didn't see anything.

Hell.

The kidnappers could have the baby anywhere, including out of the state.

"Let me see first if Colleen stayed on hold," he said.

Though Lucas wasn't sure what to tell Hailey's sister. It didn't seem a good idea to mention the bomb. However, it turned out he didn't have to make that decision, because Colleen was no longer on the line. Her car was still at the end of the road, though.

But it didn't stay there.

Colleen backed out the car, turned onto the main road and hit the accelerator. Lucas thought she had decided to leave, and he adjusted the camera angle to see if she was heading back to town.

She wasn't.

Colleen turned her car directly at the white wooden fence that fronted the ranch, and she bashed right through it. Her car went straight into the pasture. Too close to Lucas's house.

Hailey gasped. "What is she doing?" she said under her breath.

Lucas hated to think the worst, but he did. Colleen could be coming to kill them.

Dade and Gage got back into their cruiser and went in pursuit. Mason was no doubt sending someone, too, but there wasn't a lot of help to send. Most of the men were already tied up guarding the houses and the other fences, especially the back, where it would be easier for someone to launch an attack.

Colleen's car didn't make it far, though. The rain had obviously soaked the pasture, and she made it only about a hundred yards before her tires bogged down in the mud and grass. That didn't stop her, though. She barreled out of the vehicle and started running.

Directly toward Lucas's house.

He hadn't even been sure that Colleen knew which house was his, but she must have done her homework, because she was headed their way on foot.

And not alone, either.

Before Dade could get the cruiser turned around, another vehicle came up the road. A black SUV. And it looked like the same one with the attackers who'd tried to kill Hailey, Josh and him after the bombing.

"Those men are after Colleen?" Hailey asked.

Lucas didn't know the answer. Not at first, anyway. But he soon got one. The SUV didn't go after Colleen. Nor did it bog down. The driver came to a stop, and his passenger opened his door.

And the guy aimed something at Lucas's house.

It was too big to be a regular firearm, and Lucas had to zoom in on it to figure out what it was. A tear gas gun. At least, he hoped it was that and not a grenade launcher. Either way, Hailey and he had to get the heck out of there now.

Lucas closed the laptop, tucking it under his arm, and he took hold of Hailey to get her moving. It was chilly and raining, but Lucas was pretty sure there wouldn't be enough time to grab any raincoats or umbrellas.

And he was right.

There was a crashing sound of breaking glass in the living room, the side of the house that faced those thugs. Followed by another sound of the canister plinking to the floor. A couple of moments later, another canister came flying into the house.

"We have to hurry," Lucas warned her. He handed her the laptop so he could draw his gun.

Time was up, because tear gas started to spew through

the entire house. Lucas ran with her to the back door and prayed he wasn't carrying Hailey right into an ambush.

HAILEY WAS MOVING as fast as she could, but it wasn't fast enough. The tear gas was on them before Lucas and she could get to the back door.

She started to cough, the gas cutting off her breath along with burning her throat and eyes. It was no doubt doing the same thing to Lucas, but he still managed to get the door open. He already had his weapon drawn when he stepped out onto the porch and looked around. He must not have seen anyone because he pulled her out of the house.

"We can't stay here," he said.

A moment later, she realized why. Another canister came bashing into the house. Then another. It wouldn't be long before the tear gas was so thick back here that they would be coughing too hard to run.

But where?

If they ran outside, they could be gunned down.

She could see Lucas's gaze darting around while he was trying to figure that out. They had a couple of choices. They could try to make it to the side of the house where he'd parked his truck. The problem with that was it was also the side where those canister-shooting thugs were positioned.

It was where she'd last seen Colleen, too.

So that probably wasn't a good direction to go. That left the barn, a detached garage and a storage building. Beyond that was open pasture, where one of those rifle-men would be able to pick them off.

"We'll run to the garage," Lucas told her. "I have another truck there we can use to escape. Stay as low as you can and move fast."

Hailey wasn't sure she could go fast. Not with her legs so wobbly, and now that she couldn't breathe so well, it would be even harder. Still, they didn't have much of a choice.

Lucas took her hand and led her off the porch and down the steps. When they reached the yard, there was no more awning, so the rain and wind came right at them. Even though Hailey had on the hoodie, it wasn't nearly thick enough, and it didn't take long before she started to shiver. Still, she ran until Lucas pulled them behind a large oak.

Not a second too soon, either.

A shot blasted through the air and slammed right into the tree.

It wasn't just the rain that was raw and bitter. Suddenly the fear was, too. Not because the shot had come so close to hitting Lucas and her, but because she didn't want bullets being fired anywhere near Camden and the others.

More shots came, but these didn't slam into the tree. That only made the fear worse because Hailey couldn't immediately figure out where those men were shooting. Then she realized they were aiming at the cruiser that Dade and Gage were trying to get closer.

Mercy.

The shooters were no doubt doing that to stop Lucas's cousins from helping them. At least the cruiser was bullet-resistant, but she figured sooner or later, either Dade or Gage would step out so they could return fire.

Hailey considered taking out the laptop to see if she could check the security cameras, but she needed to be ready to move. Plus, she didn't want to risk getting it wet. Right now, it was still under her arm where it was semi-protected. Once they were in the garage, then she could check and make sure none of these hired killers were heading for the main house. Maybe she'd also be able to find her sister. If Colleen was innocent, then she was in grave danger out in the open with those bullets flying.

Lucas's phone buzzed, and he took it from his pocket and handed it to her. Probably so he could keep his hands free. When Hailey saw Mason's name on the screen, she answered it right away.

"Is everyone all right?" she immediately asked.

"Fine for now. I want to keep it that way. Dade told me about the bomb, the baby and Minton. As soon as Dade can, he'll move in to help. In the meantime, our other cousins, Nate and Landon, are trying to work their way to the pasture. If they get a clean shot, they'll stop the gunmen."

That was good. Hailey hoped that would happen. It wouldn't get back her niece, but it would end the immediate danger. At least, it would if these men didn't set off that explosive. But she figured they were going to use Colleen's baby as the ultimate bargaining tool to get to her.

"What about my sister?" Hailey asked. "Where is she?"

"I lost sight of her, but the last I saw her, she was moving in the direction of Lucas's barn."

Then that was all the more reason for Lucas and her not to go in there. "What about the car with Minton and the baby?"

"Still nothing on that. Grayson's coming in from town, and he'll look along the way."

Maybe they'd get lucky and could spot it. Of course, in the dark and rain, it would be hard to do.

"I can see Lucas and you," Mason went on a moment later. "Make your way to the main house when you can. You're too damn close to these dirtbags."

Yes, they were. And while Hailey desperately wanted to see Camden, she was also terrified of having these men shoot at them if they went in that direction. Plus, Lucas and she had to get to the garage first.

"I'll have the ranch hands fire at the dirtbags," Mason added. "That should keep them occupied a couple of seconds so that you and Lucas can get moving."

"But what about the shots going to the main house?" she asked.

"The ranch hands are positioning themselves so that won't happen," he assured her.

She thanked him and added, "Just keep Camden and everyone else safe." Maybe Mason and the others would be able to do that.

She relayed the information Mason had given her to Lucas, but before she even finished, Hailey heard the shots. These weren't coming from the hired killers but rather from the ranch hands. As Mason had said, it created a distraction because the gunmen were now shooting at the hands.

"Let's move," Lucas told her.

They started running. There weren't any trees or anything else right by they could use for cover, so Hailey held her breath while they were out in the open. It seemed to take an eternity to go the fifteen or so yards. The rain certainly didn't help, either, and her shoes sank down into the boggy ground.

The moment they reached the garage, Lucas took

her to the side door and threw it open. He stepped in first, his gaze slashing from one side to the other. What he didn't do was turn on the lights. Probably because it would alert the gunmen to their position. Maybe the men had been so involved with the gunfight distraction that they hadn't seen Lucas and her make their way there.

"Stay right next to me," he warned her.

She did, and while he continued to look around them, he inched his way to a truck parked at the front of the garage. The back was a workshop and storage area and was filled with shelves, tables and equipment. It would give someone places to hide. Not exactly a reminder to soothe her already raw nerves.

"I need to check and make sure no one tampered with the truck," Lucas added. "Keep watch around us."

That didn't help her nerves, either. Hailey just wanted to get out of there, but after what'd happened with the cruiser, they had to take precautions.

Lucas stooped down, and using the light from his phone, he began to make his way around the truck. She followed him while keeping watch, but Hailey didn't see anyone, thank goodness.

But she heard something.

Lucas must have, too, because he quickly stood and moved in front of her. They waited, listening. Hard to hear, though, what with the shots continuing outside, but Hailey was almost certain she'd heard something move. Or maybe it was just the wind and rain.

No, it wasn't.

There was another sound, and this time Hailey was able to pinpoint it.

Someone was in the truck.

CHAPTER SEVENTEEN

HELL. WHAT NOW?

Lucas pivoted and took aim in the direction of the truck cab. He didn't see anyone, but he was positive someone was in there.

He had known it was a risk to come into the garage, but it would have also been a risk for them to stay in the yard with heaven knew how many hired thugs now on the ranch. However, they might have gone from the frying pan right into the fire.

"Come out or I'll shoot," Lucas warned the person. But it was a warning he hoped like the devil that he didn't have to carry out. Because he didn't want to shoot in cramped quarters with Hailey.

Definitely didn't want to start a gunfight.

And he also didn't want to alert the armed thugs that Hailey and he were in the garage. That would only cause them to open fire. Or maybe launch another tear gas grenade.

"It's me," someone said.

Colleen.

Lucas groaned and definitely didn't lower his gun. "Put your hands where I can see them," he ordered.

"I'm not the one trying to kill you." Colleen added a sob. "When will you believe me?"

"I might start to believe you when you get out of the truck, hands up."

Other than another sob, Colleen didn't respond, and the seconds crawled by before she finally lifted her head. Lucas could see then that she'd been down on the seat. She lifted her hands, too.

"Satisfied?" Colleen snapped.

"Not yet. Step out, keep your hands in the air and don't make any sudden moves. Get behind me," he added to Hailey. "And try to keep watch around us in case she's not alone."

Because Hailey's arm was right against his, he felt her tense even more. He hated that he was having to put her through this, but they couldn't get in the truck until Lucas figured out what the heck Colleen was up to.

Colleen stepped from the truck, and Lucas could see she didn't have anything in her hands. She also didn't appear to be carrying a weapon. Like Hailey, Colleen wasn't wearing a coat. The rain had soaked her jeans and top, and they were clinging to her. Still, Lucas motioned for her to turn around, and when she did, he made sure she didn't have a weapon tucked in the back waist of her jeans.

She didn't.

"I told you I wasn't trying to kill you," Colleen said.

Just because she wasn't armed didn't mean she wasn't behind this attack. "Why are you in here? *How* are you in here?" Lucas amended.

"I just started running when my car got stuck. This was the first place I reached. I knew I needed to try to get to my baby, but I couldn't find the truck keys."

They were on a hook on the wall, but since Colleen

hadn't turned on the lights, either, she would have had trouble spotting them.

"Do you know where the baby is?" Lucas asked.

"No." Colleen winced when there was another round of loud gunfire. "But I have to find her. I have to save her." She made a loud sob. "Is there anything you can do to make them stop shooting? Can you try to negotiate with them or something?"

Her fear seemed genuine enough, but after the hell Hailey and he had been through, Lucas planned on hanging on to his skepticism a while longer.

"I don't have any control over those gunmen," he told her. "But there are armed ranch hands out there, and they might get them to stop soon."

Colleen looked at Hailey. "Please help me get my daughter back. Please. Just think if it were your son and how hard this would be for you."

"I have thought about it," Hailey answered. "Those kidnappers want me in exchange for the baby."

"Then do it." Colleen didn't hesitate even a second, either. Maybe because she knew there was no danger for her. But there'd be plenty for Hailey. "I'd go if they would let me."

"Really?" Lucas pressed.

"Of course."

Then he was about to put that to the test. Without taking his gun off the woman, he passed his phone back to Hailey. "Hit Redial and see if the kidnapper will answer."

Colleen's eyes widened. "What are you going to do?"

Lucas didn't actually expect the kidnapper to answer and was surprised when he heard the man's voice. "Are you ready to send out Hailey?" the man asked.

"No, but Colleen is here, and she's willing to meet with you."

And Lucas carefully watched Colleen's reaction. She didn't look annoyed or afraid. "Yes," she said. "I'll come right now. Just tell me where I need to go so I can get my baby."

"Guess Lucas told you about our little explosive device, huh?" the kidnapper taunted.

Colleen's gaze slashed to Lucas. "What is he talking about?"

"So he didn't tell you," the kidnapper continued before Lucas could speak. "Minton and your baby girl are real close to a bomb right now."

Colleen gasped. "Oh, God. Is it true? Is there actually a bomb?"

"There is. A bomb set to go off with just a flip of a switch. And if you want that to change, then convince your sister to come out and chat with us. You come, too. In fact, I insist both of you come."

Even though Colleen looked on the verge of a panic attack, Lucas blocked Hailey from going closer to her. If Colleen was truly innocent, then he'd owe her a huge apology, but for now his priority had to be keeping Hailey safe.

"What exactly do you want from the women?" Lucas asked the kidnapper.

"Any and all files they have about the DeSalvo family," he answered without hesitation.

"And then what?" Hailey added.

"Then, tomorrow morning you'll get that ransom money, and you'll get both the women and the kid."

Lucas seriously doubted it. Judging from the sound

she made, so did Hailey. Colleen was the only one of them who was clearly eager to do this.

"Let me know if the women are coming out," the kidnapper said. "Once they do, the shots will stop on our part. You'll have to make sure the Rylands and the ranch hands stop, too." And he ended the call.

"Call him back," Colleen insisted. "Have him tell me where Hailey and I need to go to get my baby."

"That's not going to happen," Lucas assured her. "Not on Hailey's part anyway."

But what was his next move?

He wanted to get Hailey to the main house, where she'd be safer and with Camden. However, he couldn't just leave Colleen here, either.

"Call Mason," Lucas told Hailey. "Let him know that Colleen is here, and I'm trying to figure out what to do with her. I also want to know if the road is clear between my house and his."

"You don't need to figure out what to do with me," Colleen shrieked. "We have to get the baby." She snapped toward Hailey. "This is all your fault, anyway. You probably have all sorts of information stashed away on Preston and Eric. Information that could send me to jail, too."

"Are you admitting to some crimes?" Lucas immediately asked her.

"No! But Hailey always had it in for Preston. I figure Eric, too. And if she hadn't been so hell-bent on putting them in jail, none of this would be happening."

Maybe that was true, but in this case, being hell-bent was the right thing to do. "Preston was a criminal. He deserved to be behind bars." And that was all the breath he was going to waste on Colleen. "Call Mason," he repeated to Hailey.

"I really am innocent," Colleen continued while Hailey located the number. "Darrin forced me to go to the hospital. He said it was the only way to get my baby. But he lied. And then he tried to kill me when he ran me off the road."

If that was true, then it was another reason Lucas was glad that Darrin was out of the picture. Hailey made a sound of agreement, probably because she felt the same, and she finished making the call to Mason. She also put it on speaker.

"What's the latest on the gunmen?" Lucas asked the moment his cousin answered.

"Pinned down, for now. But they're not budging, and I can't have the hands, Dade or the others go in any closer."

So they were at a stalemate. Well, in a way. Hailey was still in danger.

"Grayson called," Mason went on. "He spotted a vehicle just up the road from the ranch, and he's going to do a quiet approach to see if Minton and the baby are there. One of the deputies is with him."

"Tell the sheriff to be careful," Colleen blurted out.

"Who the hell is that?" Mason asked.

"Colleen. I'm in my garage with Hailey and her. Colleen was hiding in here."

Mason cursed. "And your plans?"

"Still debating that. How safe would it be for me to drive Hailey to the main house and then come back here to wait with Colleen?" That was just in case she was innocent and therefore in danger.

But Hailey was shaking her head before Lucas even finished his question to Mason. "That's too risky for you," she insisted.

"Hailey's right," Mason agreed. "When the gunmen spot your truck, I figure they'll start shooting at it."

Lucas wasn't giving up just yet on this particular plan. He wanted some distance between Colleen and Hailey. Between Hailey and those shooters, too. "Maybe the hands could continue keeping them occupied?"

"They could, but why don't you stay there for a couple more minutes. That'll give me time to hear from Grayson. If the baby is in that vehicle, I'll need to send him some help. Plus, I'd rather the gunmen not have any reason to get to the main house."

No way could Lucas disagree with any of that, but he definitely didn't like the idea of staying put, either. Maybe he tempted fate with that thought, because he heard a sound. Not one of the normal gunshots. This was more of a blast. One that he'd heard four other times before.

It was the sound of another gas canister being fired.

And this time it didn't smash into the house. It hit the garage door, and from what he could tell, it bashed into the wooden part of the door and not the glass inserts just above it. However, that didn't stop the gas from spewing in around the sides and bottom.

Mercy. Lucas definitely hadn't wanted things to go this way, but they had to move. That was especially true when the next canister came crashing through the glass.

"In the truck, now," he told Hailey and Colleen. He grabbed the keys from the wall hook.

They were already starting in that direction anyway. First Colleen. Then Hailey, who got in the middle. They were already coughing, too, and he hoped the tear gas didn't water his eyes so much that he wouldn't be able to see.

The moment Lucas started the engine, he hit the remote control to open the door, and once he had enough
clear space to get out, he gunned the engine.

Driving right into that cloud of tear gas.

But that was just the start of their troubles. Because
the gunmen started shooting at them.

HAILEY TRIED TO clear her eyes and throat so she could
help Lucas get them to safety. If that was possible. The
shots were coming at them so fast that it was like being
trapped in a hailstorm.

The bullets tore through the windshield, and Hailey
took hold of Colleen and pushed her lower on the seat.
She got lower, as well, but Lucas couldn't while driving.

Lucas cursed. "Hell, they shot into the radiator."

No doubt to disable the vehicle. But how had they
even known Lucas, Colleen and she were in the garage
in the first place? Hailey hoped it was a guess on their
part and they didn't have some insider information from
Colleen. Her sister could have called or sent those thugs
a text when she saw them come into the garage.

"Where are we going?" Hailey managed to ask Lucas
even though she was having to fight for every breath.
And she was shaking from the wet and cold. She had
such a tight grip on the laptop and Lucas's phone that
she was afraid they might shatter.

"Away from those shots. Away from the main house,
too."

Good. As much as she wanted to get to safety, it was
too risky to go in that direction. Too risky to stay put,
too, and Lucas didn't speed toward the road but rather
across the backyard and to the side of his own house.

That put an instant buffer between them and the gunmen. What it didn't do was get rid of the lingering tear gas.

Probably because the thugs sent two more canisters their way.

The gunmen were trying to flush them out, trying to force them out into the open, where they'd be easier targets.

"Watch Colleen," Lucas said to her. A reminder that he didn't trust her sister. Neither did she, and her alarm went up a significant notch when Colleen threw open the glove compartment.

"I need a gun," her sister insisted.

Hailey wanted that, too, but she hoped there wasn't one for Colleen to find. There wasn't. But Lucas took out his backup weapon, and when he handed it to Hailey, she had to shift the laptop under her arm so she could take it. Hailey put it in her pocket.

Giving her the gun earned Lucas and her a glare from Colleen, but Hailey didn't care. She preferred not to be in a closed vehicle with one of their armed suspects.

She lifted her head enough so she could adjust and pull out the laptop. She opened it and prayed the Wi-Fi signal was strong enough outside the house.

It was.

She pulled up the security camera screens so she could help Lucas keep watch. After all, the gunmen could sneak around the front of the house and attack. Hard to see much of anything, though, with the darkness, the tear gas and the rain, but at least the rain was washing away some of the gas. That should make it easier for them to breathe and see.

Despite the nightmare going on around them, Lucas's gaze met hers. For just a couple of seconds. She wanted to tell him how sorry she was that this had happened again.

She wanted to say a lot of things to him.

But since it wasn't the time or the place, Hailey went back to keeping watch. Right now, that was the best thing she could do for all of them. Too bad she didn't see something on the screens that would help Dade and the others close in on the gunmen. She switched the angle.

Nothing.

Then she switched it again, and that's when Hailey saw the movement. With the thick rain, it was just a blur, but someone had definitely moved up behind the two gunmen.

Another man dressed all in black. This one, though, was also wearing rain gear—a coat with a hood.

Hailey wasn't sure how he'd gotten there, but it was possible he'd come from the vehicle that had crashed through the fence. That SUV was only yards away from the other thugs.

"There's a third gunman," she relayed to Lucas.

And it made her wonder if there were others in the SUV. It tightened her stomach even more to think that there could be enough of them to overrun the ranch. Plus, there were the two across the road with the sniper rifles who had pinned down Josh and Sawyer.

"If any of the gunmen move," Lucas said, "let me know."

The words had no sooner left his mouth when the newcomer did move. He hurried behind a tree.

Coming closer to the ranch.

Closer to Lucas's house.

More movement caught her eye, and when she adjusted the camera angle, she saw the guy aim the tear gas launcher. No, not again. But he fired. Not one but two canisters.

Except these were different.

The gas coming from them was thicker, and it was milky white.

Hailey turned the laptop so that Lucas could see it, and he cursed. "Smoke bombs."

Hailey knew the reason for his profanity. As bad as the tear gas was—and it was *bad*—the smoke bombs could be worse. Because they could conceal the gunmen trying to move closer to the house.

And that's exactly what was happening.

The smoke began to spread, and it continued when the men fired off several more.

"Keep watch as best you can," Lucas advised her.

She would, but it was next to impossible to keep track of the men now. Maybe the rain, though, would work in their favor and quickly wash the smoke away as it was dissipating the tear gas.

A buzzing sound shot through the truck, and Hailey's heart jumped to her throat. At first she thought it was their attackers, but it was only Lucas's phone. With all the chaos going on, she'd forgotten that she was still holding it.

"It's Grayson," she relayed, looking at the phone screen. She answered it right away and put it on speaker.

"Please tell me you found my baby," Colleen jumped to say.

"No, but I'm close enough to the car to see inside. There are two men in the front seat and an infant carrier in the back. The person I don't see is Minton. Any idea where he is?"

Hailey quickly scanned through all the camera angles.

Even with the smoke, she could see Dade and the others pinned down. She couldn't see the gunmen, though, who'd been shooting and launching that tear gas and the smoke bombs.

But there was no sign of Minton.

"I don't know," Hailey told Grayson. "According to what the kidnapper showed us, he was in the car with the baby earlier."

"Yeah, but he's not there now, or if he is, he's down on the floor where I can't see him."

"Does that mean the bomb isn't there, either?" Colleen blurted out.

"I can't tell. But I'm going closer as soon as I have the backup that Mason's sending." Grayson paused. "Do I want to know how bad things are at the ranch?"

"The gunmen haven't gotten to the houses," Lucas answered.

What Lucas didn't say was—they hadn't, *not yet*. But there was always the possibility that they would unless the Rylands and ranch hands figured out a way to stop them.

"I'll call you back when I can," Grayson said before he hung up.

Hailey hoped he could get the baby out of there. That would be one less worry on their minds. Because even if Colleen was guilty, Hailey still wanted her niece far away from this dangerous situation.

"Where's the third gunman you saw?" Lucas asked her.

That sent Hailey's attention back to the computer screen. As she'd done before, she panned around the camera angles, looking at the tree where she'd last spotted him. But even when the smoke cleared a little in that area, there was no sign of him now.

Sweet heaven.

Because she'd gotten so preoccupied with Grayson's call, Hailey had lost sight of him. That could turn out to be a fatal mistake. Especially considering the gunman could be hiding in one of those smoke clouds that were drifting toward Lucas's house.

"Any chance the third gunman could be Minton?" Lucas added.

Hailey went back through what she'd seen of the man, but she had to shake her head. "I never saw him standing fully upright, so it's hard to know how tall he is. Plus he was wearing a hood, so I couldn't see any part of his face. But it's possible it's Minton. Or Eric."

However, it was just as likely that it was another thug who'd been hired to kill her.

"Grayson has to get to my baby," Colleen said.

Obviously she wasn't thinking about the third gunman. Maybe not even thinking about who was responsible for this. Her focus seemed to be solely on the baby. And she was crying.

Hailey was definitely affected by those tears, and it tore at her heart to think how much her sister could be suffering right now. She slid her hand over Colleen's, causing her sister to flinch. At first. Then Colleen gave her hand a gentle squeeze.

"No matter what happens," Colleen said, "I'm sorry for the way things have turned out."

Hailey was about to ask her exactly what she meant by that. But she didn't get a chance to say anything. That's because the passenger door flew open, and before Hailey could even register what was going on, someone latched onto Colleen and dragged her from the truck.

That someone put a gun to Colleen's head.

CHAPTER EIGHTEEN

LUCAS WHIPPED HIS gun in Colleen's direction. But it was too late. The man already had her before Lucas could do anything to stop it.

However, Lucas could do something to keep Hailey safe. He crawled over her, putting himself in front of her. He didn't lower his weapon. He kept it aimed at the guy. He also watched Colleen's reaction.

She called out for help, tried to get away, but the man only jammed the gun harder against her head. It seemed convincing.

Seemed.

But Lucas reminded himself that this could all be part of the ploy to get to Hailey. A ploy he hadn't been able to prevent because he hadn't seen the guy sneaking up on the truck.

Behind him, he could hear Hailey's breath gusting, and he knew she had to be scared. Lucas hoped, though, that she would continue to keep watch around them, because heaven knew how many hired guns could be coming at them.

"Let Colleen go," Lucas demanded, though he figured this would get zero results.

And it didn't.

The guy laughed. He was wearing a tear gas mask that covered the lower part of his face, but Lucas could see enough of him to know that this wasn't Minton or Eric. He was likely just another hired gun.

"Sorry, can't let her go," the man finally said. "Got my orders, and I'm to keep this gun on her."

"Who's giving those orders?" Lucas snapped.

"It's not my place to tell, but you'll know soon enough. The boss is on the way. He should be here any minute now, and then things will get real…interesting."

Hell. Lucas had figured as much, but it was gut-tightening to hear it spelled out for him.

"Keep an eye on the security feed," Lucas told Hailey, but he wasn't even sure there was enough room for her to maneuver the laptop around so she could look. There hadn't been a lot of time when he'd moved in front of her, and she was literally jammed against him, the steering wheel and the door.

"Don't let him kill me," Colleen begged while she stared at Lucas. "*Please*. I don't want my daughter to be an orphan."

Neither did he, but Lucas wasn't sure yet how to put a stop to this. Especially when the guy shifted the gun and took aim at him. Hailey must have seen that, because she came over his back, putting her head in front of his.

Lucas cursed at her, tried to get her to move back, but she fought him.

"He won't kill me," Hailey insisted. "Not until he's sure I've given him everything I have on the DeSalvo family. But he'll kill you."

"The little lady's right," the gunman verified. "And since I can't risk a bullet going straight through you and into her, then I have to settle for just telling you to toss out that gun."

One of the last things Lucas wanted to do was surrender his gun. But he didn't want to risk Colleen and Hailey being shot, either. So he tried to reason with this guy.

"Whatever you're getting paid, I'll double it," Lucas offered. "I can make the call now and have the funds transferred to your bank."

"That sounds real nice." The sarcasm dripped from his voice. "But doing something like that would get me killed. Besides, I'm getting paid pretty good for this. Now, throw out that gun."

Lucas felt something against his back. Hailey's hand. And it wasn't empty. She had hold of his backup weapon, no doubt a reminder that he could use that. But the problem was that once Lucas didn't have a visible weapon, this thug might change his mind about shooting.

And yes, the bullet could go through him and kill Hailey.

Even if it didn't, it could kill him, and then this thug would be able to do whatever he wanted with Colleen and Hailey.

"Time's up," the guy said without warning.

The shot blasted through the air.

Followed by Colleen's piercing scream.

Lucas felt as if someone had slugged him, and he had to fight his instincts to move away from Hailey and leave her unprotected. But it also sickened him to hear Colleen make sharp sounds of pain.

And to see the blood.

"Oh, God," Hailey said, and she would have come over Lucas if the thug hadn't pointed his weapon right at her. She stopped, freezing, but she kept repeating, "Oh, God."

"I only shot her in the arm," the man said as if that

was some huge concession. Which, in a way, it was. Because he could have just as easily killed her.

The blood spread quickly across Colleen's arm, and she looked at Lucas, silently begging him to help her. He'd wanted proof that Colleen was innocent in all of this, and the gunshot was it. He seriously doubted that she would have agreed to a henchman shooting her as part of the deal.

In the distance, Lucas heard another blast from the launcher. More smoke bombs, no doubt.

"No more warnings," the gunman said to Lucas. "Toss out the gun or I shoot her again. This time I might not be so careful where I aim."

He wasn't bluffing, so Lucas had no choice but to throw his gun out of the open truck door. Now he only hoped he could get to his backup weapon when he needed it. And he would need it. He was certain of that.

"Now what?" Lucas snapped.

"We wait." The guy glanced at the back of the house, where the smoke was still the thickest. He also peeled off his gas mask. Probably because the rain had rid them of the tear gas. Lucas's eyes were still burning, but the sensation wasn't nearly as bad as it had been.

Hailey still had his phone, and Lucas heard it buzz. Mason or Grayson was probably calling. But the thug shook his head. "Let that go to voice mail."

Hailey did, and she eased the backup weapon to Lucas's side. Ideally the gunman didn't see what was going on, but he had his attention nailed to them.

"Help me," Colleen said. She was shaking now. Maybe going into shock. And she needed medical attention. However, the only way she was going to get that was for Lucas to get rid of his thug so they could call for an ambulance.

"When I move, get down," Lucas whispered to Hailey.

He felt the muscles in her body tense. Clearly, she didn't like the idea of him moving. Probably because she knew what the outcome could be. But thankfully Hailey didn't argue with him.

Lucas got ready to launch himself at the gunman. Maybe he'd be able to knock both him and his gun to the ground. Of course, Colleen would be in the middle, and Lucas prayed she didn't get hurt any worse than she already was, but if he didn't do something fast, they'd all be dead.

His phone buzzed again, distracting him for a moment. Something bad was probably going on. Maybe that bad thing didn't include Camden, but even if it did, Lucas had to put it out of his mind and try to finish this.

He didn't get far.

Lucas hadn't even started moving when he saw something out of the corner of his eye. Someone was coming toward the back of the truck. Maybe one of his brothers or a Ryland cousin.

But it wasn't.

The gunman smiled, and while he still had hold of Colleen, he moved away from the truck door, making room for their visitor.

"Told you it wouldn't be long," the gunman taunted. "The boss is here."

LUCAS SHIFTED HIS body so that it was hard for Hailey to see. He did that so he could reach the gun she was trying to give him, but it also meant she didn't know who had just arrived. She had no trouble recognizing his voice, though.

"Finally," he said.

Eric.

She hadn't known which of their suspects would be coming at them through the smoke, but Eric certainly wasn't a surprise. But was he working with Minton? Or had he come up with this all on his own?

Whatever *this* was.

"Can we leave now?" the thug asked Eric.

Eric shook his head. "Soon, though. I'm getting another vehicle up here since your idiot comrades shot out the radiator of Lucas's truck. Not very smart, and they'll pay for that."

So Eric was planning on using it to escape. But she doubted that he and his hired gum would be leaving alone. No.

Eric would try to take Colleen and her with him, and that meant Lucas would try to stop it. He could be hurt or killed in the process.

Hailey put aside the laptop so her hands would be free in case things were about to get worse than they already were. Lucas took the gun, but there was no way he could lift it without causing Eric and the thug to shoot first. Both had their weapons aimed at Hailey and him.

"You bastard," Colleen spat out. "You took my daughter, and now you had your hired gun shoot me. And why? I erased all those files. I did everything you told me to do."

"You knew it was Eric?" Lucas asked, and he didn't sound pleased that Colleen might have withheld that from them.

Colleen shook her head. "No. But I suspected it. He

knew Preston had left me money, and taking my baby was the only way to get it back."

Eric lifted his shoulder. "You didn't deserve a penny of DeSalvo money just because you slept with my father."

"I had his child!" Colleen practically shouted, but the outburst combined with the blood loss must have drained her, because she sagged against the gunman holding her. He shoved her back up, jamming the gun against her head again.

"You think that matters to me?" Eric didn't wait for her to answer. "Because it doesn't."

Hailey saw the anger rise on Eric's face and knew she couldn't let his short fuse and horrible temper come into play here. "Why did you do all of this?"

"Isn't it obvious? I don't want to die in jail like my father. You have files and information that could put me behind bars."

True, but it wasn't for anything serious.

"You made the deal with the DA," Lucas reminded him.

"It included only the recordings from my father's office." He glanced around, no doubt looking for the vehicle that was coming for them.

Lucas's phone buzzed again. The third time someone had tried to call them in the past couple of minutes. It was no doubt important. Maybe even about Camden. But Hailey didn't answer it.

"When the FBI, CSIs or some other agency with initials analyzes the voice on those tapes, they might be able to identify Melvin here." He tipped his head to the gunman. "Melvin has worked for me for years. He has a record, and it wouldn't take much to connect him to me if they were able to match his voice."

"There was no dirty agent," Lucas concluded. "But you let your father believe there was."

"You'd be surprised what I learned from the old man when he thought he was talking to an actual agent. I made lots of money on deals where my father gave the fake guy some insider information. Of course, I had to share some of that cash with Daddy to make him think he was running things."

Yes, but Preston wouldn't have known his own son was working behind the scenes to milk him of family funds. It was all so senseless since Eric would have inherited most of it anyway.

At least, he would have, unless there'd been another child.

Oh, mercy.

"What are you going to do with your half sister?" Hailey blurted out.

That put some new alarm in Colleen's face. Probably because she'd pieced it together, as well. Eric wouldn't want any competition for the DeSalvo estate, and it was possible that the baby—and therefore Colleen—would have a claim.

"Yes," Eric said, looking at Hailey. He'd obviously seen the realization in her eyes. "And of course, you have to go, too. You know too much. Plus, I'm betting you have some dirt on me squirreled away."

Hailey was about to say that she didn't have anything else now that Colleen had deleted the files. But she changed her mind and went with something that might save them.

"If anything happens to me, the files I have will be sent to every news agency in the state," she lied.

Eric laughed, but the laughter stopped just as quickly as it'd started. "Where are the files?" he snapped. His temper was definitely showing again.

"I'm not telling you. Not until you get Colleen an ambulance and you and your hired killers are off Ryland land."

Eric's mouth tightened. "Nice try. But you're all dying. Including him." His glare slashed to Lucas. "Thanks to Hailey including you in this, she's signed your death warrant."

"Hailey didn't involve me," Lucas said, his voice low and dangerous. "*You* involved me when you tried to kill her and put my son in danger. How the hell do you possibly think you're going to get away with this?"

"Easy. I plan on pinning all of this on Minton. He's an idiot. And soon he'll be dead like the rest of you."

Sweet heaven. If Minton was anywhere near the baby, then she could be hurt, too. Or worse.

Hailey heard the sound of a car approaching from the back of the house. A moment later she saw the black SUV, the one that had brought in the gunmen. Had no doubt brought Eric, too.

"All of you will come with me," Eric insisted. "And that way I'll have some leverage to make sure Hailey gives me everything that she possibly has on me."

By leverage he meant they would become his hostages.

Eric would no doubt torture Lucas and Colleen to get Hailey to give him something she didn't have. Once he figured that out, he would indeed kill all of them. Probably Minton, too.

"Let's move," Eric said, and he used his gun to motion toward the approaching SUV.

Hailey knew that time was up. They had to do something now even though Lucas didn't have a clean shot. Eric was staying behind Colleen and his hired gun.

And Lucas did something, all right.

He sprang from the seat, barreling out of the truck, and he crashed into Colleen, Eric and the gunman.

They all went to the ground.

But the only sound Hailey heard was the shot that one of them fired.

THE SHOT WAS DEAFENING, but Lucas prayed that it hadn't hit Hailey, Colleen or him. It was hard to tell because the impact of slamming into the ground had knocked the breath out of him, and the pain spiked through him when his jaw collided with the hired gun's Glock.

Lucas hadn't wanted things to play out this way, but Eric hadn't given him much of a choice. If they'd gotten into that SUV with him and his hired killers, Colleen, Hailey and he would have soon been dead.

Colleen screamed when they fell, but Lucas still didn't know if she'd been shot again. That's because the fight started almost immediately. The thug slammed his gun against Lucas's head so hard that it probably gave him a concussion.

That didn't stop Lucas from fighting, though. The stakes were too high for him to lose. He still had hold of his gun, but it was too risky to get a shot off now. He had to get Colleen out of the way first, and that wouldn't be easy since she was trapped between Eric and him.

Eric spewed out a string of profanity, and for a guy who didn't work with his hands, he was fighting hard. He was also trying to shoot Lucas. Eric brought up his gun, but Lucas managed to knock it away in the nick of time.

Eric's shot blasted into the ground right next to Lucas.

Hailey yelled out something. Something that Lucas didn't catch, but he hoped she would stay back.

She didn't.

He saw her out of the corner of his eye. She had gotten out of the truck and had picked up his gun. The one he'd thrown out of the truck. She was trying to take aim, but there was no way she'd have a clean shot.

But Eric did.

The goon was punching Lucas, but he still managed to see Eric lift his gun again. And this time he aimed it at Hailey.

"Get down!" Lucas shouted to her.

He wasn't sure if she did—not in time, anyway— before Eric pulled the trigger again. Lucas didn't look to see where the shot had gone. Instead he shifted his weight, shoving Colleen out of the way so that he could pin down Eric.

Melvin was obviously looking out for his boss, because he walloped Lucas in the head again. More than anything, Lucas wanted to shoot the guy, but he couldn't let go of Eric to do that.

Someone fired, though.

Hailey.

She'd shot into the ground. Maybe to distract Eric and Melvin. If so, it worked in a bad way. Melvin looked at Hailey.

And he took aim.

That meant Lucas had to release Eric so he could dive at Melvin. Melvin still managed to pull the trigger, but Lucas was able to throw Melvin enough off balance that he didn't shoot Hailey. But Melvin had come darn close to doing just that.

Too close.

Lucas couldn't tell her that now because he was fighting for their lives, but later he wanted her to know that she should never take a risk like that again. Because she could have been killed. He could have lost her.

Colleen scurried away from them, and while she was holding her injured arm, she ran to Hailey. Maybe because Hailey didn't see it coming, Colleen wrenched the gun from her hand. Colleen pointed it at the men.

"Give me back my daughter, Eric," Colleen shouted. "Or so help me, I'll kill you right now."

Lucas prayed she didn't shoot, because the way she was shaking, there was no telling who Colleen might hit. His cousins were likely nearby, and a stray shot could kill one of them. It also caused his heart to slam against his chest when he saw that Hailey was trying to get the gun back from her sister. No way did he want Hailey in a struggle—any kind of struggle—where there was a gun involved.

Since every second this went on was another second when someone could get killed, Lucas threw his own gun aside so he could latch onto Melvin's. Of course, Eric took full advantage of that. He tried to take aim again, but Lucas stopped him by slamming his elbow into Eric's jaw. Eric howled in pain and dropped back down to the ground.

A shot cracked through the air.

Lucas's breath stopped, and despite being in a fistfight with Melvin, he glanced at Hailey to make sure she was all right. She wasn't. She was seemingly frozen with both Colleen's and her hands on the gun.

Melvin cursed, and he froze as well.

Lucas looked on the ground beside him and saw Eric. Bleeding. The shot that Colleen had fired had hit him in the stomach.

"You're gonna pay for that!" Melvin yelled, and he tried to turn his gun on Colleen.

Lucas didn't let that happen. He used the new surge of adrenaline that he got to grab Melvin's gun. Of course, Melvin didn't just give it up. He kept trying to aim it at Colleen. But instead, Lucas turned the gun on the hired killer.

Just as Melvin pulled the trigger.

The bullet went into his chest. Since the shot was at point-blank range, Melvin didn't even draw another breath. It killed him instantly.

Lucas didn't waste a second on the gunman. Instead, he took the guy's weapon and aimed it at Eric. He also kicked Eric's gun from his hand and took aim at him in case he tried to move. He did, but it was only to clutch his stomach and his chest.

And he laughed.

"You think this is over," Eric said, looking at Colleen and Hailey. "It's not."

That's when Lucas realized that Eric wasn't just holding his hand to his gunshot wound. He pressed something on his chest. A small box that resembled a remote control on a garage.

A split second later, Lucas heard a sound he definitely didn't want to hear.

An explosion.

CHAPTER NINETEEN

"No!" Colleen yelled.

Lucas didn't yell, but he frantically looked around to see if he could find the source of the explosion. It hadn't come from the area where the tear gas had been launched. No. This was further away. Just up the road from the ranch.

In the same area where Grayson had said he'd spotted the kidnapper's vehicle.

Colleen must have realized that, too, because despite her injury, she turned and started to run in that direction.

"Stop her," Lucas told Hailey. Though he hated to give an order like that since Colleen was still armed. It was obvious she was hysterical, and there was no telling what she might do.

Lucas checked first to make sure there were no weapons near Eric. He was bleeding, maybe dying, but that didn't mean he wouldn't be able to shoot them. It would be the ultimate way to get his revenge.

Hailey hooked her arm around Colleen's waist but didn't have a solid enough footing and her sister slung her to the ground. That meant a change of plan. Lucas scooped up one of the guns and handed it to Hailey.

"Make sure Eric doesn't get up," he told her, and he took off running after Colleen. There were possibly some of Eric's hired guns still in the area, and he didn't want Colleen shot for a second time tonight. The next bullet just might kill her.

Might kill him, too.

Lucas only hoped they didn't get caught in the middle of a gunfight.

He had to tackle Colleen, dragging them both to the ground again. This couldn't be good for her injury since she was still bleeding. But despite that injury, she fought like a wildcat.

"I have to get to my baby!" she shouted.

Yeah, Lucas understood that, but he shook his head and got in her face. "You can't go down there. It's a good quarter of a mile away, and you'll be killed."

Logic wasn't going to work here, so he just pinned her to the ground with his body and wrenched the gun from her hand. Colleen kept fighting him, punching his chest with her fists, and Lucas just let her do it while he kept watch to make sure they weren't about to be ambushed.

He looked back at Hailey. Even from a distance he could see that she was shaking, but she still had the gun aimed at Eric. Eric wasn't saying anything, wasn't moving, either. Lucas had rarely wished someone dead, but he hoped in this case that Eric was so that he would no longer be a threat to Hailey and Colleen.

But there were other threats out there.

Colleen finally quit fighting, her hands dropping to the ground, and she sobbed. The tears came, mixed with the rain on her face, but Lucas could deal with the tears as long as she didn't run out into the path of those possible gunmen. Now that he knew Colleen was innocent in all of this, he definitely wanted to make sure he kept Hailey's sister alive.

He got up, pulling Colleen to her feet, and he took

her to the truck, pushing her into the middle so Hailey could get in, as well. He wouldn't be able to drive the truck, but at least being inside it was better than having them stay in the open.

Hailey had such a fierce grip on the gun and her muscles were so rigid that it took Lucas a moment to get her moving. When he finally did, she sagged against him.

"The baby," she said.

Lucas figured she was praying that her niece was okay. He was doing the same and adding some extra prayers for Camden and the rest of his family.

"Both of you stay down," Lucas told them once he had Hailey in the cab of the truck.

She nodded, took out his phone and showed him the screen with the missed calls. All three were from Mason. Lucas certainly hadn't forgotten about them, but he wanted to keep his hands, and his attention, free in case they were attacked again.

Hailey must have understood that, because she hit the redial button and put it on speaker. Mason answered on the first ring.

"What the hell was that explosion?" Mason immediately asked.

"I'm not sure." Lucas didn't want to spell out his worst fears. "Have you talked to Grayson?"

"He's not answering his phone, and he's nowhere near any of the security cameras. Please tell me he wasn't near that bomb when it went off."

Lucas didn't know, and again he didn't want to guess. Grayson was smart, so maybe he'd made it out of there with the baby.

"The reason I called you earlier was to warn you

about Eric," Mason went on. "I saw him on one of the cameras. Is he dead?"

"Not yet. Can you call an ambulance for Colleen and him?" Lucas asked.

"Already done, and they're on the way. Dade and the others have cleared the gunmen so the medics can get through. I'll send a cruiser down to pick up Colleen, Hailey and you. Colleen is innocent, right?"

Lucas glanced back at her. "Yeah." Innocent and shaken to the core. Also still losing some blood. Hailey had peeled off her hoodie and was using it as a make-shift tourniquet.

"Good," Mason answered. "Then the three of you can come here. I'll have Dade or someone wait with Eric. Let me know the moment you hear anything from Grayson."

"I will." Lucas looked around the yard again. "Are you sure the gunmen are all out of commission?"

"All the ones on the ranch grounds. The ones across the road, too." He paused. "Don't know about Minton, though."

Yes. Lucas hadn't forgotten about him, either. Eric had claimed there was no dirty agent, and that should clear Minton's name. If Eric was telling the truth.

Lucas heard the sound of an approaching car coming from the main part of the ranch, and he automatically pivoted in that direction with his gun aimed and ready. But it wasn't one of Eric's thugs. It was Sawyer and Josh. Josh hurried out of the cruiser toward them.

"I drew the short straw," Josh said. "Go ahead with Sawyer. I'll make sure Eric doesn't go anywhere."

Lucas hated to put this on his cousin, but one look at Hailey and Colleen and he knew he had to get them out of there. He thanked Josh, and because he didn't want the women out in the open any longer than necessary, he scooped up Colleen and took her to the cruiser. He would have gone back and done the same for Hailey, but she was already trailing along behind him. He put Colleen in the front seat. Hailey and he took the back.

"I'm okay," Hailey said to him.

It was almost certainly a lie, but Lucas latched onto it. He also latched onto her. He pulled her into his arms, probably with a lot harder grip than either of them had been expecting.

The relief came. She was alive and in one piece. No thanks to Eric. That fight could have played out a dozen different ways, and in any one of the scenarios, Hailey could have been hurt or worse.

Colleen, however, wasn't faring as well. She was sobbing now, hunched over and probably in a lot of pain. Maybe it wouldn't be long before the ambulance arrived, though Lucas was worried that she might not go to the hospital until they got news about the baby.

It wasn't a long trip to the main house, but it certainly felt like one. Lucas kept watch the whole way, but thankfully he didn't see any signs of danger.

Only the aftermath.

He spotted one of the gunmen, dead, in the pasture. Not far from where they'd launched the smoke bombs and the tear gas. The goon and his fellow hired thugs had turned the Silver Creek Ranch into a war zone. That twisted at Lucas's gut. But it was also something he had to push aside.

For Hailey's sake.

Heck, for his own peace of mind.

Because he thought they could both use it, he brushed a kiss on Hailey's forehead. Then her cheek. Yes, they both needed that. Needed the real kiss that followed, too. It wasn't nearly long enough, but Lucas figured he could do better later. Later, he wanted to do a lot of things. Like tell Hailey that he had died a thousand times tonight worrying about her, and that it had driven home to him just how important she was to him.

"I'm in love with you," Hailey blurted out.

Judging from the startled look in her eyes, she hadn't intended to say that. Nor did she have time to add more, because Sawyer pulled to a stop directly in front of the main house, and that was their cue to get moving. Sawyer helped with Colleen, but before they even made it up the steps, Lucas heard two welcome sounds.

The ambulance sirens.

And his son.

Camden was fussing, and while it was obvious he wasn't happy about something, just hearing him eased the knot in Lucas's stomach.

Despite her limp, Hailey hurried in ahead of them. And Lucas let her. She looked around the massive foyer. No sign of Camden there, but he was in the adjacent family room with Tillie and Mason's wife, Abbie. Tillie was pacing while rocking Camden, obviously trying to get him to sleep. Hailey went to him and pulled him into her arms.

Camden stopped fussing right away and studied her face. Hailey was still pretty much a stranger to him, but that didn't stop his boy from smiling. He smiled even more when he looked in Lucas's direction.

Everything suddenly seemed all right with the world.

Well, almost everything. His phone buzzed, and when he saw Grayson's name on the screen, Lucas knew this was a call he had to take.

"Is it about the baby?" Colleen asked. Sawyer was trying to get her to sit, but she batted away his hands and went to Lucas.

Lucas figured it was indeed about the baby, but he wasn't sure it would be good news. No way to buffer it from Colleen, though, since she was right next to him. Because she would probably be able to hear every word anyway, he went ahead and put it on speaker.

"I have the baby," Grayson immediately said.

Lucas could feel the relief go through the room, and Hailey went to her sister to give her a hug. Colleen broke down again, crying, but Lucas figured these were happy tears.

"Is she okay? Was she hurt?" Colleen blurted out.

"She's fine," Grayson answered. "I'm bringing her to the ranch right now. The ambulance is ahead of me."

Which meant Colleen wouldn't have much time with her daughter before being whisked away to the hospital. She wouldn't care much for that, but Colleen needed medical attention ASAP. She also clearly needed to see her daughter right away, because she started toward the door and would have hurried out, no doubt to watch for Grayson. But Lucas stopped her. He didn't want any one of them outside just yet.

"What about the explosion?" Hailey asked.

"The bomb detonated after the baby was already out of the car," Grayson answered. "Minton killed the kidnapper, but he couldn't disarm the bomb, so he took the baby and ran. When I'd looked in the SUV earlier with the binoculars, I thought she was still in the vehicle, but it was only her car seat that I saw."

Good. Lucas hated that the baby had even had to go

through a nightmare like that, but at least she wasn't near the blast.

Thanks to Minton.

"Where is Minton?" Lucas pressed.

"With me."

Lucas felt no regret about that whatsoever and hoped all of Eric's hired thugs were dead or arrested. And speaking of Eric, he needed to give Grayson an update on the idiot who'd done his best to make their lives a living hell.

"Minton won't be staying," Grayson continued. "He wants to borrow a vehicle to get him back to his office, so once I'm at the house, I'll let him use my truck."

Even though Minton was innocent and had helped them by saving the baby, Lucas could understand why the agent didn't want to hang around. He hadn't exactly been friendly to Hailey and the rest of them. Plus, like Grayson, he probably had reports to write up about the attack.

"If Eric's still alive, he'll need to go to the hospital, too," Lucas said.

"Yeah. I got a call from Dade. Eric died a couple of minutes ago. The ME will come out and take care of the body. The bodies of the other gunmen, as well."

Lucas thanked him. He definitely didn't want any of his cousins or their families waking up to a giant crime scene, so maybe the bodies and the debris could be cleared out by morning.

Grayson had been right about the ambulance, because Lucas heard the siren as it made the turn toward the main house. He wished he could talk Hailey into going to the hospital, too, to be checked out, but judging from the grip she had on Camden, that wasn't going to happen.

"Maybe I can ride with the baby and Colleen in the ambulance?" Tillie suggested. Lucas wanted to kiss the woman for making the offer. "Unless Hailey and you need me here for Camden, that is."

"No," Hailey and Lucas said in unison. They'd be just fine now that the danger had passed.

Well, maybe it had passed.

"Are we sure there are no more hired killers?" Lucas asked Grayson.

"The hands and deputies are doing a final search now, but there's no one shooting. Just in case one's hiding, Sawyer and Josh are going to do a sweep with infrared, Mason's still in his office checking the security cameras."

Hailey closed her eyes a moment, nodded. She was obviously thankful for these extra security measures. It would help everyone get some sleep for what was left of the night. Everyone except Colleen. But he figured she wouldn't mind. She was alive, and her baby had been rescued.

Grayson ended the call just as the ambulance pulled to a stop in front of the house, and this time Lucas wasn't able to hold Colleen back. That's because Grayson had said he was right behind the medics. And he was. He didn't waste any time getting out and bringing the baby to Colleen.

There were more tears, of course, and Colleen hugged her daughter as tightly as Hailey was hugging Camden.

"You should go," Grayson prompted Colleen. Apparently he'd already given his keys to Minton, because the agent drove away.

Colleen managed a shaky nod, but despite the fact

she was bleeding, she carried the baby toward the ambulance. Tillie was right behind her.

"Call me when you can," Hailey told her sister. "And if the doctors keep you at the hospital overnight, I'll be there first thing in the morning."

Despite everything that had gone on, Colleen managed a weak smile and a thank-you. Maybe this was the start of a better relationship between the sisters.

"Tell Mason I'm taking his cruiser," Grayson said to Abbie. "If anyone needs me, I'll be with the ME and then at the office."

Lucas felt guilty since Grayson had a long stretch of work ahead of him. And he'd help. But not tonight. Tonight he needed to be with Hailey and Camden.

"Do you want me to take Camden?" Abbie asked.

Lucas certainly hadn't forgotten about Mason's wife being there, but he didn't understand her question. No way did he want Camden out of his sight. But Lucas looked at Hailey. Then himself. They were soaking wet, covered in mud, blood and heaven knew what else.

"You can use the showers in the guest rooms," Abbie suggested.

"In just a couple of minutes." Hailey kissed Camden's cheek, and despite the fact that he was right up against her wet clothes, he didn't seem to mind.

Abbie must have decided they needed some alone time, because she disappeared down the hall. Probably to check on her own sons.

Hailey got a few more kisses and then passed Camden to Lucas so he could do the same. It was pure magic. Somehow, just holding his son could melt away most of the misery from the past couple of days.

But misery wasn't the only thing that'd happened tonight.

"You said you were in love with me," Lucas reminded Hailey.

She made a soft sound of surprise. "Yes, *that*." Then she dodged his gaze and opened her mouth to say something that Lucas realized he might not want to hear.

"You can't take it back," he growled, and then frowned when he heard the tone of his own voice. He hadn't meant to make it sound like an order. "Please don't take it back," he amended.

Hailey didn't make another sound of surprise, but judging from the way her eyes widened, she certainly hadn't been expecting that from him. Well, Lucas hadn't expected it, either. Nor was he sure when he'd wanted Hailey's "I'm in love with you," but he definitely wanted it.

With Camden in the crook of his left arm, Lucas slid his right hand around Hailey's waist and pulled her closer. He kissed her. Not some gentle, everything-will-be-all-right kind of kiss, either. This was long and deep. Just the way he liked his kisses when it came to Hailey.

The kiss stirred the heat between them, but it did more than that. It made things crystal clear for Lucas.

"I fell in love with you shortly after we met," he said with his lips still against hers. "That hasn't changed. Never will. I want you in my bed…my life. Our lives," he added, glancing down at Camden.

And Lucas pulled back so he could see her reaction. He expected her to be stunned. Maybe even have a run-for-the-hills kind of look in her eyes.

She didn't.

Hailey smiled, slow and easy. A smile that lit up her

whole face, and she pulled him right back to her for another kiss. "Good. And you can't take it back."

Lucas had no intentions of ever taking it back. Ever.
He gathered Hailey and his son into his arms and held
on.

* * * * *

Elle James, a *New York Times* bestselling author, started writing when her sister challenged her to write a romance novel. She has managed a full-time job and raised three wonderful children, and she and her husband even tried ranching exotic birds (ostriches, emus and rheas). Ask her, and she'll tell you what it's like to go toe-to-toe with an angry 350-pound bird! Elle loves to hear from fans at ellejames@earthlink.net or ellejames.com.

Books by Elle James

Harlequin Intrigue

Mission: Six

One Intrepid SEAL
Two Dauntless Hearts

Ballistic Cowboys

Hot Combat
Hot Target
Hot Zone
Hot Velocity

SEAL of My Own

Navy SEAL Survival
Navy SEAL Captive
Navy SEAL to Die For
Navy SEAL Six Pack

Visit the Author Profile page at
Harlequin.com for more titles.

TRIGGERED

Elle James

This book is dedicated to cowboys of all shapes, sizes and sexes. These brave men and women work hard, play hard and have a sense of loyalty, decency and ethics we should all aspire to.

CHAPTER ONE

NECESSITY, BURNING CURIOSITY and a Hummer limo brought him here, but as Ben Harding sat in the leather armchair surrounded by three other men, he wondered what the heck he'd gotten himself into. He glanced around the room again. The only thing he had in common with the others was that they each wore a cowboy hat, jeans and boots.

Beyond that, he knew nothing about the men gathered in billionaire Hank Derringer's home. The Raging Bull Ranch lay in the heart of the back of beyond, South Texas, where men were tough, the drug runners were tougher and a property owner stood a good chance of getting killed riding across his own spread.

Ben had done his homework. Hank Derringer had become a recluse since he'd lost his family over a year ago in a botched kidnapping attempt. The man had made billions and continued to make more in the oil and gas industry. All facts that were easy enough to find. But why bring these men here? Why now?

Ben would have blown off the invitation to come if he'd had any other choice. His career at the Austin Police Department at an end, he'd been pounding the pavement looking for work and finding that no one, until now, wanted to hire a man who'd been kicked off the force for killing a man with his bare hands.

Did he regret what he'd done?

No.

And he'd do it again, given the same circumstances.

His gut clenched and he fought to push the rage and lingering images to the back of his mind as a tall, slightly older man joined them.

He wore a black Stetson and looked very much like the other men seated around the room. "Gentlemen, I'm Hank Derringer. Thank you all for coming to the Raging Bull Ranch." He sat near the huge stone fireplace, facing them. "I brought you here because you are the best of the best."

"Best of the best what, Hank?" The muscle-bound, blond-haired man across from Ben spoke first. He nodded toward Ben and the other two men. "And who are these guys?"

Hank tipped his head toward the man questioning him. "Patience, Thorn. I'm getting to that. For the rest of you, meet Thorn Drennan, the best sheriff Wild Oak Canyon ever had. A man the people could count on to fight for truth and justice."

Thorn's eyes narrowed. "You're forgetting—I'm no longer the sheriff."

"Precisely." Hank turned to the man with brown hair, brown eyes and a wicked scar across his right cheek. "Chuck Bolton. Your friends call you Big Tex, born and raised on a ranch near Amarillo. You know how to ride, rope and build fences like the best of them. Served two tours in Iraq and one in Afghanistan where you wiped out an entire Taliban stronghold against your commander's orders."

The man sat up straighter, his broad shoulders straining against the seams of his chambray shirt. "Got the boot and a bum leg for that."

"A man with courage and determination to fight the good fight," Hank said.

Big Tex shrugged. "I guess it depends on your definition of 'the good fight.'"

Hank moved on to the next person, a man sitting back from the rest, dark circles beneath his eyes, an intense, haunted expression in his green eyes as he stared out the window. "Special Agent Zachary Adams, one of the FBI's best undercover operatives working to stop the drug cartels along the border. Got caught in a bad situation on the wrong side of the border. Yet you survived."

"For what it was worth." The man's gaze shifted from the window to Hank. "And, just for the record, former FBI. I quit."

Hank nodded. "Right."

Derringer turned to Ben, his smile warm, welcoming. "And then there's Ben Harding, the most highly decorated officer on the Austin police force."

"*The* Ben Harding?" Big Tex snorted. "Weren't you the guy who was fired for strangling Frank Davis to death with your bare hands?"

Ben stiffened. He'd seen what the high-powered CEO had done to that young girl in a run-down warehouse on the seedier side of Austin. He'd watched him run from the scene of the crime with the child's blood on his hands and clothing. Ben hadn't cared who he was or what big company he ran. All he cared about was making the man pay for what he'd done to the girl.

Ben's stomach roiled as he recalled the scene and the memories of another very similar crime involving the deaths of his wife and young daughter.

His fingers balled into fists and he rose halfway out of his seat, ready to take on the world. "Yeah, I killed a man, what's it to you?"

Big Tex shrugged. "Just wondering."

"I read about it. Davis was a sick bastard into hurting little girls. I'd have done the same," the man called Zach said.

"You gave him what he deserved," Thorn agreed. "Why waste money on a system that would have turned him loose to do it again?"

The starch taken out of his fight, Ben sat back against the soft brown leather of the wingback chair. He was disappointed he wouldn't have a brawl to release all the tension balled up in his gut since he'd arrived. At least now he felt more of a kinship with the others in the room.

Hank's mouth twisted into a wry grin. "You are all highly trained in your fields, and because of your various circumstances find yourselves unemployed."

Ben snorted. "Unemployable."

"Wrong." Hank's lips spread into a smile. "I'm here to offer you a position in a start-up corporation."

"Doing what? Sweeping floors? Who wants a bunch of rejects?" Zach asked.

"I need you." Hank rose from his chair. "Because you aren't rejects, you're just the type of men I'm looking for. Men who will fight for what you believe in, who were born or raised on a ranch, with the ethics and strength of character of a good cowboy. I'm inviting you to become a part of CCI, known only to those on the inside as Covert Cowboys, Inc., a specialized team of citizen soldiers, bodyguards, agents and ranch hands who will do whatever it takes to see justice served."

"Whoa, back up a step there. Covert Cowboys, Inc.?"

Big Tex slapped his hat against his thigh. "Sounds kind of corny to me. What's the punch line?"

"No punch line." Hank stood taller, his broad shoulders filling the room, the steel in his eyes indisputable. The man was on the up-and-up. "Let's just say that I'm tired of justice being swept under the rug."

Ben shook his head. "I'm not into vigilante justice, or circumventing the law."

"I'm not asking you to. The purpose of Covert Cowboys, Inc. is to provide covert protection and investigation services where hired guns and the law aren't enough." Hank's gaze swept over each of the men in the room. "I handpicked each of you because you are all highly skilled soldiers, cops and agents who know how to work hard, fire a gun and are familiar with living on the edge of danger. But mostly because of your high moral standards. You know right from wrong and aren't afraid to right the wrongs. My plan is to inject you into situations where your own lives could be on the line to protect, rescue or ferret out the truth."

Ben stood, his body tense, his first reaction to the older man's words to leave and never look back. "I'm not a vigilante, despite what the news says."

"I'm not hiring you to be one," Hank said. "I'm asking you to join CCI as a protector, a man willing to fight for truth."

"Truth, huh?" Zach said. "It's hard to find people who care about truth anymore."

Hank's lips thinned. "My point, exactly."

"Tell me, why should I work for you?" Ben asked.

The older man's shoulders straightened and he looked directly into Ben's eyes. "I care about truth and justice."

He walked to the desk in the corner and lifted four folders. The first he held out to Ben. "Are you in?"

What did he have to lose? Ben had nothing to go back to in Austin. No job, no family. Nothing. Against his better judgment, Ben nodded. "I'm in."

Hank handed him the folder. "Your first assignment is on the other side of the county working undercover on the Flying K Ranch. As far as everyone else knows, you're hiring on as a ranch hand. Your job is to help get the ranch operational, but most of all to protect the woman who just inherited it."

"Sounds easy enough."

"Don't count on it. This county is in need of cleanup. I'm hoping you gentlemen will be the men to help in that effort. It's our first challenge for CCI." Hank stared at the other men. "Who else chooses to take on the challenge?"

One by one the men threw their hats in the ring and grabbed a folder.

Ben opened the file and stared down at the image of a beautiful woman with long strawberry-blond hair, green eyes and skin as pale and smooth as porcelain. His gut told him he was stepping into waters way over his head. What did he know about providing protection to a woman? He'd been a street cop, not a bodyguard. Hell, he hadn't been able to protect his own family. A knot of regret twisted in him, but he asked, "When do I start?"

"Tonight. Grab your gear and get on over there, she should have arrived today."

Ben's eyes narrowed. "You were sure I'd take the job?"

"If not you, I'd be out there doing it myself. Don't get me wrong. I won't ask any of you to do anything I wouldn't be willing to do myself."

Ben clapped his hat on his head and headed for the door. It was a job. He didn't have to like it; he just had to do it until he found something else.

"'THE COW DOG saved the little girl and became her very best friend. The end.'" Kate Langsdon closed the book and set it on Lily's nightstand. "Now it's time for little girls to go to sleep." She leaned over and kissed her daughter's forehead, her heart squeezing in her chest with the amount of love she felt for this pint-size person with the long, loose curls of silky, strawberry-blond hair, much like her own.

"Mommy?" Lily yawned and rubbed her emerald-green eyes. "Can I have a cow dog?"

"Sure, sweetie. Just as soon as we can find one as good as Jess the cow dog." Kate switched the light off on the nightstand and straightened her aching back, got up and headed into the bathroom. The past few days had been strenuous and emotionally draining, the amount of work taking the spunk right out of her. She'd driven from Houston to Wild Oak Canyon, Texas, cleaned a house that had been standing empty for two months, emptied as much as she could of the moving van she'd rented and poked through the belongings of a man she'd never known and never would.

Her father.

Tears welled in Kate's eyes. For years, she'd thought her father dead. All this time, the man had been living in South Texas on a ranch near Big Bend National Park.

Kate dug her hand in her pocket and thumbed the key she'd received a week ago in an envelope from an attorney, including a letter, last will and testament and one corrupt video disk. The day that package arrived everything in Kate's life had changed.

She pulled the key from her pocket and tossed it into her makeup kit, stripped out of her dirty jeans and climbed into the shower. She stood for a long time as the warm spray washed down over her body, releasing the stiffness from her shoulders and tempering the ache in her lower back.

She wished all her worries could wash away with the water. As she stood in her father's house, on the ranch he'd bequeathed to her, she wondered if she'd done the right thing bringing Lily here.

She'd come to start over and to find answers. For one, what did the key fit? The video had been all static and with a brief glimpse of her father, but it cut off before her father could tell her what the key belonged to. Her father's letter left instructions for her to get help from the only man he trusted, Hank Derringer, the owner of the Raging Bull Ranch in Wild Oak Canyon. He'd help her with whatever she needed.

She hadn't called Mr. Derringer at first, taking a day to digest the fact that her father hadn't died when her mother had told her. The news had been so shocking that it took that long for it to sink in. Contacting his trusted friend was the furthest thing from her mind.

Until someone broke into her apartment in Houston while she had been at work and Lily had been at day care.

When she'd come home to find the apartment she and Lily had called home for four years looking as if the place had been tossed in a Texas-size salad bowl, she'd been angry and scared.

How dare someone break into her home? Kate knew

she couldn't stay in the apartment, not after it had been violated and especially not knowing the reason. Nothing had been taken, as far as she could tell.

She'd packed up her daughter, boxed their belongings and headed west to Wild Oak Canyon and the Flying K Ranch to find the answers. How permanent this move proved to be was up to what she found, but she'd quit her job and given up her lease before she left. Either way, she couldn't go back and pick up where she'd left off.

Alone in the world except for Lily, Kate had turned to the phone number of the stranger her father had recommended.

Hank Derringer had answered on the first ring. He'd tried to talk her out of coming to Wild Oak Canyon. When she'd insisted, he'd promised to send a cowboy to her, one who could help her get the ranch back up and running and provide the protection she and Lily needed. Her cowboy would be there before they turned in for the night. Or so Hank had promised. Kate wondered what kind of protection she needed on a ranch out in the middle of nowhere.

She'd waited as long as she could to take her shower and still the cowboy hadn't arrived and probably wouldn't until morning.

When the water grew tepid, Kate turned it off and grabbed for the fluffy white towel she'd unearthed from one of the boxes she'd brought with her in the moving van. Bent over, her head upside down to wrap her long hair in the towel, her hands froze. Was that a sound downstairs?

She strained to listen.

Nothing.

Kate shrugged, worried her imagination was getting

the better of her. She continued towel drying her hair when something crashed below and a low curse followed.

Her breath caught on a gasp and her pulse raced. She'd turned out the lights on the main floor and locked all the doors before she and Lily had come up for the night. Whoever was down there was moving around in the dark. *Inside* the house.

Kate wrapped the towel around her and ran into the master bedroom she'd planned to share with Lily the first night until she could prepare another room just for her daughter.

Lily lay sound asleep, oblivious to the danger, the only light in the room the glow from the open bathroom door.

With nowhere to run, Kate quietly gathered her daughter, blankets and all, and hurried to the closet where she'd hung all of the clothing she'd brought with her next to those of her father's. Kate thanked her lucky stars that Lily slept soundly. The little girl didn't stir as Kate laid her down in the back corner of the closet, tucking the blankets around her, blocking her from view.

Once she had her daughter hidden, Kate tiptoed back to the nightstand, slid the drawer open and removed the 9 mm Glock she'd brought with her.

A board creaked on the stairs, sending Kate scurrying toward the door where she eased it closed.

Her hands shook as she alternated between holding up her towel and balancing the pistol. She wished she'd had time to dress, wishing more that she'd loaded the weapon. She prayed that the sight of it would scare a trespasser into leaving without hurting her or Lily. On second thought, she turned the gun around and held it by the barrel. Hitting the man would be better than pointing an unloaded pistol.

The doors down the hallway opened one by one. Kate held her breath as the intruder made his way toward the room she and Lily occupied. What she wouldn't give for cell phone reception.

Though, what good would it do when the sheriff wouldn't reach her ranch for fifteen to twenty minutes? She was on her own.

Where was the cowboy? Why hadn't he arrived already? Was the man moving down the hallway her cowboy? If he was, he had a lot of nerve barging in and sneaking around. He deserved the same as any thief and Kate would give it to him.

With Lily in the closet and her own hands shaking, Kate couldn't chance it. She had to divert attention and get the attacker away from the room where her daughter lay sleeping.

Kate prayed the man would give up and go away.

As she watched in horror, the doorknob turned. She wished it had a lock on it she could twist to buy her a little more time. Maybe not having a lock would work out for the better. She raised her arms and waited, her breath caught and held.

A dark figure stepped through the door. The man wore a ski mask. Anyone in a ski mask meant trouble.

As soon as his head cleared the entrance, Kate slammed the butt of the pistol down on his skull so hard the gun bounced out of her hands and skittered across the floor.

The man lurched forward and dropped to his knees.

Kate flung the door wide and leaped past the intruder.

Before she could take two steps, a large hand snagged her ankle.

Her forward momentum brought her down hard, knocking the breath from her lungs. She clawed at the carpet, kicking with all her might with her free foot, landing a couple hard heels in the attacker's face.

His grip loosened and Kate scrambled to her feet, running as fast as she could for the stairs, thankful and terrified when she heard the intruder's footsteps behind her.

She had to get the man as far away from Lily as possible. If he hurt Kate, maybe he'd leave her for dead and never find the little girl hiding in the closet.

Kate took the stairs two at a time, missing the last one, toppling to the floor and wasting precious seconds.

The man above her came crashing down the steps and leaped over the railing to land beside her.

Kate swallowed her scream, fearing she'd wake Lily. She rolled to the side, her fingers wrapping around the cord of a lamp.

She yanked the lamp toward her, grabbed the base and turned in time to see the man flying at her. He landed on top of her, knocking the wind from her.

With her hand still around the base of the lamp, Kate swung as hard as she could. The ceramic lamp made contact with the ski mask and bounced off, crashing to the wooden floor, shattering into a million fragments.

Out of options, Kate remembered the self-defense training she'd taken when Lily was little. She knew she was the only one there to defend her small daughter. With the desperation of a trapped mother bear, she freed one hand and jabbed her thumb into the man's eye.

He yelled and punched her face.

Pain radiated across her cheekbone, her vision blurred and Kate knew she wasn't going to last much longer. For Lily, she tried to hang in there, forcing the darkness back, struggling beneath the weight of her attacker.

As the intruder reeled back to hit her again, Kate squeezed shut her eyes.

Before the fist connected with her face, all the weight on top of her shifted backward.

Kate's eyes popped open.

The man in the ski mask fought against another man wearing a black T-shirt and a cowboy hat. Fists flew, and bodies banged against the old furniture. The cowboy hat flew across the room, landing in a corner.

Kate sucked in air, filling her lungs and clearing her fuzzy thoughts. She scrambled to her feet, clutching the towel around her, searching for a weapon of any kind. Her hands wrapped around the legs of an end table. She lifted it high and waited for the right moment.

The two men tumbled and flew around the room, knocking over furniture. With the lights out, Kate could barely tell who was who.

Then her rescuer hit the floor on his back and the man in the ski mask pulled a knife from his belt, the metal glinting in a ray of moonlight shining through a gap in the curtained window.

Kate's heart thudded against her rib cage.

The man in the ski mask closed in on Kate's rescuer.

Without thinking past saving the man on the ground, Kate rushed for the one with the blade and slammed the end table down over his head with enough force to break the small table into several pieces.

The attacker dropped to his hands and knees. He swung his arm out, clipping Kate in the back of her legs.

She fell hard, her head hitting the corner of a coffee table. As she landed, she heard shuffling of feet and tried to rise to see what was going on. When she lifted her head, her vision swam.

No. She couldn't give up now.

Pain radiated from the back of her head. She closed her eyes, praying for them to clear and let her get back into the fight. Lily depended on her.

Hands gripped her arms. Kate struggled, but the grasp was strong. Too strong for her to fight off.

"Shh. It's okay. I'm not going to hurt you." The voice was a deep rumble, the tone rich and warm, resonating from deep in his chest, wrapping her in a reassuring blanket.

"Bad guy?" she asked, without opening her eyes.

"He's gone." A hand brushed a wisp of hair out of her eyes. "Are you okay?" The same hand trailed softly over her cheekbone where the masked man had punched her.

Kate winced, and she opened her eyes to stare into the bluest eyes she'd ever seen. Her breath caught in her throat, and not out of fear. "Who are you?"

"Ben Harding. Hank Derringer thought you could use my help."

Thank God. The cavalry had arrived.

CHAPTER TWO

BEN STARED DOWN at the woman, her long wavy strawberry-blond hair lying in damp ringlets against the wood floor. Wrapped only in a fluffy white towel, she looked like a fallen angel, her creamy smooth skin begging to be touched, the towel riding up her shapely thighs.

"You're staring." The woman blinked up at him, her fingers pulling the edges of the towel together over her chest. She tried to sit up, pressed a hand to the back of her head and sank back. "Must have hit harder than I thought."

"I'll call for an ambulance."

She shook her head and winced. "No. I'll be all right, just give me a minute." One arm rose to cover her eyes. The top edge of the towel slipped lower over the swell of her breasts, capturing Ben's attention.

He really needed to focus on the situation, not the female lying almost naked at his feet, which proved hard when the woman had a great figure and very touchable skin. A pang of guilt and sadness knotted his gut. He hadn't felt like touching a woman in more than two years. Not since... "Any idea what the guy was after?"

"None," she answered, the arm dropping to her side. "I'm just glad he's gone and you're here. I'm Kate Langsdon." She held out a hand, a frown denting her pretty brow. "What took you so long?"

"I just got the assignment an hour ago."

"Well, Mr. Harding, I'm glad you came when you did. Any later and…" She shrugged and tried to sit up again. "I have to get up."

"You should stay put and let me call an ambulance."

"No, I have to get upstairs."

"Why the rush?"

"I just need to." She sat up, swayed and started to fall back. "Damn it, I can't be dizzy."

"Pigheaded woman." Ben caught her before her head hit the floor.

"Stubborn man," she whispered.

He scooped her into his arms and lifted her off the floor.

She tensed, her arm automatically circling his shoulder. "You don't have to carry me. I'm perfectly capable of standing on my own two feet."

"Not with a knot on your head and a crazy determination to get upstairs."

"Give me a minute and I'll argue this point." Her uninjured cheek lying against his chest belied her ability to put up much of a resistance. Her free hand struggled to keep the towel in place.

Ben ignored her protest and carried her up the stairs. "Which room?"

She sighed. "Last one on the landing. And really, I can get there on my own."

"No need. From what Hank told me, I'm the hired hand, here to help rebuild a ranch and protect its owner."

"Hank's words?"

"Right." His lips twisted, a frown creasing his forehead. "Let me do my job."

She chuckled, a smile curling her lips, making her

face shine even with the nasty bruise turning her cheek purple. "Somehow, I don't think carrying a woman to her bedroom is part of the job description." The smile faded. "But thanks."

For a brief moment the sun had shone in the woman's face, tugging at a place Ben thought buried for good with his wife and daughter. He shook the thought from his head and turned left on the landing.

When they crossed the threshold into the room, the woman twisted in his arms, her gaze darting toward the closet.

The door was open, blankets spilled from inside, some half-dragged out on the floor. "Let me down." She pushed against his arm, her nails digging into his skin.

"I will, but I'm not dropping you."

"Let me down." She shoved harder.

He lowered her feet to the floor, his arm remaining around her waist.

She stood for a moment, swaying, and then lunged for the closet, her eyes wide, her face tense. "Lily?" Her voice was strained, desperate.

"Who's Lily?" he asked.

Kate didn't answer as she dove into the back of the closet, rifling through blankets. When her face appeared at the edge of the closet door, it was pale and pinched. "Lily?" She leaped to her feet and nearly fell on her face.

Ben was there to catch her, his arms crushing her against his chest. "Who's Lily?"

"Mommy?" A tiny voice called out from the bathroom. "Mommy?"

Kate's head came up and she fought her way out of Ben's arms, dropping to her knees in front of a little girl with a mass of golden-red curls very much like her mother's drying wispy locks. She stood silhouetted against the light streaming from the bathroom, like an angel descended from heaven.

"Oh, Lily." Kate hugged the child to her.

Sweet Jesus. Hank hadn't said anything about a little girl. Ben stood like stone, his feet rooted to the floor, unable to move, forgetting how to breathe.

The little girl was about the age of Sarah before she'd been murdered. Though his Sarah was as different from Lily as night and day, they were about the same size and age.

Before Sarah had been killed. She'd been four years old. She would have been six now, if a man Ben had captured and had subsequently been released on a technicality hadn't targeted Ben and his family.

Ben hadn't been home when his wife and daughter had been brutally stabbed to death. Had he been, he'd have killed the murderer with his bare hands, just like he'd killed the man who'd murdered fifteen-year-old Angelica Garza.

Seeing Kate Langsdon on the floor holding the little girl in her arms brought back too many painful memories. Ben's feet moved one at a time as he backed toward the door. With his heart lodged in his throat, he couldn't breathe or think. His gut told him to run as far from Kate and Lily Langsdon as he could get.

Before he reached the door, the curly-haired angel noticed him for the first time. "Mommy, who's that man?"

Kate eased her hold on her daughter and looked up at Ben, the fear of a few moments ago still evident in her pale face. "That's Mr. Harding. He's the man who came to help us on the ranch."

"Are you going to help my mommy?" she asked, her

gaze open, direct, piercing the wall wrapped tightly around Ben's heart.

He yearned to run and keep running until the child's trusting eyes were erased from his mind. But he knew he couldn't leave this little girl and her mother when the intruder he'd chased off earlier might return.

"Yes, ma'am. I'm here to help your mommy." He nearly choked on *mommy*. His daughter had called his wife Mommy. His daughter had looked at him with complete trust, as if he could never let her down.

But he had. He hadn't been there when she'd needed him most. He had been all about the job, bringing in the bad guys. He'd never taken into account that the ones that got off might come back to haunt him. Until it was too late.

Kate's eyes narrowed. "Are you okay?"

No. Ben's gaze went from Lily to Kate. For a tough cop, used to facing down danger on the streets of Austin, he was more terrified of these two women than any criminal he'd ever confronted. "I'm fine." He cleared his throat. "I'll just bed down in the barn."

"No." Kate stood and swayed, her hand on her daughter's shoulder.

Before he could think through his actions, Ben was there, steadying her with a hand under her elbow, the other around her waist.

"Stay here. In the house." She leaned into him for a moment. When she'd steadied, she pulled away and looked up into his face. "Please."

Her green eyes pleaded with him, her hand on his arm burning a path through his defenses. How he wanted to leave, but couldn't. Despite his vow to never care again, he'd proved over and over he just couldn't honor that vow after all. Killing the high-powered child murderer was evidence. Damn Kate and Lily for making him care. "I'll stay on two conditions."

Her shoulders straightened. "Anything."

He scooped up the gun she'd dropped earlier and handed it to her. "First, put this away, take it to a pawn-shop or learn to use it."

She took the gun from him, keeping her body between the gun and her daughter's curious eyes. "Check. I'll learn to use it." Her chin tipped upward. "And the second one?"

His gaze swept over her, taking in the smooth lines of her shoulders, the gentle swell of her breasts and the curve of her thighs peeking out from under the terry cloth. If he had any hope of staying neutral in this situation, he had to put distance between himself and Kate. She was too damned attractive.

He forced an uninterested rise of his brows. "If I'm going to get any work done around here, you have to keep your clothes on around me."

Kate gasped, hugging the towel closer, her cheeks flaming red.

"I'll be on the couch downstairs." He stepped out into the hallway and closed the door between them with a firm click.

Kate stared at the barrier between them for a long moment, stunned at the cowboy's abrupt words and de-parture. "As if I planned to be standing in front of him in nothing but a towel," she mumbled.

"Mommy, why was I in the closet?" Lily's hand slipped into hers and tugged, dragging Kate's mind back to what was important. Her daughter.

She scrambled for an answer that wouldn't scare her

small daughter. "I thought it might be fun to pretend to be camped in a cave in the mountains."

Lily tipped her head to the side as if debating whether or not she believed Kate's lie. Then she smiled and pulled Kate toward the closet. "Will you camp in the cave with me, Mommy?"

"Oh, baby, I don't think so. I'm pretty tired and bed sounds more comfortable. You can sleep in the closet, if you want."

Lily stared from the bed to the closet and yawned, her eyelids sagging. "No, I'm tired, too. Maybe tomorrow."

Kate grabbed the blankets from the floor and flung them across the bed as best she could, tucking Lily in on the side away from the door.

As she pulled out a pair of pajamas that would fully cover her body, she thought of Ben Harding's condition. A spark of defiance shot through her and she replaced the pajamas in the drawer, reaching for the filmy light blue baby-doll nightgown she'd bought one hot, impulsive day in Houston.

She slipped the silky garment over her head, letting the towel drop to the floor, and recalled the feeling of being held in Ben's strong arms as he effortlessly carried her up the stairs to her bedroom. Her skin sizzled where his hands had been beneath her thighs and very nearly touching the side of her breast.

Now that she had time to think beyond defending her life, she realized the cowboy Hank had sent was everything a girl could dream of—tall, dark and handsome. Add a brooding, mysterious look in his blue eyes and he was devastatingly appealing.

She hadn't felt like this since…before her husband, Troy, had been killed in Afghanistan, a month before she'd delivered Lily. Four years ago. A wave of guilt washed over her for thinking such thoughts about a man who wasn't her husband. But, then, Troy had been dead a long time, she hadn't. The man downstairs had triggered a strong physical response she thought she'd never feel again.

Kate sucked in a deep breath and let it out, the tips of her nipples tight little points poking at the sheer fabric of the nightgown. She reached for the hem, telling herself that wearing the gown was asking for trouble.

Her hands stopped before they could lift it over her head. Who was she kidding? The man wasn't interested in her any more than she should be interested in him. He was there as the hired help. Hank had promised protection for her and Lily until they could figure out who was responsible for the break-in in Houston and now at the Flying K Ranch.

As she lay down on the sheets, her thoughts drifted to the man sleeping on the couch downstairs. He'd had a strange look in his eyes when he'd seen Lily. His brows had furrowed into a fierce frown, scary in its intensity. It hadn't looked like an angry frown so much as one of great pain and sorrow. What would cause such a look on a man's face?

She didn't know. In fact, Kate didn't know much of anything about her hired gun. Hell, she didn't know anything about Hank Derringer for that matter. This area was rumored to have a big drug cartel influence. Had she asked for help from one of the local mafia?

Kate lay staring at the ceiling, wondering what she'd done by bringing Lily here. Not that she'd been any safer in Houston. Not after her apartment had been ransacked.

A yawn nearly dislocated her jaw, forcing Kate to

give up trying to make sense of all that had happened. Tomorrow she'd ask the questions burning in her mind. Who the hell was Ben Harding and what kind of hired hands did Hank Derringer provide? Even more importantly, did he have any hired hands that were a little older and less attractive?

Kate rolled over and punched her pillow before settling down. Her bruised cheek reminded her of the intruder and her near miss with death. She reached out and looped her arm over her daughter, pulling her close. If anything happened to Lily, she'd never forgive herself.

Tomorrow she'd start her search for answers.

CHAPTER THREE

A KNOCK ON the door brought Ben off the couch and up on his bare feet in seconds. He must have fallen asleep after tossing and turning on the narrow couch. Every noise had kept him awake until way into the wee hours.

The sun shone through the filmy curtains, lighting his path through the boxes and furniture. From what he could see of the front porch, two men stood there in tan uniforms.

The local law enforcement.

As he pulled the door half-open, footsteps sounded on the stairs behind him.

"Who is it?" Kate descended the flight of stairs in a light blue baby-doll nightgown, pulling a robe over her shoulders that only came down to midthigh. Her creamy legs and the glimpse of her breasts through the thin material of the gown had Ben's jeans tightening.

With the door gaping, he had no choice but to open it the rest of the way.

The two men in tan uniforms stared at him, then their eyes drifted to the woman on the stairs behind him.

A flash of anger burned through his bloodstream and Ben moved to block their view as much as he could. "Can I help you?"

The bigger man stepped forward. "I'm Sheriff Fulmer, this is Deputy Schillinger. We're here to see Katherine Langsdon."

Ben's eyes narrowed. "For what reason?"

The sheriff's lips pulled up on one side in a sneer. "Now, I guess that's between me and the lady."

"It's okay, Ben." Kate laid a hand on Ben's arm and stepped up beside him. "I wanted to call on them this morning anyway. We had a break-in last night."

"Sorry to hear that. Can you describe the perp?"

She shook her head. "No, he was wearing all black and a black ski mask."

"Not much I can do to help without a detailed description."

She tipped her head to the side. "Then why did you come out?"

"Ms. Langsdon, as the only living relative of the late Kyle Kendrick, you have been served." The sheriff handed her a thick envelope, his face poker-straight.

"What?" She took the packet, her cheeks blanching, making the bruise stand out even more.

"What's this all about?" Ben slipped an arm around Kate as she opened the envelope, every protective instinct on alert in the face of the sheriff and his deputy.

"Back taxes? The will said nothing about back taxes." She looked up at the sheriff.

"Sorry, Ms. Langsdon, I only deliver the bad news, I don't create it. Your father was the one who didn't pay. Since he left the ranch to you, you're responsible now."

Ben didn't like the sheriff's tone or the way the man hit her with the notice so soon after coming to her father's ranch.

"Twenty-seven thousand?" She snorted softly. "I can't afford twenty-seven *hundred*." Kate stared at the paper in her hands. "That would completely wipe me out and then some."

The sheriff shrugged. "You might consider selling this dump. Pretty young woman like you will find it difficult to manage a place this size all alone."

It was all Ben could do to keep from punching the sheriff for his patronizing words. Ben barely knew Kate, but any woman would resent the sheriff's inference that a woman couldn't run a ranch.

"I'm not alone." Kate clutched the envelope to her chest, her chin rising. "I have Ben." She edged nearer to Ben.

His chest swelled, his arm automatically tightening around her middle, pulling her closer to him.

The sheriff's brows rose. "Hired hands don't always stick around."

"He's not the hired hand. He's…" Kate's hand waved, in search of the right word.

Afraid she'd say he was her bodyguard, Ben finished for her, "I'm her fiancé. We will be working the ranch together."

The sheriff's eyes narrowed. "What did you say your last name was?"

Ben's lips twisted. "I didn't. Now, if you'll excuse us." He moved to shut the door.

The sheriff shoved his foot in the way. "Don't cross me, cowboy."

Ben's brows rose and he stared down at the boot in the doorway. "Did you have more business to discuss?"

The sheriff stared at Ben for a long moment, then replied, "No."

"Then have a nice day." Ben glanced down at the boot and back up at the sheriff. Ben's free hand clenched into a fist, ready to take on the arrogant sheriff if the need arose. He'd seen law enforcement officers who let the power of their position go to their heads. This sheriff appeared to be one of them. He made a mental note to watch the man. He could cause trouble for himself and for Kate.

The sheriff finally moved his foot. "I'll be seeing you around Wild Oak Canyon."

Ben shut the door, muttering, "Not if I can help it."

Kate turned away, her gaze on the legal document the sheriff had given her. "Twenty-seven thousand dollars." She looked up at Ben, her eyes glazed. "That's more than I have in every savings account."

"Surely you have a thirty-day notice on it."

"Thirty days until they seize the property for back taxes owed." She shook her head. "I don't believe this. I should never have come."

"Can't you go back where you came from?" As he made the suggestion, his gut clenched. If Kate left, he wouldn't have to be around her. He could forget the way she made his body hum to life.

Kate shook her head. "No. I quit my job. They've already leased the apartment we lived in. Not that I'd go back. It's no safer in Houston than here."

"What do you mean?"

"I left Houston after my apartment was broken into and ransacked."

"In Houston?"

"Last week. The day after my father's will was read."

Ben didn't like it. Hell, she wasn't any safer in Houston than in Wild Oak Canyon. Ben resigned himself to being her protector until he could convince Hank he had the wrong man for the job. "Was your Houston apartment in a bad neighborhood?"

Kate shook her head. "I hadn't had any problems in the four years I lived there. Whoever did it tore everything apart."

"Any writing on the walls or threats?" Ben asked.

"No. They even ripped the cushions on my sofa. Every drawer was tossed, even the contents of the refrigerator."

"They're looking for something," Ben stated. "The day after your father's reading, you say? Did your father leave you anything besides this ranch?"

Kate's eyes widened. "Yes." Before Ben could question her, she ran up the stairs.

The blood racing through Ben's veins had nothing to do with whatever item she might have received from her father and more to do with the way her bottom swayed side to side and the vision of smooth, creamy skin visible along the curves of her legs. "More clothes. She damn well better wear more clothes," he muttered.

Kate paused at the top of the stairs, glancing down at Ben, her brows dipping. "Did you say something?"

"I'll get my clothes on." He strode back to the couch he'd spent the better part of the night lying awake on, thinking of the sexy legs on a woman he had no business looking at that way.

Hank Derringer was paying him to provide protection from a problem, not to become the problem or one more thing Kate had to be protected from.

He pulled his T-shirt on over his head, calling himself every kind of fool. If he had any cell phone reception at all, he'd be calling Hank and asking for a different

assignment. One with a less attractive woman and…
no kids.

"Hi."

Speak of the devil.

Ben's head poked through the neck of his T-shirt and
he stared down at the pint-size version of Kate. Light
reddish-blond curls lay in bright disarray around the
child's shoulders.

She held out a brush. "Mommy told me to brush my
hair."

Without thinking, Ben took the brush from the girl.
He'd brushed Sarah's hair so many times he could have
done it with his eyes closed. He knew just how to ease
the tangles free without making her cry.

His throat closed as an image of his dark-haired
daughter flashed into his memories. God, he missed her.

Lily looked up at him, her green eyes so like her
mother's. "Please?" She turned her back to Ben and
fluffed her mane of red-gold hair out behind her, waiting expectantly.

Just like Sarah had.

All of the air left Ben's lungs as if he'd been kicked
hard in the gut. Yet his hand moved, reaching out to
lift a lock of silky red-blond curls. He dropped to his
haunches and ran the brush along the strand, picking
out the knots with care.

He hadn't felt this emotionally wrung out since Sarah
and Julia had died. But the more he brushed Lily's hair,
the more his shoulders relaxed and the tightness in his
chest loosened.

By the time he finished working the tangles out of
the child's hair, he could swallow again. "All done," he
said just like he had when he'd brushed Sarah's hair.

"Thank you." Lily turned and hugged him tight, her fresh, baby-shampoo scent filling Ben's senses.

Over the top of Lily's head he spied Kate standing on the bottom step, her eyes round. Was that a tear trickling down her cheek?

Kate ducked her head, a hand swiping at the moisture. Seeing Ben brushing Lily's hair had hit her like a Mack truck. Lily's father had died before she was born. Kate had been a single parent from day one. Seeing someone else, especially a man, brushing her daughter's hair sent a flood of longing through her, for Lily and herself.

Lily didn't know what it was to have a daddy. Just like Kate. Kate swallowed hard on the lump forming in her throat. "Lily, sweetie, go get dressed."

Her daughter's face lit. "Are we going outside to play?"

Kate smiled and patted her daughter's head. "You can play, but I have work to do outside."

"Yay!" Lily darted up the stairs, her bright curls bouncing as she went.

Kate descended from the last step and held out her hand. "My father left this key for me and a video disk."

She dropped the key and the disk into Ben's hand.

"What does the key go to?" Ben turned it over in his fingers.

"I don't know. I've tried to watch the disk, but I couldn't get it to work. The letter from the attorney had a note from my father to contact Hank Derringer for help."

"Maybe Hank can get someone to look at the disk and see if they can pull the information off."

Lily was down the stairs again, wearing shorts, cowboy boots and pulling a shirt over her head.

"Stop, young lady," Kate ordered, afraid her daughter would miss a step and tumble the rest of the way down the stairs. "You can't go out without me, and I'm not dressed."

"Please, Mommy." Lily looked up at Kate with a slight pout on her pretty pink lips.

"I'll take her," Ben offered. "We can discuss the key later." He handed it back to her, setting the disk on an end table.

Kate curled her fingers around the key. "I'll be ready in a minute. I need to finish unloading the rental van and get it back to town."

Ben smiled and raised his hands palms upward. "I'm here to help."

Kate's heart skipped several beats as the man's smile transformed his face from frowning, brooding darkness to sunshine. "You should smile more often," she said without thinking.

Immediately, his face changed back into the brooding cowboy, his forehead creasing. "I find little to smile about these days."

Kate wondered what made him so sullen and sad but didn't want to push the issue, not when he'd thrown up a no-trespassing sign in the way his body stiffened and he turned away. He took Lily's hand in his. "Ready?"

The two left through the front door.

Yes, sir, the cowboy had issues. Hell, didn't everyone?

Kate climbed the stairs, her footsteps slow at first and speeding up as she neared the top. For the first time in months, she wanted to get outside and enjoy the sunshine and fresh air. She refused to believe the hired hand had anything to do with her sudden surge of energy.

A pair of jeans, a snug-fitting ribbed T-shirt and tennis shoes completed her outfit. After she pulled her hair up into a ponytail and settled a baseball cap over her head, she hurried out to join Lily and Ben, her steps light, eager to finish unloading and settle into her new life.

Ben and Lily squatted beside the moving van, pointing at something on the ground.

"That's a scorpion, Lily," Ben was explaining. "Don't try to touch or pick one up, they have a really bad sting."

Lily hunched over, staring at the insect crawling across the ground. She looked up and spied Kate. "Mommy, come see the scorpion."

Kate smiled and squatted beside her. With the three of them all gathered in a circle so close, her stomach knotted. This must be what it would feel like to be a family unit. Mommy, daughter and…daddy. Troy would have been a good father to Lily. He'd been so excited about the arrival of his firstborn, only to be robbed of ever seeing her.

Lily was a beautiful baby and an even prettier little girl with a grown-up sense of responsibility and a child's joy of exploring.

"The day's not getting any longer. I guess we better get this van unloaded so that I can return it to the rental center in town." Kate stood, pulled the padlock key from her pocket and unlocked the back of the van.

For the next twenty minutes, Kate and Ben worked in silence, carrying boxes and furniture into the house. Lily helped a little, then lost interest and wandered around the yard, picking flowers and investigating her new home.

Kate kept a close eye on her. After last night's break-in, she wasn't feeling exactly trusting of her new environment.

Lily had strayed to the corner of the house when Kate

and Ben hauled out the sofa with the repaired cushions she'd brought with her from her apartment.

Getting the sofa through the door took them several tries, tipping it in multiple directions, before they finally shoved the item through. When the sofa cleared the door frame, Kate tripped over a throw rug and landed on her bottom, the edge of the sofa coming down hard on her ankle. "Ouch!"

"Are you all right in there?" Ben called out over the top of the sofa.

"Yes, just not very graceful." Kate stood and put pressure on her ankle and felt pain shooting up her leg. She swallowed a yelp and lifted her end again. There was no time for injuries. The van needed to be back before three o'clock or she'd have to pay for another day's rental.

Once they got the sofa settled into the living room, Kate headed toward the door, trying to hide her limp.

Ben shook his head and pointed to the sofa they'd just placed. "Sit."

"I'm fine, just a little sore. It'll work itself out." When she tried to walk past him, he grabbed her arms and made her stop.

"Let me see." His grip was firm but gentle and his tone the same.

The warmth of his hands on her arms sent shivers of awareness throughout her body. "Really, it's fine," she said, even as she let him maneuver her to sit on the arm of the couch.

Ben squatted, pulled the tennis shoe off her foot and removed her sock. "I had training as a first responder on the Austin police force. Let me be the judge."

Kate held her breath as he lifted her foot and turned it to inspect the ankle, his fingers slipping over her skin.

"See? Just bumped it. It'll be fine in a minute." She cursed inwardly at her breathlessness. A man's hands on her ankle shouldn't send her into a tailspin.

Ben Harding was a trained professional. Touching a woman's ankle meant nothing other than a concern for health and safety. Nothing more.

Then why was she having a hard time breathing, like a teenager on her first date? Kate bent to slip her foot back into her shoe, biting hard on her lip to keep from crying out at the pain. Her head came very close to Ben's. When she turned toward him she could feel the warmth of his breath fan across her cheek.

"You should put a little ice on that," he said, his tone as smooth as warm syrup sliding over her.

Ice was exactly what she needed. To chill her natural reaction to a handsome man paid to help and protect her, not touch, hold or kiss her.

Whoa, there, girl. Kate jumped up and moved away from Ben and his gentle fingers, warm breath and shoulders so broad they could turn a girl's head. "I should get back outside. No telling what Lily is up to."

Ben caught her arm as she passed him. "You felt it, too, didn't you?"

Kate fought the urge to lean into him and sniff the musky scent of male. Four years was a long time to go without a man. "I don't know what you're talking about."

Ben held her arm a moment longer, then let go. "You're right. We should check on Lily."

Kate hurried, no, ran for the open door, her heart racing, her breathing ragged. Just as she crossed the threshold into the open breezy, South Texas sunshine, a frightened scream made her racing heart stop.

"Lily!" Kate burst out onto the porch.

The sound of engines racing up the gravel driveway greeted her. A man wearing a do-rag over his head with a bandanna pulled up over his mouth and nose straddled a huge motorcycle in the middle of the yard, holding a doll by its hair. He laughed, the sound so evil it made Kate's skin crawl.

"That's Lily's doll." Kate flew off the porch and would have scratched the man's eyes out if an arm hadn't circled her waist and yanked her back.

"Go back to the house. Now," Ben said into her ear, his voice tight around the command.

"But Lily—"

"Go." He shoved her back behind him.

Kate hesitated.

The roar of engines rose to a crescendo. An army of bikes swarmed into the yard, stirring up dust where the grass had long since died.

Kate ran for the house. Before she could reach the porch, a motorcycle cut her off. There must have been twenty bikes racing around the yard in a tight circle, trapping Ben and Kate in the center. The dust rose in a cloud, choking visibility to everything beyond.

Beyond panic, long past frightened, Kate screamed into the smoke screen, "Where's my child?"

CHAPTER FOUR

BEN HAD LEFT his Glock on top of the refrigerator in-side the house while they'd been working to unload the trailer. Now he wished he had it. Two unarmed people against a biker gang weren't good odds in anyone's ex-perience.

A rider broke the ring, circled the pair and then swerved toward Kate.

Fear for her spiked his adrenaline and he lunged to-ward the motorcyclist. Grabbing the closest handlebar, Ben twisted it hard toward the man astride. The sharp turn on the forward-moving bike caused the bike to flip over, rider and all.

Ben snagged Kate's hand and pulled her closer to him into the center of the circle.

The man he'd toppled pulled himself out of the dirt, his face bleeding from where he'd crashed into the gravel drive. He glared at Ben and Kate and roared, veins pop-ping out on his forehead.

Kate shrank against Ben. "Oh, God."

They had nowhere to go; the ring of motorcycles tightened. The man with the doll eased toward them, dark eyes glaring through the slit between his do-rag and bandanna. "You need to leave, lady, before it's too late." He ripped the head off the doll and flung it at Kate's feet.

Kate reached for the doll, but Ben held her back.

"When I make my move…run toward the house," he said into her ear. Anger surged and Ben threw himself at the lead man, knocking him out of his seat.

Kate ran.

Ben got one good, hard punch at the man's face before two goons ditched their rides and jerked him off their leader. Caught between two beefy Hispanic men, Ben struggled, twisting and kicking, determined to keep their attention long enough for Kate to escape.

Ben jabbed an elbow into the gut of the guy on his right.

The man loosened his hold.

Ben ducked beneath his arm. No sooner had he shaken free from his captors' hold than he was slammed to the ground from behind, a bull of a man hitting him low and hard.

The wind knocked from his lungs, Ben lay facedown in the dirt, willing his body to move. A foot in the middle of his back kept him from doing anything, especially refilling his starving lungs.

Kate screamed.

A shot of determination rocketed through Ben. He rolled onto his back; at the same time he grabbed the man's leg who'd planted his heavy boot into his back. With a hard twist, he sent the thug flying backward, landing hard on his butt.

Two more men grabbed him, hauled him up and yanked his arms behind him, hard enough that spasms of pain ripped through his shoulders.

The leader lumbered to his feet and stalked toward Ben. He hit him with a hard-knuckled fist, square in the jaw. Ben's head jerked back, hazy gray fog encroaching on his vision. Another punch to his gut would have had him doubling over, if he didn't have two big guys holding him up.

Through the torture, his gaze panned the yard, searching for Kate and Lily.

The bikers had broken the circle and raced around the yard, running over bushes, ramming into a rose trellis. One drove up onto the porch and ripped the porch swing from its hooks.

Another cut off Kate's attempt to get to the house.

Kate shot a glance over her shoulder and dodged to the left.

The biker sped past her and spun to renew his attack.

Ben planted his feet in the dirt and struggled, twisting and turning in an attempt to go to Kate's rescue, his mind conjuring his wife's last minutes on the earth, fighting to protect their daughter.

Then, he hadn't been there to help Julia. His job now was to protect Kate. If only he'd been more vigilant and not lulled into believing danger wouldn't strike during the daylight hours.

Hell, the fight wasn't over.

The gang leader swung again.

Ben jerked to the side hard enough that the guy on his left tripped. The leader's blow hit his own man in the cheekbone. The man yelled and grabbed his face with both hands, letting go of Ben.

Using the weight of the other man's body, Ben rolled into him and sent him flying over his shoulder.

Kate ran toward the road.

The biker who'd missed her straightened his bike and hit the gas. The back tire spun, then gripped the ground and shot forward.

Ben came at him sideways, plowing into the biker.

The bike and rider rolled over to the side, the rider moving sluggishly in the dirt.

One down, nineteen to go.

Kate ran on, but another bike raced after her.

Ben wouldn't catch up before the biker reached her.

A loud air horn broke through the roar of racing motorcycle engines, followed by a cloud of dust storming toward them on the gravel drive leading to the highway. Another air horn burst and a truck swerved around Kate, aiming straight for the biker in pursuit of the fleeing woman.

A shotgun's nose poked out of the passenger window and blasted a hole in the ground in front of the bike tire. As a result, the biker spun so fast, the back wheel whirled all the way around and out from under the rider.

The gang members Ben had thrown off caught up to him and knocked him to the ground. He came up spitting dirt and ready to tear into them. He swung again and again, pummeling one man in the face. When that one went down, he kicked out and sent the other sprawling on his backside.

Another shot rang out, peppering bird shot at the gang members.

One man yelped and sent his bike skittering out of the shooter's range.

The leader of the gang yelled something and circled his hand in the air, then pointed to the road.

All of the bikers revved their engines and rode out, leaving a lung-choking cloud in their wake.

Their leader left the yard, shouting, *"Dejar o te vas a morir!"*

As the dust cleared, the driver and passenger of the truck dropped to the ground.

Ben laughed, the effort making his split lip and sore rib cage hurt. He leaned against the gnarled trunk of a live oak tree, his knuckles bleeding and every muscle in his body screaming.

The driver was an older Hispanic man with a decided limp. The passenger, the one holding the shotgun, was a woman who could only be described as grandmotherly. Thank the Lord for help in all shapes and sizes.

Ben's next thought went to Kate and Lily.

Kate rounded the back of the pickup and ran back into the yard, tears making muddy tracks down her cheeks. "Lily!" she cried out.

A whimper sounded from the tree branches over Ben's head.

Hidden between the leaves was a little girl with a curly halo of hair, clutching a ball of fur to her chest, tears slipping down her cheeks. "Mommy?"

"Lily?" Kate skidded to a halt beneath the tree. "Oh, baby. I'm so glad you're okay." Kate grabbed a branch and started up the tree.

Ben snagged her arm. "Let me."

"I can do this."

"It would be better if I could hand her down to someone she knows."

Kate backed away and let Ben take the lead.

He ducked beneath the low-hanging branches and climbed upward. "Hey, Lily. How'd you get all the way up here?"

She hiccuped, her bottom lip trembling as she clutched the fuzz ball to the curve of her neck. "I followed Jazzy."

"Is Jazzy one of your toys?" He spoke in calm, soothing tones, careful not to grimace when a shard of pain rippled across his hands or ribs.

Lily shook her head. "No, Jazzy's not a toy."

A soft mewling erupted from the fur ball and little paws reached out to latch onto Lily's shirt.

"Jazzy's a kitten." Lily's eyes rounded as she stared down into Ben's eyes. "Can I keep her?"

Ben chuckled, his body hurting with every breath. He wanted to crush the little girl and the kitten to his chest and hold them there for as long as he could. He couldn't tell if the pain he was feeling stemmed from sore ribs, bruises or heartbreak. "You'll have to ask your mommy."

"Will you ask her for me?"

"You bet." Ben settled on a thick branch and wrapped his legs around it before he reached out. "Come on. I think your mother wants to fix you lunch or something."

"I'm scared." She glanced around at the ground below her. "Are the bad men gone?"

Rage burned in Ben's throat as hot as acid but he fought to keep it from his face and voice. "Yes, baby. They're gone." This child should not have been exposed to the violence of those men.

She leaned toward him and stopped, her arm around the kitten that clung to her, its blue eyes as big around as Lily's. "You're bleeding."

"It's okay. It doesn't hurt, just a little cut."

"I want my mommy," Lily whimpered.

"I'm going to hand you down to her. Come on. You're so brave to save that kitten. Now let me be brave and save you from falling out of the tree."

Lily smiled. "Silly, I'm not falling out of the tree."

"Your mother thinks you will." He winked. "But I know better. You're good at climbing trees, aren't you?"

She nodded, then let him grab her around the waist and lift her onto the branch he sat on. He hugged her to him, relief washing over him in such a rush that his eyes glazed over and he couldn't see.

"Give her to me, please," Kate cried.

Ben blinked several times before he loosened his hold on the little girl and handed her down into Kate's outstretched arms.

Kate gathered Lily into a hug so tight, Lily grunted. She sat on the ground in the dirt and hugged her some more, tears trickling from the corners of her eyes.

"I'm okay, Mommy." Lily patted Kate's face. "See?" Her empty hand pressed against Kate's face, urging her to look into her eyes. "I saved the kitten." Her smile broadened. "Can I keep her? Her name is Jazzy."

"Sure, honey. You can keep her." Kate dashed the tears from her cheeks and hugged Lily again. Then she climbed to her feet, lifting Lily to perch on her hip. "Come on, let's clean up."

Ben slid out of the tree and dropped to the ground beside the two, his hand going around Kate's waist. "You two going to be all right?"

"I hope so." Kate's eyes widened. "You're bleeding."

Lily grinned at Ben. "Told you."

Kate cupped Ben's cheek. "Come in the house and let me take care of your cuts before they get infected."

The light touch sent fire through his veins. Ben pushed her hand aside. "I'm fine. I'll just stay out here and see what I can do to clean up the mess they made." Anything rather than being close to Kate. She brought out too many feelings in him, feelings he'd thought long dead, emotions that made a man vulnerable.

The woman holding the shotgun waved her hands at

them. "You three go get cleaned up and let us take care of the mess. Eddy and I can set things to rights in no time. Can't we, Eddy?"

The short Hispanic man had wandered off, picking up broken bush branches. *"Sí, señora."*

Ben stepped between the woman and Kate. "Could we at least know the names of our rescuers?" He tried to smile, his lip hurting with the effort. "I'm Ben Harding, Kate's my...fiancée."

"Oh, goodness, yes." The woman shifted the shotgun into her other hand and gripped Ben's hand in a firm, capable grasp. "Margaret Henderson. But most folks 'round here call me Ma or Marge. This here's Eddy."

"Mrs. Henderson, Eddy, glad to meet you." Ben nodded at the gun. "Good shootin'."

"No boys in my family, so my daddy taught all his girls to squirrel hunt." She grinned. "And I make a mean squirrel soup."

"I'll bet you do." Ben let go of her hand. "Thank you for showing up when you did. I think they were about to get the best of us."

"I don't know. You were holdin' yer own pretty well."

Ben didn't want to argue with the woman. He'd gotten his butt whipped and Kate would be in a world of hurt had Margaret and Eddy not come along when they did. Guilt with a hint of heartrending regret tugged at his empty belly. What made Hank think a washed-up cop was the right man for this job? It had taken an old woman with a shotgun to chase off the latest threat. Some bodyguard he'd turned out to be.

Margaret smacked Ben on the back. "Twenty-to-one odds needs a little more encouragement than bare fists.

Don't let it get ya down. Question is why they were here in the first place."

Eddy stuck a long blade of grass between his lips and rocked back on his heels. "Their leader shouted *'Dejar o te vas a morir'* as he left." The man had a decided Mexican accent.

Kate shook her head. "I don't know Spanish. What does it mean?"

Eddy's gaze captured Kate's, his lips tightening for a moment before he spoke. "Leave or you will die."

KATE'S HEART SANK into her belly. Holy smokes, what the hell had she done to the bikers to warrant a death threat?

"Well, now, isn't that a nice way to welcome the new neighbors." Marge turned to face Kate, the stiff, tough persona fading with the softening of her eyes. "You must be Kate."

Kate held on to Lily, refusing to let her child out of her sight for even a moment. Her legs still shook and she couldn't keep her hand from trembling when she held it out to Margaret. "Should I know you?"

"Kate Kendrick—" the woman folded Kate's hand in both of hers "—you're the spittin' image of your father."

Kate shook her head. "I go by Kate Langsdon." She gripped the woman's hand with her free one. "Did you know my… Kyle Kendrick?" She still couldn't manage to refer to him as her father. Throughout her life, her mother had told her that her father had died in a car wreck. Growing up without a father hadn't given her any practice saying the word. And for the past four years, Lily had been without a father of her own.

"Know him? I worked for him until the day he was m—" The older woman's eyes widened and she clapped a hand over her mouth. "Sorry." Her glance moved to Lily, and her hand fell to her side. "I worked for Mr. Kendrick until he passed. He was a good man."

Kate bit her lip, wanting to refute Mrs. Henderson's statement. What man would willingly walk away from his daughter and never have contact with her? In Kate's mind, that didn't make a good man.

"Thank you for coming to our rescue." Kate smiled and turned to Ben. "Now, let's get you inside and doctored up."

The kitten Lily had been holding mewed.

An answering meow came from beneath the porch and a brightly colored calico cat stepped out of the shadows.

The kitten clawed at Lily.

"Ouch." Lily held the kitten away from her shirt.

Kate pointed to the cat. "That must be the kitten's mother."

Lily hugged the fur ball to her, her brows pulling together in a mutinous frown. "Jazzy is *my* kitty."

"Honey, you have to let her go to her mama."

"But I want a kitten."

"Jazzy will be your kitten, but you'll have to let her be with her mama until she gets bigger."

"I want her to come in the house and sleep in my bed."

"When she doesn't need her mother anymore. You can come and play with her outside until then."

The kitten dug her claws into Lily, scrambling to get to her mother.

"See, she misses her mother." Kate leaned Lily away from her. "How would you feel if someone wouldn't let you come to your mother?"

Lily stared at the kitten and the calico mother cat, meowing over and over. "I'd feel sad."

"And the kitten is sad because you won't let her go to her mother."

Lily wiggled in Kate's arms, so she set her daughter on the ground.

Plucking the kitten's claws from her shirt, Lily settled the animal on the ground.

As soon as she was loose, the kitten ran for her mother, curling in and around the cat's long, sleek legs.

"See how happy Jazzy is?" Kate knelt beside her daughter.

"Can I play with her after lunch?"

"You sure can." If the bikers weren't back or an intruder wasn't rummaging through the only home they had to go to. Kate's chest tightened. "We'll bring food out for Jazzy and her mother."

Lily slipped her hand into Ben's and one into her mother's. "I'm hungry. Can we eat now?"

Kate almost laughed at how quickly Lily forgot the bad men on motorcycles, all her concentration on eating and getting back outside to play with her kitten. How simple to be a child and forget about all the horrible things adults could do to each other.

Ben glanced over the top of Lily's head. "She'll be all right."

The biker's warning echoed in Kate's mind. "I hope so."

CHAPTER FIVE

KATE LED THE WAY into the ranch house. As soon as she passed through the door, Lily shook her hand free and ran to the bathroom. Kate and Ben followed, filling the tiny room.

Lily stood on a small plastic step, just the right height to boost her little body up to the sink. She pumped liquid soap onto her hands and turned on the faucet, splashing water over her arms and shirt. "Do kittens like milk?"

"I suppose they do," Kate replied, her voice soft, reassuring and less shaky than it had been in the yard after being terrorized by the biker gang.

Ben's gut clenched. He should have been ready—he could have handled the situation better. He reached out and grabbed her hand. "I'm sorry."

Kate's brows wrinkled. "For what?"

"Letting it go that far."

She dragged her hand out of his, closed the toilet lid and pointed at it. "Sit."

Obediently, he did, amazed at the strength in her tone.

While washing her hands, she chewed on her lip, tears welling in her eyes. She dashed them away, apparently not wanting him to see them. Tough tone and tears didn't add up. Ben's chest squeezed. This woman had been scared out of her mind, but she refused to show it.

Lily climbed into Ben's lap. "You have a boo-boo on your mouth." She poked a finger at the drying blood.

The child felt right, her legs dangling over his knee, her feet swinging in and out. As quickly as she'd come, Lily slid off his lap and left the bathroom.

"Stay in the house, Lily," Kate called out.

"I will. I'm going to my room to play with my dolls."

The sound of footsteps on the stairs echoed through the old house.

Kate snatched a clean hand towel from the shelf over Ben's head, leaning so close, the scent of herbal shampoo wafted over him.

Her breasts brushed against his shoulder and he gasped.

Kate jerked back, towel clutched in her fingers. "Did I hurt you?"

"No," he said through clenched teeth. The pain she'd caused had nothing to do with flesh wounds. She'd stirred his heart to life and that was more painful than a broken bone or knife stabbing. He'd thought his heart was firmly locked away after the deaths of his wife and daughter.

Now he sat at the tender mercy of a woman and her daughter, reminding him with every move, every touch and soft word of all he'd lost.

She dampened the towel in the water and touched the cloth to the corner of his lip, dabbing gently to remove the dried blood.

"Lily's a great kid," he said.

"I know." Kate's gaze focused on his wounds, one hand steadying herself on his shoulder. Warmth filtered through his chambray shirt to his skin. Ben's jeans tightened and his pulse quickened.

"Some bodyguard I am," he said.

When he glanced into her eyes, he caught her staring down at him.

"You were outnumbered. You couldn't fight them all."

"I should have had my gun on me at all times," he countered.

"And they might have used it on you or Lily."

"Or you."

"I'll make an ice pack for that jaw. Any other injuries?"

The longer she stood there close enough to touch, the harder it was not to reach out. "No." He shook his head and stood, wincing, his hand automatically rising to press against his ribs.

Kate's brow furrowed. "Liar. Let me see." She pushed his T-shirt up, tucking it beneath his arms.

A bruise the size of a grapefruit was making its dark purple appearance against his skin and everything beneath the mark ached.

"Damn, Ben, you could have a broken rib." She dipped the towel beneath the faucet again, wrung it out and pressed it to his side, her fingers sliding over the bruise. "Does that hurt?"

Ben grasped her fingers and held them away from his skin. "Yes," he lied. Her touch wasn't what hurt, it was the effect she was having on him. If he didn't get away soon, he'd be hard-pressed to walk away without kissing her.

"Let me take you to the clinic in town. They must have an X-ray machine." She tugged her hand free and pressed the cool towel to his side, all her focus on his injury.

Past his level of endurance, Ben tipped her chin up. "I don't need a doctor. I'm not going anywhere."

When her green-eyed gaze met his, he realized his mistake. Her lips parted, and what she might have said next faded away on a sigh.

Ben bent and brushed his lips across hers. He'd only wanted a taste. But like water to a desert flower, the more he tasted the more he wanted.

His fingers curled around the back of her neck, tugging at her hair, tipping her head back, giving him more access to her lips, her throat and the pulse beating wildly at the base. She leaned into him. Her fingers pressed against his chest, the tips curling into his skin, not enough to hurt, but enough to ignite a flame he'd thought long burned out.

As fire spread through his veins, his arms tightened around her, his lips going from soft and gentle to crushingly hard, desperate to wipe out the stab of guilt that ravaged him from head to toe.

"I'm sorry, Julia," he said against her lips. "I'm so sorry."

The woman in his arms stiffened, her mouth moving away from his, her hands pressing against his skin.

"Let go of me," she said, her voice ragged, her tone strained.

Ben backed up, his hands dropping to his sides. "I'm sorry. That shouldn't have happened."

"Damn right, it shouldn't have." Kate's hand shook as she swiped the back of her hand over her bruised lips. "I don't know who Julia is, but I'm not her." She turned to walk out of the bathroom.

Ben caught her hand. "You're right. I had no business kissing you." Not when he still had feelings for his dead wife. Feelings that amplified his guilt for having kissed this stranger. "It won't happen again."

Without facing him, she jerked her hand free. "I don't think this arrangement will work after all."

"I understand. I'll talk with Hank about a replacement this afternoon."

"Please." Her shoulders rose and fell as if she sighed deeply, then she left the room.

Ben's fists balled. He wanted to hit something, but his knuckles were already like raw meat. He wasn't sure he could handle any more pain, both physical and emotional.

Too much about Kate and Lily reminded him of Julia and Sarah. The sooner he left the Flying K Ranch the better off they both would be.

Images of the intruder on the first night and the terror of the motorcycle gang nagged his conscience. Would Kate's next hired gun take better care of her? Would he try to kiss her and forget why he'd come?

KATE RAN UP the stairs and peeked in at Lily. Her daughter sat at her little table with her miniature tea set laid out. A teddy bear and two dolls occupied the other seats.

Satisfied Lily was okay, Kate slipped past and into her own room, closing the door behind her. She leaned against the panel and pressed her fingers to her burning cheeks.

He'd kissed her. Her bodyguard had kissed her.

What had her running scared was that she'd liked it. So much so that she'd kissed him back, practically crawling up his body to get closer.

She covered her softly swollen lips and moaned.

It had been four years since she'd known the touch

of another man's kiss, the feel of big, strong hands on her skin.

Her body burned with a need she thought had been buried with her husband. Kate squeezed her eyes shut and tried to picture Troy's face, a sob rising up her throat when the only face she envisioned was Ben's.

Kate opened her eyes, her gaze darting around the bedroom to the framed photograph of her and Troy on their last vacation together. They'd gone to the coast, playing in the sun and sand as if there'd be no tomorrow. Tomorrows for Troy had ended with an improvised explosive device that detonated beside his convoy. He'd been killed instantly. One week before he was due to come home. One month before his daughter's birth. Two days before their third anniversary.

Troy smiled back at her from the photograph, his light gray eyes and sandy-blond hair so different from the dark hair and stormy-blue eyes of the man downstairs.

Kate hugged the frame to her breast, again trying to recall Troy smiling down at her as he'd kissed her goodbye. Even holding Troy's photo, Kate couldn't see him. Her mind fixated on the dark-haired, brooding man who'd come to help her keep Lily safe in their new home.

Kate set the photo on her nightstand and hurried into the bathroom. She didn't have time to worry about why her memories of Troy were fading. She had a daughter to take care of, one who needed her to make lunch.

She stared into the mirror and almost cried of fright. Her face was smudged with dirt, her eyes red-rimmed and puffy from tears of joy at finding Lily safe in a tree.

Kate scrubbed her face with cool water, brushed her hair and secured it in a ponytail at her nape. Clean-faced and refreshed, she took a deep breath and resolved to act as if nothing had happened. No more kisses would be exchanged and life would go on as usual.

When she passed Lily's room, her daughter no longer sat at her table, the tea set abandoned.

Her heartbeat quickening, Kate hurried down the stairs.

A quick perusal of the living room found it empty. Only Mrs. Henderson in the kitchen.

Fear pushed Kate out the front door.

Ben was hanging the porch swing that had been knocked down by the gang.

As soon as he settled the chain on the hooks, Lily climbed up on the swing and patted the seat beside her. "Will you swing with me?"

"I don't know." Ben glanced out at the dry Texas landscape, only his profile visible from where Kate stood. The dark circles beneath his eyes and sad, faraway look tugged at Kate's heartstrings.

"Please?" Lily batted her eyes like a pro.

Ben chuckled and smiled. "When you put it like that…sure." He settled on the swing beside Lily and looped his arm over the child's shoulder, pulling her close.

A lump the size of a grapefruit lodged in Kate's throat and she backed away, racing for the kitchen and a hand towel to dry quickly forming tears.

Marge stood at the kitchen counter, adding lettuce and tomatoes to thick slices of bread layered with lunch meat. "Ah, there you are. I hope you didn't mind me barging in and jumping right in. I worked here so many years, it feels more like home to me than my own house. I've missed coming out."

Kate's mouth watered. "Where did you get all that food?"

"I was the cook and I handled the grocery shopping for Mr. Kendrick. I figured with you just having moved in, you probably hadn't had time to visit the store to stock up. Eddy's a ranch hand. He wanted to check on the horses and cattle, so I asked him to bring me out after stopping for a few things at the market."

"A few?" Kate opened the pantry doors and checked in the refrigerator and gasped. "This isn't a few."

Mrs. Henderson blushed. "I'm sorry. It's kind of pushy of me, but I've been beside myself staying at home since Mr. K. passed. My husband retired last year and we just bump into each other too much. I *need* to work outside the home."

"I'm not sure I can pay you, and I don't expect you to work for free."

"Now, don't you worry none. Consider this a welcome home gift. And once Eddy gets the cattle rounded up and the fences mended, he'll give you a better idea of what this place can do to support you and your little one."

Tears filled Kate's eyes. "Why?"

"Like I said, Mr. Kendrick was a good man. Many times he'd spot me my mortgage payment when my man was out of work." The older woman sliced a sandwich in two and laid it on a freshly cleaned plate. "Now, you just sit right down there and have yourself a bite. You could stand to gain a pound or two." Marge patted her rounded figure. "Not that you want to put on as many as I have." She laughed and moved around the kitchen like one very familiar with its contents.

Ben entered, carrying Lily on his arm. "Someone is hungry. I wonder who it is."

Lily's hand shot up. "Me!"

He swung her up in the air and caught her.

Kate's heart warmed at her daughter's giggles. Oh, to be young enough to forget so easily. Today could have turned out very badly. Any one of them could have been hurt or killed. Thank God Lily had been climbing a tree, although Kate wasn't all that comfortable with a four-year-old climbing unattended. What if she'd fallen?

If the impact on the ground hadn't hurt her, the biker gang could have.

Ben set Lily on her feet and laid a hand on Kate's shoulder. "She's all right. I won't let anything bad happen to her."

"I know that." Kate's gaze followed Lily around the kitchen, but her mind was on the hand warming her shoulder. "I was just thinking that I should be mad at Lily for climbing a tree, but I can't find it in my heart to be. If she hadn't…" Kate glanced up into Ben's eyes.

A muscle in the side of his jaw twitched. "We'll have to do a better job of keeping an eye on her. She's a very active little girl. Aren't you, darlin'."

Marge trimmed the crust off a sandwich and cut it in triangles, then set it on a plate in front of Lily. "Eat up, half-pint."

"You'll spoil her," Kate protested.

"It's my biggest fault." Marge smoothed Lily's hair back from her forehead. "Never had any of my own. Guess I do go a bit overboard."

"It's hard not to, even when they're yours." Kate smiled at Lily. "She's all I've got."

Marge smiled. "You have Ben, too. When are the two of you lovebirds gonna tie the knot?"

Kate's face burned. She hated lying, but if it helped

keep the rest of the town off her back, she'd do it, and she didn't know Marge well enough yet to set her straight on the fake engagement. "We haven't set a date."

"No hurry, huh? Too many young couples meet each other one day, marry the next and file for a divorce within a year." Marge crossed her arms. "You're smart to wait. Seems Mr. Kendrick and your mama were in that category. Young and crazy stupid in love. Mr. Kendrick never considered whether his new bride would be happy out in the middle of nowhere Texas. She wasn't suited for the rugged life of a ranch owner. Too bad she didn't stay around long enough to find out."

"My mother never talked about my father. She told me he'd died in an automobile accident."

Marge shook her head. "Nearly broke Mr. K.'s heart when your mama left him. He didn't even know you existed until after your mother died and her lawyer notified him, or I'm sure he'd have done more to get to know you sooner."

"My mother's been dead for nearly five years. Why didn't he come find me then?"

Marge shrugged. "I asked him again and again. He just said the timing wasn't right. Might have been because he'd been doing a lot of traveling." The housekeeper leaned close. "He never said, but I think he worked for the government, secret service or something. He'd pack and leave a note that he'd be gone awhile. Never said how long, when he'd be back or where he was going."

"Any idea where he went?" Ben asked.

"I think he had business in Mexico. The man spoke Spanish like a native."

Kate frowned. How sad to learn about her estranged

father from a stranger. Especially when he'd lived in Texas all her life and hadn't bothered to get to know his daughter even after he'd learned of her existence.

"Mrs. Henderson?" Ben began.

"Call me Marge. Please."

"Marge." Ben smiled. "What exactly happened to Mr. Kendrick?"

"Now, that's a very good question. You'll get a different answer depending on who you ask."

"What do you mean? Didn't a coroner determine cause of death?"

"The county coroner is a good friend of the sheriff. He'd put whatever the sheriff wanted him to put on the death certificate."

Kate's eyes widened. "I was under the impression Kyle Kendrick died of natural causes."

"The coroner stated he'd died of heart failure."

"And you don't believe him?"

"Oh, I'm sure Mr. Kendrick died of heart failure, but the cause of the heart failure, in my opinion, had nothing natural about it."

Ben pulled up a chair at the table and sat beside Kate. "Why do you say that?"

"The man had bruising around his throat. I'm sure his heart failed when his lungs could no longer get air."

Kate gasped, setting her sandwich on the plate, all hunger forgotten. "Someone choked him?"

"I watch enough crime scene investigation shows to know a man with bruises around his throat didn't run into a door."

"Did you say anything to the sheriff?"

Marge shook her head. "If they couldn't see what was in front of them, either they're just plain stupid or were in on the killin'. Sayin' somethin' to them wouldn't bring back Mr. K., and it might have bought me the same demise."

A chill slithered across Kate's skin. "Who would want to kill him?"

"I can't even imagine." Marge tidied the counter, talking as she went. "Mr. K. was quiet, but well-liked in the community by the few who got to know him. He never had a bad word to say about anybody. He was kinda reclusive, but that could be expected of a confirmed bachelor like himself." She paused and stared out the window. "Could be someone involved in the troubles around here."

Kate frowned. "Troubles?"

"The Flying K is smack-dab in the middle of an area known for drug trafficking from across the border." Mrs. Henderson glanced at Lily. "Maybe Mr. K. got crossways with one of them. They found him here in this house. No sign of forced entry, but the place was a shambles. It was like someone he knew killed him, then ransacked the house. As far as I could tell, the only thing missin' was the computer out of Mr. K.'s office. Eddy thinks it was Larry Sites, though why Larry would take the computer…" Mrs. H. shrugged. "The man could barely read, much less find his way around a keyboard."

"Larry Sites?" Kate shook her head, trying to take it all in.

"Larry was a ranch hand here at the Flying K. Worked with Eddy. But no one's seen him since the day we found Mr. K." Marge clucked her tongue. "Poor Mr. K."

A lead weight settled in Kate's belly. "The more I hear the more I'm beginning to think Lily and I need to move back to Houston."

"Oh, honey," Marge said as she laid a hand on Kate's shoulder. "I'd hate to see you go when you just got here."

"Mommy, can I go out now?" Lily asked, her hands and face covered in peanut butter and jelly.

"Sweetie, it'll have to be later. After you wash your hands and face, we're going to town. I have some business to do there."

Mrs. Henderson was there with a clean, wet washcloth before Lily could move a muscle, scrubbing the sticky jelly from her face and hands.

"What do you say to Mrs. Henderson?" Kate prompted.

"You missed a spot." Lily's tongue slid along her lips and she smacked them loudly.

Marge laughed and dabbed at the stickiness.

Lily jumped down from her chair and skipped toward the hallway. "Thank you for making lunch, Mrs. Henderson. It was delicious."

Kate pushed her plate away and stood. "Thank you for the sandwiches, Marge." She rummaged through drawers to find something to wrap hers in.

"Don't you worry about that. I'll put it away for later. You go on. The town rolls up its sidewalks at five o'clock. If you have business there, you need to skedaddle."

"We'll find dinner in town. No need to cook anything here."

"Will do, Kate." Marge gave her a hug. "I'm glad you're here. I've missed Mr. K. and you're the spittin' image of the man, only prettier."

Kate thanked her again and hurried out of the kitchen, her mind running through all Mrs. Henderson had said.

She should have looked this gift horse in the mouth

before accepting it and moving out to Wild Oak Canyon in the middle of South Texas. Now that she was here, she had to make the best of it. First things first. She wanted to know more about her father's death and the people with whom he'd done business.

BEN FOLLOWED KATE out of the kitchen. "I have a bad feeling about this."

"You and me both." She stopped at the base of the steps. "I want to freshen up a bit, then I'll be down. I assume, as my bodyguard, you'll be coming with me to town?" This last question she spoke in a whisper.

"That's right."

"In my car or your truck?"

"My truck."

"Good. I'll meet you in five minutes." She ran up the stairs.

Ben almost groaned aloud at the sway of her hips. The woman was far too distracting for him to keep his mind on the task at hand. Julia hadn't been quite as curvy as Kate. Her frame had been slight, so much so that giving birth had been especially difficult. Their obstetrician recommended that she not have any more children due to her narrow frame and complications of high blood pressure and prenatal diabetes during pregnancy.

Ben had been disappointed, wanting a whole brood of children. But he'd hidden his regret well. The sight of baby Sarah, so perfect and pink, had been all he'd needed.

Until a brutal murderer had taken her away from him.

All these thoughts stemmed from the one short glimpse of Kate's swaying fanny.

He shook his head, squared his shoulders and climbed

the stairs behind her, heading for the room she'd assigned to him where he changed into a clean shirt and jeans.

Once he'd smoothed his hair into a semblance of order, he stepped into the hallway and ran into Kate.

He knocked into her, throwing her off balance. Ben grabbed her and pulled her into his arms, crushing her against his chest, his heartbeat hammering through his veins. Had he hit her any harder, she would have fallen right over the railing and down to the hardwood flooring.

Once he had her securely in his arms, he couldn't make himself let go. Her curves fit him in all the right places, so soft and tempting.

She looked up, her lips inches from his. "What are you doing?" she whispered.

"Keeping you from falling over the rail." Ben couldn't believe how cracked his voice sounded. "I promise to be more careful in the future."

Her tongue swept across her bottom lip, moistening it. "Please."

"Please what?" Why hadn't he let go of her already?

"Be more careful." She dragged in a deep breath and stepped free of his arms, straightening her shoulders while tugging the hem of her blouse. "I need to get to town. I want to run by the bank before they close."

He nodded, his hands dropping to his sides, the heat still burning within. "I need to touch base with Hank while we're there."

"Good. Then let's get going."

At least one of them had the wherewithal to get past the awkwardness Ben had instigated.

"I'll get Lily." Kate dodged past him like a scalded cat and ducked into Lily's room.

"I'll be in the truck," Ben called out, taking the stairs

two at a time. He breezed through the kitchen. "You need a ride back to town, Mrs. Henderson?"

"No. I see Eddy headed this way. I'm sure he'll be wanting to get home and he promised to take me. Don't worry none about locking up. I still have a key." She patted her pocket.

Ben almost frowned, but caught himself. "Are you the only one who has a key besides Ms. Langsdon?"

"As far as I know." Marge's brows furrowed. "Why?"

"Just wondered. I'll make a stop at the hardware store to buy all new locks and keys. Just for safe measure."

She nodded. "Don't want anything bad to happen to those girls."

Ben's jaw tightened. "No, we don't." Whether it was him or one of Hank's other cowboys taking care of her, it wouldn't hurt to change out the locks on the house.

He pulled his truck around the side of the house, got out and grabbed the booster seat from Kate's car, securing it in the backseat of his truck. He tucked his 9 mm pistol into the glove box.

Lily burst through the front door and skipped across the yard, all smiles, her light strawberry-blond curls bouncing around her shoulders. She wore a sundress with a bright yellow-and-white daisy pattern. She was all sunshine and happiness, oblivious to the dangers around her.

That's how a child should be—carefree and happy.

Ben's fingers tightened around the steering wheel, memories threatening to overwhelm him. Scenes in his mind he'd tried so hard to push away.

Kate followed Lily out the door. Her pretty red-blond hair was pulled up in a loose bun at the back of her head.

She wore a pastel yellow sundress and sandals, looking like spring and everything right with the world.

God, he had to get Hank to find someone else to take this job. He wasn't cut out for this. It was too soon. Every time he looked at the mother and daughter, a knife twisted in his gut. Sadly, he feared it was already too late to walk away.

Ben couldn't imagine leaving them to whatever peril the wild Texas landscape, and even wilder men who'd already threatened her, had to offer.

He opened the back door, helped Lily up into the booster seat and buckled the belt across her lap.

"I'm impressed," Kate said as she inspected his work. "You did that like you've done it before."

Ben backed away and rounded the truck, wordlessly, his teeth clenched. He'd buckled Sarah in a hundred times, careful with his precious daughter, wanting to keep her safe in case of a traffic accident. Too bad he hadn't kept her safe from her killer.

Kate climbed up into the passenger seat, her brows puckered. "Did I say something wrong?"

"No." Ben sat behind the wheel, fighting for control. Finally, he shifted the truck into Drive.

Her brow remained puckered as she sat back.

Lily fell asleep in the backseat almost as soon as they hit the highway.

Ben's grip tightened on the wheel, his knuckles turning white. His gaze panned the long stretch of road, looking for any hidden hazards, man-made or in the terrain. As knotted up as he was, he'd exhaust himself before nightfall. He inhaled and let the breath out slowly, willing himself to relax.

When they neared the town of Wild Oak Canyon, he had his control back.

Until Kate spoke, her soft tones warming him inside and out. "I believe the bank is on the next corner."

Ben shook his head. "We're stopping at the sheriff's office first."

CHAPTER SIX

KATE CLIMBED DOWN from the passenger seat before Ben could come around and open her door. He insisted on lifting Lily out of her booster seat. Still sleepy, the child stirred and lay across Ben's shoulder. Her eyelids fluttered, then closed.

The sight of Lily sleeping so peacefully on Ben's shoulder was sweet and disturbing. On the one hand the three of them gave the appearance of being a family. On the other, Ben wasn't a fixed variable in Lily's life. When they figured out what was going on and cleared the threat, Ben would be gone. Lily would wonder what she'd done to chase him off. She might even blame herself. Kate reached out. "I'll take her."

Ben turned away, refusing to give up Lily. "Let her sleep."

It only made sense. Kate wasn't too happy, knowing this was temporary. They'd made the mistake of claiming Ben was her fiancé. In a town the size of Wild Oak Canyon, that little tidbit would already have made its rounds.

Kate led the way into the sheriff's office, determined to take charge of this situation, starting with reporting the biker attack.

Deputy Dwayne Schillinger sat in a chair behind a desk, his feet propped on a stack of paper, his hand curled around a burger. "Well, well. To what do we owe the pleasure of your visit so soon?" The man let his boots drop to the floor with a thump and laid his lunch in the wrapper.

"I want to report another attack on my property and a death threat," Kate said.

"What kind of attack might that be?" Dwayne wiped his hands down the sides of his uniform, leaving a streak of yellow mustard. He finally pushed out of his chair and stood.

"A gang of bikers rode through my yard, attacked Ben and damaged property. As they left, they shouted out a death threat."

"Can you describe the men?"

"They wore bandannas around their faces and they rode motorcycles." Kate's fists clenched. "I think they were Hispanic."

"That's not much to go on. Without more detailed physical descriptions, I can't go out and arrest anyone. You have to do a little better than that."

Kate let out a frustrated huff. "Don't you know the people of this county? There can't be that many and surely you know who owns motorcycles and who doesn't."

Ben stepped up beside Kate and added softly, "One of the men had a tattoo of a snake. It wrapped around his wrist and forearm."

"Now *that* I might be able to do something with. Sounds like Guillermo Ramirez. His friends call him Snake."

A shred of relief rippled through Kate. A name for her attacker was better than nothing. "I suggest you arrest him for trespassing and assault."

"As soon as I can find him. Like his nickname, he's pretty slippery and difficult to track."

Kate fisted her hands on her hips. "I have a child living with me. I don't want this to happen again. Are you going to do your job and track down the man? Or do I need to call in the state police?"

Dwayne patted her arm. "Now, don't get your panties in a wad, young lady. We take our work seriously out here. We'll get right on it."

Kate nodded to the stack of papers on his desk. "Aren't you going to take notes, a statement or anything?"

"Don't need to." He tapped a finger to his temple. "I'll remember."

Kate dragged in a deep breath, closed her eyes and counted to three. "Thank you for caring." She turned and marched toward the door.

As she reached for the knob, the deputy called out, "Wouldn't have to be scared for yourself or your daughter if you weren't living on the Flying K."

Kate spun. "And what's that supposed to mean?"

Deputy Dwayne shrugged. "Nothing good's come of living at the Flying K. Look what happened to your father."

Kate walked back toward the man. "Are you telling me my father didn't die of natural causes like the medical examiner claimed?"

Dwayne's squinty eyes rounded. "No, ma'am. Just saying it ain't a healthy place to raise a family."

"You know something I don't?"

The deputy raised his hands. "No, ma'am. Just saying."

"I suggest you find this Snake guy and arrest him.

That would go a long way toward making the Flying K a healthier place to live." Kate left the building.

Ben followed, chuckling. "Nice."

"I don't need your patronization. I need answers." Kate stomped to the truck and yanked on the handle. Her nail bent back for her effort and the door remained closed. "Dang it!"

"Mommy?" Lily's eyes fluttered open. "Why were you yelling at that man?"

All the starch went out of Kate. "Oh, sweetie. I was just a little disappointed with him." Inside she bit hard on her tongue. "A little disappointed" was a huge understatement.

Ben clicked his key fob and the locks on the truck popped up. "Bank next?" His mouth twitched on the corners.

If Kate wasn't mistaken, the man was fighting a smile.

A shot of anger flared and died as she tried to picture her tirade with the deputy from Ben's view. Okay, so it must have been amusing to the man to see a woman dressed in a sundress and sandals rip into Deputy Dwayne with all his self-importance, attitude and mustard tracking down his shirt. "Smile and I'll serve your teeth on a platter," she warned, her own lips quirking upward. After the tension of the night and early morning, she could use a good laugh, even at her own expense.

"I wouldn't dare." Ben settled Lily in her booster seat and stepped back, allowing Kate to buckle her daughter in.

Her mood a little lighter, Kate climbed into the passenger seat and leaned back. "Not the bank yet. I want to go to the county tax assessor's office. There has to be a mistake about my father's back taxes."

Ben drove the three blocks from the sheriff's office to the county offices. When he pulled up in front of the building, he left the engine running. "I have a call to make. Will you be all right on your own for a few minutes?"

"Hopefully Lily and I will be safe inside the county offices. When we're done there, we'll go next door to the bank. Take your time." Kate climbed out, lifted Lily from her seat and took her hand, entering the cool interior of the county offices.

"Can I help you?" An older woman with gray hair and a pair of glasses perched on the end of her nose smiled a greeting.

"I hope you can." Kate pulled the letter from her purse and laid it on the counter. "I need information on the Flying K Ranch and any taxes owed on the place."

The woman grimaced. "Ma'am, I'm sorry but the computer is down and has been for two days now. The technician hasn't been able to fix it and we're waiting on someone from state to help." She pushed a form toward Kate. "If you'd like to fill out this form and leave it with me, I'll check the records as soon as I have access."

Kate sighed. "Thanks." While Lily stood patiently beside her, Kate filled out the form, then showed the woman her driver's license and a copy of the deed to the ranch as proof of ownership.

"Do you know when they'll have the system back up?"

"Not a clue. Check back tomorrow. Hopefully it'll be up then."

"Thank you." Kate left, Lily's hand clasped in hers,

no less tense than when she'd entered the building a
few minutes earlier. No use obsessing over a downed
computer; she had only thirty days to come up with
the cash, should she need it. No time like the present
to see what the bank could do for her. She entered the
cool, brightly lit bank lobby, her shoulders back, a smile
pasted on her face.

ONCE THE TWO GIRLS were out of the truck, Ben glanced at
his cell phone. Two bars. *Here's hoping.* His cell phone
had been such a big part of his life in Austin. Out here
in South Texas, he was lucky to use it at all.

He hit the speed dial for Hank Derringer and held his
breath, not letting it out until the device sent a ringing
sound back to him.

"Howdy, Ben," Hank answered.

"We need to talk."

"I take it you've met Kate?"

"I have." He inhaled and let out the breath before
jumping in. "I need you to reassign me."

A long pause met his request.

"Did you hear me?" Ben prompted.

"I did. Only I've already assigned the other three
members of CCI to cases." Hank cleared his throat and
continued, "Is something wrong with Kate?"

"No. It's just that I'm not the right man for this particular job."

"I have full confidence in your abilities. I didn't
choose you for this case by acci—"

"You didn't tell me she had a child." Ben cut him off,
not wanting to hear Hank's arguments.

"Ah." That one word said it all.

"I'm not cut out to play bodyguard to this woman

and her little girl. You need someone who…that… Well, damn. Get someone else."

"This has to do with Julia and Sarah, doesn't it?" Hank asked softly.

It was Ben's turn to leave dead air between the two of them. He swallowed hard on the giant lump clogging his throat before he could croak out his answer. "Yeah."

"Look, Ben, it was exactly the reason I hired you for this job. You have more of a stake in this case, more of an understanding of what's at risk, than anyone else on the team. I picked the right man."

"I can't do it."

"Yes. You can." Hank's voice softened even more. "I heard about the intruder last night and about the biker gang attack this morning. I wish I could send someone else to help you, but I just don't have the resources yet."

Ben snorted. "Good news travels fast, doesn't it?"

"What can I say? It's a small town and I have a few friends."

"In the meantime I'm stuck, is that what you're telling me?"

"You've met Kate and Lily. You've seen a little of what they're up against. At this point, could you really walk away?" Hank left a pregnant pause for Ben to respond. When he didn't, Hank went on, "I stand by my decision. I think you're the right man for the job."

"So it's take this one or resign?"

"You're not the kind of man to resign, if I read your dossier right."

Damn the man. He'd done his homework. He knew Ben more than Ben knew, or would admit to knowing, himself.

"Is that all you have?" Hank asked.

"No, can you use your connections to run a background check on Larry Sites and Guillermo Ramirez?"

"Had a check done on Larry Sites when the man disappeared after Kendrick's death. Newspapers reported that he was suspected of Kendrick's murder, that he's wanted for questioning. Otherwise, he didn't have an arrest record."

"Know anything about Ramirez? The man has a snake tattoo on his arm. He seemed to be the leader of the biker gang attack."

"I'll get an official background check on him, but from what I know, he's a thug for hire. It's rumored he works for whatever cartel will pay him the most. He's walking a thin line doing that. I'm surprised someone hasn't put a bullet in him yet. Part of it has to do with his ability to disappear. We suspect he slides across the border when it's hot on this side."

"Nice." Ben's fingers tightened on the cell phone. Kate was in a lot more trouble than just a biker gang harassing her. "Let me know when you find my replacement. Until then, I'll do the best I can."

"Thanks, Ben. Kate and Lily need you out there." Hank clicked off.

Ben sat for a long moment, staring at the street, heat waves rising from the asphalt, making mirages rise up before his eyes in wavering images of his dead wife and child.

Maybe it was the heat waves, maybe it was the tears. Ben blinked and Julia and Sarah disappeared.

He fought the urge to step on the accelerator and drive. Out of town, away from this job, from Kate and Lily. Hell, out of Texas altogether.

Instead he placed another call while he still had reception.

"Jenkins speaking."

Ben immediately recognized the voice on the other end of the connection as Detective Jenkins of the Austin Police Department. "Jenkins, Ben Harding here. I need some help."

"Ben? Is that you?" Jenkins pitched his voice low, almost to a whisper. "Man, where are you? As far as anyone knows you fell off the face of the earth."

"I'm in South Texas near a little town called Wild Oak Canyon."

Jenkins chuckled. "I guess it's true, then. You did fall off the face of the earth. What can I do for you?"

Ben jumped in. "Who's handling my case?"

"Man, you know I'm not at liberty—"

"Damn it, Jim. Who's handling it?"

Jenkins sighed. "Masters was assigned after you left."

"Anything new?"

"Not much. I think Masters tracked down the man who supplied the girls to Frank Davis. We don't have much, other than hearsay, so we haven't made an arrest yet."

"Girls?" All he knew about was the one Davis had killed.

"Apparently Davis was more deviant than originally suspected."

Ben's hand tightened around the cell phone. He wanted to kill Davis all over again. "Who was the supplier?" he asked through clenched teeth.

"You know I can't give you that kind of information. You're not on the force anymore."

Ben slammed his palm against the steering wheel. "When did you start following all the rules?"

"When you got fired." His tone was flat, final. "Why do you want to know?"

"I killed a man for killing a girl. I want to know it wasn't in vain. From the sound of it there are more women and girls being trafficked."

The silence on the other end indicated he'd gotten his friend's attention.

"Who supplied the girls to Davis? If they are victims of a human trafficking ring, it has to stop."

"I don't like going against department rules."

"Lives could depend on this." Ben's hand tightened on the receiver as he waited for his friend's response.

"Look, we know that. Masters is working the case."

"So let me help. What's it going to hurt?"

"You, me… I don't know, but I don't like playing both sides of the law."

"I'm no rogue and I doubt I could get into much trouble way down south where I am, but if there's any way I can help, I will."

After a long pause, Jenkins said, "His name is Rolando Gonzalez. He's here in Austin, but we suspect he has connections to the Mexican Mafia. As a matter of fact, he's got family in South Texas. Let me pull the file and get back with you. If you could do some looking around while you're down there, we might get more on him and who he's working for. Just don't do anything stupid."

Like killing him before they could get information out of him? Ben knew he'd gone beyond his limit on Davis. Seeing that girl lying on that cot, beaten, bleeding and past help… Ben stared out the window, his heart racing as if he was there all over again.

A movement on his right jerked him back to the present.

Kate and Lily exited the county tax assessor's office, waved at him and walked next door to the bank. If Hank got him off this case with Kate, he would have time to check out the lead Jenkins was talking about.

"I don't get reception out on the ranch where I'm working, so leave a message on my cell. If it's urgent, contact Hank Derringer." Ben left Hank's number with Jenkins. "I'll be waiting for that information."

"Will do. And Harding…stay safe. If this is as big as I think it is, you don't want to get caught in the cross fire of the Mexican Mafia."

Hell, he couldn't afford to get in the middle of the Mafia, not when he had Kate and Lily to protect. He'd wait to make any inquiries until Hank found a replacement.

"I NEED TO take out an equity loan on my father's—my ranch and open a three-thousand-dollar line of credit until I can withdraw money from a CD I set up for Lily's college." Kate leaned forward, her anger building with each time Art Manning tapped his pen to the loan application form in front of him.

"I'm sorry, Ms. Kendrick."

"Langsdon."

"Ms. Langsdon. I'll have to perform a complete credit check on you and have our corporate underwriters approve this before I can give you an answer. In the meantime I suggest you open an account here. We can't loan money to anyone who is not a current client of our bank."

"I see." Kate stood. In the meantime, she was running low on cash and she needed money to pay Eddy and Ms. Henderson's salaries, not to mention putting food on the table and all the deposits she'd needed to get the electricity and gas switched over to her name.

"While your underwriters are thinking about it, I'll be thinking about whether or not to open an account." She gathered Lily's hand in hers.

"Ms. Kendrick."

"Langsdon."

"Without a job and a current income, I doubt the underwriters will take your application seriously."

"The land isn't enough collateral to secure a mortgage?"

"Not given the history of that particular parcel and its location."

"You mean I won't be able to get a loan?"

He shook his head. "I doubt it."

Kate breathed in and let it out before speaking again. "Thank you for your time, Mr. Manning."

She headed for the door, ready to be out in the heat, away from the stuffy air-conditioned atmosphere of the bank building.

"You look like your father." The voice belonged to a businessman dressed in a tailored suit leaning against the stand containing blank deposit slips.

Kate's steps faltered and she glanced at the man, her eyes narrowing. "Seems to be the consensus. If you'll excuse me…" Impatient and tired after a sleepless night and the fright of the morning, Kate had no intention of stopping to chat and she veered to the side.

The stranger stepped out, blocking her path to the

exit. He stuck out his hand. "I'm Robert Sanders. Your father and I were friends."

To avoid being outright rude, Kate clasped the man's hand and shook it briefly. "Nice to meet you, Mr. Sanders. I'm Kate."

"Kate Langsdon." He held on to her hand longer than Kate wanted, then let go. "You have his eyes."

"I thought the hair was the dead giveaway."

"Your father's hair was much darker." Sanders raised a hand to touch one of Kate's curls.

She backed away.

The man's hand fell to his side. "But the green eyes are unmistakably his. I believe your mother had blue eyes, did she not?"

His comment took the wind out of Kate's sails. "You knew my mother?" So far, no one in town had mentioned her mother. Most people she'd run across in Wild Oak Canyon mentioned Kyle Kendrick, but not her mother, as though she'd never been there.

"No, but your father had a picture of his ex-wife on his desk. You don't look much like her at all."

That made Kate smile and her gut twist at the same time. "My mother always said I was a constant reminder of my father."

"Your mother must have been a very special woman. Your father never married after she left."

A spike of anger flared in Kate's gut. She'd loved her mother until the day she'd died. But if she had one regret in her relationship, it was that her mother had chosen to lie to her about her father, claiming he was dead, instead of alive and available if she'd wanted to meet him.

Kate suddenly felt stifled in the bank. "If you'll pardon me." She wanted out. Knowing Ben was waiting made her all the more anxious to leave, ready to get back to safe territory.

That thought gave her pause.

Damn.

After only one day, she'd come to rely on the strength and presence of Ben. If things didn't get better soon, she ran the risk of becoming too dependent on him.

Since her husband's death, Kate had been hesitant to date, unwilling to drag her daughter through relationships that wouldn't last. Not many men wanted to date a woman with a ready-made family.

Not that she wanted to date Ben. But the close proximity of a bodyguard could lead to the same outcome. Lily could become attached.

As she stepped around Mr. Sanders, the man handed her his business card. "I feel somewhat responsible for the well-being of my friend's daughter." When she didn't take his card, he lifted her hand, laid the card in it and curled her fingers around the paper. "Please, if there is anything I can do, don't hesitate to call."

Kate clutched the card. "Thank you." When she turned to leave, his hand caught her elbow.

"If you don't mind, I'd like to visit the ranch and make sure you're doing okay out there all alone."

"That won't be necessary."

"I insist."

"I'm not alone. I have my…fiancé staying with me. I'm quite all right."

Sanders's eyes narrowed fractionally, then his brows rose. "So, wedding bells are in the near future for you, are they?" He grasped her hands again. "Congratulations, my dear. I'm so happy for you."

Kate pulled free of Mr. Sanders's grip. "Thank you."

She snatched Lily's little hand and turned away, hating the lies she was telling this town, but feeling more comfortable with the fact that Ben's presence would keep her safe. At least it might make others think before they set foot on her property. The more the people of the county thought a man lived there full-time, the better off she was. A lone woman on a ranch could be considered a target. Especially a ranch in cartel territory.

Houston was looking better every minute. But Kate had come too far to turn back now. She wanted to find out why her father had died. If he hadn't died of natural causes, Kate wanted to know who had killed him and why.

BEN HAD HIS hand on the gearshift ready to pull away from Wild Oak Canyon, to start a new life…elsewhere. As he flexed his arm to move the gear, Kate pushed through the glass doors, leading Lily by the hand, a troubled expression on her face.

Instead of driving away, Ben found himself climbing down and opening the rear passenger door before Kate reached the vehicle. The slump in her shoulders and the dullness in her eyes plucked at his heartstrings more than he cared to admit. "I take it that meeting didn't go well."

"County computers are down until further notice, so I struck out there."

Ben lifted Lily into her seat and buckled her belt. "We can come back tomorrow."

"Then the bank…" Kate stepped on the running board and slid into the passenger seat. "I only asked for a home equity loan to help me catch up in case I owed back taxes, and a line of credit loan to last me long enough so that I can sort through my father's will and cash in some

TRIGGERED

certificates of deposit I have set aside for Lily's college fund." She snorted. "You'd think I'd gone in there asking for a fortune."

Ben didn't trust himself to comment. His insides churned. He didn't want to admit to Kate how close he'd been to leaving her and Lily in Wild Oak Canyon. What kind of coward left a woman and her child to fend for themselves?

Once they were all in the truck and belted, Ben rounded the truck and climbed into the driver's seat.

Kate sighed. "I guess the only good thing out of those two stops is this." She held up a business card. "This Robert Sanders claimed he was a friend of my father's and gave me his card in case I needed anything."

Ben reached for the card. "Let me see that."

Kate handed it over. "Looks legit."

Robert Sanders of Sanders Homes. Real Estate Broker and Construction.

Ben turned the card over, then handed it back to Kate. "Let me have Hank check him out before you get too chummy."

Kate nodded and slid the card into her purse.

Ben would keep an eye out for Sanders. If he really was a friend of Kyle Kendrick, he shouldn't be a threat to Kate. But then Kyle's place hadn't been broken into. He'd known his attacker.

Ben shifted into gear and pulled out onto the road.

"I need to stop at the hardware and feed stores for the things Eddy wanted me to get." Kate pulled a sheet of notepaper from her purse. "He handed it to me on the way out of the house." She glanced over her shoulder at Lily. "Then we can go to the diner and have supper. Would you like that, Lily?"

Lily's eyes widened, a smile lighting her face. "Do they have milk shakes?"

Kate let her daughter's happiness wash over her and she smiled back. "I don't know, but we'll find out."

"Can I have a chocolate milk shake?" Lily's feet bounced on the seat back.

Ben laughed. "We'll see when we get there."

In less than an hour, they had what they needed loaded into the back of the truck.

"Guess it's a good thing *you* drove today. I haven't had the chance to go through my father's barn and see if he had a truck. This ranching thing is all new to me."

"I can help you there."

"I thought you were a bodyguard. Were you a cowboy in your former life?"

"I grew up on a ranch." He'd loved living on a ranch, riding horses and raising cattle. But his family didn't own the ranch. Once his father's health declined to the point he could no longer handle the hard work, they'd moved to Austin where both his parents died in a multicar pileup on the interstate the week after Ben graduated from college.

"So is it true, once a cowboy, always a cowboy?" Kate's question pulled Ben back to the present.

He wasn't looking at her, but he could feel Kate's direct stare, and it made him uncomfortable. Why did she have to ask so many dad-burned questions?

He didn't respond with anything more than a shrug.

Her lips twisted. "Nice to know. You must be a man of many talents. Anything else you'd like to share with me?"

"No." Ben pulled into the parking lot of Cara Jo's Diner. The timing couldn't have been better. He shouldn't have shared anything about his existence before Kate. None of that existed anymore. Not his parents, not his wife and child and not his work as an Austin police officer.

His slate was clean. What he did with his life now was the only thing he could do.

Start over.

A pretty young woman wielding a broom swept the sidewalk in front of the diner and smiled brightly when Ben stepped from the truck. She stopped to reach into a big cardboard box. When she straightened, there was a round-bellied puppy in her arms. "Howdy. I don't suppose ya'll want a puppy."

Kate had just set Lily on her feet and reached back into the truck to retrieve her purse, a hand holding on to the child's.

Lily wiggled free of Kate's grip, squealed and ran for the box. When she tried to step up on the curb, her sandal caught and she tripped, her little body slamming into the sidewalk.

Before Kate could reach her, Lily raised her arms for Ben to pick her up, tears streaming from her eyes.

Ben gathered her in his arms and cradled her. When he glanced up, his gut clenched at the paleness of Kate's face. He tried to pry the little girl's arms from around his neck, but she wouldn't let go. "Don't you want your mama?"

Lily buried her face in his shirt. "No, I want you."

CHAPTER SEVEN

LILY'S KNEES AND HANDS were scraped and bleeding. Her big emerald-green eyes filled with tears. "Am I gonna die?"

Ben smiled down at Lily. "No, baby, you'll be just fine."

Kate's heart skipped a few beats. A pang of jealousy tugged at her. But more than that, her chest tightened at how quickly Lily had assimilated Ben into her life. When he left, he'd leave a hole in her daughter's world that Lily wouldn't understand. She wouldn't be fine.

"Let's get her inside." The woman with the broom set the puppy down in the box and leaned her broom against the wall. "I have a first aid kit in the kitchen."

As Ben stepped into the diner, Lily practically crawled over his shoulder. "I want to see the puppies," she cried.

Kate followed Ben. "After we clean up your boo-boos, sweetheart, you can see the puppies."

"Can I hold one?" She sniffled and rubbed her arm over her nose.

Kate handed Lily a tissue from her purse. "If the nice lady says you can."

The broom lady chuckled. "My name's Cara Jo Smithson. And yes, you can hold one."

Lily grinned, her tears disappearing.

"So you're *the* Cara Jo?" Ben asked. "You're not what I expected as the owner."

Cara Jo laughed and batted her eyes. "I hope you mean that in a good way." The diner owner glanced over her shoulder at Ben, her footsteps slowing.

Kate had a sudden urge to scratch Cara Jo's eyes out for flirting with Ben. Then she had to remind herself the engagement was just a big fib. She had no hold on Ben and no right to be jealous if he flirted with the stunning Cara Jo. "The first aid kit?" Kate prompted.

"Oh, yes. This way." The woman marched to the back of the dining room and through a swinging door. Cara Jo held the door for Ben, Lily and Kate. "The washroom is at the rear of the kitchen. The first aid kit is in there under the sink."

Kate assumed the lead, stepping past shiny stainless-steel preparation tables and a huge gas stove.

"Let's get you fixed up." Cara Jo eased past Kate and Ben and entered the employee washroom, where she reached beneath a counter for a large, red plastic container with a big Red Cross sticker plastered to the top.

Ben set Lily on the countertop.

Kate moved to stand beside Ben, her hip so close it rubbed against his. A shot of awareness winged through her and she almost pulled away.

Cara Jo pulled bandages, sterile gauze and an accordion of alcohol prep pads from the kit, handing them to Kate.

While Kate dressed Lily's wounds, Ben distracted the child. He smoothed the red-gold curls out of Lily's face. "How many puppies do you have in that box, Cara Jo?"

Kate smiled, glad Ben's words captured Lily's attention, drawing it away from what Kate was doing.

"There are five, but one is already spoken for."

"What breed are they?"

Cara Jo laughed. "Purebred mutts, as far as I can tell." She opened an alcohol pad and handed it to Kate. "The vet seems to think they're a mix between Australian shepherd and border collie. All I know is that they're fuzzy and cute as can be. I'm having a hard time letting them go. But one dog in the family is enough when I'm working so much here at the diner."

Kate wiped the alcohol pad across Lily's skinned knees.

Lily grimaced and reached for the knee. "Ouch."

Ben caught her hand before she could touch the cleaned wound. "You're doing so well, Lily. I didn't know you were such a big girl. So far, not a single tear."

"Big girls don't cry, do they, Mommy?" Lily darted a look at Kate.

Kate could feel the next sentence coming before her daughter even said it.

"Big girls can take care of puppies, can't they?" Lily's eyes rounded, her head tipping up and down.

Kate's brows furrowed. "I don't know. Puppies are a lot of work. Someone has to feed them every day and take them outside a lot until they learn to go out on their own."

"I can do that." Lily's eyes widened, her bottom lip pouting outward, just a little. "Can I have a puppy, Mommy? Please."

"You just found a kitten. Isn't a kitten enough?" Kate couldn't resist her daughter's sad puppy look. And now that they lived on a ranch, not in an apartment in Houston, she had no excuse. A puppy was a definite possibility. Still, it meant committing fully to living in Wild

Oak Canyon. A puppy in a Houston apartment wouldn't work for Kate or the puppy.

"Let Mommy think about it, Lily," Ben said.

"Ben's right." Kate could have kissed Ben, the thought strangely appealing, more so than she wanted to admit. "I need to think about it."

Lily slumped.

"Hey, why the sad face?" Ben chucked a finger beneath her chin. "She didn't say no."

Teardrops shimmered on Lily's eyelashes. "She didn't say yes."

Kate shook her head, smiling. "I want to think about it."

"They'll be ready to wean from their mother any day now," Cara Jo added. "I hope they all have a home soon."

"Based on the one you were holding up before Lily fell, I'm sure they'll be snatched up," Ben said.

A bell jingled from the dining area. "If you two can handle this, I've got a customer. By the way, my special this evening is meat loaf and mashed potatoes, if you plan on staying for dinner."

"We can handle it from here," Ben reassured her. "And yes, we're staying for dinner."

Alone with Ben and Lily in the washroom, Kate's body tingled at the man's nearness. Heck, his broad shoulders practically filled the small space and his strong, capable hands dwarfed hers as he held her daughter.

Fingers fumbling, Kate applied a bandage to the sore knee, then bent and kissed the covered injury. "There, all better."

"Not quite." Ben pulled the rubber band from Lily's ponytail that had been hanging drunkenly to one side.

Strands of silky golden-red curls fell loose about her shoulders. "Can't let this brave young lady walk out of here with a lopsided pony." Carefully, he bunched the hair into his hand, smoothing all the lumps, and secured it again in the band.

Kate's breath caught and held throughout the process. Clearly, the man had done this before. She didn't know anything about Ben. For all she knew, he could be married with a little girl of his own. A family he'd soon go home to.

Her stomach flip-flopped, a sense of impending loss leaving an empty space inside. How could this be? The man was nothing more than a hired gun, a bodyguard to protect her. He'd only been around for a day.

Kate had never believed in love at first sight. Not that what she was feeling was anything like love. Respect, maybe. The man was strong, self-assured and handy to have around in a fight...or fixing a little girl's hair. That pretty much summed up her knowledge of Ben Harding. That, and he'd been a first responder for the Austin Police Department in his past life. What had made him leave to go work for Hank Derringer as a bodyguard for hire? The little bits of information she'd gleaned from the quiet man only made Kate want to learn more.

"Come on." Ben swung Lily up in his arms. "If it's all right with your mother, we'll go see those puppies now."

"I was thinking dinner would be a good idea."

The disappointment on Lily's face made Kate reconsider. "Okay, but only for a few minutes. I'll order our food while you two play with the puppies." She raised questioning brows at Ben. "Anything you'd like in particular?"

For a long moment, he stared down at her, with Lily

perched on his arm. His blue eyes smoldered, his gaze lowering to somewhere south of Kate's nose.

Her pulse quickened, her mouth going dry. Kate ran her tongue across suddenly parched lips. "Food…what kind of food would you like?"

His mouth twitched. "Cara Jo's mention of meat loaf and mashed potatoes sounded great. I haven't had meat loaf in a long time."

"Meat loaf it is." Kate couldn't get out of the washroom fast enough. Heat suffused her entire body at the thought of Ben's full lips, that blue-eyed gaze bearing down on her, reminding her she was more than just a mother. She was a young woman with needs and physical desires she'd thought long gone with the death of her husband.

In an attempt to get her ragged breathing under control, Kate sat at one of the empty booths and waited for Ben and Lily to step outside before she dared follow them with her gaze.

"You're one lucky lady." Cara Jo stood at her elbow, a pad and paper in her hand.

"How so?" Kate wasn't feeling so lucky. At the moment, she felt trapped by her own raging hormones and latent desires.

Cara Jo spread her hands, palms up. "Why, your husband, of course."

"Fiancé," Kate corrected.

Cara Jo glanced out the big window at Ben squatting beside the box, handing Lily a puppy. "That man's hot, and he's really good with your daughter."

Kate's gaze followed Cara Jo's. "Yes, he is." Too good with her daughter and too handsome for Kate's own good.

"Let me know if you ever decide to give him up."

"Why?"

"He's just the kind of guy I'm looking for."

Kate's teeth ground together and she fought to keep from saying something stupid like *he's mine, keep your greedy hands off him.* Once again, she had to remind herself that she had no claim on Ben and that he wasn't even her fiancé. "You'll be the first to know," she said through tight lips.

Cara Jo laughed. "Lighten up. I'm not going to steal your man. He's in love with you, not me."

If only.

Kate's eyes widened and she almost jumped up from the table and ran. What the hell was she thinking? Ben wasn't her man. They'd only known each other for a day. He didn't—couldn't—love her and she'd better get such crazy thoughts from her head before she did something even more stupid, like falling for the big guy.

"Are you ordering for yourself or your family?"

"All of us." Kate had let the family comment slip right by so easily without trying to correct Cara Jo. At this point, she couldn't retract the lie without backtracking with the sheriff's office and anyone else who'd spread the rumor.

"So you're the folks who've moved onto the Flying K Ranch? I'm glad."

Kate's gaze shot to Cara Jo's. "You are? Why?"

Cara Jo shrugged with the hint of a smile. "Gets kinda lonesome out here in the middle of nowhere. There's not nearly enough women our age to talk to." Cara Jo's smile widened. "A girl could always use a friend."

Kate's eyes misted. "Thanks. I was feeling a bit overwhelmed by the acres of land between me and my nearest neighbor."

Cara Jo's sunny face darkened. "I hear you had some trouble out your way."

"Someone broke into the house the first night I was there."

"And what's this I heard about a motorcycle gang tearing through your yard?" Cara Jo shook her head. "What's with people? It's as though they're trying to scare you off or something."

"I'm getting that feeling, too. I just don't know why." Kate tipped her head to the side. "Did you know my father?"

"A little. He stopped by the diner for supper occasionally." Cara Jo gazed into Kate's eyes. "You have his eyes. I remember them being a pretty shade of green."

"So people say. I wouldn't know." Kate glanced toward Ben and Lily. "I never met the man."

"Really?" Cara Jo's pretty brow furrowed. "I think he traveled a lot. He never said much when he came in, but he was always polite and tipped well. He had a great smile, but apparently he didn't talk to anyone else about his life or what he was up to on the Flying K. He was a recluse."

"I wonder why he didn't get to know his neighbors."

Cara Jo leaned closer. "Some say he was involved in the Mexican Mafia. I'm usually a good judge of character. I didn't see it in him."

"I wish I'd had the chance to get to know him." Her comment was no more than a whisper.

Cara Jo's frown deepened. "Yeah and if wishes were horses..."

"...beggars would ride," Kate finished.

The diner owner bent toward Kate and hugged her with her free arm. When she straightened, she swiped at moisture in her eyes and laughed. "Hey, what say we do lunch sometime?"

Warmth washed over Kate. Nobody in Houston had volunteered to be her friend. Rarely had she gone out to lunch with anyone other than Lily.

She'd been casual acquaintances with her coworkers at the hobby store where she'd been employed. Scraping out an existence for her and Lily on what little she made and the money from her husband's life insurance became an exhausting job. Spare time was spent with her daughter, going to the parks and zoo.

"I'd love to do lunch." Kate smiled up at Cara Jo. "Maybe you'd like to get out of town and come visit the ranch? I can make a mean grilled cheese sandwich." Kate glanced around the diner. "I'm not a grand cook."

Cara Jo snorted. "And you think I am? I have the usual. If I change things up, I get complaints. People can be such creatures of habit."

"Cara Jo," a gray-haired older man called out from a booth on the other side of the entrance.

"I'll be right with you." Cara Jo grinned. "Don't be surprised if I show up on your doorstep real soon. In the meantime, what's your poison?"

Kate gave her new friend their order and sat back, admiring the tall, curvy young blonde's happy efficiency at handling her customers.

A squeal from outside drew Kate's attention.

Lily squatted on the wooden planks of the front porch, reaching out to a rambunctious black-and-white pup that nipped at her fingers. She jerked her hand away from the dog's sharp teeth and giggled.

Ben sat back on his haunches, smiling at the child. Every once in a while, his smile dimmed and his gaze grew somber.

Kate sat forward, studying the man.

The bodyguard had dark wavy hair hanging down to his collar. His square chin and lean, muscular body spoke of strength and discipline. But those smoky-blue, brooding eyes held too many shadows. Someone or something had hurt this man.

Kate closed her eyes and told herself she didn't want to know who and what had caused him so much pain. She couldn't keep them closed long. Lily squealed again and Ben's rich laughter made her want to go outside and join them.

"You should go see the puppies. They're too cute to miss." Cara Jo was at her side again. The diner owner set three glasses of ice water on the table and utensils wrapped in bright red cloth napkins. "Your food won't be ready for a few minutes. Go on before I do. That man is too yummy to be left alone long."

"No, I'll just wait here." Kate was already too aware of the man and the magnetism that pulled at her.

Lily giggled again, making Kate's heart leap.

"Have it your way, but those puppies will steal your heart." Cara Jo walked away to tend to another customer.

Lily squealed again, and Ben's laughter followed. Unable to resist, Kate rose from the booth seat and pushed through the front door out onto the porch. "Okay, you two are having entirely too much fun. Let's see what you've got."

Ben grinned up at her, the shadows gone from his eyes. "I think Pickles is her favorite."

"And which one is Pickles?" Kate dropped down on her knees and peered into the large cardboard box.

Five fluff balls growled in their puppy voices while tearing at a stuffed toy that had seen better days. Each puppy had its own unique coloring. Three were the mottled gray, white, black and red of the Australian shepherd. Two were black-and-white like a border collie.

In the corner closest to where Lily stood, one of the black-and-white pups leaped against the side of the box.

"Look, Mommy, Pickles has pretty blue eyes." She dangled her hand in the box and Pickles snapped at it, his high-pitched bark playful.

Lily laughed and hid her hand behind her back, looking up at Kate with shining eyes. "Can we take him home? Please, Mommy."

Kate lifted the puppy from the box and held him in the air. The gyrating ball of fur wiggled its way out of her hand. Kate caught Pickles before he hit the ground, her heart lodged in her chest. "You are a mess, little fellow."

"No, he's not. He's happy you picked him." Lily pointed at Pickles's long black tail tipped with white. "See, he's wagging his tail."

Kate held the puppy up to her face. The little fellow licked the air, trying to get her nose, making her laugh at his persistent attempts.

Raised by her mother in a small condo in the city, she'd never been allowed to have a pet. No one was home to take care of it for hours and her mother thought it was unfair to animals to be left alone for so long. That and they could barely afford to put food on their table, much less buy food for a dog.

Kate hugged the puppy to her chest. Closing her eyes,

she inhaled the unique scent of puppy fur and puppy breath. The defenseless pup reminded her of a time when she held Lily in her arms, alone in the maternity ward. She'd clung to her baby, after the miracle of her birth, realizing Lily was the only person she had left to love in her world.

Tears welled in her eyes and she blinked to keep them from falling. When she looked up, her gaze met Ben's.

All the pain of her own loneliness shone back to her like a mirror in his eyes.

Ben stood, his jaw tightening until a muscle jerked on one side of his face. "I'll wait in the truck."

Her heart squeezing in her chest, Kate asked, "What about supper?"

"I'm not hungry," he called out without looking back.

CHAPTER EIGHT

BEN WALKED AWAY. He would have run if he thought it would help. But no matter how far he ran, he couldn't escape the image of Kate staring at him through tear-soaked eyes.

As he dropped down off the porch, the sound of Lily's voice reached out to him, slamming another bullet into his heart. Sarah had been that enthusiastic, filled with a beautiful love of life. His daughter had been the joy of his existence.

For a few short minutes, he'd let Lily into his heart, laughing for the first time in two years. Letting her happiness revive his dead heart. Guilt swamped him, dragging him into that bottomless pit he'd crawled into after he'd discovered his wife and daughter murdered in their home.

How could he let another little girl fill that void?

And Kate's tears had touched him like nothing else since Sarah's death. He shouldn't be having these feelings. He'd lost his chance at love. He'd squandered it by not being there to protect them. Instead he'd been chasing his career as a cop, fighting to keep criminals off the street.

Ben jumped into his truck and slammed his door, then he hit the steering wheel with his palm so hard, pain reverberated through his hand and up into his arm. He welcomed it, using it to refocus on why he was there.

He had to regain his self-control or risk the lives of the people he was there to protect. No matter what, he couldn't let Kate and Lily suffer the same fate as his family.

"YOUR DINNER IS READY." Cara Jo appeared in the doorway. Her smile turned into a frown. "Where'd Ben go?"

"He's waiting in the truck. I'm sorry. We're a little tired from all the excitement last night and this morning. Could we get the meal to go?"

"Absolutely. Give me a minute and I'll bring it out."

Kate returned the puppy to the box and then fished in her purse for her wallet, extracting enough cash to pay Cara Jo for the food and a tip. "I don't need any change."

"Honey, consider it my gift to the new girl in town."

"I insist. This is your livelihood." Kate placed the money in Cara Jo's hand and closed her fingers around it. "Please."

Perhaps the other woman saw the moisture in Kate's eyes, because she didn't press the issue. "Okay. Give me a minute."

A couple minutes later, she returned with a bag filled with take-out boxes. The heady scent of hot food wafted beneath Kate's nose and her belly growled. "Thank you. And please, come out whenever you'd like."

Lily stared down into the box, her lip trembling. "Can we take him home?" She looked up at Kate, pressing her hands together like she was praying.

"Not today, sweetie. Pickles has to stay with his mommy for a few more days."

"Then can we bring him home?"

"If he's not one of the puppies Ms. Cara Jo has promised to someone else."

Lily's gaze shifted to Cara Jo. "Can I have that one?" She pointed to Pickles, who'd resumed jumping against the side of the box, barking at Lily.

Cara Jo smiled. "You're in luck. He's still available."

Lily squealed and jumped up and down.

Anxious to leave and find out what had made Ben depart so abruptly, Kate reached out and hugged Cara Jo. "Thanks for everything. I look forward to seeing you soon."

Cara Jo patted her back. "Let me know if I need to bring my shotgun out with me. You stay safe."

Kate slid her purse strap up over her shoulder. One hand held on to the bag of food while the other grabbed Lily's little fingers. "Come on, it's time to go home."

Ben stood beside the truck, his head bent, his hat tipped low, shading his eyes.

As soon as she stepped off the porch, he opened the back door and swung Lily up into her booster seat, buckling her in place. Wordlessly, he took the bag from Kate and settled it on the back floorboard, out of range of Lily's swinging legs.

Kate climbed into the front passenger seat and closed the door, unsure how to broach the subject of his sudden retreat.

When Ben slid in behind the wheel, he didn't look at her; instead he backed away from the diner and headed out of town on the highway leading to the Flying K Ranch.

"Just so you know, I asked Hank to find a replacement for me." His soft-spoken words took a moment to register.

When they did, Kate's head jerked toward him, her heart hitting the bottom of her stomach. "Why?"

"I'm not the right man for this job."

After the craziness of the day, the invasion of her home by a faceless man and the biker gang threats, Ben's announcement scared her the most. Tremors rippled through her body. A chill that had nothing to do with the truck's air-conditioning wrapped around her and she shook uncontrollably. Keeping her voice as even as possible, she remarked in a tone she hoped sounded unconcerned, "You've done pretty darned good so far."

"Nevertheless, when he's got someone else lined up, I'll be leaving."

What could she say to that? Her logical left brain said to leave it, nothing she could say would convince him to stay if he really wanted to go.

Her emotional right brain urged her to beg him to stay. He'd saved her more than once and she trusted him to do it again.

Instead, she whispered into the darkness, "Why did you walk away from Lily, me and the puppies?"

At first she didn't think he'd heard her and she let it go. Maybe she didn't want to know after all. What if he answered that he didn't like children or that he didn't like her? Nothing made sense. The way he'd been so happy and laughing with Lily led Kate to believe he liked children.

"I couldn't handle it." Ben's words broke through the frigid darkness.

Her heart already strained from his announcement that he'd be leaving; Kate wanted to know more than he was giving her. First she glanced over her shoulder at Lily.

Her baby's head dipped toward her chest, her eyes closed, chest rising and falling in deep, even breaths. Blessedly asleep, unaware of Ben's announcement that he'd be leaving.

Anger cleared Kate's head and forced her to sit up straighter. "Just what is it that you couldn't handle? Is it the constant threats out at the ranch?"

He didn't answer, ratcheting up Kate's annoyance with him for his vagueness and her desire to get to the bottom of the issues.

"Is it me? Am I too demanding?"

He shot a glance at her. "No, it's not you."

"Does Lily have you running scared? I can see that. Most four-year-old children terrify me. Especially ones who idolize me and dog my every step."

Ben's lips curled on the corners in a hint of a smile that never reached his eyes. The light from the dash didn't reflect in their dark depths. "No, Lily is a beautiful little girl."

Kate sucked in a deep breath and let it out between clenched teeth. "If it's not the situation and it's not me or Lily, what the hell had you running?"

Another long pause lasted a couple miles.

Kate turned away from Ben and stared out at the darkness. Only she couldn't see past the glass reflecting her image and Ben's behind her.

The man stared straight ahead, his eyes smoky dark, the shadows beneath them deep and disturbing.

"I lost people I loved." His voice was agonizingly deep, and the words spoken so softly Kate thought she'd imagined it.

She turned toward him, studying his face. Had he spoken or had she imagined the words?

His hands gripped the steering wheel so tightly his knuckles had turned white. That and a tick in his jaw were the only indications of something going on more than him driving the truck.

"Who did you lose?" Kate asked, daring to believe she'd heard correctly.

"My wife and daughter. Sarah was Lily's age when she and Julia were murdered."

All the air left Kate's lungs and a weight settled on her chest that crushed the will from her. Julia. The name he'd called her when he'd kissed her. "Oh, God. I didn't know." She reached out and touched a hand to his arm.

Being with Lily had to be killing him.

Kate's worst nightmares had been those where she'd lost Lily, but every time she'd awakened to realize it had only been a bad dream.

Ben had lived it.

Her stomach roiled, the pain of loss almost as palpable as if she'd lost Lily. She swallowed hard on the giant lump choking her throat. "I'm sorry." Kate's voice caught on a sob. She looked back at Lily, counting her blessings, knowing that every minute she had with her little girl was precious.

Ben didn't have that anymore. His Sarah was gone.

Her bodyguard, the man who'd protected her and Lily, drove on as if he hadn't spoken at all. His face inscrutable, his lips pulled into a tight line.

As they turned off the highway onto the road that led to the Flying K Ranch, movement caught Kate's attention out of the corner of her eye. Before she could react, something hit the passenger-side door with the force of a freight train, flinging Kate sideways. If not for the seat belt, she'd have slammed into Ben and possibly gone through his window.

Lily screamed from the backseat as the truck lurched sideways and skidded across the road toward the ditch.

Ben fought to keep the vehicle on the pavement, but the driver's-side tires bit into the shoulder before he could right the vehicle.

Kate barely had time to straighten before the truck was hit again. All she could see before she was tossed against the restraining belt was a dark grille and the glass of headlights that hadn't been turned on.

Ben cursed, grinding his foot to the accelerator, trying to get away from their attacker. The impact pushed them off the road and down into the ditch so fast the truck teetered on two wheels.

Her breath caught in her throat as the truck wavered, then dropped to all four tires, the jolt flinging her against the door.

Lily cried out.

"Hold on, baby," Kate called out.

Switching the truck into four-wheel drive, Ben gunned the gas pedal. The tires slipped on the gravel, then the knobby treads dug into the dirt and the truck shot back out onto the road.

The dark, steel-gray haze of dusk surrounded them.

Kate twisted in her seat, peering into the semi-darkness of a cloudy starless evening. Behind them, taillights gleamed, two specks of red racing back toward Wild Oak Canyon.

Lily cried softly in the backseat.

The danger past for a moment, Kate unbuckled her belt and crawled over the front seat into the back.

Ben flipped the overhead light on. "Is she all right?"

He drove slowly toward the ranch, his gaze darting to the rearview mirror.

Kate cupped her daughter's face.

Other than silent tears trailing down her cheeks, Lily appeared to be okay. "We're okay, aren't we, baby?"

"Want me to take you two back to town?" Ben offered. "We could report in to the sheriff's office and let him know what happened."

"No. I don't want to risk being out of the vehicle if that guy returns. I just want to go home." She sat in the middle of the backseat beside Lily, holding her child's hand. Soon the tears stopped and Lily fell back to sleep.

Kate trembled in the darkness, afraid of staying where someone obviously didn't want her. She was pissed off that she was being forced out by thugs.

When they arrived at the ranch, Kate unbuckled Lily.

Ben opened the door from the outside and draped Lily's sleeping body over his shoulder.

Kate dropped to the ground, her body stiff from being hurled around the interior of the cab. Her shoulders were sore and her right breast was tender from the force of her body hitting the shoulder strap of her seat belt.

While Ben carried Lily into the house and up the stairs to her bedroom, Kate went from room to room, switching on the lights. When she reached the kitchen, her hand paused on the light switch.

A noise in the pantry captured her attention.

A moment before, she'd been so tired she could barely stand. In an instant, she was on alert. She flipped the light switch on and grabbed for the broom she'd propped beside the door early that morning.

She waited for the next sound that would indicate where the intruder stood.

Her teeth clamped down hard on her lip to keep her from screaming.

A loud click sounded from the pantry and the lights blinked out.

"Kate?" Ben called out from the staircase behind her.

Kate flipped the light switch and nothing happened.

Then something moved in the direction of the walk-in pantry. A door thumped open and footsteps scuffled across the tile.

"Stop or I'll shoot." Kate held the broom up like a shotgun. Her eyes had yet to adjust to the darkness. All she could make out was a shadowy form.

"Then shoot," a voice called out. He lunged for the back door and ran out before Kate could do anything.

And what could she have done? The broom wasn't a gun. At best she could have thrown it at him. At least he hadn't attacked her.

"Kate!" Ben's voice echoed in the living room. "Where are you?"

"In the kitchen. I'm okay."

"What happened?" Footsteps sounded on the wood floor in the hallway and Ben skidded to a halt behind her, his hands reaching out to gather her into his arms. Ben crushed her to his chest. "You scared the hell out of me. Why didn't you answer me the first time?"

"We had an intruder in here. I didn't want him to know where I was."

"Are you all right?"

"I'm fine." *Now that you're here.* She leaned back against him, wrapping his arms securely around her middle.

He turned her in his embrace and tipped her chin up. Already her eyes were adjusting to the limited lighting. A soft blue glow poured in through a nearby window as clouds skittered across the sky, freeing the moonlight.

Kate stared up into Ben's dark eyes. "Why is this happening?"

"I don't know." He smoothed a hand over her cheek and it found its way to the back of her neck. He tugged her hair, tipping her head backward, making her lips more accessible to his...kiss.

Ben's mouth closed over hers, sending wave after wave of sensations rippling through Kate's body.

Her hands climbed up his chest, twining around his neck. She applied pressure, wanting more, needing him to deepen their connection, to warm her body with his. To chase away the shadows of fear making her tremble.

His tongue twined with hers, thrusting deep, sliding long and slow, in and out.

When his hands slipped downward, over her shoulder blades and to the small of her back, she didn't protest, couldn't tell him to stop. Not when all she wanted was for him to shove her up against a wall, wrap her legs around his waist and drive deep inside her.

How long had it been since she'd made love to a man? Since before Troy had left for war. Almost five years. More than any woman should have to grieve.

BEN'S MEMBER STRAINED against the stiff denim of his jeans, pushing against the button fly, waging a war for freedom. His hand tangled in Kate's thick, lush curls, cupping the back of her head as he bent her over his arm and took what he wanted in the form of a kiss. But it wasn't enough.

The lingering shock waves of adrenaline pulsed through his system, urging him to take action. With no enemy to attack and no imminent danger, his relief could only be derived from making mad, passionate love to this woman whose body warmed his hands and awakened desires long buried.

Kate melted against him; her hands smoothed down the back of his neck and then squeezed between their chests. Her fingers searched for the buttons on his shirt, opening one after the other until she slipped through the opening and touched his skin.

Cool, slim fingers set off a string of explosions inside Ben, sparking nerve endings to life.

Before long, she had all his buttons undone and was tugging his shirt out of his waistband.

Ben found the hem of her dress and pulled it up over her head, tossing the garment to the floor. A black lace bra was all that stood between him and her perfectly rounded breasts.

When her hands locked on the top button of his jeans, his heart skipped several beats and he sucked in a raw, ragged breath.

He closed his hands over hers. "No."

She froze and glanced up, her green eyes shadowed. Then her chin dipped and she backed away. "You're right. I shouldn't have done that. I'm sorry."

Ben's hands fell to his sides, regret burning in his gut. He couldn't let himself be distracted, not with Kate's and Lily's lives at stake. He reached around the wall, feeling for the light switch, and flipped it.

Nothing.

"Know where the breaker box is?" he asked.

"I saw it in the pantry earlier today. The intruder must have known where to look because that's where he was hiding."

"This has got to end." Ben felt his way through the kitchen to the pantry he recalled from unloading Kate's furniture and supplies. There was a sound of rustling fabric, a drawer opened and closed behind him and a beam of light clicked on.

"This might help." Kate, now redressed, followed him into the closet-size room and shone the light on the breaker box. Her presence in the tight confines of the tiny space lined with canned vegetables and boxes of cereal only made matters worse.

He was so tense, he fumbled with the handle to the breaker box before he could get it open and find the tripped switch.

Once the switch had been returned to the on position, light poured through the open pantry door.

Kate backed out, turning off the flashlight. "Just so you know, there are several flashlights in the drawer at the end of the counter here." She slid the electric torch into the drawer and closed it, her hands shaking.

Her gaze slipped up to his, her eyes wide and haunted. "I won't attack you again. I promise."

Ben leaned in the door frame of the pantry. "You didn't attack me. If anything, I was all over you. I've never wanted to kiss someone as much as I wanted to kiss you."

Her brow furrowed. "Then why...?"

"It's wrong. I won't be here long and I don't want to lead you on in any way."

She nodded. "Good, because I'm not in the market for a man. I only need a bodyguard. I don't know what came over me. Must have been the adrenaline rush. Don't worry. I'll leave you alone."

When she turned to leave, Ben shot forward and captured her arm. "Don't get me wrong." He lifted her chin and stared down into her flashing green eyes. "I wanted to kiss you. And I still do." He bent until his lips barely touched hers.

Kate's gaze caressed his mouth, then her eyes rounded and she backed away, spun and ran up the stairs.

It took every ounce of Ben's self-control not to follow her.

CHAPTER NINE

AFTER LYING AWAKE in her bed with her eyes wide open and her mind spinning until the early hours of the morning, Kate finally fell into an exhausted sleep.

Not until Lily skipped into her room the next morning did she open her eyes and squint at the sun shining through her window.

"Oh, baby. I should be up by now to fix your breakfast."

"Mrs. Henderson fixed it for me."

Kate sat up, the T-shirt she'd slept in bunched around her. "She did?"

"Uh-huh. Can I go outside and play?"

Before her daughter finished her sentence, Kate was shaking her head. "Not until I'm up and dressed. You're not to go outside without me or Mr. Harding. Do you understand?"

Lily sighed and crawled up on the bed. "Could you hurry? I saw a lizard on the front porch."

Kate ruffled Lily's strawberry-blond curls. "No rest for the weary, is it? Okay, okay. I'm getting up. Why don't you go down and help Mrs. Henderson in the kitchen?"

"Okay." Lily rolled to the edge of the bed and dropped onto the floor.

The patter of her feet warmed Kate's heart and made her want to get out of bed and join the day.

The fear of the night before faded with the steady heat of the midmorning sun.

She quickly brushed her hair, secured it in a low ponytail at the base of her head and washed her face. A glance at her wan complexion in the mirror triggered her to dig in the drawer full of cosmetics for powder, blush and a little mascara. No sense looking like death.

Not when there was a handsome man close by. One who'd admitted to wanting to kiss her.

Excitement filtered through her body as she thrust her feet into jeans and pulled them up over her hips. A soft rose T-shirt and pointed-toed pink leather cowboy boots completed her outfit. She hurried from the room and down the stairs to the kitchen, peeking into the living room and ranch office on the way. If she were honest with herself, she'd admit she was looking for Ben.

"He's outside in the yard with Lily," Marge said as she appeared at the kitchen door.

Kate started. Having another person in the house took some getting used to. "I was looking for Lily."

"She's out there with Mr. Harding. They are too cute together. He's hangin' a tire swing for her. Eddy's out rounding up strays. We got here two hours ago."

Kate peered out the window over the kitchen sink at the man hanging from a tree branch. He expertly tied a rope to the branch, then swung out of the tree to land on his feet beside the four-year-old.

Lily grinned up at him, clapped her hands and giggled. "Do it again, Mr. Ben. Do it again," she cried, loud enough Kate could hear her muffled words through the window.

"He scrubbed an old tire he found out back with a brush and dish soap and he found a length of rope in the shed." Mrs. Henderson dried a pan as she gazed out the window, a smile lifting the corners of her mouth.

The image of the man and child made Kate's heart ache. Lily really needed a father figure. She needed a man in her life to teach her to be adventurous, to show her how to make things and climb trees.

Kate chuckled. Not that the child hadn't learned something about tree-climbing on her own. Kate's smile faded. And thank goodness she had. No telling what the biker gang would have done had they found her outside alone.

A chill shook Kate's body.

"Got a plate of scrambled eggs warming in the oven. Sit yourself down while I pop bread in the toaster."

Kate sank into a chair at the big kitchen table. "You don't have to go to the trouble."

"Now, don't argue with me. I like doin' for others. Makes me feel useful. Oh, by the way, your telephone is working now."

Kate hopped out of her seat. "Good, I want to call the sheriff."

"Oh, honey, I heard about your intruder last night. Ben— Mr. Harding already put a call into the sheriff's office reporting the incident. He said they were sending a deputy out today to look around."

Dropping down to the seat, Kate shook her head. The man was always a step ahead of her.

Marge continued talking as she scooped eggs onto a plate and set it in front of Kate. "I checked around to see if anything had been taken. I could swear I had several cans of soup and tuna I'd planned on using for lunch today. And the loaf of bread I'd laid out was gone." She shook her head. "Looked to me like someone who was hungry slipped in and took what they needed."

"Why wouldn't that person just knock on the door and ask for food? Why steal it?"

"Could have been undocumented immigrants." Marge's brows dipped. "Sometimes a steer will go missing. No telling what's been taken since Mr. Kendrick passed. Eddy said the cattle are all over the ranch. It'll take him days to account for what's left of the herd."

"I suppose I could learn to help him. Do you think Lily would be all right out riding along with us?" Kate had ridden horses a couple times, but she was by no means an expert. Lily had never had the opportunity.

"I could keep her here with me. I'm sure we could find plenty for her to play with around the house."

"I don't want to be a bother."

"No bother. I love little ones." Mrs. Henderson set a glass of orange juice beside Kate's plate. "Eat now. Better to make your decisions on a full stomach."

Kate ate the scrambled eggs and toast, enjoying being waited on for the first time since her mother died. She carried her plate to the sink and ran it through the warm soapy water Mrs. Henderson had used to clean the dishes. No dishwasher in this house.

"Look, he's got the tire up." Mrs. Henderson pointed out the window.

Lily lay on her belly through the hole of the old tire, swinging and laughing out loud.

Her happiness made Kate's heart lighter. She deserved to have a yard to play in and a real home, not an apartment in a busy city.

What would it take to find the ones responsible for

trying to run them off the property? Kate wanted a place to call home, for herself as much as she wanted it for Lily. This ranch was the only thing her father had ever given to her, and she'd be damned if she let anyone take it away.

Determination and a sense of purpose flowed through her veins, giving her the inspiration she needed to fight for what she wanted for her and her baby. "Mrs. Henderson, do you know the number for Cara Jo's Diner?"

"Sure do."

Kate called her new friend Cara Jo. Then she brushed her teeth, stopped in her bedroom for her pistol and a box of ammunition. She shoved the box into her pocket. She held the pistol behind her back, then headed outside to fulfill her promise to herself.

Ben lifted Lily out of the tire and set her on the ground.

Her hair was falling out of her ponytail and she wore a thin coating of dust and a smile. "That was fun. Can we do it again?"

"After a while, sweetie." Kate dropped a kiss on her tousled hair. "Right now, I want you to go inside and help Mrs. Henderson bake cookies."

Lily squealed and ran for the house.

Kate inhaled and let out her breath in a slow, steadying release. "I want to take you up on that offer."

Ben's gaze dropped to her lips. "What offer?"

Heat spread throughout Kate's body at the thought of Ben's kiss. She shoved the image aside and squared her shoulders. "I want you to teach me to shoot my gun." She pulled the weapon from behind her back and held it out.

Ben touched a finger to the tip of the barrel and

pointed it away from him. "You start by never pointing a gun at someone unless you want to shoot them."

"It's not loaded." She dug the box of ammo from her jeans pocket and held it out in her other hand.

"Trust me. Make it habit not to point a gun at anyone, loaded or unloaded, unless you intend to shoot him."

"Okay."

Ben took the weapon from her hands and inspected it. "Do you own cleaning supplies for this?"

"Yes."

"Good, it looks good for now, but after we shoot, it'll have to be thoroughly cleaned." He tipped it back and forth and weighted it in his grip. "It's a nice 9 mm Glock. Where did you get it?"

"It was my husband's." She'd almost made him get rid of it when she'd discovered she was pregnant. After his death, she couldn't bring herself to sell it. Now she was glad she hadn't. "Is it a good brand of gun?" she asked.

"One of the best." Ben clicked a button and the magazine dropped out of the handle. He caught it with his other hand. "Let me see the rounds."

Kate plunked the ammo box in his open palm, careful not to touch him, afraid to set off another bout of uncontrollable lust. That would be a disaster, considering he didn't want anything to do with her. Hadn't he said he was leaving as soon as Derringer arranged a replacement?

Ben loaded the bullets into the magazine. "Make sure your bullets are pointing toward the barrel of the weapon." He showed her how to slip the magazine into the handle and how to release it. Then he handed the gun to her. "You do it."

She didn't care how basic the lessons were, she

wanted to learn and get it right the first time. When Ben left, Kate's and Lily's lives depended on Kate's ability to protect them.

Kate held the weapon, searching for the magazine release button. When she found it, she released the magazine and it fell to the ground.

"You'll want to keep your weapon as clean as possible." Ben chuckled, the sound warming Kate's insides.

As Kate bent to retrieve the magazine, a vehicle rumbled down the gravel drive, stirring up a cloud of dust.

"Must be the sheriff's deputy." Ben took the Glock from her and reassembled it, stuffing it into the back of his waistband.

The SUV pulled to a stop. The cloud of dust drifted to the ground and Deputy Schillinger climbed out. "I hear you had another intruder."

"We did," Kate responded. "He was here when we got home after dark yesterday."

Schillinger had a lump of tobacco stuffed between his teeth and his lower lip. He spit a dark stream of nasty juice on the ground at Kate's feet. "Did you see who it was?"

Kate stepped backward, her breakfast roiling in her gut. "No, he didn't happen to announce himself or show his face. He did get away with some pantry staples and bread."

"Probably illegals."

When Schillinger looked like he would spit again, Kate frowned. "Do you mind?"

The man paused, then let loose anyway, wiping a dark drop from his chin. "Not at all."

Kate stared at the mess on the ground and back at

the deputy, then crossed her arms. "And let me guess…
you can't do anything without a full description." Kate
let out a tight breath. "I don't know why we bother to
call you. I'll turn this over to the Customs and Border
Protection guys. Maybe they will do something. Thank
you for your time."

Another vehicle approached. It slid in beside the deputy's SUV and Cara Jo's long, lithe form stepped out.
"Hi, Kate. Got a surprise for Lily." Cara Jo pushed her
shoulder-length blond hair back behind her ears, opened
the back door and reached in, extracting a black-and-
white puppy from the backseat.

Lily burst from the house, racing toward Cara Jo.
"It's Pickles! It's Pickles!" She skidded to a stop in the
gravel and reached up.

Cara Jo laughed and handed her the puppy. "You have
to be very careful with puppies. They're smaller than us
and can be hurt easily."

"I'll be very careful. I promise." Lily clutched the
squirming puppy against her chest and ran to Kate's
side. "Look, Mommy, Pickles is here."

"That's great, honey. Can you take him in the kitchen
and get Mrs. Henderson to help find feeding bowls?
You can get one of the boxes we used to pack and use
it for his bed."

Lily ran toward the house, the puppy flopping in her
arms.

Cara Jo joined the group of adults. "What's happening?" She glanced at the deputy. "What are you doing
here, Dwayne?"

Kate could have laughed at the way the deputy's lips
thinned at being called by his first name. "I was called

in on business." His chest puffed out a bit more and he looked down his nose at Kate's new friend.

Cara Jo's brows rose and she turned to Kate. "Business?"

"Unfortunately, the sheriff's department is better at serving papers than they are at finding intruders." Kate gave the lawman a pointed look. "If you're not going to dust for prints or at least write down a statement, I see no further need of your services."

Dwayne's eyes narrowed. "This isn't the place for a woman. You really should consider selling before the bank takes the ranch."

"The bank's not taking anything." She didn't know how, but she'd find a way to come up with some money.

"Then you might want to leave before anything bad happens to you or your little girl."

Ben slipped an arm around Kate's waist. "She's not going anywhere she doesn't want to."

"Besides, it's ridiculous to even consider leaving," Cara Jo said with a snort. "Give up a ranch because the sheriff's department is too scared or lazy to do anything about the growing crime rate in the county?" She hooked Kate's arm and stared at the deputy. "Why are you on the force if you can't do your job?"

Dwayne's face bloomed a ruddy red, his eyes narrowing at Cara Jo. He shifted his attention to Kate. "Think about it, Ms. Langsdon."

Ben's arm dropped from around Kate's waist and he stepped toward the deputy, his fists clenched.

Kate grabbed his hand and slipped it back around her. "He's not worth it."

Schillinger turned and marched to his SUV, climbed

behind the wheel and spun out in the gravel on his way out of the drive.

"That man always has a sour look on his face," Cara Jo remarked.

Kate laughed. "I thought it was just me."

"No, it's definitely him." Ben brushed a lock of Kate's hair back behind her ear.

"Thanks for being here for me." Even if Derringer had sent him, Ben had gone above and beyond on more than one occasion. Kate couldn't imagine having to deal with everything that had happened on her own.

"I need to make a call. You going to be all right for a few minutes?" He gazed into her eyes.

Her heart flipped at the worry reflected in his eyes. "I'm fine. Cara Jo's here."

"Go on. We need time for girl talk." Cara Jo waved Ben toward the house.

Once he left them, Cara Jo faced Kate. "Now, what's this about the county foreclosing on your ranch?"

Kate shook her head. "You don't want to know."

"I wouldn't have asked if I didn't care." Cara Jo touched a hand to Kate's arm.

Cara Jo had it right, Kate had needed someone she could talk with and Ben wasn't necessarily the right person. He was the hired help. He couldn't dig her out of her financial hole. Nor did she want him to. She dragged in a deep breath and let it out. "The sheriff and Deputy Schillinger served me with papers that the county is going to seize the property for almost thirty thousand in back taxes."

"Holy moley." Cara Jo flattened a hand to her chest. "That's a lot of cash."

"Yeah." Saying the amount out loud made it sink in

all the more, threatening to overwhelm Kate. "I just need time to figure things out. Hire a lawyer or something. But the local bank probably won't loan me any money to keep things going in the meantime."

"I've got a loan on my diner through that bank. But then I grew up here. They know me."

Kate sighed. "I'm an unknown and not a very safe bet." She glanced around at the barn and outbuildings. "And I'm sure the rumors about the attacks aren't giving the bank faith in my abilities to run a ranch and protect my interests."

"You can't help that someone is attacking you." Cara Jo nodded toward where Ben had been. "And you have your fiancé living here. Ben looks fully capable of handling any difficulty."

"Having Ben here didn't help me one bit in the eyes of the bank loan officer." Kate snorted. "I don't even have enough to pay Eddy and Marge until I can get my hands on my daughter's college fund."

"How much do you need?" Cara Jo propped her hands on her hips. "I can't afford thirty thousand, but I can spot you some money until you can get to yours."

Kate's chest swelled, her eyes filling. "No, I can't take advantage of you like that. You barely know me. I'll figure things out. Heck, I've only been here a couple days. Things are bound to get better."

"Sometimes things get worse before they get better. But then, don't let me be the downer here." Cara Jo hugged Kate. "The offer's open if you need it."

"Thanks." Kate gave her a watery smile. "I'll wait and see what the county assessor says when the computers come up again. No use borrowing trouble. I have enough as it is."

From the hallway where the phone was located, Ben could keep an eye on Kate and Cara Jo outside. He dialed Derringer.

"Hank, Ben here."

"Got the phone line hooked up at the Flying K, did you?" Hank asked.

"It's working."

"Good. Had some news on that DVD you sent to me. My contacts in the state crime lab may just be able to recover what was on it. They told me they should have it by this evening. Whatcha got?"

Ben watched as Kate and Cara Jo hugged. What were they talking about? "Can you do some digging on Deputy Dwayne Schillinger and a Mr. Robert Sanders?"

"Why?"

"Schillinger's been out here twice to investigate break-ins, and done nothing but warn Kate to leave."

"Hmm. That doesn't sound right."

"That's what I'm thinking."

"I'll get my contacts on the deputy. I take it you had another break-in last night?"

Ben's hand tightened on the receiver. "We did."

"Anyone hurt?" Hank asked.

"No, he left without attacking."

"As for Robert Sanders, he's pretty well-known in the area, what with his ties to real estate and construction. But I'll have my folks do a little digging to see if he's got any dirt hiding under his rug."

The pounding of horse hooves made Ben glance toward the south. "Hank, I gotta go. Let me know if anything comes up."

"Will do. And, Ben, be careful out there. Ranches

can be like islands. You're out in the middle of nowhere with no one to depend on but yourselves."

"I know that. And the local authorities aren't helping at all."

Ben hung up and burst through the door as a horse and its rider galloped across the dry grasses toward the house.

"That's Eddy." Mrs. Henderson stood on the porch, wiping her hands on a dry dish towel. "He's in an all-fired hurry."

Kate was halfway to the fence, with Cara Jo following, when Ben leaped off the porch.

Eddy's mount galloped across the dry Texas paddock of sparse grass and scraggly vegetation. By the time he reached the gate, Kate was holding it open for him.

Ben ground to a halt beside her. "What's wrong?" Ben asked.

Eddy slipped from the saddle, his boots hitting the ground, stirring up a puff of dust. "Found several steer carcasses along the southern boundary."

CHAPTER TEN

"I DIDN'T KNOW if you wanted to come out and inspect, or if you wanted me to notify the sheriff's department and let them handle it." Eddy waited for Kate's response.

Kate glanced at Ben. "I don't think the sheriff will be much help. Let's get out there and see what we've got." Kate headed for the barn. "Oh, wait.... Lily." Kate performed an about-face and headed back to the house.

Just inside the kitchen door, Lily held Pickles to her cheek as she stood beside Cara Jo.

"Kate, go on, do what you have to do." Cara Jo waved Kate toward the barn. "Don't worry about Miss Lily. She and I are going to start training Pickles. Aren't we, dear?"

Lily nodded. "Mrs. Henderson's making treats for Pickles."

Kate bit down on her lip. "Are you sure?"

Cara Jo smiled. "Absolutely."

"Don't you have to be at the diner?"

"Not today. I give myself a day off every once in a while. I can do that." She smiled. "I'm the owner."

"Thanks." Kate spun and hurried to the barn where Eddy and Ben stood.

Her first time in the barn, Kate stared around at the tack hanging from hooks on the walls. "Is there a four-wheeler or a horse I can ride?"

Eddy shook his head. "No four-wheelers, but I've got a couple horses in the stalls in the barn."

Ben captured her arms and turned her to face him. "You're not going. You need to stay and look after Lily."

"You saw what Marge is capable of." Kate nodded toward Eddy. "She wields a powerful shotgun, doesn't she?"

Eddy slapped his hat against his thigh. "Scares me, if that's whatcha mean." He slipped a rifle into the holster on his saddle.

Kate felt a little better knowing they'd be heading out with a little more firepower than her Glock, which was tucked neatly into Ben's waistband, along with the one he wore on a shoulder holster over his blue chambray shirt. She made up her mind. "Lily will be fine with Mrs. H. and Cara Jo will be there as well to entertain her and keep an eye out for trouble."

Ben crossed his arms. "Sounds like you thought this through."

"I did."

"I still don't think it's a good idea."

Her brows rose. "Why not? This is my ranch, and it's my responsibility to see to the safety of the people and animals on it." She stepped toward one of the occupied stalls. "I'm going."

Ben followed, his boots stirring the dust around her. "Have you ever ridden a horse?"

"Plenty," she lied. Well, it wasn't a lie if "plenty" meant five times in her entire life.

"Right." Ben's one-word response told Kate he didn't believe her for a minute.

Eddy led a horse from the middle stall. "This is

Lucky. She's a little older and as calm a horse as we have on the Flying K."

"As compared to what?" Kate asked as she stared up at the horse, thinking the mare was bigger than any of the horses she'd ever ridden.

"She's been out roaming the pastures since Mr. K.... left." Eddy breathed deeply, his jaw tightening. "She won't be hard to ride."

Kate refused to be intimidated by the animal's size. "You'll have to show me where everything is."

Eddy led the way to the racks of saddles stored in the tack room. He nodded toward a brightly colored blanket. "If you'll toss that over Lucky's back, I'll handle the saddle."

Rather than push the point and take the saddle herself, Kate led the way back out to the horse and eased the blanket across Lucky's back.

The animal eased sideways, whickering softly.

Kate stepped away and let Eddy settle the saddle on the horse's back. She studied Eddy's moves, committing them to memory for the next time when she'd insist on doing it herself.

"When you cinch the girth on Lucky, do it a couple of times. She likes to blow her belly out. If you don't do it more than once, she'll fool you and when you get going, the saddle will slide to the side, dumping the rider."

Kate nodded. "I'll remember."

Once Eddy had the saddle securely fastened, he handed the bridle to Kate. "You can do this."

Kate nodded, trying to remember, from the five times she'd ridden at a farm outside Houston, how to slip the bridle between the horse's teeth and over its head.

Eddy walked away, calling over his shoulder, "She'll

bite down to keep you from getting it between her teeth. Stick your thumb in the corner of her mouth to get her to open."

While Eddy adjusted the girth on his horse, Kate worked at sliding the bridle between Lucky's teeth. After several failed attempts, the horse stomped her feet and swished her tail, slapping at Kate like a pesky fly.

"You're going to wear this bridle," Kate said between gritted teeth.

In her peripheral vision, Kate could see Ben walking toward her. She'd be damned if she couldn't accomplish this one little task. With her teeth clenched as tightly as Lucky's, and the bridle held in one hand, Kate shoved her thumb in the corner of the animal's mouth and tugged.

Lucky smacked her lips and her teeth opened wide enough for Kate to slide the bridle between her teeth and loop the strap over her ears. "There. That wasn't so bad, was it?"

The mare opened and closed her mouth as if adjusting to the metal bit.

Kate tightened the strap beneath Lucky's chin and the one around her head. When Lucky was ready, Kate walked her to the barn door and glanced at the stirrup, wondering how in hell she was going to get her foot up that high. She glanced around the barnyard, spying a wooden step close to a hitching post. She tugged the reins, urging the horse to follow.

Lucky straightened her legs, refusing to move.

Ben had saddled a gray Arabian gelding and stood in the barnyard watching Kate struggle with the mare. "Need a hand?"

"No, I have this," she insisted.

"Lucky doesn't like the step." Eddy led his gelding out and swung up into the saddle.

Ben closed the distance between Kate and himself.

An uncontrollable surge of excitement swept over her, setting Kate's nerve endings alight.

"Let me help," he whispered. "It by no means implies you need it." Ben stooped, cupping his hands.

Kate leaned close. "I don't like relying on you." She stepped into his palms.

"Why?" He rose, lifting her high enough to toss her leg over the saddle.

"Because you won't always be there. I'll have to take care of myself and Lily." She held on to the saddle horn with one hand.

Ben nudged her calf.

His fingers touching her, even through the thick denim of her jeans, had her blood racing through her veins. She held her leg well out of his way while he adjusted the stirrup on the right and rounded the horse to adjust the left. When he had it positioned correctly, he guided her foot into the stirrup. Then he handed Kate the reins and stepped back.

Lucky danced to the side, setting loose a swarm of butterflies in Kate's belly. Now was the time to admit she hadn't ridden a horse in over ten years. But she clamped down hard on her bottom lip and held on for dear life.

Ben swung up in his saddle, turning the gelding all in one smooth motion, like he'd done this a thousand times before.

Since he'd grown up on a ranch, he probably had.

Her back ramrod-straight, Kate nudged Lucky with her heels and followed Eddy to the gate.

Ben covered the rear.

Eddy leaned down and pulled the lever, opening the gate.

Lucky bolted through and set off at a gallop.

Her heart in her throat, Kate pulled back on the reins, wishing she hadn't been so quick to say she'd ride out. No matter how hard she tugged on the leather straps, her efforts only slowed the mare marginally.

Ben and Eddy caught up to her before she'd gone far.

The ranch foreman passed her and led the way to the southwest corner of the ranch.

Ben and his gelding kept pace beside her.

"This is the first time you've been out to see what you now own?"

She nodded. The thought of all that she could see around her belonging to her seemed a bit overwhelming. "What do I do with all this?"

"That's why you hire people like Eddy to take care of the horses, cattle and whatever else you decide to raise."

"I've never been one to sit back and watch others do all the work. It bothers me to have Mrs. Henderson cooking meals and cleaning up after me. I've never had anyone wait on me. Not even my own mother." Kate stared at Eddy's back, wondering what it meant to be a working rancher and if she had what it took to do it.

"Ranching is hard work."

Kate sat up straight, though her tailbone was beginning to hurt. "I'm not afraid of hard work."

"It's twenty-four hours a day, three hundred and sixty-five days a year."

She smiled. "So is parenting."

"Lily needs a mother to take care of her."

"And I need to make this place operate at a rate that can support us. Otherwise, I'll have to find a job to support *it*. And out here in South Texas, I doubt there are jobs that pay enough to support a woman and her child, much less her ranch."

Ben touched the brim of his hat. "You have a point. Owning a ranch is a big responsibility. Are you sure you want to bite off that much?"

Kate frowned at him. "Now you're sounding like Deputy Schillinger. I'm not a quitter."

"What about the danger?"

"I'm not a quitter," she repeated, staring ahead at Eddy.

"What about Lily?"

Kate bit down on her bottom lip. That was the rub. Had it just been Kate, she'd have jumped in with both feet ready to rip into anyone stupid enough to try to run her off her land. Now she had a child to protect. And she had to give Lily a home.

Funny how, after only two days, she'd started thinking of the Flying K as home. Her home. Though she still didn't know much about the man who'd lived here, the man who'd been a big factor in bringing her into this world, she felt a tenuous connection to him and wished not once but a hundred times that she'd had the opportunity to know the man. "Lily needs a place to call home."

"Isn't home where the heart is? Wouldn't she be happy anywhere as long as she's with you?"

Anger bubbled up in her chest. "Are you trying to talk me into leaving?"

"No, I'm trying to figure out why you want to stay when all you've gotten out of it so far is threats and attacks."

As quickly as it rose, the anger ebbed away. "I've also made a new friend." She smiled. "And I met you." She glanced at him, her brows rising.

Ben's gaze remained forward as if he avoided hers. "That's not much of a bonus."

"I think so." She gave him a moment of silence before asking, "I understand we're a painful reminder of your family. But is it that bad that you still want to leave us?"

"Damn it, yes." His response startled the horse beneath him.

The gelding sidestepped, bumping into Kate's.

Ben's leg brushed against Kate's calf. He jerked the reins to the left and the horse danced away. But the brief contact had been enough to leave Kate's breath ragged, her hands shaking.

For a few long moments, Kate rode in silence, her heart hammering against her ribs. Ben wasn't afraid of evil men with guns. He feared her and Lily. It all made sense.

He'd lost his wife and daughter. Seeing Kate and Lily had to be tearing him apart. Kate's heart tightened as if someone had hold of it, squeezing mightily. She'd lost a husband she'd loved with all her heart. Kate couldn't imagine losing her spouse and her daughter all at once. She doubted she'd be strong enough to go on living.

Ben was afraid to care again.

Eddy shouted and kicked his horse in the flanks. Black buzzards rose from the ground ahead, their huge wingspan filling the air, stirring dust into a cloud.

Relieved to have something else to concentrate on, Kate eased her horse forward, bringing the mare to a halt beside Eddy.

The stench of decaying flesh almost knocked her out of the saddle. Kate gasped and sucked in another lungful of the putrid air. She pulled her shirt up over her nose and breathed through the fabric.

Spread across the ground was the carcass of a black Angus steer, mostly picked over by the scavenger birds who'd located this meal.

Eddy and Ben dropped out of their saddles and squatted beside the dead animal.

"Whoever killed it used a knife." Ben pointed to the smooth edges of cut skin on what once had been the steer's throat.

Kate gagged and swallowed hard to keep from vomiting. She sucked in a deep breath through her shirt and let go of it. Then she grabbed the saddle horn, slipped her feet from the stirrup and slid down the horse's side, landing with a thump on her butt.

Ben was beside her, grasping her beneath her arms. "You all right?"

"I'm fine, except for my damaged pride." She stood and brushed the dirt from her hands and backside. "Who would have done this?"

"Considering they cut away the biggest chunks of meat, I'd say someone who was looking for a meal. *Madre de Dios.*" Eddy rattled off a couple sentences in Spanish before he shook his head and stood.

Ben was circling the dead animal. "There are footprints all around." After a moment he looked off into the brush to the south. "They lead toward the canyon."

"Shouldn't we follow them?"

Ben shook his head. "Only if you want to die."

A shiver rocked Kate's frame. "You think the people who killed this cow would shoot at us?"

"No, but they might slit your throat to keep you from disclosing their location."

"Oh." Kate wrapped her arms around her middle, the warmth of the day turning cool. "What now?"

Eddy looked out over the land. "We need to herd all the strays closer to the ranch house and barn where we can keep a closer watch on them."

"Doesn't that limit the amount of grazing?" Kate cast a glance at the dry land, where vegetation was sparse.

"Do you have a better suggestion?" Ben asked.

Kate stared across at Ben and Eddy. "We could call in the Customs and Border Protection and have them run interference until they get the drug trafficking under control."

"We'll report it," Ben said. "But getting the illegal activity under control won't happen overnight." He gathered his reins and led the gelding away from the dead steer. "In the meantime, we need to do like Eddy said. Otherwise you'll continue to lose cattle."

Eddy glanced at the sun tipping toward the horizon. "We can start tomorrow. It's getting late and we shouldn't be out here after dark."

Kate walked her mare a few steps away from the carnage and reached high for the saddle horn, dragging herself up enough to get her foot in the stirrup. At last she was able to sling her leg over the saddle. Proud she'd gotten up by herself, she almost cried when she noticed the reins hanging from the bit down to the ground.

A soft chuckle sounded beside her.

Ben walked across the dry ground, bent to retrieve the reins and handed them up to her without a word. That quirky smile almost made her want to kick him. At the same time it made her insides heat with want. She pushed aside her desire and focused on the next step.

The three of them rode back the way they'd come, with Eddy taking the lead again.

Halfway back to the barn, Ben shouted to Eddy, "Go

on ahead. Kate and I are going to do a little target practice."

Eddy chuckled. "Can you wait until I get out of range?
I prefer to remain in one piece."

"You bet." Ben reined in beside Kate and dropped to
the ground. He grasped her around the waist and lifted
her out of the saddle.

When she opened her mouth to protest, he covered
her lips with a finger. "I know you can get down all by
yourself. Just humor me. It'll be faster and you won't
need to spend any more time with me than you have to."

She rested her hands on his shoulders as he let her
slowly slide down the front of his body until her feet
touched down. Kate clamped hard on her tongue, afraid
she'd say what she really thought. That his hands on
her waist had been deliciously sexy, the broad fingers
spanning her middle, his muscles flexing and the ease
with which he'd lifted her had left her breathless. But
not nearly as air-deprived as the feel of his body against
hers as she'd slid down him to her feet.

She'd do best to keep her mouth shut and get this lesson over with. The more time she spent alone with Ben,
the more she couldn't imagine him leaving. Dangerous
ground to be sure.

BEN REGRETTED LIFTING her from the saddle as soon as his
hands closed around her. He compounded the regret by
letting her body brush against his. Now all he wanted
was to do it again, only this time for her to wrap her legs
around his waist, her breasts pressing against his chest.

He pulled the Glock from his back waistband and
checked the safety.

Kate stood with her back to him. She'd pulled the

rubber band from her hair, letting it fall free around her shoulders. After she'd finger-combed it several times she gathered the long tresses in a bunch.

Ben shoved the pistol into his pocket and pushed Kate's hands aside, plucking the band from her fingers. In two quick motions he had the ponytail secured. His hands dropped to her arms, turning her to face him.

She blinked up at him, her lips parted, full and kissable. "You do that like a natural."

"Comes from having a daughter, much like Lily." His hands fell to his sides and he turned away.

He strode several feet away from Kate, needing the distance to keep from pawing her like a teenager. His member strained against the tight confines of his denim jeans. God, he wanted the woman. Instead, he scanned the terrain, searching for a target.

"Kate," he called out.

She came to him, her hands twisting together, her brows just as knotted. "We can do this another day," she said.

"No, you need to know how to use that gun if you plan to keep it."

"Okay." Kate nodded. "Show me."

He handed her the Glock and wrapped her fingers around the grip, lacing one finger over the trigger.

Her body shook against him.

"Think of it as an extension of your arms." He helped her cup her trigger hand with the palm of her empty hand and raised her arms.

"Look down the barrel and line up the sight with the target."

"What am I aiming for?" she asked, holding the gun steady.

"See the prickly pear cactus there with the three lobes facing us?"

"Yes."

"Aim at the top center lobe. Once you have the sights lined up, press the trigger slowly."

Her pulse hammered through her veins. "Will it kick?"

"Not much."

"How much is not much?" she asked.

"Just shoot it and you'll find out."

She aimed the barrel toward the cactus, breathed in, then out, then closed her eyes and pulled the trigger.

The pop wasn't as loud as she'd expected and the kick wasn't bad at all. She focused on the cactus, noticing all three lobes remained intact. "Did I miss?"

"Yes, and you scared the crap out of me." He pushed his cowboy hat back on his head and circled behind her, his arms coming up on either side. "Let's do it again. Only this time, keep your eyes open."

Ben spooned her body with his, bringing his arms up on either side of hers. His hands closed around her fingers and he inhaled her unique scent of honeysuckle and citrus.

His groin tightened and he knew he was in trouble.

CHAPTER ELEVEN

BEN'S BREATH STIRRED the tendrils of hair hanging loose from her ponytail. Kate leaned her back against the solid wall of muscles that was her bodyguard cowboy. The warmth of his arms around her reassured and scared her all at once.

What would it be like to lie in his arms naked?

Her hands shook so badly, she thought she might drop the gun.

"Are you afraid?" he whispered.

Yes, yes, she was afraid. Afraid of falling in love with a stranger. Afraid of investing her emotions in someone who would leave as soon as the threat was neutralized. Afraid she and Lily would be heartbroken when the dust settled on the Flying K Ranch. "N-no," she lied, "I'm not afraid."

"Good. This time keep your eyes open and caress the trigger like a lover."

Holy shotgun blasts! Was he kidding her? All his words did was make her even more aware of the ridge of his fly pressing into her buttocks. She wanted to caress something, and it wasn't the trigger of her 9 mm Glock.

Perspiration beaded on her forehead. "Is it getting hotter?"

"You bet." His hand curved around her again. "Ready?"

Oh, hell, yes, but not for what he was thinking.

Focus, woman. Hell, how could she when she had the hottest cowboy in Texas wrapped around her?

Think of Lily. Images of her daughter brought Kate back to the real reason for her shooting lessons. Living alone on a ranch, she had to have the ability to protect herself and her daughter.

Her hand tightened around the grip and she forced air into and out of her lungs, focusing her concentration down the short barrel, lining up the sights with the target. Then, like Ben said, she stroked the trigger, keeping her eyes wide open.

The weapon kicked backward and Kate almost dropped it.

The acrid scent of burned gunpowder filled her nostrils and she blinked to clear her vision.

"I'll be damned." Ben leaned to her side and stared at her, his brows furrowed. "Are you sure you haven't done this before?"

"No." Dear God, his face was close enough to kiss. So much for maintaining focus on the lesson. "Why?" Her voice cracked and her body trembled.

"Take a look." He faced what was left of the cactus. The top, middle lobe had a hole blasted through it.

Kate squinted, afraid she was seeing things. Sure enough, there was a smooth round hole, dead center. A thrill of excitement rippled through her. "I did that?"

"You did." He chuckled. "I think you've taken me for a ride. How many times have you handled this gun?"

Kate shook her head, floored by her accuracy. "Other than using it to hit the intruder over the head the other night, never."

"I believe you have a promising career ahead of you as a sharpshooter or sniper."

"It was luck." Kate laughed shakily.

He nodded toward the cactus. "Do it again, only this time, aim for the right lobe." His hands fell to his sides and he backed away.

Standing alone, she didn't feel as confident or steady. But she also wasn't distracted by body contact. She looked down the barrel and lined up the right lobe in her sights.

"Remember…caress the trigger." Ben's words slid over her like melted chocolate in the dry Texas heat. Her hand tightened around the grip and the trigger and the weapon discharged.

Kate yelped. "Dang. I wasn't ready." She glanced at the cactus. "Did I hit anything?"

Ben chuckled. "The dirt in front of the plant."

Widening her stance, Kate glared at Ben. "I'm going to get this."

He nodded. "I have no doubt."

"Shh." This time her hands didn't quiver, her body didn't budge and the bullet nicked the lower corner of the lobe she'd aimed at. Her gaze shot to Ben. "Does that count?"

"If it had been a man, you most likely would have hit him where it would hurt him." Ben grinned. "That's good."

Kate couldn't look away. When Ben smiled, his entire face lit up and his blue eyes shone bright and clear. She tipped her head to the side. "I like it when you smile."

Immediately, his mouth straightened and he glanced away. "Adjust how you line up the sight based on where it hit last time, and keep practicing." Ben strode to where they'd tied the horses.

Kate took her time and fired again. The bullet bit into

the top corner of the cactus lobe. Her concentration alternated between the target and Ben. He'd gone from happy to glum in seconds and it was driving her nuts.

"You know, it wouldn't kill you to smile more often." She cast a glance over her shoulder at the silent man.

He flipped the stirrup over the saddle on his horse and he tightened the girth before he muttered, "Have to have something to smile about."

"I heard that." Kate lined up the sights and squeezed off another round. The bullet pierced the center of the right lobe. Kate smiled and looked back at Ben, careful to point the nose of the pistol away from him. "How about waking up every day?"

"What about it?"

"Aren't you happy when you wake up every day?" Kate continued. "How can you be unhappy when the sun is shining?"

"The sunshine makes it incredibly hot out here in South Texas."

Kate fired off the remaining rounds in her ten-round magazine. Some of the shots went where they were supposed to, others hit the dirt in front of and behind the cactus plant, never touching it. When the last bullet was spent, she hit the magazine release button and caught the magazine before it hit the ground. The sun dipped low on the horizon, lengthening Kate's shadow.

She crossed to where Ben stood holding his horse's reins and stared up into his eyes.

The shadows were back and his jaw was tight, a muscle twitching in his left cheek.

Before she could overthink her reaction to his somber look, Kate smoothed her hand over the twitching muscle. "You must have loved her a lot."

Ben grabbed her wrist so fast, Kate cried out. "I loved Julia and I loved Sarah," he said, taking her gun in his other hand and tucking it back into his waistband. "But nothing I do now will bring them back. Nothing. They're gone."

His fingers hurt where he crushed her wrist, but Kate couldn't pull it free, nor could she back away from the intensity of his gaze.

"Julia and Sarah died, Ben." She pressed a hand to his chest. "But they never left you."

Silence settled like dust between them.

For a long moment, nothing stirred, neither one of them moved.

Then Ben yanked her hard against his chest, his lips crashing down over hers, his mouth claiming hers in a savage kiss. He let go of her wrist, one hand cupping the back of her head, the other clutching her bottom, grinding her pelvis against the hard ridge beneath his fly.

When he let her come up for air, his lips moved over hers, sliding along her chin. "I loved my wife."

"Yes, you did. But you didn't die with her."

"I know, damn it." He grabbed her arms and shook her. "I should have."

"No, Ben. You're still here for a reason."

His head whipped up. "What for? To punish me for failing to protect them?" He shoved her away from him. "I wasn't there for them."

"You didn't kill them."

"I could have stopped him."

"You couldn't be everywhere. He'd have found a way."

Ben stalked away, breathing hard, his face a ruddy red. Kate's heart squeezed so hard in her chest, she thought she might have a heart attack. The anguish in Ben's face, the agony in his tone, ripped her apart.

"We need to go. It's getting dark."

When Ben passed her to get to his horse, Kate touched his arm.

He shook off her hand. "Don't." His glare scorched her.

Kate flinched, drawing back her hand as if he'd burned it. "I'm sorry. I shouldn't have brought it up."

He snorted and swung up into the saddle without offering her a leg up.

Kate managed to mount on her own, struggling to keep Ben's anger and withdrawal from bringing her all the way down. The man had some issues.

Hell, so did she. Only she'd had four years to work through them. Two years and a wake-up call in the form of Kate and Lily hadn't been enough time to lessen Ben's loss. He was still mourning his wife and child and nothing Kate could do or say would mend that kind of broken heart.

As Kate turned her mare north toward the house, a light blinked from the south. A shot of adrenaline raced through her system and she tugged hard on Lucky's reins, wheeling her around to face south again.

"Did you see that?" Kate glanced over her shoulder at Ben.

Lucky jerked her head and whinnied, trying to get Kate to turn back toward the barn.

Ben was already a few yards north when he reined in and twisted in his saddle. "See what?"

"A light." Kate pointed. "Out there."

Ben urged his horse around and came to a halt beside Kate. "Where?"

As dusk settled in around Kate, her eyes adjusted to the darkness. A flash of light blinked on, then off, a tiny pinprick on the horizon. "There." She gathered her reins. "Should we go check it out?"

Ben studied the light. "No."

"But—" The light grew more steady, pointed directly at them.

"No, looks like they're headed this way and we don't have time to outrun them." He spun his horse and dug in his heels. "Come on."

Kate stared at the light a fraction of a second longer. It was getting bigger. Which meant Ben was right, the vehicle causing the light was headed their way. Whether it was friend or foe, Kate had no intention of sticking around to find out.

She swung Lucky around and took off after Ben and his gelding, letting Lucky have her head.

Ben raced across the ground, dodging cactus, sage and saw palmetto. When he came to a dry ravine, he reined in so fast, Kate's horse struggled to stop in time. Tire tracks led down the banks and back up the other side.

Ben was off his horse and reaching for her reins before Kate had time to think. "Why did we stop?"

"We won't make it back to the safety of the ranch before they catch up. We have to find a place to hide." He reached up, grabbed her around the waist and pulled her off the horse. "Hurry."

Ben took the reins of both the horses and ran down the banks, following the meandering creek bed.

Kate hurried after him, slipping and sliding on the loose gravel and rocks. "Do you think whoever is out there is dangerous?"

"You want to stick around and find out?" he said over his shoulder.

Kate closed her mouth, conserving her energy to keep up with Ben's headlong race down the wash.

When he came to a point where the creek bed curved north at a huge boulder, he tugged the horses behind the outcropping and tied their reins to a scrubby root. They were a good two hundred yards from the tracks. "Stay here."

Kate skidded to a halt, breathing hard. "Why? Where are you going?"

"Back to see who's trespassing." He turned and started back the way they'd come.

Kate laid a hand on his arm. "Not without me, you're not."

"It'll be dangerous."

"It's my land. I need to see what's going on." She let her hand slip down to his.

"It's safer staying clear." The darkness was settling in around them and the stars popped out of the sky one at a time.

Kate couldn't read the expression in Ben's eyes, but she wouldn't let him go without her. She dropped his hand and crossed her arms. "If you don't take me with you, I'll follow you anyway."

Ben sucked in a deep breath and let it out. "You're a stubborn woman."

"I've been known to be. Are you going to stand around arguing or are we going to go and find a good place to hide closer to the road?"

"I don't like it."

She snorted. "So noted."

"Then stay behind me and keep quiet."

"Yes, sir." Kate popped a salute that was all but lost on him as he turned and jogged back down the creek bed, hunkering low so that he wouldn't be seen over the banks.

Kate followed, copying his technique, her heart pounding, her breathing erratic. What was she getting herself into?

All she knew was that she didn't want to be left behind while Ben risked his life to see what was going down on her ranch.

Light glinted above them, casting a beam over the top of their heads.

Ben came to a sudden stop and flung his arm out, catching her before she barreled past him. "We hide here."

He ducked behind a boulder no bigger than a sheep and dragged her down beside him. Ben pulled the Glock from the back of his jeans and handed it to Kate. "Don't use this unless I tell you to." He removed his 9 mm from his shoulder holster and held it in front of his face.

Kate's hand trembled. Sure she'd been practicing shooting, but the thought of pulling the trigger on a person...

Her shoulders stiffened, her resolve strengthening as she thought of Lily. She'd do whatever it took to protect the ones she loved.

The rumble of an engine grew louder and the light brighter. Then it angled down the creek bank and came to a grinding halt, dust flying all around, forming a hazy glow in front of the truck. The driver turned the vehicle off and silence engulfed the scene.

As the dust settled, Kate peered at the back of the pickup. Four men perched on the sides, wielding what looked like automatic weapons, the type used by the military.

Kate gasped, then clamped a hand over her mouth and stared wide-eyed as one man hopped out, his feet crunching as he landed in the gravel. He stretched, his gun arm rising high into the night sky. He said something in Spanish and the driver responded.

Another man, brandishing a similar weapon, dropped down and shone a flashlight in a wide beam around the pickup, turning it slowly toward the position where Kate and Ben lay.

Ben whispered, "Close your eyes."

Kate squeezed them shut and ducked her head low behind the boulder.

The crunch of gravel grew louder. Kate fought her instinct to look up and see how close the men had come, but she was afraid that if she looked, the flashlight would glint off her eyes and give away their position.

"Brille la luz aquí!" a voice shouted closer than Kate had imagined.

Ben pressed his lips to her ear. "Don't move," he whispered.

He didn't have to worry. She froze, holding her breath, waiting for the men to move away.

Light shone on either side of the boulder.

Then a loud bang blasted through the night and kicked up dust around where Kate hovered. She bit hard on her tongue to keep from crying out.

Footsteps crunched closer and then a heavily accented voice called out. *"Serpiente para cenar!"*

Men laughed and the light bobbed skyward.

The footsteps moved away.

Kate let go of the breath she'd been holding and dared to peer around the side of the boulder.

One man had his gun slung over his shoulder and he held a long fat snake out to the side, speaking in rapid Spanish. The driver and the other gunmen laughed.

The crackle of a radio broke through their merriment and the driver responded to the call. When he finished, he waved a hand out the window. *"Vayamos!"*

The snake man dropped the reptile and leaped over the side of the pickup. The other men leaped in beside him. The truck pulled up the other side of the wash as another set of lights crested the bank behind them and dipped down into the creek.

In that one instant the light from the second vehicle illuminated the truck in front of it. Kate could see into the first truck's bed.

Huddled low and holding on to one another were several women and young girls.

One cried out.

One of the gunmen slapped the girl. *"Silencio!"*

Kate lurched forward, her heart lodged in her throat.

Ben captured her arm and dragged her back to the ground. "Don't move." He pushed her back to the ground and started to get up himself.

This time she caught his arm and held on to Ben. "There's too many of them."

"Alto!" The gunman with the flashlight shone the beam over the creek bed for a long moment, the light hovering over the top of the small boulder.

Kate ground her teeth and fought her instinct to leap out and scratch the man's eyes out who'd slapped the girl. But even she knew it would be crazy. They outnumbered

Kate and Ben and outgunned their two pistols. Taking a stand would be suicide.

After a moment, the gunman waved the driver on and the truck topped the incline and pulled away. The second truck lumbered down into the ravine and up the other side, revealing the back filled with four more gunmen and from the dark forms hunkered low in the bed, another load of people.

Ben lay still for a long time, even after the second truck exited the creek and moved off across the desert.

"Why didn't we stop them?"

"My duty is to protect you. We were outnumbered. The best we can do is get back to the ranch and report this to the Customs and Border Protection."

"But those women and the girls…" Kate stood and brushed the dust off her jeans.

"Coyotes would just as soon kill them, ditch them and save their own butts." Ben headed back down the creek bed toward where they'd stashed the horses.

Kate was left to follow, wishing with all her heart she could have done more to protect the frightened people in the back of the trucks.

Ben untied the horses, bent to give her a boost up and swung up into his saddle without speaking another word.

They hurried across the dried grasses, dodging cacti and stumpy palmetto palms illuminated by the sparkling blanket of stars in the sky.

"Do you think they could be the people responsible for killing the steer?" Kate called out over the thrumming of horses' hooves.

"Probably."

"We should have stopped them."

Ben shot a glance her way. The moon had begun to

rise, reflecting light off Ben's eyes. "The only way we'd go back out there at night is with a full contingent of soldiers and the Customs and Border Protection agents leading the way. Even then, *you're* not going out there."

A chill gave her gooseflesh as she recalled the guns every one of the men carried.

Ben urged his horse into a gallop, cutting off any further conversation.

Kate dug her heels into her horse's flanks, her gaze panning the horizon, searching for the lights of the two vehicles. Her breathing returned to normal only after the glowing windows of the ranch house came into view.

They rode up to the gate at full gallop.

Eddy stood ready, swinging the gate open for them. "You two are in a hurry. Run into trouble?"

"Two trucks full of gunmen and people." Ben dropped down off his gelding. "We had to lay low until they passed."

"You did right getting back here." Eddy nodded toward his horse. "I was getting worried and was about to come out searching for you."

Kate led her horse into the barn. Before Ben or Eddy could offer to help, she'd flipped her stirrup up over the saddle and loosened the girth. Not so hard. She could get used to riding the range and checking on cattle.

When it came time to haul the saddle off the horse, Kate tugged, expecting it to be difficult. But she pulled too hard and the saddle slid right off, the weight sending her flying back.

Ben's arms circled her waist, steadying her.

Kate leaned into him for a moment, appreciating the solid muscles and the earthy scent of a man who'd been working with horses. She could get used to having him around.

Kate pushed away. "We need to get up to the house and call the CBP." She ducked around Ben and hurried to deposit the saddle in the tack room before she did something stupid…again.

Brush in hand, Eddy stood beside Kate's mare. "I'll take care of the horses. You two head on up to the house."

"Thanks." Ben hooked Kate's arm and led her out of the barn and up to the house.

She was kind of glad to have him so close. After hiding from gunmen, the night's shadows caused her a lot more heebie-jeebies than ever before. Before she'd seen the two truckloads of coyotes and women, Kate had been more than ready to call this place home and make a stand for the land her father left for her and Lily. But now…

Kate and Ben only made it halfway across the yard when Lily burst through the screen door and raced down the steps. "Mommy!"

Ben let Kate's arm drop. "I'll make the call."

"Thanks." Kate gathered Lily up in a bear hug and swung her around. "How's my sweetie pie?" She held the child longer than normal and inhaled the scent of baby shampoo. An image of the women and girls in the backs of those trucks had been indelibly etched in her memory. She couldn't imagine being so desperate she'd subject Lily to the danger of stealing across the border in the middle of the night with men who'd just as soon take the money and leave them for dead.

"We made cookies. I found a horny toad, but it got away. Pickles piddled in the hall twice and he's asleep now." Lily glanced over Kate's shoulder at the barn. "Can I ride a horse?"

"Not now, baby."

"When?"

"Another day." A day when Kate felt more comfortable about the horse she'd be riding, and after they found the gunmen traversing her land and jailed them where they couldn't traffic humans or drugs ever again. Maybe then she could be more certain about making the Flying K their home forever.

"Come see our cookies." Lily wiggled out of Kate's arms and ran for the house.

Kate followed Ben and Lily into the house.

Once inside, Ben headed for the hallway.

Kate entered the kitchen where Lily showed her the cookies she'd made with Mrs. Henderson and Cara Jo.

Cara Jo was stacking cooled cookies in the cookie jar. "I'm so glad you two made it back when you did. I was about to call the sheriff."

"I'll tell you about it after Lily is in bed." Kate glanced around. "Where's Mrs. Henderson?"

"Her husband picked her up an hour ago."

"Thanks for staying with Lily. I owe you."

"I enjoyed it as much as I think she did."

"Now, let me see if these cookies are edible." Kate grabbed a cookie from the pile and bit into it, her empty stomach rumbling. "Oh, yes. They are wonderful. Snickerdoodles?" she asked.

Lily laughed. "How did you know?"

"My mother used to make these." Tears welled in her eyes at the memory of her mother and the weekends they'd spent making cookies and hanging out when she was little like Lily. At times like this, she missed her so much it hurt.

Kate glanced at the clock. "Holy smokes, it's way past your bedtime, young lady."

"I already had my bath. Miss Cara Jo let me stay up until you got home so that I could show you the cookies."

Cara Jo winced. "I hope you don't mind. She was so excited."

Kate shook her head. "Not at all. But now it's time for bed."

Lily danced ahead of Kate. "Can Miss Cara Jo read a book to me?"

"I'm sure she would like to get home sometime tonight and it's a long way back to town."

Lily grabbed one of Kate's hands and one of Cara Jo's and looked up at them both with her wide green eyes. "Please?"

Cara Jo laughed. "I'd love to and it'll give you a chance to wash up and have dinner."

"You're sure?"

"Absolutely." She swung Lily's arm. "Lily and I are best buds, aren't we? Why don't you grab Pickles and let's get her settled in her box upstairs."

Lily chased Pickles down the hallway and up the stairs.

Kate hugged her new friend. "Thanks, Cara Jo."

"Really, Kate. I love Lily, she's a great kid." Cara Jo climbed the stairs behind Lily, leaving Kate at the bottom.

Ben slipped up beside her. "I made the call. They're sending out a chopper to see if they can locate the trucks."

Kate faced him, her heartbeat speeding up at his proximity. Why did this man she'd only known a very short time have that kind of pull on her? "Any chance they'll find them?"

"The trucks have a big head start in the amount of time it took us to ride back to the ranch." He shrugged. "They could be just about anywhere by now."

Kate rested her hand on the banister and stared up the stairs, her heart heavy. "Do you think they're helping illegal immigrants or trafficking women?" Kate gazed into Ben's eyes.

His brows dipped low and a muscle jerked in his jaw. "As far as I could see, there were only women and girls in those trucks."

"Dear Lord." Kate sagged and her stomach roiled. "We should have stopped them."

"No. We were outnumbered and not as heavily armed." Ben gripped her arms and turned her toward him. "Let the Border Patrol deal with it. They have the resources and the weapons necessary to handle the coyotes. Had we intervened, we would only have made matters worse."

"Still…"

"Have faith in the CBP."

"Do you?"

Ben's lips tightened. "At this point, I have to. I have to focus on you. I can't risk your life chasing after bad guys." He turned and would have walked away, but Kate put a hand on his arm.

"Ben, what happened out there?"

"What do you mean?"

"Between us." She stopped, her gaze dropping to where her hand touched his arm. "Before the coyotes… The kiss."

He stiffened, drawing up to his full height. "What

happened out there…shouldn't have. I won't let it happen again."

Kate braced her palms on his chest. The solid muscles beneath his shirt made her long to run her fingers across his naked skin. "I shouldn't have encouraged it. But…"

"It won't happen again. I'm here to protect you and Lily. Nothing more." He backed away, his tone brooking no more argument, his face set in stone.

Kate tucked her hands in her pockets to keep them from shaking. She wanted to say more, to tell him she'd felt his response, he wasn't immune to her. Instead, she turned and walked up the stairs.

IT TOOK ALL of Ben's self-control to keep from going up the stairs after Kate. He wanted her so badly it hurt and the turmoil it was causing inside him was more than he could stand.

Kate was as different from Julia as night from day. She'd already proved she wasn't afraid of anything. When the gunmen had shot so close to them, Kate hadn't fallen apart like a lot of women would have. She'd held steady and stayed low.

He wondered what Julia would have done. What she had done when she and his daughter had been…

Ben's breath lodged in his throat when he realized he couldn't even remember Julia's face. He closed his eyes, but all he could see was light auburn hair, glinting like copper in the sun.

Ben stepped out onto the porch.

Eddy was coming up from the barn. "I have the horses settled in for the night and gave them an extra section of hay."

"Thanks."

Eddy climbed the steps and stood beside Ben, staring out into the night as he rocked back on his boot heels. "Well, I'll be heading home unless you think I need to stay."

"No. Go on home. I'll take it from here."

"Think she'll stay?"

Ben didn't have to ask who Eddy was talking about. "Kate's a pretty determined woman."

Eddy nodded. "If she's anything like her father, she won't give up easily."

No, she wouldn't, but in this case, maybe she should. The situation was too dangerous.

"I'll be goin'. *Buenas noches.*" Eddy climbed into his pickup and drove away, leaving behind him a deep silence.

Darkness closed in around Ben as he crossed to the barn, checked inside, made a pass around the outside and the perimeter of the other outbuildings.

When he was satisfied there were no intruders, he climbed the steps to the house and went straight to his room. He grabbed fresh jeans and a clean shirt and ducked into the bathroom down the hall.

When he emerged, he peeked in at Lily, who lay sound asleep, her puppy in a box beside her bed, also asleep.

Sounds from the kitchen drew him down the stairs when he should have gone straight to bed.

Kate stood with her back to him at the kitchen counter, wearing a worn T-shirt and frayed denim shorts, and she was barefoot. Her hair hung in limp, wet strands, dampening the back of her shirt. "You can wash your hands in the sink, here. Your plate will be ready in a moment."

Knowing it was a mistake, yet unable to help himself, he crossed to the sink and stood beside her. He squirted dish soap onto his fingers and cleaned his already clean hands. He couldn't resist any excuse to be closer to her.

As he dried his hands, she smiled at him.

"Sit. Cara Jo left after reading two books to Lily. Mrs. Henderson left the best roast beef and potatoes you've ever tasted warming in the oven. I'll have a plate full for you in two shakes."

Kate stood within reach and, if he was right, she wasn't wearing a bra. Dear God, he wanted her.

Ben swallowed hard and backed up several steps. "I'm not hungry." For food.

When she turned with a heaping plate in one hand and a glass of iced tea in the other, she frowned. "No argument. You need to eat." She set the plate and glass on the table and pointed at the chair. "Sit."

Too tired to argue, or maybe just too tired to fight it, he sat in the designated chair. Two candles stood in the middle of the table with a box of matches beside them. Ben struck the tip of a match against the matchbox and applied the flame to the wick.

"Sorry, forgot the silverware." Kate dived for a drawer, pulling out a knife, fork and spoon. She hit the light switch on the wall, plunging the room into an intimate hazy glow.

She returned to his side and leaned over him to place the utensils beside his plate.

He couldn't take anymore. He grabbed her around the waist and sat her in his lap. "Do you have any idea what you're doing to me?"

Her eyes widened, her mouth opened in an O, and her cheeks turned a pretty pink. She sucked in a breath and let it out, her blush deepening. "Based on where I'm sitting, I could hazard a pretty good guess."

"Damn it, Kate, I promised it wouldn't happen again."

She sighed. "Some promises were meant to be broken." Her gaze dropped to his lips.

Her words, the way she said them, and that shift of her attention was his undoing. "What am I supposed to do with you? You set me on fire."

Her lips turned upward and she smiled. "Burn, baby, burn."

Laughter rumbled up inside him. He fought the happiness, fought to control a surge of hope. In the end, he lost and grasped her cheeks between his hands, kissing her like she was the buoy that would bring him back to the surface of the sea of sorrow he'd been wallowing in since Sarah's and Julia's deaths.

Her fingers pried loose the buttons on the front of his shirt, one by one. She didn't break the kiss until the last button was freed.

Ben's hands slipped beneath her shirt and up her back. As he'd suspected, she wasn't wearing a bra. Heat rushed to his loins, his member straining against his fly.

Kate shoved the shirt over his shoulders and down his arms.

Ben's fingers slid along her sides and upward to cup her breasts. When his fingers found the taut nipples, he paused. "Lily?"

"Will sleep until morning." She kissed his chin, her lips sliding downward to caress his neck, her breasts pressing into his palms.

Even the child conspired against Ben. With nothing but his memories standing in his way, Ben lost the fight. He shrugged the shirt off his arms and lifted the hem of

Kate's T-shirt up and over her head, flinging it across the table. Then he lifted her, spreading her legs wide to straddle his hips. In the soft candlelight he gazed down at her, drinking her in like a man dying of thirst.

"Don't stop now." She raised his hand to her breast. "I'm not good at starting over. I married my high school sweetheart. I don't know how to flirt. I never had any practice."

"You're doing a hell of a job." He rolled her rosy nipples between his thumbs and forefingers.

Her back arched, her hair slipping down to her waist, curling as it dried.

"You should eat." She gasped as he took one nipple between his teeth and nipped.

"I am."

"Food, silly." Her fingers wrapped around his head and held him where he was, her thighs tightening against his sides.

"The only thing I'm hungry for is you." He stood, bringing her up with him, wrapping her thighs around his middle.

Her arms circled his neck as she spread kisses along the column of his throat.

Ben carried her up the stairs to her bedroom, kicking the door open softly so as not to disturb Lily and Pickles.

He set her on her feet and stripped her shorts down her long legs.

Kate stood for a moment, bathed in moonlight peeking through the window. Her tongue swept across her lips, her gaze traveling over him and downward. "You're a bit overdressed." Her fingers closed around the metal rivet of his jeans. She pushed it through the hole and slid the zipper downward, slowly, her fingers brushing against his erection.

Past rational thought, he swung Kate up into his arms and, one-handed, flung back the comforter.

About to lay her against the sheets, he paused.

A movement out of the corner of his eye and a dry rattling sound shot adrenaline through him and he jumped back.

"What? Oh, my God!" Kate clung to him, her arms clamped around his neck, her gaze on the bed. "Is that what I think that is?"

Coiled against the cool white sheets was the biggest rattlesnake Ben had ever encountered. And it was angry.

CHAPTER TWELVE

KATE STIFLED A SCREAM as she clung to Ben, holding her arms and legs as far away from the snake as she could. She'd have crawled over Ben's body and run if he hadn't been gripping her so tightly. "Do something," she cried.

Ben chuckled, struggling to maintain his hold on her squirming body. "I have to put you down before I can take care of the snake." He strode to the door. "Turn on the light."

Kate flipped the light switch.

The snake on the bed rattled again, perhaps angry at having his sleep disturbed.

Kate shot a glance all around them, searching for friends of the snake in her bed. The floor appeared clear of any other slithering creatures. "Put me down."

Ben dropped her feet to the floor and steadied her. "Are you okay?"

She crossed her arms over her breasts. "No. There's a snake in my bed. A poisonous one at that."

"You can wait in the hall if you like."

"No." She didn't want to leave Ben's side. If anyone could handle a tough situation, it was Ben. "What are you going to do?"

"Get rid of the snake," he said, his tone matter-of-fact.

"How?"

He didn't answer. Instead he approached the end of

the bed, careful to stay out of striking range of the big rattler. He pulled the top sheet and comforter completely off the bed and shook them.

Nothing fell out.

Kate lunged for the sheet and shook it again, before wrapping it around her body.

Ben eased the elastic corners of the fitted sheet off the end of the bed. Circling wide, he repeated the process on the other end of the bed, then he gathered the ends and pulled them together quickly before the snake could slither out and onto the floor.

Carrying the fitted sheet like a bag, he held it away from his body and descended the stairs.

Kate followed, checking the floor before she took every step. She stopped at the top of the stairs, shivering in the air-conditioning.

Ben continued down, stepping out the front door onto the porch. "I'll be back. Don't touch anything until I can check your room over."

Kate held her breath until Ben returned, letting it out as he appeared again in the doorway.

"The snake?"

He closed the door and glanced up at her. "Dead."

Kate heaved a sigh. "Thank God." Then her heart thumped against her ribs. "Lily." She dashed into her daughter's room, slapping the light switch on the wall.

Ben burst through the doorway behind Kate.

Kate gathered Lily up in her arms and held her while Ben checked her bedding and room thoroughly.

"Mommy?"

"Shh, baby. Go back to sleep."

Pickles whined in his box.

"Can Pickles sleep with me?" she asked, her voice groggy, a fist rubbing over her eyes.

"No, baby. Pickles has his own bed."

"I want Pickles to sleep—" A huge yawn interrupted Lily's protest. She snuggled down in Kate's arms and fell back to sleep.

The puppy turned around in his box three times and dropped down, his head draped over his paws.

Ben straightened the bedding and waited for Kate to lay the child down. Afterward, he tucked the sheets around Lily and pressed a kiss to her forehead.

Kate swallowed hard on a knot in her throat.

Ben had kissed Lily, the gesture so natural and right it took Kate's breath away.

When he straightened, his gaze met hers. He nodded toward the door.

Kate stepped out into the hallway, tugging the sheet up securely over her breasts, embarrassed about her behavior. She'd more or less encouraged Ben to make love to her. Hell, she'd practically thrown herself at him. Her cheeks burning, she pulled the door halfway closed and turned toward her bedroom.

Two steps in that direction and she stopped, a huge tremor shaking her so hard her teeth rattled.

Ben's hands settled on her bare shoulders. "What's wrong?"

"I can't go back in there."

"I'll check it out."

"Thanks, but it won't make a difference. I won't be sleeping in there tonight."

"I've disposed of the snake."

"Yeah, but you can't take the image out of my head."

"You can sleep in my room."

"No. You need your sleep more than I do."

"We both need sleep." He cupped her elbow with his warm, strong palm and led her past Lily's room to his.

Once inside the doorway, Kate stopped and stared at the four-poster bed, images of a naked Ben flashing through her mind. "No. I can't do it."

"I'll sleep on the couch downstairs."

"I can sleep on the couch."

"And if something happened to you downstairs, I might not hear anything."

Kate trembled. "I just won't sleep then."

"Don't be ridiculous. Take the bed." He urged her forward, stripped the comforter back and checked the sheets. "See? No snake."

A shiver racked her body yet again. "I can't get that rattler out of my mind. I almost crawled into bed with a snake." She shivered again.

He shoved a hand through his hair. "If it helps, I'll stay with you until you go to sleep."

She glanced at him, her brows pulling downward. "What we were about to do…"

"Don't worry. I'll only stay until you go to sleep. Nothing else."

"I don't know."

"For crissakes." Ben scooped her up in his arms and tossed her on the bed. "Go to sleep before I forget myself again." He turned his back on her and paced the floor.

Kate adjusted the sheet around her body and moved to the farthest side of the bed. "And I'm supposed to sleep while you pace?" She shook her head.

He stopped and shoved a hand through his hair. The button on his fly remained undone, the zipper halfway down.

Despite her best promise to herself, Kate's gaze ze-
roed in on the dark hairs peeking through. The shivers of
dread for the snake changed to the shivers of the kind of
excitement she'd felt before the snake had come on scene.

Her gaze rose to capture Ben's, staring down at her.

He groaned. "I can't do this."

"Then don't." Kate fluffed the comforter, checking
beneath it one more time before she settled in, her eyes
wide. She turned her back to Ben and feigned sleep.
After a moment or two, a sensation of something crawling across her leg made her sit up in the bed and drag her
legs up to her chin. She shook the blanket again. Nothing fell out or slithered across the bed.

Kate peered over the top of her sheet-covered knees.
"Why are you still standing there? The couch is downstairs. I don't need you." Her voice trailed off. The hell
she didn't need him. It was destined to be a long, scary
night.

His hand rose to the light switch. "Want me to turn
out the light?"

Her hand went up immediately. "No!"

Ben sighed, crossed the room and sat on the edge of
the bed.

"What are you doing?"

"Going out of my mind. What does it look like?" He
swung his legs, jeans and all up onto the bed. "Come
here." Ben gathered her in his arms, pulling her body
up against his. "Go to sleep."

"I can't."

"Yes, you can. Close your eyes and picture Lily playing with her puppy."

Snuggled against Ben, one hand resting on his bare
chest, Kate tried. Instead of her daughter, all she could

imagine was trailing that hand across his taut muscles, finding and pinching the hard little brown nipples.

She closed her eyes, inhaling the fresh, clean scent of soap and man. Her hand slipped over a rib, then another, inching south to the waistband of his jeans.

Ben captured her hand. "This can only lead to one thing."

"You think?"

In a flash, he shoved her onto her back, pinning her wrists above her head. "I loved my wife, Kate. I don't need another woman in my life."

"Then why are you lying on top of me." Her gaze met his unflinchingly. She arched her back, her pelvis rubbing against the hard ridge beneath his jeans. "And why are you so aroused?"

He closed his eyes, his breath coming in short, ragged pants. Then his mouth descended on hers. His hands found the edge of the sheet over her breasts and yanked it downward, peeling it from her body, until she lay naked and trembling. Not out of fear, but in anticipation of what would come next.

She raised a hand to his zipper, sliding it lower until his erection sprang free, hard and straight.

"I didn't want this to happen," he said through gritted teeth.

"So noted." Kate's hand circled him, sliding along his length, dipping inside the denim to cup him, massaging his member. "What are you going to do about it?"

He leaped from the bed and stood with his back to her, breathing hard.

She rose behind him, her hands caressing a path, curving around his shoulders, down his sides to his narrow hips. Kate circled around to his front, beyond caring what he thought of her brazen behavior, beyond patient…ready to take him inside her.

She wanted him to fill the void she'd been living with for so long.

Kate pushed his jeans over his hips and down his legs, her hands caressing his buttocks, his thighs and the sharply defined calves.

He stepped free of the denim and threaded his hands in her hair, dragging her to her feet.

She let him, her body sliding up his, skin-to-delicious-skin. Every nerve ending burned, fire radiating from her core outward.

He cupped the back of her thighs and lifted her, wrapping her legs around his waist. "Stop me now."

"I can't." She wove her fingers into his hair, dragging his head downward until their lips met. "I need you."

His member nudged her opening, the tip sliding in. "Wait."

"Really?" Her thighs tightened around him, lifting her up.

"I have protection in the nightstand…by the bed." He groaned and lifted her off him, laying her across the bed, her legs draped over the side.

Kate reached into the drawer and removed a strip of foil-packaged condoms. She tore the packet open with her teeth and rolled the condom over him, her hand cupping him at the base.

Ben stepped between her legs, grabbed her wrists and pinned them over her head, his erection poised at her entrance. "You make me hotter than the Texas sun."

"That makes two of us, then." She wrapped her legs around his waist and tightened, driving him in.

He slid all the way inside, the smooth, slick sensations so erotic, he threw his head back and drew in a deep, steadying breath.

Then he pulled back out and slammed in again, settling into a fast, smooth rhythm.

As the friction increased, heat built and tingling sensations rippled through Kate's body. Her back arched off the bed, her thighs clenching with each thrust until she pitched over the edge, crying out his name.

His fingers dug into her hips as he plunged in one last time. Ben held steady, his face tense, his muscles bunched and his member throbbing against her channel.

As they tumbled back to the earth, Kate's legs disengaged from around his waist and dropped over the side of the bed.

Ben eased her up on the mattress and lay beside her, spooning her body with his.

"Stay with me?" she begged.

His hand rested on her naked hip. "As long as there are no regrets in the morning."

She sighed. "No regrets." Kate snuggled in his arms, feeling more safe and secure than she had since her husband left for war. If only she could count on this to last.

Sadly, she knew she couldn't.

A single tear slid down her cheek and dropped onto the sheet. How could a man come to mean so much to her in such a short time? Was she desperate for male companionship? Or was it *this* man that made her feel this way?

It didn't matter. When his replacement came, Ben would leave. She'd be on her own again.

But for now, he kept the boogeyman and the snakes away while warming her backside.

Kate closed her eyes and fell asleep.

BEN LAY FOR a long time, his arms around Kate's naked body, holding her like they belonged together. Making love to a woman had that effect on him. That had to be the explanation for his sudden desire to stay with her, to become a part of her and Lily's lives.

But that wouldn't be fair to either one of them. He'd had a wife and daughter. He'd loved them both so much it still hurt to think about them. How could he begin to love someone else as much? He couldn't. It wasn't possible. Was it?

Kate stirred against him, her bottom brushing sensitive areas, stirring desire so strong he couldn't suppress it.

He'd asked Hank to find his replacement. What if he did? Could Ben walk away and leave Kate in the hands of someone else? Could he trust that other agent to take care of Kate and Lily, to protect them from whoever was after them?

His arms tightened around Kate, his chest squeezing tight. He couldn't desert them. Not now. Not when they needed him most.

The sound of a puppy's cries pulled Ben from his thoughts. Pickles had to be missing his mother.

Ben slipped out of the bed and stood, gazing down at Kate as she lay deep in sleep, caressed by the moonlight streaming through the window. Her long hair looking more auburn in this light as it splayed across the pillow, her lips parted as if she fell asleep whispering.

Ben brushed a strand of hair from her cheek and bent to press his lips to hers.

"Sweet dreams."

He slipped into his jeans and zipped them, then padded barefoot to the next room.

Lily lay splayed across her bed, her foot dangling over the side.

Pickles looked up at Ben, his soulful blue eyes begging Ben to rescue him from his grief and loneliness.

Ben scooped up the puppy and the box and headed down the stairs to the couch. He understood how Pickles felt. Torn from the ones he loved, but surrounded by the possibility of a new family.

In the night, everything seemed more overwhelming than during the light of day.

As he lay on the couch, his feet hanging over the arms, Ben cuddled the puppy against him and turned over the day's events in his mind.

Two things stood out, touching him with a cold hand of dread.

A gang of coyotes was using the Flying K as a place to traffic human cargo.

Secondly, that snake hadn't gotten into Kate's bed on its own. Someone had put it there.

CHAPTER THIRTEEN

KATE YAWNED, STRETCHED and glanced around her room, disoriented at first. Her tender breasts rubbed against the sheet and she remembered where she was—in Ben's bed—and that she was naked.

"Mommy?" Lily called out.

Kate scrambled to her feet, wondering where Ben had gone. She had just wrapped the sheet around her body when Lily ran by the open door.

"Mommy?"

Her frightened cry spurred Kate forward. "Lily, I'm here."

Lily stopped at the top of the stairs and looked back. "Where's Pickles? He's not in his box."

Kate smiled and shrugged, relieved her daughter hadn't asked why she was in a different room and wrapped in a sheet. "I don't know. Let me get dressed and I'll help you find him."

"Lily?" Ben's deep voice echoed up the stairs.

Kate moved to peer over the banister railing at the man.

He stood barefoot, wearing nothing but his jeans. The sight of his naked chest sent Kate's pulse skittering into crazy palpitations. An image of herself lying naked with him spread warmth throughout her body, and extra fire to one place in particular.

He shot a heated glance at her before he held the puppy up for Lily to see. "I have Pickles down here."

"Pickles." Lily ran down the stairs, her hand trailing along the railing, wild, light red hair flying out around her shoulders.

A sharp tug in the region of her heart made Kate press a hand to her chest. How like a family they were. She had to remind herself that it was nothing but an illusion. A fantasy bubble destined to pop when life returned to normal.

Ben handed Lily the puppy. "I've already taken him outside. He should play all right inside for a few minutes. Stay in the house, please."

"I will." Lily set the puppy on the floor and ran into the living room, squealing as Pickles chased after her, barking in his shrill puppy voice.

Which left Ben staring up at Kate. He stepped up one of the stair risers. "How are you this morning?"

Kate gathered the sheet around her body, a flush of warmth burning up her neck into her cheeks. "I'm fine."

He climbed two more steps, his gaze pinning hers. "Any regrets?"

Her eyes widened, her heart pounding so hard, she could hear it banging against her eardrums. "No regrets." She swallowed hard and forced herself to ask, "And you?"

When Ben cleared the top step and stood with her on the landing, Kate stepped away until her back bumped against the wall.

"None." Ben advanced slowly. When he stopped, barefoot and toe to toe with her, he reached out and touched the rise of her breasts above the sheet. "Seems you were wearing this last night."

A smile fluttered across her lips, shyness weighing on her words. "I think I need a new outfit."

"I kind of like this one." His fingers tugged on the end, untucking the edges.

Kate inhaled, her breasts rising as Ben unfolded the sheet, exposing her body to his piercing gaze.

"Oh, yes. I like this outfit." He bent, capturing a nipple between his teeth, nipping lightly.

Kate's hands feathered through his hair, pressing against the back of his neck. She closed her eyes, letting the rampant waves of desire swarm over her.

"Mommy?" Lily's voice brought her back to earth with a jolt.

Kate jerked the sheet closed, stepped around Ben and leaned over the railing. "What is it, Lily?"

"Pickles had an accident."

A chuckle rose up her throat. "I'll be down in a moment to help you clean it up." When she turned toward her bedroom, Ben blocked her path. She blinked up at him. "You heard Lily, the puppy had an acci—"

Ben lifted her chin with a crooked finger and kissed her hard, his tongue darting out to capture hers in a brief caress.

As quickly as he'd possessed her, he let her go. "I'll take care of the puppy." Then he left her on the landing and padded down the steps, entering the living room in search of Lily.

Kate stood still for several seconds, unable to get her bearings. Hell, she'd been unable to form coherent thoughts since Ben had come into her life. If she wasn't careful, she'd fall in love with a man who still loved his dead wife. And where would that leave her?

Kate eased into her bedroom, on the lookout for anything that slithered or rattled. The room remained silent as she dressed for the day in jeans, a white button-down shirt and cowboy boots. She pulled out the key her father's attorney had given her at the reading of the will and decided it was time to look for whatever it belonged to.

Perhaps when she found the lock, it would unveil the reason why someone wanted her off the property and away from Wild Oak Canyon.

As Kate gathered her ponytail in place, corralling her wild curls with a rubber band, the telephone at the bottom of the stairs rang. She decided to forgo makeup. It wasn't as if she was trying to impress anyone. Certainly not Ben. He wasn't sticking around. What had happened last night wasn't the stuff relationships were made of. Ben was a bodyguard. Kate was the job. When she no longer needed his protection, he'd be gone.

If she was smart, she'd discontinue this sex-only connection with the bodyguard. It wasn't fair to her, to Lily or to him.

With a deep breath, she hurried down the stairs and lifted the phone on the fourth ring. "Hello."

"Kate, it's Cara Jo."

"Hi." Kate's heart warmed at the sound of her new friend's voice.

"Just wanted to let you know the local church in Wild Oak Canyon has a Mother's Day Out program. Lily might enjoy playing with children her own age a couple times a week."

"Wow, that would be great. What days?"

"Tuesdays and Thursdays from nine until three o'clock." Cara Jo called out to someone on her end of the phone.

"Are you at the diner?" Kate asked.

"I am. It being Thursday, I thought I'd let you know early enough to get Lily in today, if you had a mind to." She chuckled softly. "Purely selfish reasons, I assure you. If you come to town, you could join me for lunch and do a little shopping without having to drag poor Lily around."

"That sounds good. I could run by the sheriff's office again and report the dead cattle, for all the good it would do."

Cara Jo snorted. "At least you'd have a record of it."

"Right." Kate glanced at Lily playing on the floor in the living room with Pickles. The little puppy had as much energy as the four-year-old.

Nothing like jumping into the community. And Lily was used to playing with the children she'd met at the day care in Houston. Kate made the decision. "I'll check it out today. If all goes well, I'll meet you for lunch."

"Make it around eleven-thirty. Twelve to one-thirty is our busy time and it gets hard to find a seat."

"Will do." Kate hung up, ran back up the stairs and grabbed play clothes, shoes, barrettes and a hairbrush from Lily's room.

When she returned to the first floor, the living room was empty.

Sounds of voices and laughter came from the kitchen.

When Kate entered, she was struck by how natural the scene appeared.

Lily sat in a chair on a stack of books, digging into a bowl of cereal. Ben sat beside her with a plate of eggs, bacon and toast. Mrs. Henderson busied herself at the stove, talking to both of them with her back to the room.

Kate smiled. "Good morning."

"Oh, Kate, dear. Sit. I have breakfast for you." Mrs. Henderson lifted a fry pan full of fluffy, yellow scrambled eggs and faced her. "Did you sleep well?"

Kate's face heated. "Yes. I did." *Minus the snake and the musical beds and making love to Ben.* She had slept well once she'd fallen asleep in Ben's arms. She refused to meet his gaze, but out of the corner of her eye she could see the way his lips twitched.

If he smiled now, she'd throw something at him.

Instead he shoved a forkful of eggs into his mouth and chewed.

"Lily, how would you like to make some new friends today?" Kate asked, hoping to pull attention off her red cheeks and focus it on her baby girl.

Lily set her spoon beside her bowl and lifted her cup of milk. "Yes, please."

Kate continued for Ben's benefit, "There's a Mother's Day Out program at the local church. Cara Jo from the diner suggested it, thinking Lily might like to meet some of the local children. I think it's a good idea."

Ben nodded. "Eddy had a few things he'd like picked up in town. We can take the truck."

"I'll take my car, you can follow. I think I'll be safe in town and I might want to do a little shopping while there."

Ben frowned. "Are you sure you don't want me to drive?"

"I don't think it's necessary." Kate remained firm. If Ben was leaving, she needed to get around on her own and not be afraid. "Nothing's going to happen in a town full of people."

Ben's brows didn't rise. "I'm not thrilled with the idea of taking two vehicles. Seems a waste of fuel and time.

But as long as you wait for me to follow you back to the ranch, I suppose it's okay."

Kate almost smiled. For some strange reason, she liked pushing his buttons. But she understood his reasons. It was his job to protect her and Lily. "I'll let you know when I'm ready to head home."

Fifteen minutes later, she'd finished her breakfast, brushed her teeth and Lily's, and gathered her keys and purse.

Ben waited outside beside his truck, his brows dented in what appeared to be a permanent frown. He'd already switched the booster seat into the backseat of her car.

Lily ran to his arms. "Pickles cried when I put him in the box."

"Mrs. Henderson will let him out to play once we leave. He'll be fine until you get home." Ben tucked her into the safety seat and buckled the belt over her lap, then pressed a kiss to her forehead.

Kate stood back, once again amazed at how comfortable the two were together. Already, she predicted it would be hard on Lily when Ben left.

Kate climbed into the car and pulled out onto the highway bound for the little town and the church where Lily would spend the day doing what kids did—play.

The drive was uneventful and Kate relished the time alone with Lily. It gave her the opportunity to think through what had happened the night before. She never would have thought she'd be so quickly attracted to a man, and never had she dreamed she'd jump into bed with a stranger after knowing him such a short time. Having married her high school sweetheart, Kate hadn't dated as an adult. One thing was for sure, she wasn't setting a good example for Lily. Still she didn't regret the magic she'd experienced with Ben the night before.

Kate parked in front of the church.

Ben parked on the passenger side of Kate's car. He got to Lily before Kate and lifted the child out onto the ground, tucking her hand in his.

Kate took Lily's other hand and they walked into the church together.

At the administrative office, Kate filled out paperwork and let them make a copy of Lily's shot records. When it came to filling out the emergency data card, she paused. She wrote down her home phone number and her cell phone number, but the cell number was only reliable sometimes. "If you can't get me on my cell phone, call Cara Jo's diner and ask for me or leave a message with Cara Jo. I'll check in there."

"Leave my cell number, too, as backup." Ben recited his number and Kate wrote it on the form.

Kate and Ben walked with the administrator to the classroom Lily would be in. Six children ranging in age from three to five gathered around tables, wearing cute little aprons. They were elbow-deep in finger painting.

Lily was so excited, she didn't even say goodbye.

Kate left the building, happy that her daughter would have a fun-filled day with children her age.

"Now what?" Ben asked.

"I want to stop by the county assessor, do a little shopping and then meet Cara Jo for lunch." She shot a glance his way, but didn't linger on his handsome face, afraid she'd ask him to stay with her. "What about you?"

"While you're in town, I can take care of reporting the dead cattle to the sheriff's office. At least get it on record. I need to run out to Hank's and check on the status of that DVD. Then I'll drop by the hardware store for the items Eddy needed for the ranch."

Kate glanced at her watch. "Meet back here at three?"

"Three." He caught Kate's arm as she turned away. "Don't go anywhere else without notifying me first, will you?"

"I won't." Her arm tingled where he touched her. Damn. The man had her tied in knots and wanting so much more. Things she shouldn't be thinking in broad daylight came to mind more than she cared to admit. With her thoughts on her bodyguard, she wasn't focusing on what was important. The nutcase causing her grief and the human trafficking happening on her own land.

"Three o'clock." She scooted away from his grip on her arm and climbed into her car. After shifting into Reverse, she left the parking lot, cranking the air conditioner up to chill her suddenly flaming cheeks.

She stopped by the county tax assessor's office to discover no change in the computer situation. They expected someone out that afternoon to work on it.

After she left the county offices, Kate spent thirty minutes in the General Store, exploring the aisles, getting familiar with what Wild Oak Canyon had to offer. It wasn't a huge department store, but they sold jeans, chambray shirts and cowboy hats. That and a few odds and ends in fencing supplies and plain pantry staples, fresh bread and milk. After she'd gone up and down each aisle, it was time to meet with Cara Jo at the diner across the street from the General Store.

When Kate pushed through the diner's door, Cara Jo dashed by her, carrying three heaping plates of food.

"Sorry, one of my waitresses called in sick. I have to work the lunch crowd." She set the plates on a table in the corner where three men dressed in jeans and chambray shirts sat with their forks and knives ready to dig in.

On her way back past Kate, Cara Jo gave her an apologetic frown. "Sorry. Can we do a rain check on our lunch?"

"That's fine. I ate breakfast not long ago."

"Oh, please sit, have lunch. It's on me." Cara Jo whooshed by and grabbed another two plates from the window into the kitchen.

Kate glanced around at the busy establishment. She didn't want to sit by herself, and she didn't feel like sitting with strangers.

Robert Sanders occupied a booth near the far corner, sitting across the table from the sheriff, their heads bent close, intense expressions on their faces.

Kate didn't see herself getting into a conversation with the two men. And they appeared to be discussing business. She caught Cara Jo on her next pass. "I'm going to head out to the ranch. I have some things to do out there. I'll be back in town around three to get Lily. I'll stop by then for a cup of coffee, if you have time."

"Oh, sure. Three will be our slow time. I'll see you then." Cara Jo was off again, snatching up a carafe of steaming coffee and a pitcher of ice water.

Kate left the diner and stood outside on the sidewalk. She dug her cell phone out of her purse and dialed Ben's number. The call went straight to his voice mail. She left a message, or at least hoped she did. With spotty reception, she wasn't sure she stayed connected throughout her call.

With nothing else to do, not feeling like shopping and with nobody to talk to, Kate decided to do what she'd told Cara Jo she was going to do and head back out to the ranch.

Lily would be happily playing with her new friends and Ben was busy doing errands and updating the sheriff's deputies and Hank Derringer.

A little lonely and a bit anxious, Kate couldn't stand around and wait for someone to show up or free up to babysit her. She still had a lot of unpacking to do. Mrs. Henderson would be there and now that Kate knew how to handle the Glock, she would be just fine.

Kate jammed her hand into her jeans pocket, searching for her car keys and found the mystery key her father had left her.

She could spend time searching the house and surrounding outbuildings for the lock the key belonged to. Kate climbed into her car and headed out of town to the ranch. The wind had picked up, buffeting her little car around. With few trees or hills to block the wind, it blew through, hard and fast and filled with fine grains of sand that pinged against the windshield.

In broad daylight, Kate didn't expect to be accosted. But then she hadn't expected a biker gang to show up in her front yard the first morning after she'd arrived. Just to play it safe, Kate kept alternating watching the pavement ahead and behind in the rearview mirrors. Anytime she passed a road connecting to the highway, she studied it carefully, looking for suspicious vehicles, lurking, waiting for her to pass by, alone and vulnerable.

She'd be glad when she got back to the ranch with Mrs. Henderson and Eddy.

Kate gripped the steering wheel so tightly, her knuckles turned white as she struggled to quell her rising fears and to maintain control of the little car being tossed around by strong southerly winds.

By the time she drove through the gate and up to the ranch house, Kate's fingers were cramping. And all for what? Nothing happened on the highway and no biker gang greeted her at the house.

As Kate climbed out of the car, her hair escaped its neat ponytail and whipped around her face and neck.

A rumbling-on-gravel sound made her turn and face the driveway she'd driven in on. Another vehicle turned off the county road onto the gravel drive far enough away that she couldn't make it out, but close enough to send a flash of fear through her.

Her brows furrowed, Kate hurried toward the house, scraping her mind for the location of the pistol and shells.

"Oh, good. You're here." Mrs. Henderson met her at the screen door, her purse hooked over her shoulder. "Mr. Henderson forgot to tell me he had an appointment at the clinic today and the Customs and Border Protection folks called a while ago to say they were on the way out to check on your reports of lights and dead cattle. I'd stick around and answer their questions, but now that you're here..."

"How long did the CBP say they'd be before they got here?" Kate asked.

"There they are now." Mrs. Henderson pointed down the drive.

The vehicle Kate had seen came into view. A big, white Hummer H2, with knobby tires and a green stripe, spit up a wide cloud of dust on the gravel drive.

"When they called about an hour ago, I thought it would be no problem. Eddy said he'd meet them at the barn when they came in. I had just pulled a pie out of the

oven when David called to say he was picking me up."
The older woman glanced over Kate's shoulder. "That
should be Dave now. I wasn't sure what to do with the
puppy when I left so it's a good thing you showed up
when you did." She gave Kate a half smile. "Sorry. My
husband can be forgetful. That's why I go to his appoint-
ments with him."

"Don't worry. I'll be fine without you."

Her eyes narrowed and she looked past Kate.
"Where's Mr. Harding?"

"He'll be along in a bit," Kate fudged. No use detain-
ing Marge when her husband had already driven out to
pick her up.

"I can't leave you alone. Mr. Henderson will just have
to go on without me." Marge let the purse slide down
her arm and turned in the doorway.

"No, really. I'll be fine. Eddy's around here. The Border Protection is here. And if that's not enough, Ben
gave me lessons on how to fire my pistol. It turns out
I'm a pretty good shot. You go on with Mr. Henderson.
He needs you more than I do."

The older woman's brows dipped. "Are you sure?"
She glanced around the immediate vicinity of the ranch
house as if expecting someone to be lurking in the shadows. "I don't feel right leaving you like this."

Kate rested her hand on Mrs. Henderson's arm. "You
don't have to baby me. I can handle myself and Ben will
be along shortly."

"Okay. But do be careful." She squeezed Kate's
hand and descended the stairs. "I'll be back to fix dinner around five."

"Don't make the trip out again. I can cook, you know."

Another near lie. She wasn't that good, but Mrs. Henderson didn't have to know that.

Marge patted her purse. "Well, then, I'll see you in the morning."

"Thanks, Mrs. H." Kate sighed as Mr. Henderson got out of the driver's seat and rounded the front of the car to open the door for his wife. He waved at Kate and climbed back into the car and turned it around, headed back to the highway and town.

Kate admired the way the old couple relied on each other for things. They loved each other, which was evident in the way the old man took care of Marge and she him.

When Troy had been alive, Kate had never quite pictured them growing old together. Now she supposed that she'd never had enough time on her hands to dwell on such things, what with her pregnancy occurring so close to when they'd gotten married and then Troy leaving before even Kate knew she was with child.

Kate stood in the yard as the officers stepped out of their SUV and strode across the ground to her.

One of the officers held out his hand. "I'm Officer Mendoza with U.S. Customs and Border Protection. Are you Ms. Langsdon?"

"Yes, that's me."

"We're here to review recent reports of suspicious activity in the area."

"I take it the helicopters didn't find the two trucks last night?"

"No, ma'am." The spokesman of the two pulled a notepad out of his pocket. "Could you or your husband show me where you saw the dead cattle?"

Kate let the husband comment pass by without comment. "Your best bet will be to have my foreman show you where you can find the dead cattle and the ravine where we saw the two trucks."

Eddy chose that moment to cross the barnyard, slapping his cowboy hat against his leg, dust rising and whipping away with the wind.

Kate brought the CBP officers up to date on what had happened on the ranch, from the attack in the house, the home intrusions, biker gangs and dead cattle to the truckloads of people.

Mendoza shook his head. "I suggest you get a good guard dog and a bodyguard."

"Got the bodyguard. Working on the guard dog." Her lips curved as an image of Ben came to mind and at the thought of Pickles being a guard dog.

Mendoza glanced over her shoulder and around the yard. "A bodyguard isn't much good if he's not around to guard you."

"He's on his way back from town," Kate lied, realizing she'd been stupid to leave Wild Oak Canyon without him. Without Marge as backup she only had Eddy to protect her should someone cause trouble.

When Kate had told them all she knew, she paused, waiting for their response.

Officer Mendoza closed his notepad and slid it into his shirt pocket. "Could you show me where you found the carcasses?"

Kate turned to Eddy.

"Sí." Eddy eyed the men. "I have extra horses in the barn."

The officer smiled. "Thanks, but we'll stick with the SUV. It gets in most places the horses can go."

Eddy didn't respond, his gaze roving over the huge

tires and fancy paint job of the CBP vehicle. Then he shrugged. "You'll have to follow me and my horse." He turned and walked away.

Mendoza grinned. "He always so talkative?"

Kate smiled. "He has to warm up to you."

"How long have you owned the Flying K?"

It was Kate's turn to smile. "A grand total of a week."

Eddy had mounted his horse and stood waiting by the gate to the pasture.

"Guess we better get going." Mendoza nodded at Kate. "Thank you for your time."

"Hope you find the trucks. I'm worried about the passengers as hot as it gets out here." Kate watched as the Hummer cleared the gate and Eddy closed it behind them.

Once the group disappeared across the pasture, Kate dug the key from her pocket and performed a systematic search of the inside of the house, fitting the little key into every lock on the off chance it was the right one. She checked behind furniture, paintings and beneath rugs for any hidden doors.

The attic had been particularly creepy, with spiderwebs and a thick layer of dust. The hot Texas sun had heated the top of the house so much Kate had broken into a sweat as soon as she'd pulled down the attic access door and climbed to the top. After checking out two old trunks and an antique desk, she retreated to the air-conditioned second floor.

She let the attic door close on its springs. So far she'd struck out on finding the lock inside the house. She headed out the front door, letting the screen slap closed behind her.

Living in Houston had conditioned Kate to the con-

stant noise of urban life. Here, the silence was only interrupted by the wail of wind against the windows. When
she stepped out on the porch, the strong westerly breeze
hit her with a heated blast, slapping her hair around her
head. As far as Kate knew, she was the only person
within miles of the ranch house. That gave her a kind of
lonely, distant feeling. A quick glance at her watch told
her she didn't have much time to check out the rest of
the buildings if she wanted to be back in town on time
to pick up Lily at the church and have a cup of coffee
with Cara Jo.

She descended the steps, blinking the sand and grit
out of her eyes. Choosing the shed closest to the house as
a place to start looking, Kate kicked up dust as she trod
across the dry Texas soil and flung open the door to the
small building. The interior was packed with an ancient
riding lawn mower, an antique car probably dating back
to the 1940s, a variety of spare parts and equipment, a
large rollaway toolbox and fishing poles.

After the bright sunshine, the interior was dark and
deeply shadowed. She flipped the light switch beside
the door and nothing happened. She'd need a flashlight
if she planned to explore in the outbuildings. How long
had it been since anyone had been inside this one? At
least long enough to accumulate a thick layer of dust.
Which, in this part of Texas, could be as little as a day.
At the least, she could check out the toolboxes. They appeared to have tiny locks on some of the drawers.

The shed had no windows and only the one large door.
Kate opened it wide and leaned a cement block against
it to keep the wind from slamming it shut.

Then she stepped through, blocking the sun for a moment. She hugged the shadows, allowing for as much light as possible.

First, she tried the toolboxes. The key didn't fit the two locks, so she moved on. Kate squeezed between the front of the antique car and the wall of the building to get behind it. A scorpion skittered over a concrete block and down the side into a shadow.

Kate hated scorpions, having been stung more than once living in Houston. A shiver slithered across her warm skin. She'd have to warn Lily about the dangers of picking up rocks and things.

On the other side of the antique auto hung a rack of fishing poles. Below the rack, on the dirt floor was a tackle box with a keyhole on the front.

Ready to try anything, Kate stuck the key in the hole and turned it.

The lock clicked open.

A rush of excitement filled her and she dropped to her knees to better see what might be inside. The lighting behind the car was minimal, dust particles gleaming in the air. Kate held her breath as she laid her hands on the box, her pulse hammering through her veins.

Careful to look for scorpions or black widow spiders, she eased the lid back. From all she could see with the shadows and limited light, it was what it looked like. A fishing tackle box. The top compartment was loaded with dusty lures and faded rubber worms.

Kate let go of the breath she'd been holding. "Why would he leave me a key to a fishing tackle box?"

She sat back on her haunches and lifted the top compartment, exposing the bottom of the container.

Once again her breath hitched in her throat. Beneath a filet knife and a pair of pliers lay a mix of lures and lead weights. Buried among them was a slim silver thumb drive.

Was this it? Was this the item the key was hiding? Kate moved the knife and pliers aside and fished the thumb drive out of the box.

She shoved the data storage device into her pocket and stood.

The heavy shed door slammed shut, cutting off the light, throwing Kate into complete darkness. She reached out a hand to steady herself against the antique car and waited for the wind to blow the door open again so that she could see to find her way out.

The door didn't open.

Kate felt her way back around the old car to the front, her shirt catching on a nail protruding from the wall, ripping through the fabric and tearing into her skin. She screamed and nearly tripped over the forgotten concrete block the scorpion had scurried beneath.

Heart racing, afraid she'd brush against something deadly, sharp or creepy, she moved around the wall until her fingers brushed against a hinge. Finally, she'd reached the door.

Wind whistled through the cracks, a dark, lonely sound.

Kate leaned against the door and pushed. It didn't budge. She tried again, this time putting her full weight into it. The door remained closed. She stepped back, tucked her shoulder and slammed into the door. She bounced back.

As the truth dawned on her, her heart sank to her stomach. The door had been locked from the outside.

CHAPTER FOURTEEN

BEN SAT ACROSS the desk from Hank. "That's what's been happening."

"Too much for young Kate to handle alone." Hank nodded. "I'm glad you've been there to protect her." He leaned forward. "I received word from one of my connections in Customs and Border Protection. They found a dead woman on a ranch adjacent to the Flying K two weeks ago. From what they said, she was an illegal immigrant. How she got there, they would only guess. She died of exposure and dehydration."

"Damn." Ben shook his head. "A dead woman, dead cattle, intruders. You think they're trafficking humans across the Flying K and don't want Kate to interfere?"

"Sounds like it. A deadly situation if Kate gets in the middle. The immigrants aren't who she needs to be worried about. It's the coyotes who bring them across. They don't care who they have to kill to get paid."

"Hank, we only saw young women in the backs of those trucks."

Hank glanced up at Ben. "If they're trafficking young women, we have an even bigger problem. Someone stateside is harboring them and possibly selling them to underground sex dens."

Ben clasped his hands together to keep them from shaking. "Like the one we busted in Austin. I caught one of their suppliers, Marcus Mendez. The bastard got off on a technicality, then he came after my family. Think these are connected?"

"Could be." Hank leaned back in his chair. "I spoke with the regional director of the CBP. They didn't find the trucks you and Kate saw last night."

"Damn it." Ben stood and paced in front of Hank's desk. "I should have stopped them there."

"You had Kate to protect and you were outnumbered." Hank rounded his desk and laid a hand on Ben's shoulder. "You did the only thing you could. Now that you know they're running a human trafficking trade across the Flying K, you have to keep Kate from stumbling into them."

"I'll try but she was real upset by what we saw." Kate had a mind of her own and might try something dumb to help those girls. Ben blew out a long breath and dragged a hand through his hair. "I should be with her now."

"Where is she?" Hank asked.

"I left her at the diner. She should be okay there for a little while." Only now he wasn't so sure. Trouble had been following Kate since she'd arrived in this part of Texas. "Before I go, anything on the video?"

"As a matter of fact, we did make a little headway." He clicked the keyboard on his computer and then nodded toward the flat-screen television mounted on the wall behind Ben. "Look at this."

Static filled the screen, then a wavering image of Kyle Kendrick blinked into view.

"Hello, Kate. If you've received this video, something has happened to me and I'm either dead or missing and presumed dead. I couldn't leave without letting you know that of all the regrets in my life, you and your mother are my most heartfelt."

After a short pause, he continued.

"I can't say that I lived a good life. I didn't go to church, I wasn't a pillar of the community and I avoided jail on more occasions than I'd care to remember."

Ben sat back, his heart squeezing in his chest as he imagined Kate watching this video and her reaction to seeing the man on the screen for her first time.

"Then I met your mother and everything changed. I wanted to be a better man. I wanted to make her proud of me, and I thought I could. But I was in too deep. The people I worked with had me. Imagine being married to the mob. In this case, the Mexican Mafia cartels."

Ben whistled, noting the haggard expression, the dark circles around the man's eyes. Eyes that looked so much like a haunted version of Kate's. "What a life."

"I married your mother, thinking I could shake their influence. I thought I could just quit, stop running drugs and start fresh." The man in the video shook his head. "I was wrong and it almost got your mother killed." He ran a hand through his hair and tipped his head back, squeezing shut his eyes. "I had to let her go. To send her away. I didn't know she was pregnant with you. If they'd known how much I cared for her and anything about my unborn child, they'd have used it against me. I couldn't contact you, couldn't talk to your mother. I had to shut the door to that part of my life completely or risk your lives. It was the hardest thing I've done in my entire life."

Kyle Kendrick stared into the camera, his eyes narrowing. "When the DEA cornered me in Vegas, I knew it was over. They would have sent me to jail, which, in retrospect, might have been easier. Instead, they gave me a chance to redeem myself. If I would become their informant, they wouldn't lock me up." Kyle snorted. "I should have let them send me to jail." Kyle shook his head slowly.

"Once I started ratting out the leaders of the cartels, I knew my days were numbered. But I hung in there, trying to find out who the stateside head honcho was."

Ben shot a glance at Hank.

"I've come so close I might be in trouble. I'm sending this video in case something happens to me. I wanted you to know how much I loved you and your mother."

After another short pause, Kyle continued.

"In the envelope with this video is a key. It unlocks a tackle box you'll find in the shed with the old Cadillac. In the bottom of the tackle box is a flash drive. It contains all the notes I used to nail the members of the cartel and the work I've compiled leading up to the discovery of the stateside crime boss. At the time of this video, I know there are things happening in the area. I leave this information with you in the event of my untimely but fully expected death. The data is encrypted, so you'll need to hand it over to someone who can break the code. What you do with it is up to you. Toss it, ignore it or hand it off to the DEA, I don't care. Just don't get involved. I would hate to think my work once again puts you in danger."

Ben narrowed his eyes and focused on the screen.

"As I was saying, several factions are active. Drug running and human trafficking. The coyotes who run the people across the border referred to the stateside connection as *Diablo Patrón,* the devil boss. I think I know who's responsible, but haven't accumulated enough evidence to nail him. If what I think is true…" He looked at his hands clasped in between his knees. "Let's just say, I want to verify before I call in the Feds. The stakes are high. Whatever happens to me, know that I deserved what I got. Whatever you do, don't get tangled up in this mess. And watch out for the following men…"

As Ben leaned forward, the picture on the screen tilted.

Kyle Kendrick lurched forward to catch the camera, but missed, and the machine fell to the floor with a loud crash. Then static and gray squiggles filled the video screen.

"Who?" Ben leaped to his feet. "Who was she supposed to look out for?"

Hank stood, as well. "That's the kicker. Nothing else was recorded. Or Kendrick thought he'd finished recording his message and didn't. He must have been in a hurry to get the disk in the mail."

"Holy hell." Ben paced to the end of the French doors and back across Hank's spacious wood-paneled office. He stopped and faced the older man. "She needs to leave now. Go back to Houston, get the hell out of Texas. If the cartel finds out about the flash drive, she's dead."

"Scared the hell out of me, too." Hank walked around the desk and laid a hand on Ben's shoulder. "And there's one other thing I wanted you to know."

Ben looked into Hank's eyes. What else could go wrong?

"I hired another cowboy with the skills necessary to take over for you with the Langsdon woman. You don't have to go back there. He's here on the ranch. I can send him immediately."

Ben pressed a hand to his gut as if he'd been punched. "No."

"Are you sure? He has a stack of medals and credentials almost as impressive as yours."

"No." Ben straightened. God, what was he doing? He had an out. He didn't have to go back to the Flying K and be around Kate, whose body and soul reminded him of all he had to live for. He wouldn't have to face Lily, the child who'd worked her way into his heart in such a short time and left him open to her unconditional love and the heartbreak of leaving her behind when the job was done.

"I'll see this one through," Ben said. He headed for the door before he could change his mind, or before Hank could pull rank on him and change it for him.

"What about the video?"

Ben stopped. "Do you have it in a format I can show Kate?"

"Do you have a computer?"

"Yes."

Hank dropped into his desk chair, plugged a flash drive into the side of his monitor and clicked his keyboard. A moment later he yanked the flash drive from the monitor and handed it to Ben. "Be careful out there. Don't hesitate to call me in or to notify the DEA if things get out of hand."

"Don't worry. I'll be in touch." Ben left, climbing into his truck with a sense of impending doom.

Kate had come to the Flying K with the hope of starting over, of providing a good home for Lily. She'd ended up in a hotbed of danger.

Ben couldn't get back to her fast enough. Thank goodness she'd stayed in town.

The drive back to Wild Oak Canyon passed in a flash, considering Ben broke every speed limit the whole way.

Thank goodness the county sheriff couldn't hope to patrol all the roads leading into the community with so few on staff.

Once in town, he pulled into the diner, his gaze searching for and not finding Kate's car. His heart skipped several beats, but he refused to let himself get worked up. He unbuckled his seat belt, dropped down to the pavement and looked around.

Cara Jo stepped out of the diner, her brows furrowed. "Oh, thank goodness you're here."

Ben's adrenaline spiked. "Why? Where's Kate?"

"She left right before lunch to head back to the ranch. She promised to be back in time to pick up Lily, but the woman in charge of the Mother's Day Out program called and said Kate hadn't come and Lily was the last one there. I tried to call you, but you didn't answer. I tried Kate's home phone and there was no answer. I was just about to get Lily myself, but I was afraid I wouldn't be on the list of people allowed to collect her."

Ben was already back in the truck and pulling out of the parking lot by the time Cara Jo finished talking. He whipped out onto the street, drove the few blocks and skidded to a stop in front of the church.

The woman he'd met earlier stepped out the front door of the church, holding Lily's hand. She turned and locked the church.

"Mr. Ben!" Lily jerked her hand free of the woman's and ran toward him, her arms outstretched.

Ben gathered her to him and lifted her off her feet.

"Thank goodness you're here. Lily was upset and worried you had lost your way." The woman looked around Ben. "Is Ms. Langsdon with you?"

"No, she had something come up and asked me to

pick up Lily," Ben lied. He held Lily close, his heart aching for the child who'd thought she was forgotten.

Lily leaned back, tear tracks dried on her cheeks. "Can we go home now? Pickles missed me."

Ben nodded. "Yes, we can." He thanked the woman and tucked Lily into the backseat of his truck, buckling the seat belt over her lap. He didn't have the booster seat, but the buckle would have to do until he got back to the ranch and found Kate.

She'd promised not to go back until he could go with her. And why wasn't Mrs. Henderson answering the phone at the ranch?

Questions swirled in his mind throughout the drive out to the Flying K. When he came within sight of the house, he spied Kate's car sitting in the drive.

Nothing moved. No one came out to greet them.

Ben shifted into Park and climbed down. He lifted Lily out of the backseat and carried her to the house. The front door was unlocked. When he pushed it open, he called out, "Kate?"

As soon as he set Lily on her feet, she ran for the kitchen where Pickles's shrill barks created such a loud ruckus, Ben could barely hear himself think.

The house was a disaster. Drawers had been pulled out of the kitchen cabinets, pots and pans lay strewn across the floor.

"Pickles!" Lily cried out. "Where's Pickles?"

A high-pitched whine sounded from behind an over-turned chair.

Ben found the puppy's box wedged between a cabinet and the chair and lifted it out, puppy and all.

Lily leaned over the box and let the puppy lick her fingers. "Oh, Pickles, did you miss me?"

Ben checked the pantry and locked the back door, then lifted Lily in his arms. "Sorry, sweetheart, we'll come back for Pickles in a minute."

He didn't want to leave the little girl alone until he was certain whoever had turned the house upside down was no longer there. He carried Lily from room to room.

The child clung to him, probably sensing all was not right. "Mr. Ben, why is the house a mess?"

Ben tried to think of something that would make sense to a child and not frighten her. "Someone must have been playing with things and didn't put them away."

"Where's my mommy?" Lily trembled in his arms and he held on tighter, anger burning below the surface. No child should be afraid to come home.

A quick look around the house, both upstairs and down, confirmed his suspicion. Kate wasn't there and not a single room had been left untouched. Even Lily's room had boxes overturned, clothes flung across the floor and pillows torn open.

By the time he got back to the kitchen, Lily was sobbing quietly. "I want my mommy."

"Tell you what. I bet I know someone who could do with some hugs."

He entered the kitchen and set Lily on the floor.

Pickles barked in his shrill little voice.

Lily ran to the box and lifted the puppy into her arms. "Oh, Pickles." She hugged his neck and held him tight until the puppy squirmed loose and tore out across the floor.

Lily laughed and ran after him into the living room.

Ben followed. Of all the rooms, this one seemed the safest for now. "Stay in the living room, sweetheart. I'll be right back."

He hated leaving the four-year-old alone in the ransacked house, but he didn't know what to expect outside. He jogged to the barn first.

The stalls were empty. He checked the number of saddles in the tack room. All were there and Eddy's truck wasn't in the barnyard. Had Kate gone with Eddy?

Ben couldn't think of a logical reason why she'd leave with Eddy.

Pulse pounding, Ben emerged from the barn and yelled, "Kate! Kate!" He made a complete circle around the barn and scanned the pastures nearby. A few horses trotted over, hoping for a treat. But Ben saw no sign of Kate.

Unwilling to leave Lily alone any longer, he ran toward the house, heart heavy and desperate to find the spitfire redhead. "Kate!"

Moving fast to get back to the house, Ben almost missed the noise coming from the shed.

He ground to a stop and held his breath so that he could hear even the slightest sound.

There it was again. A muffled cry.

"Kate?" He jogged to the shed, careful to limit the crunch of his boots on the gravel.

"Ben! I'm in here," a voice called out, followed by pounding on the wooden door.

Kate.

Ben grabbed the door and yanked. It didn't budge. A latch had been slid home after the door had closed. The wind could have closed the door, but then someone on the outside had to push the bolt through the hasp.

He slid the latch to the side and jerked the door open.

Heat hit him at the same time as Kate's body plowed into his chest.

Her face was red and she wasn't perspiring.

"Holy hell, Kate, how long have you been there?"

"I don't know. It was dark. I must have drifted off. But it seems like forever." She leaned heavily against him and smiled up at him through pale lips. "I could use a drink of water."

He scooped her into his arms. Her skin felt hot and dry. It had to be over a hundred and twenty inside the shed. If she'd been in there for several hours, the sauna-like atmosphere could have killed her.

Ben carried Kate toward the house.

"Lily?" Kate's big green eyes gazed up at him.

"She's inside playing with Pickles." Ben's mouth was set in a grim line. "Why did you leave town?"

Kate nestled closer to him, shrugging. "I don't know. I didn't really feel like shopping. I wanted to find out what the key belonged to." She wiggled against him, jammed her hand into her pocket and drew out a small silver flash drive. "I found this."

Ben's eyes widened. "Ah, you found your father's data."

Kate's brows furrowed. "How do you know about it?"

"Hank's team has been busy. I have something for you to watch as soon as we get you hydrated and cooled off."

"I'm fine. Show me."

He shook his head. "Not until I know you're okay."

When they entered the house, Lily ran past, followed by a nipping, barking Pickles. "Hi, Mommy. Someone made a mess and didn't clean up." She stopped in the middle of the floor so fast, Pickles plowed into her. "Why is Mr. Ben carrying you?"

Kate smiled at her daughter, then glanced up at Ben, her brows raised. "Why *are* you carrying me?"

Ben smiled at Lily. "Because I'm big and strong."

Lily giggled and raced off, Pickles nipping at her heels.

Kate moved against him. "You can put me down."

"I will." He glanced at the stairs, then the couch and decided he wouldn't convince her to get in a cool shower. Not when he had news about her father and with Lily playing on the ground floor. Ben laid her on the couch. "Stay."

Kate laughed shakily. "I'm not a dog." Then she looked around the room. "Holy cow."

"Yeah, and it doesn't get better."

Her shoulders sagged. "Will this ever end?"

Her sad expression was almost his undoing. "Sit tight. I'll be back with a tall glass of ice water and a cool rag. But only if you stay."

"I may not be a dog, but I can be bribed." Kate settled back against a tattered throw pillow, her skin cooling in the air-conditioned room.

By the time Ben returned, Kate was shivering, her teeth chattering together so hard she thought they might crack. "I don't know what's wrong with me." Pain stabbed through her calf. She jerked up to a sitting position, grabbed her leg and doubled over. "Ow!"

"What's wrong?" Ben set the ice water on the table.

"Cramp." She tried to rise and fell back against the couch, too dizzy to stand. "I need...to...stretch." She pressed one hand to the cramped muscle, the other to the bridge of her nose.

"Just lay back." Ben pressed her firmly against the cushion, stretched her legs out straight, slid her shoes off her feet and pushed her toes up.

"Ow! Ow! Ow!" Kate reached for his hand, but

couldn't quite get there before she fell back against the pillow. Soon, the cramp eased and she lay still, her breathing shallow, the pain gone. "How'd you do that?"

"Works on a charley horse. Figured it would help you with the cramp." He lifted the glass. "Now, let's get some fluids inside you and you'll feel better." He helped her to a sitting position and slid in behind her to hold her up while she drank.

She wanted to drain the glass, but Ben wouldn't let her.

"A little at a time. Otherwise you'll just barf it up."

She snorted. "That would be attractive."

"In between sips, you can tell me what happened."

"Before you say anything, I'm sorry." She sipped from the glass, gathering more words as the fuzziness cleared from her head. "I shouldn't have come home by myself."

"Then why did you?"

"I can't rely on you to always be here for me and Lily. I have to be able to handle things on my own."

"When we find out who's behind all the threats. Not a moment sooner."

"I know, I know." Because he was there and she couldn't lie back against the pillows, she let herself lean into the hardness of his muscular chest. "I should have waited for you. And I will from now on." As soon as the words left her mouth, she knew they were a lie. Ben wouldn't be there for her *from now on*. "Or at least until we figure out who's doing this," she added.

"My most immediate concern is getting you hydrated." He pulled her closer and urged her to take another sip.

"Don't worry. I think I could drink a bathtub full of water."

"What happened?"

"I was looking for a lock the key would fit into and had just found the tackle box in the shed and the flash drive inside it when the door slammed shut. I'd propped the door with a concrete block. Guess it wasn't enough for the gusts of wind."

Ben's arm tightened around her. "It was more than the wind. Someone closed the door on purpose and locked it from the outside."

Kate glanced up, the glass of water forgotten, another tremor shaking her. "Someone locked me in there on purpose? There weren't any windows to let any air in."

Ben's body stiffened beneath hers. "You could have died if we hadn't found you soon enough."

Kate placed the cool glass against her lips, her thoughts on Lily as she plowed through the living room, the puppy chasing after her. "I can't afford to die, Ben. I'm all Lily has," she whispered.

Ben took the glass from her and set it on the table within her reach, then he laid her back on the couch.

She wanted him to hold her longer until the chill of what had almost happened dissipated.

He stood, looking down at her with a frown pulling his brows together. "You're going back to Houston."

Kate tried to push to a sitting position. "Says who?"

"It's not safe here."

"I have nothing left for me in Houston."

"You have Lily."

She started to say something, but bit down on her lip instead. He had a good point. "I can't go back to Houston. It's not any safer. Remember? Someone ransacked my apartment there. I'll bet it has something to do with what's on that flash drive I found."

"You can't tell anyone about it. No one."

"Okay."

"And at least consider leaving here until the dust settles."

She wanted to tell him to quit telling her what to do, but before she could he pressed a finger to her lips.

"I'm not trying to be a jerk. I'm worried about you and Lily. When I came back here and couldn't find you…"

She grasped his hand and held on to it. "I'm glad you did. Mrs. Henderson wasn't due back until tomorrow morning and Eddy could be out until dark working with the cattle. That reminds me."

Ben stared down at her. "Reminds you about what?"

"The CBP was out here investigating the cattle carcasses and asking questions."

Ben's mouth tightened. "Hank says they found a woman's body on the ranch adjacent to the Flying K two weeks ago. She appeared to have been an undocumented alien."

Kate's stomach dropped. "Dead?"

He nodded.

"Wow. I really am in the middle of this, aren't I?" She sat up and waited for the dizziness to clear. "You said you got information off the DVD my father left?"

"We did." He pulled the flash drive from his pocket. "Where's your laptop?"

"It's in a satchel in my bedroom." She sat up and leaned forward, but before she could rise, Ben pressed a hand to her shoulder.

"I'll get it." Ben collected the laptop from her bedroom and returned to the living room where he booted up the system and plugged in the flash drive. "Have you had lunch?"

"No. Marge said she left a pie on the counter and to help yourself." She didn't glance his way, her eyes trained on the screen. When it came up with her father's image she drew in a sharp breath, her heart squeezing so tightly she was afraid it would stop. "That's him? That's my father?"

CHAPTER FIFTEEN

BEN ENTERED THE KITCHEN, the sound of the video barely reaching him. He figured he'd chosen the coward's way out by ducking into the kitchen while Kate reviewed her father's first and last words to her. Ben tried to block the words from his mind and Kate's reaction by keeping busy.

As he glanced around, he noted that the back door swung wide open on its hinges, the hot Texas wind blowing into the house. The countertop was empty, no pie there, only a few crumbs. Perhaps Kate had been mistaken. The pantry door also hung open. When Ben peered inside, he noted cans lying sideways on the shelves and strewn across the floor. Someone had been in a hurry to get in and get out of the kitchen. Another unauthorized entry. Since the front door most likely hadn't been locked when Kate left the house to look into the shed and barn, it wasn't a forced entry, but an entry nonetheless. The other break-ins had been just that. The doors had been locked. Whoever had come in hadn't broken a window. He'd used a key or jimmied the lock.

Could it have been the same person responsible for locking Kate in the shed? Ben had stopped by the hardware store and picked up all new doorknobs and keys for the house. He'd gotten enough copies to give Mrs. H. one and one for himself and Kate.